ENTHRALLED

THE SPIDER'S MATE #2

TIFFANY ROBERTS

BLURB

He conquered her, but he is the one enthralled.

Ketahn hadn't wanted a mate. Fate gave him Ivy Foster. Now, he wants nothing more than to enjoy his little human.

But fate is not content to make things so simple.

With an enraged queen searching for him, Ketahn knows the Tangle is not safe for his mate. They need to leave. Yet Ivy will not forsake her people, and he cannot condemn her compassion. When they wake the other humans from their death sleeps, Ketahn now has more mouths to feed, and the strands of his web are in danger of snapping.

To keep Ivy and her people safe, he must placate the queen that hunts him. He must venture into Zurvashi's domain and face her wrath—and her desire.

The strength of his heartsthread, his bond with Ivy, will be tested.

Ketahn refuses to let that thread break even if he must sever all the rest.

To all our fellow monster lovers, thank you for taking a chance on us.

To Sam Griffin, our talented artist, we love and appreciate you more than you know.

CHAPTER 1

"The Queen's *Khan'ul* Claw is dead," Ketahn rasped in vrix. "By the Eight, what have I brought upon us?"

Ivy clutched the spear shaft against her chest. Darkness was closing in around her, made deeper and more sinister by the blood red light in the corridor, and she found herself battling an irrational certainty that it would swallow her up.

Her chest constricted, making her rapid breaths painful, and the pounding of her heart echoed in her ears. Fear and adrenaline were bitter on her tongue.

Please don't let him be hurt.

Taking in a slow, shaky breath, she set the spear on the floor and eased toward Ketahn. The stench of rancid water thickened as she neared the jagged break beyond which the floor sloped down. It was impossible to tell the difference between the blood and the black water pooled on the floor. Fortunately, the gloom made the vrix body lying beneath Ketahn indistinct enough to prevent Ivy from fixating upon any details.

A strained growl rumbled in Ketahn's chest. That growl culminated in a torrent of snarled words in his language, all spoken too quickly and ferociously for Ivy to make out much of anything.

Ketahn stomped two legs on the dead vrix, grasped his spear, and tore it free from the corpse's back. There was no pretending the dark liquid that spurted out was anything but blood. Ivy gasped and stumbled back as the blood splashed at her feet.

A sharp shake of Ketahn's weapon flicked the gore from its head. The sounds of little bits of flesh hitting the water were sickeningly mundane.

"He will not have you," Ketahn said. "She will not have me."

Ivy swallowed hard and lifted a hand to touch Ketahn's arm. "Ketahn?"

He stiffened for an instant; that stillness offered no warning of what came next. She was only vaguely aware of the sound of Ketahn's spear falling as he spun around, swept Ivy into his arms, and pulled her against him in a crushing embrace. Ivy wound her arms and legs around him as though it was the most natural thing in the world, as if she'd done so a million times over a thousand lifetimes.

None of the unpleasant smells in the air mattered now. When Ivy inhaled, she filled her lungs with Ketahn's spicy scent, and it was enough.

One of his hands petted her hair, smoothing it down, as he buried his face between her shoulder and neck. After a harsh exhalation that warmed her shoulder and blew strands of her hair backward, Ketahn drew in a ragged, desperate breath. He slipped his forelegs around her and brushed them along the backs of her thighs.

Catching a fistful of her hair, he tugged back on it, angling her chin up as he strengthened his embrace. "And she will *never* have you," he rasped against her throat.

"No one is taking me away." Ivy closed her eyes. "I'm yours, Ketahn. No one has me but you."

He shivered, and the vibrations rippled through her. Ivy

knew she was all that was keeping Ketahn together, all that was keeping him calm. Tangling her fingers in his hair, she held him, taking comfort in his nearness, in the way he stroked her hair, her back, her body. She longed to will everything away, everything except him, but all this was no less real than it had been when she'd first awoken in this alien world weeks ago.

She'd boarded the *Sominium* to escape her past. There was no escaping the present.

"Are you hurt?" she asked.

"No."

There were more layers woven into that simple word than Ivy could possibly unravel, but she knew at least that he was being truthful.

"Who was he, Ketahn?"

His hold on her strengthened a little more as a fresh growl rolled through his chest. "Durax. He was the queen's. He was her *Khan'ul* Claw. Her hunter."

"And he wanted to take you to her?"

Ketahn grunted affirmatively. The sound was cut through by a low buzz, a bitter edge, a hint that there was still more he wasn't saying—or wasn't yet ready to say. "We must go, Ivy."

He straightened and lifted his head, meeting her gaze briefly before raking his eyes over her. His mandibles twitched. They glistened in the hellish red light, and Ivy had no doubt of what they were covered in.

She had no doubt of what *she* was now covered in.

With another frustrated growl, Ketahn cast a final glare at the fallen vrix, removed a hand from Ivy to collect the spears, and carried her into the stasis room through which they'd entered the ship.

He set her down on her feet, though he didn't take his hands off her.

Ivy was just as reluctant to release her hold on him. An emotional maelstrom raged inside her. She'd seen, done, and felt so much today that it seemed like a lifetime had passed since she'd woken in Ketahn's arms that morning. Part of her longed for numbness; the death, the sorrow, and the fleeting taste of hope had been too much.

But numbness was an all-or-nothing deal, and she didn't want to dull her feelings for Ketahn even a little. Her bond with him was all that kept her going.

Frowning, she looked up at him. "We…we can't just leave the other humans."

"We must." He withdrew from her and sank down on the debris-strewn floor. "Come, my heartsthread."

Without his hands on her body, the cool air swept over Ivy unhindered, leaving an uneasy tingling beneath her skin. She shivered and glanced over her shoulder. The gash in the hull was like the toothy maw of a huge monster, leading only to darkness and the unknown.

Ivy hurriedly stepped around Ketahn and climbed onto his hindquarters, scooting as close to his torso as she could. She wrapped her arms around Ketahn's middle. He rose, settling a big hand over both of hers. She didn't care that his skin was sticky with blood—she just needed the comfort of his touch.

"Do you think there were more hunters with him?" she asked.

"If so, they are not close. Not yet." Taking a spear in each pair of hands, he strode forward.

"Are…are the other humans safe here?"

Somehow, fresh tension rippled through him, and he made one of those low, inhuman sounds that Ivy felt more than heard. "You are safe. I cannot say more."

Were it not for the blood—Durax's blood—drying on her skin where Ketahn had unintentionally smeared it, Ivy might have pressed him on the matter. But she'd seen more than enough to understand this wasn't the time or place to do so.

She held tight as Ketahn passed through the opening. He moved with deliberate slowness and care, both spears at the ready. Even when he pushed aside the dangling pieces of conduit and cabling, he was entirely silent. But she knew his outward calm was a façade.

His hearts pounded, their pulse flowing into her through all the points of contact between their bodies, faster and stronger than usual.

There'd be a lot to talk about when they got home. She could only hope Ketahn would be open with her.

The air was immediately hotter and thicker outside the ship. Ivy had an unnerving sense of crossing into a new, alien world for the first time, and a pang of all the associated horror and excitement struck her chest, but it was backward.

The *Somnium* seemed alien and otherworldly to her now. This jungle, for all its dangers…well, it was hers.

Ketahn ceaselessly scanned their surroundings as he walked to the side of the crater, seeming to focus especially on the walls and tangled plant growth overhead. Ivy kept her gaze moving too, though her vision was filled with shadows upon shadows, contrasted only by glimpses of blue sky stolen through breaks in the vegetation.

At the side of the crater, Ketahn passed her the spears. Ivy didn't look at their black stone heads, knowing Ketahn had yet to clean them. She laid the spear shafts across her thighs and handed him the silk rope. Working in unison, they secured the rope around their waists, lashing their bodies together.

Surprisingly, her hands had only trembled a little as she'd worked the knots and twists.

Climbing out of the pit was slower than descending to the bottom, but Ivy was grateful that she wasn't forced to look down at all. She didn't dare look back until they were perched on a wide, solid rock at the top.

For an instant, she spied the dull orange glow of the ship's exterior emergency lighting far below, making it look like the pit was filled with hungry flames beneath the plant growth.

Ketahn took the spears from her and strode away from the crater at a brisk pace. Even with the ship out of sight, Ivy felt it; it was the lingering fear of a potent nightmare, it was the flickering flame of hope for a brighter future. And she was bound to it as surely as she was bound to Ketahn, the tether stretching with each of his steps.

He wasted no time in ascending the trees and delving into the jungle, moving with a blend of speed, alertness, and caution that suggested thinly veiled paranoia. His eyes were in constant motion as though he were trying to watch every direction simultaneously, and he treated every sound like it had been made by a potential threat.

And none of that seemed to slow him down much. Within a short while, what meager sense of direction she'd managed to establish was obliterated, and she had no idea where they were or where they were heading, only that his route was drawn-out and almost circuitous.

Thanks to all the time she'd spent with him in the jungle, she knew what he was doing—obscuring his trail, making it as confusing as possible for any would-be pursuers.

When Ketahn descended to the jungle floor and stopped on an unfamiliar stream bank, the sky bore the first orangey tinge of evening. Had they truly been out for so long?

He shifted both spears into one hand and began untying the rope from around their waists. Ivy helped him, their hands moving in concert. Ketahn was still searching their surroundings as he wound the rope into a small, tight coil.

"We will wash and drink. Then we go," he said.

Climbing down from his back, Ivy swept her gaze around before bringing it to rest on Ketahn. "What does *Khan'ul* mean?"

"It is like first, but more. The *Khan'ul* Claw leads the queen's hunters."

ENTHRALLED

She cringed. An important vrix then. "Are you in trouble, Ketahn?"

He chittered, and Ivy wasn't sure whether she should be reassured by the hint of humor beneath the bitterness in the sound. Turning to face her, he removed the pack she was wearing with his free hands, set it aside, and flattened a palm on her lower back, nudging her toward the water.

"Much before he came to us, my heartsthread."

With a frown, she bent forward and lifted her feet one at a time to untie the soiled strips of silk wrapped around them. "Because you wouldn't mate the queen?"

Ketahn caught one of her elbows, steadying her as she removed the strips. His gaze continued to roam. "Yes."

"But it's worse than that now, isn't it?"

"It is…most worse." He fixed his eyes upon her, and his mandibles twitched. "I was to claim her yesterday."

Ivy's brows creased. "What?"

With an unhappy trill, he stuck the spears in the ground, turned away from her, and strode into the stream. He sank down until the water was up to his waist and plunged his hands in, scrubbing the blood off his hide. His movements conveyed a touch of urgency and aggression.

As soon as he'd cleaned himself—including his face and mandibles—he glanced over his shoulder. "Come, Ivy."

With her stomach in knots, she stepped into the cool stream and waded toward him. The water gradually rose around her legs and hips and was nearly to her chest when she drew close enough for Ketahn to pluck her up and sit her on his folded front legs, putting the waterline back at her belly. The wet silk dress molded to her body.

Ketahn's hands were as gentle as ever despite the restlessness thrumming in him as he washed the blood from Ivy's hair and skin, caressing her cheeks, massaging her arms and hands. It was a lover's touch, and it spread warmth through her. But

7

when he looked down at her dress, his mandibles fell, and the growl he produced was equal parts frustrated and sorrowful.

He delicately caught some of the fabric and drew it away from her skin, brushing his thumb over a red blotch on the silk. "There is nothing she does not stain with blood."

Ivy frowned. Cupping some water in her hand, she brought it up to his cheek and washed away the bit of blood seeping from the wound. She didn't care about the dress. All that mattered was that Ketahn hadn't been seriously hurt. A dress could be replaced; he could not.

She captured his jaw between her hands and forced him to meet her gaze. "Tell me what's wrong, Ketahn. Don't keep secrets from me."

Ketahn huffed and lifted a hand to Ivy's hair, combing his claws through it slowly. Even if his face couldn't convey much emotion, his eyes were brimming with it. When he spoke, there was a resignation in his voice that seemed so at odds with the male she knew. "Yesterday was the High Claiming. It is a day when worthy male vrix try to claim mates, just before the great storms bring the flood season. There are…*althahk* that must be followed. Things that must be done, that are always done. Gifts and shows of strength and skill. Yet it always ends in conquering. In claiming."

"And the queen wanted you to claim her?" Just saying those words made the knots in Ivy's belly tighten further. She didn't like the thought of Ketahn being with someone else, of those gentle hands stroking another body. She knew this emotion—jealousy—and it made her feel ill. It also made her even more conflicted about what she felt for Ketahn.

"More than want."

"Why didn't she just claim you herself if she wants you so badly?"

"She wants only the most strong male, and wants all vrix to know her male is the most strong. If she claims me, I will seem weak. But if I conquer her, we will both prove strong, and it is known that our hatchlings would carry that strength."

Ivy stroked her thumbs along his jaw. "And now? What will happen now that you didn't claim her and killed her lead hunter?"

"Her anger will shake the Tangle," he said, mandibles falling. He tipped his forehead against Ivy's and wrapped his lower arms around her, drawing her close against his chest. "But she will never know of you. She must *never* know. I will keep you safe, my heartsthread, from the queen and everything else."

CHAPTER 2

KETAHN STARED at the den's entrance. The sliver of morning light at the edge of the cloth-covered opening was dull gray, but it was radiant compared to the shadows lingering inside.

The rain was a subdued pattering that had neither intensified nor diminished since it had begun in the middle of the night. Normally, it would have been soothing, but it had yet to offer Ketahn any comfort.

He and Ivy had reached the den just before dark yesterday. It had felt like the shadows of what had occurred—and what might yet come—had followed them through the Tangle. Conversation had been sparse; exhaustion had claimed Ivy not long after they were inside, and she'd lain atop him to sleep. But Ketahn's weariness had not been so merciful. It had tormented him through the night, had prowled on the edges of his awareness, taunting him, beckoning him repeatedly, but it had not accepted his submission.

And the muted rain had not been nearly loud enough to silence his chaotic, raging thoughts.

Ketahn shifted to lean his shoulders more comfortably against the wall. Ivy's breath remained slow and even, fanning lightly across his chest, and her limp body remained tucked securely upon his. He smoothed a hand over her silky hair.

He'd been somewhat eased by having Ivy safe and in his arms, but even she could not banish the trouble in his hearts—because she was in danger. The threat to his life mattered only in that it was an equal threat to hers.

Through the night, he'd considered the situation. He'd struggled to explore every possible solution, to find some way to make it all work out without giving up everything he'd ever known—or rather what little he had left. Ultimately, it had become a matter of weighing all those things against each other.

Ivy won out. He'd known it even before he'd thought about any of it, had known she would always be his first choice. He cared immensely for his sister and friends, but Ivy—sweet, fragile, compassionate Ivy—was his mate. She was his everything. She came before all else.

There was but one thing to do. Ketahn only hoped it wouldn't be too late, that they hadn't already run out of time.

With a sleepy hum, Ivy stirred. She breathed in deep and stretched, the hand resting upon Ketahn's chest sliding up to wrap around the back of his neck as she extended her legs down on either side of him. Releasing that breath in a sigh, she relaxed and caught the strands of his hair in her fingers, idly twirling them.

Her movements, however small, reminded him of her bare, warm skin against his hide, of her softness, of her comforting weight. None of that had been enough to lull him to sleep last night, but he doubted he'd ever sleep again without Ivy whether she was lying atop him or merely in his arms.

Since he'd claimed her, she'd taken to sleeping without clothing, bundling up upon him beneath a large blanket to share warmth during the colder nights. Without that, without her, something would always feel absent. Some piece of him would forever be missing.

Ketahn glided his hand down her back, sliding the blanket down along with it. The rasp of his rough palm across her skin was more welcome than all the jungle's music.

Despite the heaviness of his thoughts, despite his weariness, despite everything, Ketahn's stem stirred behind his slit. He covered her rounded backside with his palm and pressed her firmly against him.

Ivy's breath hitched. Her fist closed on his hair, and she drew her knees up, opening her thighs wider in invitation. "Mmm... Morning."

Ketahn drew in a deep breath. The air was already thickening with the scent of her desire, which was perfectly complemented by the rain smell that had filled the den through the night. His blood heated, his claspers curled around her hips, and his stem strained against his slit.

Resisting the urge to mate with her—resisting her—would not be easy. He wanted more than anything to sink into her hot, wet depths, to lose himself in her embrace, in their mating.

But each new drop of rain hitting the top of the den was another moment lost, never to be reclaimed. Another moment for the queen and her Claws to search for him.

He forced his claspers to withdraw from her and shifted his lower hands to her hips, pressing her even more firmly to his pelvis in the hope that it would keep him from spilling forth. All it did was coat his slit in her essence. A shudder wracked him.

Ivy lifted her head and met his gaze. His eyes must have revealed his turmoil because she frowned and scrunched her brow. Releasing his hair, she flattened her hands on his chest and sat up. Her long, pale golden hair tumbled over her shoulders. Ketahn's eyes dipped to her breasts, lingering on her pink nipples, then trekked farther down her belly to the small patch of hair and her slit—which already glistened with dew.

His fingers flexed on her hips. To resist the urge to cup her breasts, to stroke her nipples and watch them harden, he settled his upper hands upon her thighs.

"I'm your mate," Ivy said, calling his attention back to her face. Taking hold of his upper hands with both of hers, she removed them from her thighs and brought them to her breasts. "Take comfort in me, Ketahn. Use me. Let me be what you need."

Her words, spoken so gently, smashed down the final barriers of his resistance, and his desire burst free like the torrential rain of a sudden storm. His thoughts and concerns were swept away, leaving only his burning need for his mate, his Ivy. His heartsthread.

His upper hands kneaded the tender flesh of her breasts as he lifted her with his lower hands, which remained clamped on her hips. The instant she was up, his stem tore free of his slit, throbbing with the frantic rhythm of his hearts and slick with secretions. He groaned.

As his need flared, he saw it reflected in Ivy's eyes, their blue now fierce and passionate. Consuming. And he longed to be consumed.

Ketahn slowly lowered Ivy until the tip of his stem pushed inside her; then he pulled her down fast, burying himself in her tight, hot depths. Clutching his wrists, she threw her head back with a gasp. He hissed at the overwhelming pleasure of being inside her. It was unlike anything else. Her body welcomed him —her soft flesh clamped around him, quivering and drawing him deeper as her weight sank fully upon him. His claspers hooked around her thighs and strengthened their hold, pushing him in farther still.

It was bliss and punishment. The pressure in his stem would unmake him, would be his doom, but the pleasure was worth it. He longed to remain this way forever, to remain inside her, to keep their bodies joined as tightly as their heartsthreads were woven, and yet he craved more.

With a low growl, he dropped his gaze to the where their bodies were connected. She was stretched around him, and that tiny nub that brought her so much pleasure was clearly visible, beckoning him, begging his touch. Her dew mingled with his slick, covering his slit and glistening upon her thighs. Soon enough, it would be joined by his seed. He would fill her until she could take no more—and then he would give more all the same.

He braced his forelegs under her knees and forced her legs wider. The brush of his fine hairs against her skin gave him a fresh taste of her, of her sweet flavor and enticing scent, and sparked the frenzy within him. His chest rumbled with an anticipatory trill.

As he lifted her body, creating a wave of pleasure that coursed along his stem and straight to his core, Ivy released a soft moan and raised her head.

Their gazes met.

Whatever they exchanged in that instant was beyond words —it was not for his waking mind to know. Because some part of him, mysterious and instinctual, understood what was between them. Some part of him sensed the impossible strength and breadth of their bond. And that bond was all that mattered.

He slammed her down onto his stem. She moaned again, sex clenching and body curling forward, and threw her hands against his chest to rake his hide with her blunt nails. Ketahn growled and lifted her again, hammering her onto him with increasing speed and desperation. Fire swirled in his blood and flooded his loins as all his rage, frustration, and fear was burned into passion and desire.

One of his hands moved up to catch a fistful of her hair, and he tugged her head back, baring her neck. He dipped his head to trail his tongue along one side of her neck, greedily lapping the salty-sweet sweat from her skin, while the tip of his mandible fang grazed the other side.

Ivy shuddered. It rippled into him, drawing a raw growl from his throat.

"Ketahn," she breathed. "Don't stop. Oh please, don't stop."

"Never," he rasped.

He quickened his pace, his breaths ragged and snarling and Ivy's moans high-pitched and fevered as they raced to their peaks, their bodies moving in frantic but fluid desperation. Each time his pleasure seemed to reach its limits, he growled and pushed harder, faster, clawing for ever more—and Ivy did the same.

Ketahn's release came like a lightning strike, and it drew out like rolling thunder as he roared her name. Ivy came at the same instant, her whole body tensing around him, and her nails pressing hard enough to spark tiny pricks of delicious pain on his chest.

She cried out and collapsed upon him, writhing as her sex clutched his shaft mercilessly. His stem unfurled within her and thrummed, pumping his seed into her, coaxing her core to accept what it was given. He wrapped his upper arms around her and clamped both lower hands on her backside, pressing her firmly onto his pelvis to keep himself buried as deep inside her as possible.

Even with him holding her still, the quivering of Ivy's inner walls was more than enough to draw out more of his seed, to draw everything out of him.

He tipped his head back against the wall and closed his eyes, relishing the small movements of their bodies and the immense pleasure they created. He said her name again in a long, low rumble, letting it—letting *her*—devour his senses utterly as he drifted on the current of euphoria.

When the overpowering rush of ecstasy eased, and his Ivy lay limp and panting upon his chest, Ketahn purred and brushed his face over her hair, breathing in her scent. It was stronger and sweeter now, mixed with his own to create the fragrance that embodied their bond.

But as much as he longed to savor this moment with his mate, the fading pleasure quickly succumbed to the harshness of reality. He'd eluded his troubles for a short while, but they had not been resolved. The situation remained unchanged.

Memories flashed through his mind's eye. Takarahl and the queen; the pit with its crashed ship; the Tangle and the battles he'd fought years before; all the blood he had shed. The images crashed over him like cold water poured onto a dying fire.

Lifting his head, he opened his eyes to look down at his mate. Ivy's cheek was upon his chest, her lips parted as her rapid breaths flowed over his hide, and her thick, dark lashes were resting on her cheeks. The meager light was enough to make strands of her tousled hair shine a brilliant gold. She was as beautiful as always—even more so with each passing moment.

More than anything in Ketahn's world, she was worth protecting. At any cost.

"We must leave, my heartsthread," he said.

She hummed and wrapped her arms around him, rubbing her cheek against his hide. "We can gather food and water later. I like where I am." As though to prove her words, she ground her sex against his slit and took his stem deeper still.

Ketahn tensed, releasing an involuntary trill as his mandibles spread. He still could not understand how such a seemingly insignificant motion could rouse such sensation—not that he would complain about it. But it was no longer the time for such pleasures.

He forced firmness into his voice. "We need to leave the den, Ivy."

She raised her head and looked at him. Her hair was disheveled, her cheeks were flushed, and there was a small crease between her eyebrows. "What do you mean?"

"The Prime Claw will not be the last to search for me. This part of the jungle is no longer safe."

"You said no one knows where your den is but your sister."

"There are signs all around that will lead them here if they look. In time, they will find this place. We cannot remain here."

With a frown, she placed her palms upon his chest and pushed herself up, making him ease his hold on her. "What about the others? The humans?"

Ketahn's mandibles twitched, and his fingers tensed with the instinct to draw her close again. He only barely resisted. "They must be left to their slumber."

Ivy stared at him, silent, but Ketahn saw the change in her eyes, saw the passion they'd shared only moments before hardening. She shoved against his chest and lifted herself. His seed spilled from her, dripping down her thighs and his stem to pool around his parted slit. She winced, but that didn't deter her as she climbed off him, snatched up the silk blanket, and drew it around her as though putting a barrier between them.

His hide felt immediately cold in her absence, and he found himself fighting a new urge to tear the blanket off and throw it out of the den. He wanted *nothing* between him and his mate.

"No," she said with just as much firmness as he had used—if not more.

His claspers drew in against his pelvis, and his stem retreated into the shelter of his slit. Flattening his hands on the floor and the wall behind him, Ketahn righted himself, moving his legs to the sides and rising to stand over Ivy. "This is not to be argued, female."

She tilted her head back and locked her eyes with his. "It needs to be argued, Ketahn. We can't just leave them there to die."

"I cannot keep you and seven more humans safe, Ivy," he growled, thrusting his arms to the sides. "With two, the jungle is bountiful. With nine it will be unforgiving."

"And how many do you feed when you bring meat to your people?"

"It is not merely a matter of food. Clothing, shelter, tools—"

"All of which they can work for!" Ivy brought her hands to her face, covering it as she took in several deep, measured breaths. When she lowered her hands and spoke again, she did so calmly. "Humans are not useless. We can hunt, fish, build, and survive. We learn quickly. We adapt. We are different from you, physically weaker than you, but we endure, Ketahn. And they are people. *My* people. You can't expect me to move on and carry the guilt of leaving them behind when there's a chance to save them."

Water was gathering in her eyes as she spoke, sharpening the emotion already filling them. Ketahn felt his heartsthread pull taut.

"So let the guilt be mine," he said tightly, raising a hand to smooth down her hair. "I would rather that than the guilt of failing to keep my mate safe."

"That's not how it works, Ketahn. You know that's not how it works."

He dipped his hand to her cheek and brushed the pad of his thumb across her soft skin, trying to ignore the strengthening constriction in his chest.

Ivy grasped his wrist, turned her face, and pressed a kiss to his palm before looking back up at him. "I'm not asking you to choose between taking care of me or them. I'm…I'm asking you to just…give them a chance. Please? Thousands of the people on that ship have already died. These ones survived. Like me. They deserve a chance at life, even if it's not the one they sought."

All he could do was stare into Ivy's eyes as her words sank into him. If the Eight had led him to that pit, if they had led him to find her—if they had put her there to begin with, knowing that Ketahn would one day come across her—then was it not possible that the other living humans were there for a reason, also? Ivy had been destined to be Ketahn's mate. Believing that surely meant the other humans had some greater purpose.

If she had survived a journey across the stars, across a distance far beyond Ketahn's ability to measure or comprehend, to arrive here in the Tangle for him…the other humans also had destinies awaiting them.

But it was so much. Too much. The risks of taking on seven more humans, seven more people who would require food, shelter, and teaching, who would be noisy and clumsy and, potentially, lack all of Ivy's kindness and compassion, were immense.

She squeezed his wrist. "If we leave them, they will die. Once the power runs out on the ship, that's it. The cryochambers will fail. They'll just be gone." Her eyes searched his. "Could you leave your people behind if you knew they'd die?"

That question was like a blow to his hearts. He clamped his jaw shut, mandibles drawing together, and lowered his head to tip his headcrest against her forehead. He could not lie to her. He could not pretend that he wouldn't ultimately make the same choice she wanted him to make if their roles were reversed.

"I could not," he rasped.

Ivy settled a hand upon his chest over his hearts. "Then please, Ketahn, just give them a chance."

There would be no denying her—Ketahn's ability to do so had passed and would never again present itself. But *how* was he to fulfill her wishes in this? How, while the Queen's Claw would be searching for him, while he could not go to Takarahl for supplies?

He needed time to prepare, and that was not available in any abundance.

Ketahn slipped his fingers into her hair, cupping the back of her head. "I…must think on this, my heartsthread."

"Thank you." Lifting her face, she pressed her lips to the seam of his mouth.

A kiss. A sweet human kiss. He relished it for its simplicity, its intimacy, for the passion it sparked, and found himself wishing he had lips so he could return his mate's kisses properly. He satisfied himself by wrapping his arms around her and drawing her close.

Something struck the outside of the den with a heavy thump. Ketahn released Ivy immediately, whipping around to face the entrance even as he spread his arms and forelegs to shield her. His hearts raced, but his mind was clear—protecting Ivy was all that mattered, and he would not lose of focus on it.

"What was that?" she whispered.

"A falling branch, perhaps," he replied, though he knew that was wrong the moment he said it.

The sound repeated, this time striking a different part of the den—the underside. He felt the faint vibrations of the impact through his legs. Not a branch, but a rock.

Only one creature in the Tangle would throw rocks at his den.

"We are not alone, my *nyleea*."

CHAPTER 3

CALM ENVELOPED KETAHN, easing the wasteful tension in his muscles even though it did not slow his pounding hearts. His perception expanded rapidly, like a jesan flower blooming to the silver moonlight. Every sound, every scent, every vibration and movement, no matter how small, was caught in the web of his awareness.

Including the dull, barely perceptible tapping of a leg on a branch somewhere below the den.

He felt Ivy's breath upon his back, little more than a suggestion of moving air by the time it reached him, as he crept toward the opening. He felt the slow, ceaseless drumming of rain atop the den sending tiny pulses through the woven wood. His nose holes were filled with the varied scents in his den—the cloying smell of moist dirt and plants, the fresh fragrance of the rain. But stronger than everything else was a sweet, blended fragrance—that of his mating with Ivy.

Ketahn took hold of his barbed spear, which was leaning against the wall beside the opening, and grasped the hanging cloth.

He'd known time was short, that the Claws would eventually

find this place despite its distance from Takarahl, but he never could've guessed they'd come so soon.

Ivy's presence radiated behind him, coursing up and down his spine with skittering heat. He glanced at her over his shoulder. With one hand, he gestured for her to remain in place. He pressed the pointer finger of another hand over his mouth.

She nodded. Her skin was pale, her eyes wide, her stance stiff and uneasy. If not for her tousled hair and the lingering pink on her cheeks, she wouldn't have looked at all like she'd been well mated only moments before.

As though in remembrance, his stem stirred behind his slit, flooding his pelvis with a deep ache that spread into his lower abdomen. His claspers twitched and drew in firmly against his slit, increasing the already building pressure behind it.

But there was danger outside. Not just this unexpected visitor, but a whole jungle full of threats to his mate—and within that jungle, an entire city under the command of the wrathful queen he'd defied. Ketahn pressed the tips of his mandibles together and turned away from his mate.

He shifted himself to the side of the opening, readied his spear—though he would not have a clear throw unless he exited the den—and tugged the cloth aside.

The jungle, currently drab, gray, and dripping, opened before him. He angled his gaze downward.

A lone figure stood on the thick branch below, a female vrix who appeared especially large and solid in the mist. She was wrapped in a swath of dark green silk that covered her shoulders, neck, and most of her head, but it did not hide many of her adornments—gold, beads, and gemstones. Nor did it cover her eyes, which were vibrant purple even in the gloom.

Ahnset stared up at Ketahn, holding a few rocks upon one of her upturned palms. Her war spear was in one of her other hands, standing tall beside her. While she maintained that posture, it was hard to see her as anything but a servant of the queen.

That last notion kept him from feeling much relief. She wasn't a Claw, that was true, but a Queen's Fang didn't seem any better right now. Not even a Fang that happened to be Ketahn's broodsister.

"Come down, broodbrother," she called just loudly enough to be heard over the rain.

Ketahn grasped the frame of the opening, digging his claws into the woven branches. He swept his gaze across the surrounding jungle. "Were you followed?"

Ahnset gnashed her mandibles, making that new band around the right one glint with a dull reflection. "That is what you choose to say to me?"

Ketahn's mandibles spread, and wood splintered under his fingers. He growled. "Were you followed, Ahnset?"

She folded a pair of her powerful arms across her chest, her eyes taking on the cold, stony cast of a Queen's Fang. "No. Come down."

The bitter heat that flowed through Ketahn was wholly unrelated to the heat Ivy had kindled in him earlier. His hatred of the queen only deepened in that moment. Would that Zurvashi had never existed, that he would never have found himself in a situation where he was forced to question his trust in his broodsister.

"Are you certain?" he demanded.

"Protector, shield you, broodbrother, for you are fraying the threads of my patience," Ahnset grumbled. "I am certain, though your recent actions did not make it easy to accomplish."

Had the Queen's Claw already learned of Durax's demise? Was it possible that the Prime Claw had already been discovered by his comrades?

A shard of panic pierced his chest, but he forced it away. Panic would not protect Ivy. "And what actions are those?"

"You know well, Ketahn. You have angered her enough this time that she has tasked the Claw with finding you."

Ketahn cursed himself for a fool; of course Durax had not been found. The Prime Claw lay in a place no other vrix ever ventured, a place into which Durax had gone only in pursuit of Ketahn. Had Durax been accompanied by more Claws, they'd have been awaiting Ketahn at the top of the pit…and yesterday's journey home would have been made through a river of bloodshed.

"She must value their lives little," he said.

"Come down here, Ketahn. Such things should not be shouted into the Tangle no matter how far we are from Takarahl."

Growling, he released his spear and began drawing himself through the opening. His movements roused a lingering scent, drawing it into the air anew—the mating scent.

He halted with only his head and upper shoulders through the opening. The light rain would not be enough to wash that fragrance from his hide, not that he wanted to do so to begin with. Should he draw too near to his broodsister, she would undoubtedly detect the scent—and she would know it for what it was despite the unfamiliar elements Ivy contributed to it.

"I am unwell," Ketahn said, retreating into the den without removing his gaze from Ahnset. "I have no desire to worsen it in the rain."

Another deception. How many more lies could he tell his sister, his friends, himself, before he was crushed under the weight of them?

Even with the distance between them, Ketahn saw Ahnset's eyes soften, and her mandibles twitched downward. "What happened, broodbrother? Illness or injury?" She took a step toward the nest, tilting her head back farther to keep her gaze locked with his. "Come down, and I will tend to you."

"No," he replied quickly. "It is nothing that will not be healed with rest and quiet."

"Allow me to at least—"

"Say what you have come to say, broodsister, and be on your way."

Her mandibles sagged, and a shard of guilt pierced Ketahn. Again, he fought the instinct to go to her; again, his hatred for the queen intensified. But he could not blame Zurvashi for the way he had spoken to his broodsister.

"Ahnset, I—"

"No, Ketahn. I do not wish to hear your excuses or apologies. What good are they?"

Her words latched onto that shard of guilt and twisted it in the wound. Part of Ketahn knew he deserved the pain. But that did not eliminate his anger or fear—his fear that he might lose his mate so soon after finding her.

Ahnset pulled the cloth hood back, revealing more of her head. "It is nothing I have not said to you already. It is nothing you wish to hear."

"I have told you, Ahnset. Allow this to remain between me and the queen."

"That is not the way of things, broodbrother, and you know that."

Ahnset's words echoed Ivy's so closely that Ketahn found himself unable to produce a response; for an instant, he could almost see the strands of fate binding everything together, arranged intricately by the Weaver in ways no vrix was meant to understand.

"What happens to you affects those who care about you," Ahnset continued. "You cannot pretend otherwise. And the queen...she slew three of the males who attempted her during the High Claiming. I will not see your mangled remains wrapped in a shroud to be laid beside them."

Ketahn's mandible's trembled, his teeth ground together, and his claws again sank into the den's branches. "Ahnset, do not—"

"You must make this right, Ketahn." Ahnset's voice had taken on a tone somehow firm and gentle at once, the same sort of tone their mother had sometimes used when her broodlings had tried to defy her. "There is still a chance to appease her. She sees you as hers already, and she will forgive you should you atone."

"Atone?" Ketahn snarled, drawing himself partway through the opening again. "The only one who has done wrong is Zurvashi herself."

Ahnset was as unmoving as the statues in the Den of Spirits, her gaze fixed upon him. "We are all that remains of our bloodline, Ketahn. The others have long since been laid understone in their shrouds or claimed by this jungle. And you tell me by your deeds that I must lose you too."

A low, troubled trill sounded in his chest. The rain falling upon his hide was colder than anything he'd ever felt, but he did not allow himself to shiver. "I will not join them, Ahnset."

She released a heavy breath and adjusted her hold on her spear, letting it lean at a skewed angle as her rigid stance crumbled. "You need not continue along the strands you have spun, broodbrother. It is not too late to stride a different path that will not end in your destruction."

Ketahn had not heard such resignation and sorrow in Ahnset's voice in years—not since she'd learned of their mother's death.

"This will not be my end, Ahnset," he said, the heat of his fury warring with the chill of his guilt. "Zurvashi will not be my end."

Ahnset stared at him for a few more heartbeats before tugging her silk wrap back over her head. "You cannot hide from this, broodbrother. Not for long."

She turned away and strode along the branch. The blunt end of her spear thumped on the bough with a steady rhythm that faded as her form grew indistinct with distance. Rage and sorrow tore at Ketahn's hearts from all directions, pulling and shredding like a pack of xiskals fighting over a fresh kill.

The queen had threatened the threads still tying Ketahn to Takarahl; it felt as though one of them was already frayed. The thread he'd foolishly believed could endure anything.

A small hand settled on his hindquarters. The gentle touch roused Ketahn from his dark thoughts. He blinked away the raindrops that had run into his eyes, shook his head to shed more water from it, and slipped back into the den.

He turned to find Ivy there, her eyes gleaming with concern and sadness.

You cannot hide from this.

Ketahn wrapped his arms around his mate and drew her against his chest. Emotions welled inside him, each more over-whelming than the last, each only heightening the rest, and all he could do was squeeze his eyes shut and curl over his little mate, seeking comfort in her warmth, her softness, her scent.

He tightened his embrace as Ahnset's words echoed in his mind.

You cannot hide from this.

Ivy clung to Ketahn, her strong hold expressing everything he felt. Finding her had been like discovering a new world—and now it felt as though that world were crumbling.

You cannot hide from this.

We are all that remains...

"They are all gone," he rasped, only then realizing that he'd never mourned the family and friends he'd lost to Zurvashi's ambitions—he'd allowed himself only to hunger for justice. For vengeance.

"You're not alone," Ivy whispered, her breath hot across his hide. "You're never alone, Ketahn."

You cannot hide from this.

You're not alone.

Ketahn drew in a deep breath, filling his lungs with Ivy's scent, with the heady fragrance of their mating, with the familiar smells of the place that had been his home for seven years. Takarahl had been his home before this den, and…and there would be another after this. A place with Ivy.

He could not hide, but he was not alone.

CHAPTER 4

THUNDER SHOOK THE DEN. Its wood creaked and groaned, and the cloth at the opening billowed and flapped despite being secured at all four corners. Ivy started and curled up tighter in the shelter of Ketahn's body, burying her face against his chest. Her blunt nails dug into the hide of his sides.

He petted her hair with one hand, tucked the blanket around her with another, and strengthened his embrace further. She lay atop him, just as she always did when they slept—but the time for sleep had not yet come. Despite the thick shadows imposed by the storm, midday was not long past.

It felt as though a full eightday had passed since Ahnset's visit that morning.

The thunder boomed again, vibrating into Ketahn's bones and swallowing all other sounds, even those of the hammering rain and howling wind. He felt air flow over his hide as Ivy gasped, felt the small, frightened sound she released. And he felt her trembling even after the thunder had faded.

"You are safe, my heartsthread," he said, wrapping a third arm around her as he continued to smooth her hair.

She relaxed, easing the bite of her nails. "I know. Sorry."

Ketahn brushed his knuckles across her cheek and tucked wild strands of her hair behind her ear. "Do not be sorry. I understand."

His mate did not care for thunderstorms. He could not blame her for that; unsettling at best, storms were displays of the raw power of the Eight. Or…were they simply displays of the power of the Tangle? Perhaps he would ask Ivy what her people thought caused such storms. He doubted there could truly be so many monsters in the sky for the gods to battle them so often.

But he spent little time on such thoughts, and he had not allowed himself to wonder if the gentle rain having given way to this fierce storm was a sign of things to come—a sign that the peace he and Ivy had enjoyed was at an end. A spiritspeaker might have said so, as they were ever eager to see the will of the Eight in all things, but Ketahn would not concern himself with that now.

He and Ivy had spent the day together in the den. They'd completed the few minor tasks that had been available, had shared two meals, and had talked, but much of their time had been spent in quiet. In contemplation.

Not even his beautiful, alluring Ivy had been enough to distract Ketahn from his thoughts.

Idly, he slipped his fingers into her hair, grazing her scalp with his claws in slow, tender strokes.

Ahnset had been correct. He could not hide, and he could not hide Ivy. At least not while they remained so close to Takarahl. Yet the problem wasn't that they were unable to hide forever—it was that they could not hide for now. Even the queen had her limits, and her Claw had lost their best tracker in Durax. There were many places in the Tangle even some of the bravest vrix refused to go.

Ketahn would brave any place, any danger, for his mate.

The true challenge was that he'd be traveling not only with

Ivy but an entire pack of humans. Clumsy, small, weak, inexperienced humans. Ketahn's thoughts had returned to that fact over and over again. Remaining here was dangerous, venturing deeper into the Tangle was dangerous, but only the first option guaranteed eventual conflict.

Moving the humans beyond Zurvashi's reach would require preparation and supplies that would take Ketahn two or three moon cycles to gather. But with the flood season looming just ahead—or perhaps just overhead, were this storm its start—he didn't have that much time. The pit could flood in a matter of eightdays, if not far sooner.

Ivy was competent and determined, a fast learner, and it would be a great boon if the other humans were similar, but it still would not be enough to travel as quickly as was necessary.

He tucked his chin against his chest, looking down at his golden-haired mate, and raised his mandibles in a smile.

Yes, Ahnset was right...but so was Ivy. Ketahn was not alone. And the time for reluctance had long since passed. The time for secrets had passed. If his trust in his friends and his sister had been shaken, it was not the fault of the queen or anyone else—only Ketahn was to blame. He alone had lost sight of their bonds. He had allowed those threads to go untended for too long.

And he could not deny that he wanted his kind to become acquainted with Ivy's. He wanted vrix and human to come together in peace, so that both could find happiness and fulfillment. Some part of him, practical and cold, didn't think it was possible or worth the trouble, but he had to believe otherwise.

He didn't want to sever his remaining ties to the vrix. He didn't want to leave everything he'd known behind forever. Ketahn would do so for Ivy without hesitation, but if there was another way...he had to try it, didn't he?

And Ketahn was weary of hiding his mate from the world. He was weary of keeping her tucked away like some secret treasure, like something to be hoarded. He wanted others to see her —to see her radiance, her otherworldly beauty, her kindness.

He wanted the world to see that he'd been blessed by the gods themselves with a mate beyond compare.

If not the world…then at least the vrix he cared about.

Fresh thunder cracked across the sky, and the den swayed and dipped in a strong gust of wind. Ivy released a shaky breath. Its warmth bloomed over his chest. She turned her head and rested her cheek against him, maintaining her solid grip on him. Ketahn's claspers extended around her hips, anchoring her to him.

As the thunder's echoes died, he said, "I have thought upon it, my heartsthread."

"Thought on what?" she asked. "How to make the den more secure?"

Ketahn's mandibles fell, and a low growl sounded in his chest. "Our den is secure, female."

"You sure? That web was looking pretty thin in some spots."

"You are welcome to spin fresh strands to repair it, my *nyleea*."

"Sorry. Humans don't spit webs out of our butts."

"A flaw I will overlook considering how good a handhold your butt makes," Ketahn said, dropping a hand to her backside and squeezing the plump, rounded flesh.

Ivy giggled and lifted her head to look at him. Her eyes still held a glimmer of fear, but it had softened considerably. He knew she was seeking a distraction, something to keep her mind off the raging storm.

She slid her hands up from his sides and smoothed her palms over his chest, tracing the planes and ridges of his hide with her fingers. "You do like my butt…among other things."

He cupped the back of her head in one hand. "There is no part of you I do not like, Ivy."

Pink stained her cheek. She smiled softly and looked down,

settling her palms over his hearts. "So if you were not thinking about how to keep us from falling to our deaths, what were you thinking about?"

"How to protect and provide for all your humans."

Ivy's breath hitched, and her wide eyes snapped up to meet his. "Does that mean...we're going to wake them?"

"Yes, but before that..." Something constricted in his chest. He knew what he had to do, but the weight of it, the risk of it, had not fully hit him. He placed a hand on each of her cheeks, stroking his thumbs just beneath her lips. "Do you trust me, my heartsthread?"

She covered one of his hands with her own and pressed her cheek more firmly into his palm. "With my life, Ketahn."

His mandibles twitched as a deep, powerful warmth flooded him from within, combating the tightness in his chest. "To do what you asked, I must ask my friends to help. Perhaps...to join us, if they will, when we leave this place. That will mean showing you to other vrix, my heartsthread."

"If you trust them, then so do I." The corners of her lips curled up. "I mean, you haven't eaten me yet, so..."

Ketahn squeezed her backside once more as his claspers skimmed down to curl around her thighs. "No, but I will always drink my fill of my sweet mate."

Her cheeks darkened further, and it didn't take long for the scent of her arousal to reach him. It was proof of how much his mate enjoyed his attentions. His stem stirred behind his slit, thrumming with that now familiar ache, and he released a long, low purr.

But this was not yet the time. Not until she knew what he meant to do.

Ketahn smoothed her hair back with one hand. "Ivy, to do this, to help the humans...I must go to Takarahl."

In an instant, the color that had blossomed on her cheeks disappeared, and her grip on his hand strengthened. "But that...

that…" Her breath quickened as fear returned to her eyes. "What about the queen, Ketahn? You can't go back to her."

Her expression pained him like nothing else could have. "I must, Ivy. She will keep searching if I do not, and that will make it much harder to gather supplies and make ready for travel. If they are like you, the other humans will be weak when they first wake. They will need time to gain their strength and adjust to this world. We cannot do as we must if the Queen's Claw is raking the jungle. We need time."

Ivy released his hand and reached out to cradle his jaw. "What about Durax? And what will the queen do to you when she sees you?"

Ketahn removed his hand from her backside and slowly ran it up and down her back. "They will not know of Durax. He is in a place no vrix will go. As for the queen…" He released a huff. "I cannot know what she will do. But I am familiar with Zurvashi, and I think she will be…interested in my bold return. That will give us time. I will be sure to inform my friends of what is to come."

She frowned down at him, and her eyes, alight with concern, flicked between his. "You'll be okay?"

"Nothing will keep me from returning to you, my heartsthread."

Ivy stroked her thumb along his jaw. "And she won't…force you?"

It took him a few moments to decipher her meaning; for all the very specific words in Ivy's language, she often spoke in ways that barely suggested her true meaning. Her question made his hide prickle with an unpleasant tingling. The thought of Zurvashi attempting to claim him…

With a snarl, he rolled aside, flipping Ivy onto her back atop the bed of furs and fluffed silk. He positioned himself over her, caging her in with his arms and pressing his bulging slit between her thighs.

"I will *never* let that happen," he growled, rubbing his face along her neck and drawing in her sweet scent. His claspers clutched her close.

She shivered and wrapped her arms around his neck.

"I am yours alone, my Ivy. No other may claim me."

Ivy turned her face toward him and pressed her lips to his headcrest. "Just be careful. Please."

Ketahn lifted his head and brushed his mouth across hers, sampling the faintest taste of those plump, pink lips. Being careful would mean not going at all. It would mean abandoning Ivy's kind and his own to carry her off into the Tangle where they could never be found. It would mean being selfish, taking what he had conquered. It would mean keeping her like the pet he'd briefly thought her to be.

But he could not do that to her. He could not let his mate's tender heart be filled with such grief and guilt, which surely would take root and grow into resentment. No, there would be no fleeing now. This was the time to turn and face his enemy directly. A path was laid before him, the strands were clear, and he knew how to protect his mate and her people.

All he had to accomplish was the near impossible—appease the queen without submitting to her until the humans were ready to travel.

CHAPTER 5

THE TANGLE WAS peaceful around Takarahl. The beast songs were unconcerned, even pleasant, and a warm breeze rustled the leaves overhead, allowing scattered, flickering beams of sunlight to break through. What glimpses of the sky could be caught were either soothing blue or dappled with fluffy white.

Only lingering droplets on leaves and the puddles in places the sunlight would never touch evidenced the recent storm, which had kept Ketahn and Ivy in their den for another full day after he'd shared his plans with her.

There was no hint of the corruption festering understone only a short distance away, where Queen Zurvashi's rule crippled the vrix of Takarahl.

Ketahn held himself unmoving in a shadowed hollow well above the ground. His vantage allowed him clear view of the rock formation jutting from the jungle floor below.

The rock was circular from above, though its rough sides had clearly never been shaped by vrix hands. It wasn't strange in that it was a huge, solitary stone amidst the roots and trees; there were many large rocks and stony outcroppings throughout the Tangle. But none matched this one, most of all because of the deep, smooth-sided pool resting atop it. The cool water, flowing from an underground spring, ran ceaselessly over the pool's edges and fed into a small stream.

It was like a giant cup that never emptied. The Gods' Cup, some called it.

Lifting his gaze from the stone, Ketahn scanned the jungle. Though this place was known to the vrix, especially in legend, it was rarely visited. The clearing around it had shrunk in the years since Ketahn had first come as a broodling, and the path bridging it to Takarahl was very nearly lost to jungle growth.

But if all went as planned, it would receive several visitors today.

Ketahn had arrived early this morning, after a brief stop at the hidden passageway that ran beneath Moonfall Tunnel. Midday had already crept by. Such waits would not normally have bothered him, but each moment had made him more aware that he was apart from Ivy. His yearning for her always made focusing difficult, and that difficulty was heightened by the fact that she was alone and too far away for him to protect her. All he could do was remind himself that caution was the best means of returning to her safely and, soon enough, putting all this behind them.

Well, remind himself of that and hope that he would be able to return to their den today. The risk of what he intended to do was immense, and he expected he'd soon be told how much of a damned fool he was. As long as he was able to communicate with his friends, as long as they agreed to help, as long as they would care for Ivy should Ketahn's plan result in capture or death, the risks were acceptable.

They had to be.

The sun was halfway between midday and sunfall by the time Ketahn heard a distinct sound—blackrock striking blackrock, a high, sharp clacking that echoed between the trees in a brief but distinct beat.

Ketahn extended a pair of arms out of the hollow and answered with a series of clacks of his own, produced with a blackrock knife and a loose spearhead. A third rhythm sounded from nearby, ending in a brief but familiar flourish that marked it as having been made by Telok.

Despite the uncertainties awaiting him, Ketahn smiled. He hoped it was not foolish to imagine a day in the near future when more vrix knew what a smile was and what it meant. He hoped it was not foolish to long for a day when more vrix would have reason to regularly wear such expressions.

Movement beyond the edge of the clearing caught his attention. He watched as three vrix prowled through the undergrowth, moving slowly so as to produce as little noise as possible. The lead vrix, with bright green markings on his black hide, stepped into the clearing several segments ahead of his companions.

Telok.

Rekosh and Urkot emerged nearly side-by-side, keeping stride with one another despite the differences in their builds; Rekosh was tall and spindly, while Urkot was short and stout.

The three vrix studied their surroundings with alert eyes. Ketahn was glad to see it. He'd expected as much from Telok, who'd hunted in the Tangle for most of his life, but it seemed that Urkot and Rekosh had not lost their instincts after years of living and working understone in Takarahl.

"Where is he?" Urkot asked, his low voice barely carrying to Ketahn over the spring's gentle murmuring.

Telok grunted and angled his gaze up. "Somewhere high."

After a final glance around the clearing to ensure there were no unexpected guests, Ketahn emerged from hiding. Telok's eyes snapped to him immediately.

Ketahn tucked away the spearhead and knife and climbed down. Though there was a great deal to trouble his thoughts, Ketahn's spirit rallied as soon as he was standing before his friends.

"A few moments more and I would have found you," Telok said with a chitter, folding his lower arms across his chest as he planted the butt of his spear in the dirt.

Ketahn chittered, thumping a foreleg against Telok's. "If you must believe that to hold your mind together, I will not argue."

"The two of you stand here and jest," Urkot grumbled, "while the Queen's Claw prowls this very jungle in search of you, Ketahn."

"We cannot fault a fool for finding amusement wherever he turns," said Rekosh, his mandibles twitching with a soft chitter of his own.

Ketahn fought the urge to smile as he stepped to Rekosh and Urkot, brushing a foreleg against each of theirs in greeting. "You have already called me a fool, and I have yet to share my plan."

Mirth danced in Rekosh's eyes. "What have I told you? Always a thrill in your company, Ketahn."

"Would that the Protector had beaten some sense into you both." Urkot stomped on the ground. "The queen is in a rage, and you, Ketahn, are the source of her anger."

"Is that not the usual way of things, Urkot?" Rekosh asked.

"He is right to be concerned," said Telok, who kept his eyes on Ketahn. "This is a rare mood, even for her."

Ketahn's mandibles sagged. His mood fell along with them and then beyond, and he made no attempt to combat the change. As much as he wanted to enjoy this time with his friends, there were pressing matters to attend. He strode to the brim of the Gods' Cup and dipped a pair of hands in, scooping up water to pour into his mouth. The cool, clean liquid was refreshing; there was little water as pure as this in all the Tangle.

Urkot moved closer, placing a rough hand on Ketahn's arm.

"It is more than the queen that troubles you, as though she weren't enough."

"Indeed." Rekosh came close also, leaning a shoulder against the exterior of the rock formation. "Else you would not have left your mysterious message."

"And it is only by chance that I happened to check the undertunnel today." Telok caught some of the spilling water in his cupped hands and splashed it on his face with a content trill. "And even then, we might never have understood it."

Rekosh lifted a hand, palm skyward with long fingers slightly curled. "*The Hunter, the Shaper, the Weaver; parched, even the Eight must quench their thirst.*"

"Sounds like a nonsensical shard of some sacred writing," said Urkot as he rinsed pale stone dust from his hands. "And Shaper guide your hands, Ketahn, but your marks were barely readable."

"Writing has never been a talent of mine," Ketahn replied, turning away from the pool. "I learned only at the insistence of my mother."

Rekosh chittered. "We know. You complained about it every day when we were broodlings."

Ketahn grunted. "That seems an exaggeration."

"My memory seems to match Rekosh's," said Telok.

When Ketahn looked to Urkot for support, the broad shouldered vrix only twitched his mandibles and said, "One would never believe you a steady-handed hunter based on your writing alone. More likely a hatchling playing with a lump of charcoal."

Ketahn swiped a hand through the air and hissed. "The stone upon which I left those marks was small, as was the charcoal with which I made them."

"Of course," Rekosh said. "How could we expect your best work under such conditions?"

Though Rekosh's expression was unchanged, Ketahn heard what Ivy called a *smirk* in his friend's voice.

"Surely you must have called us here because you prefer our barbed insults to the spears of the Claws," said Telok.

"Difficult to choose between the two," Ketahn replied. "At least I feel no guilt in retaliating against the Claws."

"Do not pretend you feel any with us, either." Telok tapped Ketahn's leg with his own.

"Truly, Ketahn, what brings you here?" asked Urkot.

"Anywhere within an eightday's travel of Takarahl is somewhere you ought not be at present," said Rekosh. "Furious as she is, the queen is likely to scent you even from here. She will burst out of the ground like a monster of old to devour you at any moment."

Ketahn longed to find the humor that was undoubtedly in those words, but it eluded him. Zurvashi really was as some monster out of legend—huge, powerful, merciless, and without end to her appetites. But this was one beast the Eight were unwilling to slay, and no mortal vrix seemed able to stand against her either.

He refused to surrender to her regardless.

"I do not ask this lightly, my friends," Ketahn said, meeting the gaze of each of his companions in turn. "I need your aid."

Those words came out dry and raw; they had been expectedly, disappointingly difficult, because their simplicity was deceptive. They felt like an admission of weakness, an acceptance of inadequacy.

Telok's mandibles twitched and drooped, and he tilted his head. "I cannot recall you asking for aid even once in all the time I have known you, Ketahn, for as often as you have given it."

"Do you see? I was right." Urkot tapped his fingers against his chest, but there was neither malice nor arrogance in his gesture and voice. "Something is wrong. Something apart from the queen."

Rekosh made a thoughtful buzz, regarding Ketahn with narrowed eyes. "I knew something was amiss when you came to my den to weave. Had we not received that unannounced visitor, I would have extracted the information from you then."

"Regardless"—Telok scanned the edges of the clearing, high and low, before looking back at Ketahn—"we are all here now, and it is best not to linger."

Ketahn nodded, not realizing the gesture had no real meaning to his friends until he'd completed it. "Rekosh is right."

Urkot growled.

"I always am," Rekosh said, then cocked his head. "About which part, specifically?"

Now Ketahn searched the edges of the clearing. The Tangle, ever dangerous, had never felt so threatening as it did with Zurvashi as his enemy. "I would do best to be beyond her reach. Far beyond."

Urkot absently brushed his lower hand across the surface of the rock formation. "You mean for us to help you flee?"

"I do. I will require supplies for a long journey." Ketahn released a huff. Even now, the words caught in his throat. He did not want to share Ivy, even the idea of her, with anyone. "Supplies for…several travelers."

"Several?" Rekosh pushed away from the stone to stand straight. "Ketahn…"

"Do you…do you mean for us to come along?" Urkot asked.

"I cannot ask that much of you." Ketahn extended three legs, brushing one of them against each of his friends' forelegs. "But I cannot deny that your company would be welcome."

"This relates to whatever it is you have been hiding, does it not?" Rekosh asked.

"It does."

"You have kept something so grave from us?" Urkot huffed and stomped again, sending up a faint cloud of dust. "We are here to share your burdens, Ketahn. A web cannot hold with but a single thread any more than a tunnel can stand with a single support."

A gust of wind swept through the clearing. A branch snapped somewhere nearby, creating more noise as it fell through leaves and other branches. All four vrix turned their heads toward the sounds, and all four were motionless and silent for several heartbeats afterward, watching, listening.

"The wind," Rekosh whispered. "Ever eager for mischief."

"We must not tarry much longer," said Urkot, turning back to Ketahn.

"The wind bears the scent of another storm." Telok's voice was low and distracted. When Ketahn glanced at him, Telok was looking skyward to where the gaps in the jungle canopy displayed far more cloud than earlier.

"A storm is certain," Ketahn rumbled.

"Come then." Rekosh eased closer, curiosity sparking in his eyes. "Tell us. Else our imaginings are bound to be far worse than the truth."

"I…" Ivy flashed through Ketahn's mind's eye, and warmth flared in his chest. All his desire and adoration for her flowed through him freely, and his instincts—to protect her from everything, from everyone—flared in response. Any male was a threat, a potential challenger.

But not these males. Not his friends.

A long, slow breath escaped him. He shoved aside some of those instincts and glanced at his friends' faces. "It will be easier for you to see for yourselves."

"Have you recently developed a fondness for riddles?" Rekosh asked, leaning closer still as though to study Ketahn's eyes.

"I have kept something hidden from you, and I mean to amend that, but it is not a thing words can rightly explain.

Come to my den tomorrow near sunfall and all will be made clear."

"We shall come, Ketahn," said Urkot, crossing his forearms before his chest to invoke the Eight; the gesture was incomplete due to his missing lower left arm.

Rekosh and Telok mimicked the gesture.

"What do you need of us until then?" Telok asked.

Ketahn told them the items he hoped to obtain. Though some certainly must have seemed strange—especially all the blackrock, leather, cloth, bone needles, and waterskins—none of his friends questioned him. Nor did they question the directions he gave them to find his secluded den.

"You must smuggle those items out of Takarahl a little at a time, so as not to arouse suspicion," Ketahn said afterward.

Rekosh clicked his mandible fangs. "You need not point out the obvious, Ketahn."

"I will not, when you no longer have that far off light in your eyes."

"Pay no mind to that." Rekosh waved a hand. "I was simply wondering as to the nature of this secret. Who have you been hiding away? A secret mate, perhaps?"

Ketahn was not sure how he held his calm in that moment. Rekosh had guessed it with apparent ease, but he would never guess the full truth—that Ketahn's hidden mate was a creature from somewhere amongst the stars.

"You will see soon enough, Rekosh, and it will be more shocking than any of the gossip you have ever heard in Takarahl —and it will seem more unreal."

"Even more so than the rumors that the queen has an identical broodsister locked away in her chambers who she bleeds a little every day?"

Ketahn cocked his head to the side. "What? Rekosh, what nonsense is this?"

"Ugh." Urkot thumped Ketahn's hindquarters with the tip of

a thick leg. "Please, Ketahn, do not excite him. It is I who must always listen to his chattering when he is in such a state."

Rekosh, Ketahn, and Telok chittered, but the humor faded all too quickly. The storm scent, though still faint, was stronger now than it had been only moments before. Much as he would have liked to linger and speak with his friends of less weighty matters—or return to Ivy—there was more to be done.

"We had best depart," Ketahn said, "but I must ask one more thing of you before we do."

"Anything Ketahn," Urkot said.

"Whatever you need," offered Telok.

Rekosh gestured, quite gently and gracefully, for Ketahn to continue.

"When I set out for my den, I will leave another message in the undertunnel. Should you not find one by the time you are ready to depart tomorrow…I ask that you make the journey to my den regardless and care for what you find there as though it were the most precious thing in all the jungle."

Because as far as Ketahn was concerned, Ivy *was* the most precious thing in the jungle—the most precious thing in all existence.

"Ah, it is a secret mate, is it not?" Rekosh buzzed. "Perhaps a previously unknown heir to Takari's bloodline?"

Urkot tapped Rekosh's leg. "Enough, Rekosh."

"Where are you going now, Ketahn, if not straight back to your den?" Telok asked, narrowing his eyes.

Ketahn released a slow, heavy breath, stood a little straighter, and glanced toward Takarahl. He curled his hands into fists. "I go to have an audience with the queen."

Utter silence gripped the clearing; even the spring seemed to go quiet.

"Shaper, unmake me, you damned fool," Urkot growled.

At the same time, Telok pressed a hand over his face. "By their eightfold eyes…"

With those words, the conversation seemed complete. Ketahn chittered, though he felt little amusement. The weight of his friends' gazes was immense, but he knew he could rely upon them. He knew, come what would, at least Ivy would be safe.

In the end, that was all that mattered.

CHAPTER 6

KETAHN WAS WRAPPED in two shrouds as he crept along the corridor—one of black silk to hide his distinct purple markings, and one of a hunter's calm and focus to steady his hands and sharpen his senses. From beneath the shadow of his hood, he peered toward the end of the winding passageway.

Life-sized statues of Takarahl's former queens stood on either side of the corridor, each in its own alcove. The glowing crystals at the base of each statue illuminated the hall. Lush, flowing swaths of silk hung on the walls and ceiling, much of it decorated with intricate embroidery and dyed the queen's favorite shade of purple.

The purple she'd started a war over.

Old rage crackled under the surface of Ketahn's calm, but he refused to let it out. He refused to let it deter him from his purpose.

The corridor straightened after this bend, and the mats on the floor—wicker with interwoven silk of exactly eight different colors—led all the way to the chamber at the end.

The chamber's huge stone doors were open. The gems and gold inlaid on their carved faces glinted in the light of the nearby crystals. Memories flashed through Ketahn's mind unbidden, a torrent he could neither halt nor divert.

His hands curled into fists, still clutching the shroud. Few common vrix ever walked here in the queen's sanctum, from which the city was truly ruled. The chamber with the big doors was but one of many along these corridors, but it was one he remembered well—the Council Chamber, where Ketahn had stood many times years ago as Zurvashi, her advisors, and her Primes had planned every move of her war with Kaldarak.

He'd first stepped into that chamber as an eager young hunter, inexperienced but having already proven his skill against the thornskulls. He'd last exited it as a scarred warrior shattered by what he'd lost, held together only by the strength of his bitterness and the heat of his fury.

Today he would enter that chamber again as Ivy's mate, determined to destroy the shadows that had so long loomed over and within him with the radiance of his joy at having her as his own.

A pair of Fangs guarded the entryway. They stood in rigid, disciplined stances, holding their long war spears in their right hands. The Council Chamber behind them was lit with the flickering blue-green light of burning spinewood sap. The glow cast the two figures inside the chamber, both females, in an unnatural light, obscuring their features and making them look like shades caught between the realm of the living and the realm of spirits.

Those figures were conversing, but the cloth and wicker in the wide hall muted the echoes that were so prevalent throughout the rest of Takarahl, and Ketahn could not make out what the two were saying. Yet he did not need to hear or see clearly to recognize the larger of the two figures.

Zurvashi.

He felt the queen as surely as though he were bound to her by a silk rope around his neck; he was being drawn toward her.

Ketahn narrowed his eyes and barely contained a growl. If the Eight had guided him to Ivy, had willed him to take her as his mate, to bind himself to her forever, they'd also bound his fate to the queen. One of those bonds was hope, joy, kindness, passion and desire. The other was despair, sorrow, cruelty, fury and hatred. His connection to Zurvashi was the one thread in his life he was eager to sever.

Keeping low, he moved forward just enough to duck into the alcove behind the nearest statue, following the silent but insistent guidance of his instincts. Infiltrating this deep into Takarahl had been no easy task; the tunnels were bristling with more Fangs than he'd seen since the war, and he'd glimpsed several Claws prowling the city, as well.

But Rekosh's suggestion—a black shroud, a stooped posture, and a stilted gait—had proven as effective as it was simple in navigating Takarahl's common spaces.

The true challenge lay just ahead, and Ketahn would overcome it.

Adjusting the shroud to cover himself more fully, Ketahn waited, marking time by his steady heartbeats. The patrolling Fangs who'd passed him several moments before would reach the other end of the corridor soon…

If all went to plan, Ketahn would have only a moment to act.

Not for the first time, he reflected upon the foolishness of this. He knew that he was taunting death, that he was perched on the edge of disaster, but it was the boldness of this endeavor that made all the difference.

Heavy steps, accompanied by the clanking and jingling of golden adornments, sounded from the direction from which he'd come. He glanced toward the sounds. A Fang strode around the bend, her war spear held at the ready. Ketahn did not recognize her, but she looked young—perhaps as young as he and his broodsister had been when they'd been swept up into the war against Kaldarak.

He shifted his position to watch as the Fang approached the Council Chamber. The second figure in the room, having heard the commotion, walked to the open entryway. The light of the crystals fell upon her face, granting Ketahn his first clear view of her. Prime Fang Korahla.

"A disturbance, Prime Fang," the younger female announced as she halted before Korahla and assumed a stiff pose.

Korahla glanced past the younger female. "Of what sort?"

"A mess just inside the entrance to the corridor. Something was smashed."

"So clean it." Despite the dulled echoes, Zurvashi's voice carried out of the Council Chamber, rumbling with fury, firm with authority, and still somehow hollow with indifference.

Korahla's mandibles twitched, but she did not look back at the queen. "Need more information," she said almost too quietly to hear.

The young Fang replied, but her voice was too low for Ketahn to understand her words. Yet even from this distance, he could see Korahla's eyes harden.

"You two," the Prime Fang growled, rousing the door guards to attention.

Ketahn tensed; Korahla was an elite warrior with keen senses and a shrewd understanding of battle. If anyone could stop him before he reached his goal, it was her.

"Go with her," Korahla continued. "Get someone to clean up and tell the exterior guards to search the area."

Ketahn sank lower still, pooling in the shadows and watching the Fangs through a narrow gap in his shroud. Prime Fang Korahla stood at the center of the entryway, looking more unmovable than the stone around her, as the other Fangs hurried along the corridor in the direction of Ketahn's little *gift*.

Korahla narrowed her green eyes and folded her lower arms across her chest. Ketahn willed her to move, whether it was to rejoin the queen or accompany the other Fangs; so long as he was able to get into the chamber before she spotted him, it didn't matter where she went.

"This matter need not concern you," the queen said. "Return to me."

The Prime Fang held her position. "There are crushed mender roots in the hall, my queen. Who would it be but him?"

"Any one of the worms his defiance has inspired."

"I know none so bold as he."

Zurvashi snarled. "Ketahn has shown his true spirit. He cowers in the Tangle as though it can shield him from my wrath."

Korahla turned to face the queen. "That is not his way, Zurvashi."

"Do you question my judgment, Korahla?" The indistinct figure of the queen moved within the chamber, the sickly light briefly reflecting in her eyes.

"No, my queen," Korahla replied tightly. "I simply advise caution."

The queen turned away again, waving a hand dismissively. "If you are so concerned, join the others. Waste your time. So long as you are out of my sight, I care not. But know that you would do best not to cross me again, Prime Fang or not."

Movements stiff, Korahla offered the queen an apologetic bow before setting off down the corridor. Only then did Ketahn's hearts quicken.

Foolish was not nearly strong enough a word to describe what he was doing. He would have to ask Ivy if there were any human words to better describe this.

Korahla's stride was measured, dignified, and powerful, carrying her rapidly closer to him.

Moving as carefully as possible, Ketahn grasped the knife he'd tied to his waist beside the pouch that had carried the mender roots. His quarrel was with Zurvashi alone, and he had no wish to battle Korahla... But the thought of being taken without a fight was intolerable.

As the Prime Fang drew near, Ketahn spied something that made his concerns vanish for a moment—a golden band around Korahla's left mandible, identical to the one his broodsister had been wearing on her right mandible lately.

He clenched the knife grip. Anything for Ivy. *Anything*. But drawing blood before he reached the queen would only guarantee that he never left Takarahl again, and fighting Korahla would be like fighting an elder sister—or like thrusting a spear into an old friend's back.

Her pace slowed, and her back stiffened. Her mandibles drew together haltingly, as though with immense effort, and spread apart. A low growl rumbled in her chest; she was close enough now that Ketahn felt the sound as clearly as he heard it. The leather grip of her spear creaked unhappily within her strengthening grasp.

Prime Fang Korahla lifted her upper left hand and touched the pad of a finger to the gold band on her mandible. She let out a heavy breath, and some of her tension seemed to fade. Ketahn released his hold on the knife; Korahla strode onward.

The moment she was out of sight, Ketahn snapped his attention to the Council Chamber. Zurvashi stood within, her back to the doorway, leaning over the raised slab at the center of the room. The blue-green firelight still granted her an unsettling air.

Ketahn rose and stalked forward, keeping his steps light and holding the shroud snug around his body. He followed the wall toward the chamber—toward fate. But whatever the gods had planned, he would ensure this was only one more strand in the tangled web of his fate, not an end but a crossing point leading to something more.

Leading him back into the Tangle, where his ultimate fate—

his heartsthread—awaited him in the hanging den he'd called home for seven years.

A cold calm slowed his hearts as he approached the entryway, absorbing his rage and turning it into something new, something solid and sharp. He'd not made a sound in his approach, and the queen had not moved.

Ketahn's hand itched with want to draw his knife. This was a chance to catch her unaware, to change Takarahl forever—and taking that chance would mean never seeing Ivy again, for there was but one way out of here…and it would be blocked by a great many Fangs.

He entered the Council Chamber, shoved back the memories threatening to rise to the surface, stomped down the instincts urging him not to turn his back on the beast before him, and turned to slam the doors shut. The sound of them closing echoed in the chamber and pulsed through the floor. Before the echo had stopped, he swung down the thick wood beam to bar the door.

He spun to face Zurvashi. She hadn't moved from her place, but her posture had stiffened, and her mandibles were parted.

"The last of my mercy was spent on Sathai," she said, scraping her claws atop the stone slab. "Her death was swift. But you will suffer for provoking my ire, and before I am through, you will wish you had learned from her mistake."

Ketahn let his hands fall to his sides. The shroud had felt like armor as he'd made his way here. Now it felt as though it was heavier than solid stone and yet offered no more protection than a blade of grass.

"Speak your name. It will be remembered for only as long as it takes to wipe out your cowardly bloodline." Zurvashi stood up straight and twisted toward Ketahn, a malevolent gleam in her amber eyes as they fell upon him.

Her mandibles twitched, and she chittered. The danger in her stance diminished, but only by a thread's width. "A male?

And it seems you have already brought a death shroud. Convenient, as there will be no one to weave one for you before your flesh has rotted off your bones."

Though unease fluttered in his gut, Ketahn grasped the silk shroud with one hand and pulled it off.

The queen's mandibles fell, and she tilted her head.

"You," she growled, taking a step toward him. "Shall all I just said stand? You deserve nothing less than destruction."

Yet Ketahn knew Zurvashi well enough to recognize the glint of curiosity in her gaze. He needed to prey upon it. He needed more time.

"You will do no such thing, Zurvashi," he said, filling his words with as much coldness and authority as he could muster.

One of her hands had lingered atop the slab; she dragged it off as she took another step toward him, raking her claws over the stone surface. "You seem to have forgotten, little Ketahn, who rules this place."

He chittered, somehow preventing the sound from being wholly flooded by bitterness and hatred. "I know well, Zurvashi."

The fine hairs on her legs bristled, and her adornments jingled as she tensed. "And what was your queen's command?"

Instinct demanded he reject her along with any notion that she could command him. There was only one female he would serve, and he'd do so gladly. Zurvashi would never be Ivy.

"To return for the High Claiming and conquer her," he said.

"Did you obey?" Zurvashi took another step closer; only the stiffness in her legs betrayed her intention. She leapt at Ketahn, unleashing a growl that would've halted an enraged yatin in its tracks, her fingers curled and claws ready to strike.

Ketahn darted aside. He felt the air move, displaced by Zurvashi's passing body, felt the floor shake as she came down in the place he'd been standing. She slammed all four hands against the doors to stop herself. The doors rattled, and something cracked; Ketahn couldn't be sure whether it was the wood beam or the stone itself.

She turned to face him again, her mandibles wider than ever, their fangs and golden rings gleaming in the eerie light. Korahla and the Fangs would know now. Ketahn had to end this before they managed to get into the chamber.

"You made me look like a fool," the queen snarled, pushing away from the doors.

"I am doing what you need," Ketahn replied.

Zurvashi lunged at him. Her speed might have been surprising had he not seen it so many times before. He jumped aside, narrowly avoiding her huge, grasping hands, and put on his own burst of speed to leap atop the stone slab and skitter to its far side. The tips of his legs disturbed what the queen had been brooding over—a crude chalk map of the jungle around Takarahl.

"You mean to tell me what I need?" Zurvashi roared. She moved toward the slab, and one of her legs caught in the long cloth that had been wrapped around her waist and draped over her hindquarters. With a frustrated grunt, she tore the silk off and threw it away. "I tell you what I need, and you do all it takes to deliver! That is the way of this world. *My* world."

"You demanded I conquer you," Ketahn said, rising fully to tower over her for once. "You demanded a worthy male. Obedience is not what you need of me, Zurvashi. You need an equal."

"Insolent, grub bellied little—"

"I could have vanished into the Tangle with ease," Ketahn growled; even now, he and Ivy could have been far, far away from here. "I could have been done with you and Takarahl forever. Do you believe I did not anticipate your wrath?"

She narrowed her eyes and curled her hands into fists, chest heaving with her heavy breaths. "You are a fool, cursed by the Eight with so much talent and potential but none of the wisdom to apply it."

She was off balance. Ketahn wasn't sure he'd ever seen her like this, but he had to press his advantage.

He strode toward her, stopping at the edge of the slab. "Yet here I stand, Zurvashi, at the heart of your sanctum."

"My Fang has failed me."

Muffled voices came from the corridor, followed shortly by a heavy bang on the doors. This time, the wood beam did crack, though it did not yet yield. Zurvashi didn't so much as flinch; she just stared at Ketahn.

"No," he said. "They were simply pitted against a superior opponent."

A hungry light sparked in the queen's eyes. "You, little Ketahn, are bold. Bold beyond reason."

Ketahn spread his arms to the sides. "As a conqueror must be. You do not need a male to submit to your will, Zurvashi. You need a male who will face you directly…and elevate you in doing so."

The words tasted of ash on his tongue, but they were necessary.

She took a leisurely step closer. "You assume I will forgive how you have slighted me?"

Everything within Ketahn revolted against him, demanding he not do what he intended, but he reminded himself it was for Ivy. For Ivy, he needed to placate this female. For Ivy, he needed to convince the queen.

He stepped down from the slab and closed the distance between himself and Zurvashi, refusing to betray even a hint of how difficult each step was. She angled her head down to hold his gaze.

Another slam on the doors; another crack of breaking wood.

"I will conquer you, Zurvashi. I will give you all you deserve. And you will know that the male you wanted is unrivaled. The High Claiming means nothing. The queen should not be conquered alongside so many common females."

She stared into his eyes. Her scent filled his lungs upon his next breath, having already taken on the heady strength that had almost been his undoing in the past. He braced himself, preparing to battle its influence.

Zurvashi's scent struck him with its full force, invading every thread of his being as though it were being plunged into him on the points of a thousand spears. Despite his anticipation of its effect, that smell produced a spark in his core, coaxed heat into his groin, and whispered seductively to the very instincts he'd hoped to silence.

It threatened to rob him of his willpower. It threatened to claim him on a level beneath his waking mind, beyond his ability to choose.

Ketahn couldn't submit. He couldn't betray his mate—he *would* not. Ivy was his. Though she was so wildly different from Ketahn, from any vrix, she was his, and he wanted no other. The queen's scent was powerful. The deep-rooted instincts responding to that scent were powerful.

But there was nothing as powerful as Ketahn's heartsthread, nothing as powerful as his bond with Ivy.

Those bestial instincts grew into longing—and that longing was for Ivy and Ivy alone.

"Eight days," he said. "And then I will deliver unto you eight gifts worthy of a queen. Then I will conquer you, Zurvashi."

She betrayed nothing now—the veteran warrior queen at play. One of her hands shot up and clamped around his throat. Before he could react, she'd caught three of his arms in her other hands.

More shouting came from the corridor, followed by a slam on the door like a crash of thunder. Zurvashi lifted Ketahn. Briefly, only the tips of his rearmost legs were touching the floor, and all he could do was grasp her forearm with his free hand.

She slammed him down atop the slab. His back took the

brunt of the impact, but the greatest pain was at the point where his hindquarters met his torso, which was hit by the slab's edge; it felt like a blade. Then Zurvashi was over him, pinning him with her body, crushing him, forcing his legs aside with her own and filling his vision with her face.

She brushed a foreleg along one of his. "What is this scent that clings to you? I have never smelled its like…"

Ketahn fought back a growl as a strangling vine of dread coiled around his insides. He thought he'd scrubbed all the smells from his hide before coming to Takarahl, thought he'd been thorough enough. But Ivy's scent must have clung to him despite his efforts, and he did not want Zurvashi to have it, did not want her to know *anything* about his mate.

"Strangely sweet." Zurvashi's mandible fang brushed the side of his face as she dipped her head to sniff his cheek. Her pelvis pressed down on his; their slits brushed together, hers radiating stunning, beckoning heat.

Impossibly, the queen's scent intensified. She shifted her hips, rubbing her slit forcefully against his, and he felt her flesh part, felt that heat flare. Lust sparkled in her amber eyes.

"What have you been up to out there, Ketahn?"

Ketahn clenched his claspers toward one another, closing his slit as tightly as possible.

Zurvashi's gaze darkened, and she pushed down harder.

He made a noise; whether it had been a word or a shapeless sound of rage didn't matter, as Zurvashi silenced him by squeezing his throat.

With a final boom, the wood beam snapped, and the stone doors burst inward.

"I should pluck you apart one limb at a time," Zurvashi hissed.

Fear pressed in around Ketahn's hearts, but he did not allow it to take root. Ivy was all that was important, and his friends would take care of her. They would keep her safe.

He held the queen's gaze unwaveringly despite the pain, despite the burning in his lungs, despite the revolting pressure and friction she was exerting on his slit. There was shouting and movement all around, but he afforded it no attention.

"But I am intrigued now," Zurvashi purred. She lifted her head, trailing a line of pain across his cheek as she dragged her mandible fang away, slicing his hide just under the cut Durax had inflicted. "You surprise me, Ketahn. I trust you will demonstrate that my choosing you was the correct decision. You have a single eightday." Her grip on his throat strengthened. "Then my patience is no more."

She slapped a pair of hands on his chest and shoved herself off him, forcing the breath out of his lungs. His vision swam as he fought for air, as he clawed at wakefulness and willed away the darkness encroaching on the edges of his consciousness. He could not succumb; he needed to return to Ivy. He needed to hold her in his arms and let her scent overcome Zurvashi's, needed to forget about all this, if only for a short while. And then he had to act, because this had only reinforced what he'd already known—he had to get Ivy and the others far away from Takarahl with all possible haste.

"There shall be a reckoning for this failure, Korahla," the queen said. "All of you, out. And be sure our dear little hunter finds his way back into the jungle."

"Yes, my queen," someone said in a gruff, familiar voice. The Prime Fang.

Powerful hands grasped Ketahn's right arms and pulled him up off the slab. Though his joints threatened to buckle, and his head felt as though it were spinning, he managed to get his legs beneath him and find some semblance of balance.

Those hands belonged to Korahla. She kept hold of his arms and moved beside him, half guiding and half dragging him forward. "Back to your postings," she growled.

Ketahn barely registered the movement around him. He was

focused mainly upon two things—keeping his legs in motion as Korahla led him into the corridor and the next actions necessary to achieve his goals. He'd gained an eightday, but that time came at a high price, and it would depend entirely upon Zurvashi's whim.

He was so, so tired of being subject to the queen's tempers.

The sooner Ivy and the humans were ready to travel, the better. They didn't have months to learn and prepare like she'd had.

"You accursed fool," Korahla grumbled. "Your sister best not have had part in this."

"She did not."

Korahla huffed. "Good. I do not know whether she will be glad or appalled to hear of all this, but at least she will not require reprimand."

Ketahn glanced at the gold band on Korahla's mandible again, this time thoughtfully. After a moment, he chittered, the sound surprisingly genuine. "Both."

"By the Eight, Ketahn, I pray you know what you are doing."

He couldn't say whether he did or not, but he was certain of one thing—*why* he was doing it.

And he'd be back with his reason, his Ivy, soon.

CHAPTER 7

THOUGH IT HAD ONLY BEEN four days, it was strange to once again be standing in the bright white stasis room, the one part of the *Somnium* untouched by time. Ivy swept her gaze over the cryochambers on either side of the room. Out of twenty, only seven were functioning. Seven remaining humans—eight counting Ivy herself. They were all that was left. Five thousand hopeful colonists cut down to eight.

Ivy clutched the strap of her bag. Sweat dampened her palms, and apprehension swirled in her stomach. She'd wanted this, but now that she was here, she was nervous. She was about to pull seven people out of stasis and introduce them to a harsh, alien world that was home to giant talking spider people, and on top of that, she had to be the one to tell them that any friends or family they might have had on this ship were very likely dead.

It's the right thing to do.

She knew it was. There was no way that Ivy could have gone on with her life knowing that everyone left here would die within two years. They deserved a chance.

Ivy just...didn't know how to go about waking them.

"What is wrong, my heartsthread?" Ketahn asked from behind her.

"I'm scared."

He placed a hand on each of her shoulders and gently guided her to turn around. Once she was facing him, he cupped her cheeks between his lower pair of hands. "Nothing will happen to you. I will protect you, Ivy. Always."

Regardless of her stinging tears, she kept her gaze locked with his as she turned her face into his palm. In this bright room, his eyes were so vibrant a purple, gleaming with tenderness and affection, but even the powerful artificial lights could not overcome the shadows in the depths of his gaze. He'd suffered at the hands of the queen yesterday, and the weight of everything was clearly taking its toll on him.

Guilt and doubt flooded her, sour and thick in her belly. *Was she doing the right thing? Was she being selfish? How could she allow Ketahn to suffer like this just to assuage her own remorse?*

"My *nyleea*," he rumbled, stroking the pad of his thumb over her cheek. "Tell me. What troubles you?"

Her chest constricted, and for a moment, it was hard to breathe. Despite what he'd been subjected to, despite all he'd endured for her sake, Ketahn's only concern was for Ivy.

She flattened her palm on his chest over his hearts. Her vision blurred as those tears filled her eyes. "Am I doing the right thing? Am I... Should we just go? Right now, far away from here, far away from the queen, to somewhere you'll be safe?"

He chittered; the sound was warm and gentle, a little amused and a little sorrowful. "We will go, Ivy. Soon. But this"—he lifted his chin, gesturing at the pods behind her—"is right. You are right. We cannot leave them to die, not when they have a chance to live."

Ivy stepped closer to him. Ketahn dropped his lower hands from her face and wrapped his arms around her. One of his forelegs came forward and brushed intimately along her calf. His fine hairs were soft, teasing her bare skin.

"I'm scared because I…I don't know how they'll react. I don't know how I'll make them understand without making them panic. How I'll keep them calm, keep them focused… I don't even know if they'll listen to me."

Ketahn tilted his head. "Why would they not listen?"

She frowned, dropping her gaze. "Because I'm…no one. As far as this colony was concerned, I was just going to be a laborer and a breeder. I don't have any special skills, don't have any special knowledge, don't—"

Ketahn silenced her by pressing a finger to her lips. Once she met his gaze again, he leaned down to tip his forehead against hers. "You have survived the Tangle for many eightdays, my heartsthread. You have taken lessons on hunting, trapping, tracking. You know more about the jungle than any of them."

Ivy drew in a slow, deep breath, and let it out in a shaky exhalation. "Because I have you."

"And you will always have me. But you are enough. Do you know what I say, Ivy?"

Warmth filled her chest, easing some of the tightness there. "I do."

He brushed the seam of his mouth across her forehead in a delicate kiss, holding her just a bit closer as he did so. "Good."

She savored his embrace, drawing all the strength and comfort she could from it. When he relaxed his hold, Ivy turned and once more faced reality. She set her bag on the floor, stepped to the nearest functioning cryochamber, and gazed down at the woman sleeping within.

"Her name is Ahmya Hayashi," Ivy said, studying the woman's delicate features and long, black hair. "I met her during training."

Ketahn moved into place beside Ivy. "She is a friend?"

"Kind of? I think I was too scared to let anyone get close, and she was really shy and usually kept to herself. I think…I think if I had allowed it, we could have become friends."

"The chance has not passed."

Ivy stared down at Ahmya's face, and her lips curled into a small smile. "No, it hasn't."

Dropping her gaze to the control panel at the front of the pod, she tapped the screen. At the bottom was a red button which read *EMERGENCY AWAKENING*.

The pod's interior lighting came to life, illuminating Ahmya.

"Colonist Ahmya Hayashi, number four three six," said the computer in a disembodied voice from overhead. "Normal vitals. Confirm emergency awakening sequence."

Curling her fingers into her palm, Ivy drew her lips into her mouth, bit them, and took in another calming breath before tapping the button again.

"Emergency awakening initiated," the computer said. The floor beneath Ivy's feet vibrated just enough for her to feel it. The tubes connected to Ahmya emptied of whatever vital fluids had been flowing through them and retracted, and the interior of the cryochamber filled with mist.

"Subject being awakened without recommended adjustment period," the computer continued. "May suffer temporary lethargy, nausea, dizziness, disorientation, fatigue, and difficulty concentrating. Please consult a medical technician to report any issues."

The pod hissed, repressurizing, and then the clear lid swung up and backward. The mist dissipated as the pod's bed rose, lifting Ahmya so she lay at forty-five-degree angle. Still, she slept.

Ivy was tempted to reach out and touch her to see if she was real. Though one hundred and sixty-eight years had passed since they'd left Earth, it had only been two months since Ivy had been awakened. It was still a long time without seeing another human being, wondering all along if she was the only one left.

Stepping away from Ahmya, Ivy repeated the process with the other six colonists. There were three other women—Ella Lewis, Callie Wright, and Lacey Anderson—and three men—William Reed, Cole Walker, and Diego Rodriguez.

None of them stirred. Their eyes remained closed, and they continued to sleep peacefully. Ivy had been like this when Ketahn had stumbled upon this place and accidently released her. He'd stolen her from here, and she'd woken face-to-face with a monster in a dark, unknown place. She remembered her terror. While she expected confusion from these survivors when they regained consciousness, they'd at least be in a familiar place, and that would help calm them as Ivy explained everything. Except…

"Ketahn?"

He'd been staring at the humans with his mandibles twitching faintly, but he looked at Ivy upon hearing her speak. "Yes, my heartsthread?"

"I…think it would be best if you left."

His eyes flared, and he turned to face her fully. "I will not leave you."

"It would only be for a little while."

Ketahn gestured toward the open pods. "I do not trust them. Not with you, Ivy."

Ivy stepped closer to him and clasped a hand around his wrist, gently pulling it to her chest to place his palm between her breasts, over her heart. She felt the light prick of his claws and the roughness of his palm against her skin. "I will be fine. Trust me. Please?"

He cupped the back of her head in one big hand and held her gaze. "I trust you. Not them. I cannot protect you if I am away."

"I'm not asking you to go far." Ivy lowered his hand and slipped her arms around him, pressing her ear against his chest.

She closed her eyes, allowing his hearts' rhythm to soothe her, and when his arms encircled her, she felt safe and sheltered. "Do you remember how I acted when I first saw you?"

An unhappy sound rumbled in his chest, making it clear that he did indeed remember.

"They'll be sick and weak when they wake, and if you're the first thing they see, they'll be frightened too. I'll be fine." She opened her eyes and tipped her head back to look up at him. "Just let me talk to them, tell them what happened, and prepare them for what they're going to see. Then I will introduce you to them."

He stared into her eyes, his gaze unreadable. His mandibles drooped, but the nod he offered was firm. "I will see to Durax. Better the others do not see what remains of him."

"Thank you."

Ketahn caught her chin. "You will call for me if you need me."

"I will."

When he bent down, she instinctively stood on her toes to press her lips against his mouth, gifting him a lingering, tender kiss that neither of them seemed eager to break.

She couldn't lie to herself; she didn't want him to go, especially considering that he'd been gone for most of yesterday, leaving her alone in the den, worried sick over what would befall him while he was in Takarahl. Their parting now, though almost insignificant in comparison, roused those same feelings.

It was Ketahn who finally pulled away. Gently, he hooked a few loose strands of her hair with a claw and tucked them behind her ear. "I will see you soon, my heartsthread."

She smiled at him, and he lifted his mandibles in his version of the expression. Then he released his embrace, turned, and left the room, his steps whisper-quiet on the hard floor.

Despite being surrounded by seven other people, Ivy felt more alone in that moment than ever before.

CHAPTER 8

TIME PASSED at a crawl after Ketahn left, and Ivy spent it in silence amongst the sleeping humans. It would've been easy to mistake this room for a morgue—it was so still, so silent, and the air was almost chillingly crisp after weeks in the hot, humid jungle. Even the living humans were unmoving.

And it didn't help that there were twelve pods serving as caskets for people who were gone forever.

Ivy ran a hand through her hair, tugging it back from her face as she glanced around. Releasing a slow breath through her mouth, she returned to her bag, crouched down, and opened it. She removed the two waterskins and the various fruits and dried meats from inside. With nothing else to do, Ivy sat down with her back against the wall and waited.

The silence stretched, eerie and lonely, giving Ivy's mind far too much time to wander, allowing her anxieties far too much space to multiply. Her last fulltime job had been as a cashier at a grocery store. She really wasn't qualified to be tending to and briefing anyone in this situation. What if she said or did something wrong? What if she...what if she messed up, and somebody got hurt or died because of it?

Pressing her lips together, she struggled to hold back that fear, that worry. She was doing *something*. That made a difference, didn't it?

And I have Ketahn.

He'd done so much for Ivy, even though he hadn't known anything about her or her species. She'd watched him be devoured by helplessness and despair when she was sick, and she'd watched him push through it, doing everything and anything he could to help her. That was the example she had to follow.

If she didn't know what to do, she had to do what felt right. And this felt right, despite all her misgivings.

Still, that didn't stop Ivy from desperately hoping that one of these people had training that would help get them through this —and that they all recovered their wits soon.

A strangled gasp broke the silence, startling Ivy. Though Ahmya had been the first to be brought out of stasis, it hadn't been her to make the sound. It had come from across the room. Shoving away from the wall, Ivy snatched up one of the water-skins and stood.

Ella Lewis was breathing heavily, her eyelids fluttering. Her fingers curled, digging her nails into the padding of the pod's bed. "H-how long...does it take to...fall asleep?" she asked. Her voice was rough and weak, just like Ivy expected from someone who'd been unconscious for nearly seventeen decades.

Ivy hurried toward Ella and placed a hand upon her shoulder. "Shh. You actually just woke up. I need you to take some deep, steady breaths, okay? Try to relax."

"Okay," Ella said. She drew in a deep breath, and her brows creased as she released it shakily. Her skin was coated in a sheen of sweat despite the cool air. "I feel sick."

Ivy brushed the woman's brown hair from her pale face and tucked it behind her ear. "You...you might feel that way for a little while. It's a side effect of being brought out of stasis, but you'll be fine, okay? Just try to stay calm and keep breathing."

Ella slitted her eyes open. It took a few moments for them to focus on Ivy, pupils dilating and contracting repeatedly. "Are we there? We're on Xolea?"

A pang struck Ivy's heart. She caught her bottom lip between her teeth as she felt the sting of tears in her eyes. What was she supposed to say?

No yet, Ivy. Wait until the others wake. Wait until they've shaken some of the effects of the stasis.

Lifting the waterskin, Ivy opened it and brought it to Ella's mouth. "Here. Take a sip of water, Ella."

The woman parted her lips and allowed Ivy to help her drink. Ivy didn't let her have too much; just enough to soothe a parched mouth and throat before withdrawing the waterskin. Ella's eyelids drifted shut.

"Just relax while we wait for the others to wake up, okay?" Ivy said.

"Okay," Ella replied. Even that simple word came out unsteady and uncertain.

A low groan came from behind Ivy. She turned to see a man with shoulder length blonde hair raise a hand to his head and press his fingers to his temples and massage them. Cole Walker.

"Fuck." Dropping his hand, Cole opened his eyes and grasped the side of his pod, pulling himself out. His bare foot came down with surprising steadiness on the floor. The foot that followed was not quite so stable.

Cole's balance crumbled. He managed a single, staggering step, body reeling, before falling onto hands and knees. "Ah, shit."

Ivy rushed to him, crouched, and took him by the arm as he struggled to get back up. "Here, I'll help you sit. You need to take it slow."

"I'm okay, just need a…" His words were slightly slurred, and whatever he'd meant to say never came out. Once he was sitting, he ran a hand over his face and let out a puff of air. "Didn't think it'd be this bad. Worst hangover I ever had."

Ivy smiled sympathetically. She knew exactly what he meant. "This is just the beginning. It can get worse." She held the water-skin out to him. "Here, have a drink of water. I have some food too, but we'll wait until your stomach can handle it."

Cole accepted the waterskin and took a long, deep drink, tipping his head back and nearly teetering backward in the process. He wiped his mouth with the back of his hand and drew in a shuddering breath, only then glancing at the water-skin itself. His brow furrowed. "Guess they really pinched pennies with some of this equipment, huh?"

"It's...a long story. I know you're confused, but I'll explain once everyone wakes up."

"Confused?" Cole blinked a few times. "Why would I be—" He looked up at Ivy then, and his mouth hung open for a moment. "You're way hotter than the tech that put me under."

Ivy chuckled, and a hint of warmth flooded her cheeks. "Sit tight, okay? Everyone else should be waking up soon, and I'll need to help them. Do you want to take another drink?"

Keeping his blue eyes on her, he brought the waterskin to his mouth and took a longer swig than the first before handing it back to her. "Thanks."

Slowly, the others awoke, each in their own unique states of disorientation and weakness. No one was quite as bad off as Ella, who remained lying on the bed of her pod, her skin glistening with sweat. Still, the worst Ivy had to deal with was Diego Rodriguez's awakening—after she helped him down from the cryochamber, he managed a couple steps, leaning on her heavily, before doubling over and vomiting on the floor.

The air filtration system was working well enough to cut down the scent within a few seconds, but that little whiff was all it took to make Ivy's stomach churn. She led him away from the mess, keeping her lips pressed together and telling her stomach, *Not now, dang it!*

She gave everyone water, nearly emptying two of the water-skins she and Ketahn had brought along in the process, helped some of them move into more comfortable positions, cleaned the mess on the floor, and waited. The information she had to share with them was right there, gathered in a dense, weighty lump of dread in her chest, but she dared not say anything yet. Not until they could understand.

And when will that be? Even after all this time, it's still hard for me to wrap my head around it.

"Did they skip my shift?" William Reed asked. "I was supposed to... I swapped with Johnson. Was supposed to cover for him."

He was sitting at the base of his cryochamber with his elbows on his knees and his hands on his temples, raking his fingers absently through his close-cropped black hair. His dark skin was beaded with sweat, but he seemed far more alert than Ella. Though he wore the same white undershirt and underpants as everyone else, his shirt had a blue Homeworld Initiative logo on it over his heart.

He was part of the crew.

"And shouldn't we be undergoing medical exams right now?" Diego asked. "It doesn't seem right that we're just sitting here like this."

"My head feels like it's going to split in two," Lacey Anderson said. She was sitting against the wall, head bowed and clutched between her hands, her long red hair spilling down in front of her.

"I think mine already did," Callie Wright replied from where she lay on the floor next to her pod, her mass of long black curls spread out around her head. "If you find any bits of gray matter scattered on the floor, that's mine."

Ahmya chuckled softly but it quickly turned to a groan. She

was sitting in her cryochamber with her arms around her legs and her head resting on her knees. "Don't make me laugh. It hurts."

"Is th-this normal?" Ella asked. Her clothing was damp with sweat, and she was shivering.

Ivy pulled one of the blankets out of her pack and unfolded it as she approached Ella. "It's normal. I went through the same thing."

"Kinda expected more to be going on when we woke up," Cole said. He alone of the freshly awakened survivors had dared to get to his feet again, though he hadn't strayed more than a couple steps from his pod. "Don't we have shit to do?"

He waved a hand toward the neighboring cryochamber, which was still closed. "And why aren't these lazy assholes up yet?"

That lump in Ivy's chest twisted and expanded. She draped the blanket over Ella, who clasped it close to her body.

"Really, man?" asked Diego. "We've all been asleep sixty years. They're not any lazier than you."

William narrowed his eyes as he swept them over Ivy. "Were you transferred from a different stasis room? I thought Alicia Hilstad was our assigned med tech."

"She's not a med tech," Callie said. "She's one of us. Non-crew, I mean. I remember her from training. Ivy, right?"

A few of the others turned their attention toward her.

"Yeah, my name is Ivy. Ivy Foster. And I'm...I'm not a crew member."

Lacey tilted her head and squinted her green eyes. "Are we supposed to have like, visual hallucinations? Why does it look like she's wearing a spider web?"

Cole's eyebrows fell low. "If you're not part of the crew, why the hell are you waking us up?"

Ivy self-consciously ran her palms down the sides of her silk dress. "I have something really important to explain to you all, but I need you to stay calm, okay?"

"Oh, God," Ella groaned.

"That can't be good," said Diego, running his hands over his short black hair.

Taking in a deep breath, Ivy clasped her hands in front of her and looked down at the floor. "We're not on Xolea. We… didn't make it."

Though everyone seemed to gasp, whisper, or mutter something in response, their replies were all similar in tone—at once disbelieving and despairing.

"That…that can't be right!" Lacey said.

Ivy turned her face toward the closed cryochamber beside her. "The others aren't awake because…we're all that's left."

Cole scowled, stepped closer to the neighboring pod, and peered down. His eyes flared and he stumbled back, bumping into his open cryochamber. "Oh, fuck!"

"What?" Callie dragged herself up to her feet to look inside one of the sealed pods. She slapped a hand over her mouth, stifling a small cry, as her dark eyes rounded. "Oh, God. Is that a fucking corpse?"

"I was the only one who could wake you all up," Ivy continued, forcing the words out, "and I had to. The *Somnium* is losing power. If I'd left you in your cryochambers, you all would've been dead in two years."

"That's just…it's not possible," Cole said, giving himself a visible shake before facing Ivy. "Five thousand people, right? How could we be all that's left of five thousand people? This is… this is some kind of drill or something, right? A test? The Initiative just wants to see how we perform under pressure?"

Ivy shook her head. "I don't know how it happened, but the ship crashed. What you see in here"—she waved toward the closed door—"it's different out there. It's worse."

"How did you wake up?" Diego asked.

Ivy rubbed a palm over her arm. "Someone…else woke me. A native to this world."

"S-So we're not alone?" Ahmya asked, her eyes shiny with tears.

"Where are they?" Callie asked.

"I'll introduce you to him soon," Ivy said. "I just thought it was best to…wait."

"Did you guys not fucking hear what she said?" Cole demanded, striding forward purposefully. It didn't take long for that stride to falter, and he only barely caught himself on his cryochamber, sweeping his hair back from his face to reveal cheeks reddened with exertion. "A native. To this world. A fucking alien."

His words hung heavy in the air, and Ivy was suddenly aware of Ketahn's presence on the other side of that door—and again, she doubted whether this was the right thing to do. Ketahn had shown her nothing but kindness and patience since she'd awoken. She'd done her best to give him the same.

But not everyone was so open-minded. She certainly hadn't been, not at first. And she didn't *know* these people, didn't know what they were like, couldn't guess how they'd react to him.

That weighty silence was broken by William, who, with a soft grunt, pulled himself onto his feet. He didn't look at the cryochambers he used to support himself as he walked to the control console at the end of the room; he just kept his feet moving in a slow, pained, but determined rhythm.

"Are we really on an alien planet?" Ella asked Ivy, her voice whisper soft.

Ivy looked down at the woman. There were dark circles under Ella's eyes.

Ivy nodded and placed a comforting hand on the woman's shoulder. "I'm sorry. I know it's not good news, but we're alive, right? That's something."

"Fuck," Cole growled, dropping down to sit at the foot of his cryochamber.

When William reached the console, he touched the controls, and a holo screen appeared before him, filled with its errors and alerts. He muttered a curse, braced one hand atop the control panel, and used the other to press the status report icon on the display.

"All systems—" the computer began; William silenced it with the touch of another icon as information streamed across the screen.

"What, are we not allowed to hear it, too?" asked Cole.

"If he's the only one who knows what he's doing, just shut up and let him do it," said Lacey, who once again bowed her head and obscured her face with her hair. "You do know what you're doing, right?"

William didn't answer. Though his back was turned to everyone, Ivy recognized something in his posture, a certain stiffness—shock. Horror. The slow absorption of crushing information. At one point he was prompted to enter a code, which he did as though in a daze, and more text appeared on the display.

The room was silent again but for the breathing of the eight survivors. Ivy dropped her gaze to the floor. Her feet were wrapped in strips of silk that was dingy and stained now, and soon enough would be too tattered and worn to be of much use for anything. Socks and shoes were already little more than a distant memory. Were she to stop and consider it, she would've been amazed at how quickly she'd adapted to life on this planet.

But how would the others do? Would they find lives here that they thought were worth living? Would they accept this situation, adapt to it, and find some way to thrive?

Or would they lose their wills to live at all?

Will they hate me for waking them?

A sound roused her from her thoughts, and she glanced up

to see William shuffling back to the group, wearing an unsettlingly blank expression.

"So?" Cole said. "What the fuck is going on, man?"

"It's, uh…" William let out a long breath. "It's just like she said. The system is on the verge of failure, but most of the info is still there. This stasis room is the only one still operational on this part of the ship."

"This part? So does that mean there could be survivors in the other sections?" asked Callie.

William began to shake his head, but stopped the gesture to shrug instead. "I don't know. The uh, the ship broke apart. The computer lost contact with the other sections when that happened, and it doesn't have records on them."

He staggered back to his cryochamber and eased himself onto the floor with his back against it.

"Is help coming?" Ahmya asked.

Tipping his head back against the metal pod, William pressed his lips together and closed his eyes.

"No," Ivy gently answered. "The emergency signal is inoperative, and the navigation system has no idea where we are."

Ahmya's bottom lip trembled, and she lowered her face to her knees. Her body shook with her quiet sobs.

"So…what happened? Why the did the ship break apart?" Diego asked, his voice weary and laced with fear.

"I don't know," William replied. "Some kind of collision. Meteor or something? I don't have access to all the information. But the *Somnium* was designed with these big compartments, it's supposed to be a safety feature or something. They all have their own power and life support systems in the event of an emergency, so damaged portions of the ship can be sealed off. That's the only reason we're still here, I guess. The integrity of this section was just enough to get us through the crash."

"What the fuck was the crew doing during all that?" Cole asked.

"Everything they could," William said.

"Bullshit! We're fucking crashed on an alien planet, man, so don't give me that. What the fuck were you doing asleep? Shouldn't you have been helping?"

William squeezed his eyes tighter shut and muttered a response.

"Can't fucking hear you," Cole growled, grabbing his pod as though to lurch to his feet again. "Wanna speak up?"

"He said he was in stasis," Lacey snapped. "Didn't you pay attention to the seminars? The crew were working in shifts along the way."

"How does it do us any fucking good if they were in stasis when shit hit the fan?"

William's features grew taut. His lips trembled, his nostrils flared, and his jaw muscles ticked.

"Stop it!" Ivy stepped forward, glaring at Cole. "For all we know, the crew was dead before we even crashed. And if they weren't, I'm sure they did everything they possibly could to protect us. It's not William's fault, and trying to put the blame on him isn't going to change what happened."

Cole stared at her, but after a moment he sank back onto the floor.

Uncomfortable quiet settled over the group again, broken only when Callie asked, "How long have we been here?"

Ivy sighed and turned her palms up in front of her. "I don't know how long it's been since we crashed here, but it's been one hundred and sixty-eight years since we left Earth."

"The collision was one hundred and twenty-two years ago," William said. "Not sure about the crash, but I don't think it was long after that."

Over a hundred years crashed on this planet. That was plenty of time for Ketahn's ancestors to have turned the crash into a thing of myth.

"Jesus," Callie breathed, letting her head fall back against the wall and closing her eyes.

Ivy caught her lower lip between her teeth. As much as she wanted to let everyone come to terms with this in their own time, as much as she wanted to allow them to ask all the questions they must have had—and she still had so many, herself—she couldn't forget Ketahn's urgency. They were operating on borrowed time.

"Your name is William, right?" she asked.

William opened his eyes and glanced at her. "Yeah. Usually just Will, though. And you're…Ivy."

She smiled at him. "I am. Do you know if there are any supplies we can access? Food, tools, clothing, medicine, anything."

He nodded and gestured toward the control console. "Every stasis room has a small cache of emergency supplies."

She looked in the direction he'd indicated. Surely enough, there was a sealed wall compartment beside the console with a blue cross painted on its door. She hadn't noticed it the last time she was here, not that she could blame herself—there'd been quite a bit on her mind, to say the least.

"It'll last longer with only"—he sucked in a sharp breath, ran his tongue over his lips, and exhaled—"with only eight of us, but it's still not much."

Ivy nodded. If those compartments were in every stasis room, that meant there were potentially more supplies elsewhere, but she didn't want to think about entering those silent, tomblike chambers right now.

"How long have you been awake, Ivy?" Lacey asked. "You look…healthy."

Ivy turned toward Lacey to find the woman studying her with her dark brows furrowed. "I've been awake for almost two months. At least, I think so. The days feel a bit longer here than they are on Earth."

"Why didn't you wake us sooner?" Diego asked.

"I didn't know about you. The, uh, native who found this place took me from here. When I regained consciousness, I was already outside. He only just brought me back here. Ever since I woke, I thought I was the only human left."

"So where is he now? This native?" Callie asked. Her skin had taken on a grayish pallor.

Ivy glanced at the door. "He's waiting for me. I thought it'd be better to give you time to, well, wake up. He's...different."

Understatement of the millennium there, Ivy.

"I don't think any amount of time is going to prepare us to meet a fucking alien," said Cole.

"It'll just give our imaginations time to run wild," Callie said.

Running her gaze over the survivors, Ivy drew in a steadying breath. She could never silence all her doubts and misgivings, but she wouldn't let them hinder her purpose here, and she wouldn't let much more time be wasted.

These people were just like she had been—confused, directionless, and running low on hope. In their perspectives, they'd lain down yesterday expecting to wake up on a beautiful new world to begin brand new lives. And she'd just told them that a hundred and sixty-eight years had passed and everything they'd dreamed about had been taken away in what seemed like a blink of their eyes.

Her attention lingered on poor Ella. No one looked like they felt very good, but she looked like she was suffering from a terrible case of the flu. Considering the injections they'd all received before boarding the ship, that was unlikely.

"Do any of you have medical training?" Ivy asked.

"We got a crew member here," said Cole, turning his still angry gaze toward Will.

"I'm a computer tech," Will said. "I got nothing beyond the same first aid training all of you received."

"What the fuck use are—"

"I'm a nurse," Diego said, raising his voice to cut off Cole. "My head is still fuzzy, you know? But I think enough of it is second nature that I can get by for now."

Ivy offered him a smile. "All right. Diego, could you take a look at Ella? See if there's anything you can do for her?"

Diego flattened a hand on the floor and pushed himself up onto his feet, shaking his head as though clearing it.

As Diego made his way to Ella's pod, Ivy stepped over to Will. "Could you get the emergency supply compartment opened?"

Will blinked a few times, looked up at Ivy, and then turned his attention toward the marked compartment. "Yeah. Yeah, I can."

"Thank you. We can figure out what we have to work with." Ivy offered Will a hand and helped him up. "Can someone help him take stock?"

"I'll do it," said Lacey, bracing an arm on the pod beside her to stand up. She strode over to join Will at the compartment, her steps noticeably steadier than what some of the others had displayed so far.

"Thank you, Lacey." Ivy moved back to Ella. "You're going to be okay. I felt pretty crappy for a while when I woke up, too, but it'll pass."

Ella opened her eyes and looked up at Ivy. Shivering, she smiled wanly as Diego checked her pulse at her wrist. "I've had worse. Nothing can keep this farmgirl down."

Ivy returned the smile, nodded at Diego, and returned to her and Ketahn's packs, from which she removed a large, rolled up leaf. Flattening the leaf on the floor, she spread the fruits, nuts, dried meats, roots, and mushrooms upon it.

"I didn't have a scanner on hand, but through a little trial and error and with a lot of help, I know this is all safe to eat," Ivy said. "Your stomachs might need some time to wake up, but if you start feeling hungry, take whatever you like."

Callie rose and carefully walked closer. Once she was next to Ivy, she lowered herself onto the floor with a soft grunt. Just that little bit of physical activity had winded her. "Help from the natives?"

"Just one."

"Are there others?"

Ivy kept her voice low. "There are, but I haven't met them yet. We're…being cautious."

Callie's eyes rounded, but she nodded. "Not exactly comforting, but I understand."

"Are they…bad?" Ahmya asked, easing down from her pod to join them.

"They're people, like us. They just look different," Ivy said. "And well…*we're* the aliens to them. Ketahn, the one I've been with, is kind and patient. He's kept me safe, and he's taught me how to survive. He's willing to do the same with all of you as we try to find our place on this planet. So please, when you see him, keep that in mind."

Callie nodded again, flicking her gaze over Ivy. "Well, from the looks of you, I'd say things are working out. You look like you're glowing."

Ivy fought the blush threatening to stain her cheeks and lowered her eyes. All she could do was think back to this morning—waking up with Ketahn's long purple tongue between her thighs. She didn't think mentioning *that* would go over well with these people, especially once they saw him.

"Believe it or not, I've been happy here. My life on Earth was pretty shitty, but despite everything that's happened, I'm genuinely happy."

"That gives me hope," Ahmya said softly, tucking a strand of hair behind her ear. "I mean, I…I feel a little numb right now. Shock, I think? But if you can find happiness here, I'm sure we can too. We left Earth to start over on a new world…isn't this kind of the same thing?"

Callie snorted, but there was a good-natured smile on her lips. "Yeah, but we were supposed to have electricity and prefab housing. I think we're going to be short a few luxuries here."

"I have to admit, I do miss toilets," Ivy said with a grin.

Callie and Ahmya groaned.

CHAPTER 9

SOME FOOD and a little more time to adjust to the situation seemed to help most of the freshly awakened survivors. Apart from Ella, whose condition remained unchanged, everyone looked a little more lucid, alert, and calm by the time they'd finished eating a mix of the jungle foods Ivy had brought and some of the rations that had been in the emergency supplies.

Even Cole had settled down, offering a mumbled apology to the group for, in his words, "Losing my cool, or whatever."

They now had a stock of medical supplies, long-lasting food, hydration packets, blankets, jumpsuits, footwear, and several tools that could prove useful out in the jungle. That stock would be bolstered once they checked the other caches that were still accessible, though Ivy wasn't sure whether the food and medicines in the other rooms had spoiled.

It was a start, and it would take some of the burden off Ketahn as far as having to immediately provide for seven extra people.

But that still left one big challenge for today, and it was one Ivy had dreaded more with each passing minute. It was just as Callie had said—time was giving Ivy's imagination more space to run wild. And she'd already thought up about a million ways the first meeting between Ketahn and these bedraggled, weakened humans could go wrong.

Still, that dread wasn't stronger than her desire to see him again, to touch him, to speak with him. Even knowing he was nearby, she missed him.

"Hey, uh...Ivy? You got a minute?" Cole asked from behind her.

Ivy turned to face him and smiled. "I might be able to spare one, but my schedule's pretty booked."

He chuckled and stuffed his hands into the pockets of his jumpsuit, which he'd put on as soon as they'd been passed out. If he'd tried to hide the way he ran his gaze over Ivy's body, he failed miserably. It made her all the more aware of how little she wore in comparison to the others. She gripped the short skirt of her dress.

"Just wanted to say that I didn't mean to get heated with you," he said. "All the training they gave us, it really doesn't prepare you for when shit actually goes wrong, you know?"

"I know, and I'm not holding a grudge or anything. I get it. I mean, I *really* get it." Ivy glanced around the room at the other survivors, who sat quietly talking among themselves. "I had quite a rude awakening to put it lightly."

"I can't even imagine. A fucking alien, huh?"

Ivy looked back at Cole. He stood at least a foot taller than her, with a chiseled nose and jaw, full lips, thick eyebrows, and deep blue eyes. His athletic, broad-shouldered frame filled out his jumpsuit appealingly. He was attractive—more than attractive, he was gorgeous. But she felt nothing toward him, not even an inkling of desire.

Am I truly in love with Ketahn?

What else could it be? There was a sexy man of her own species standing in front of her and she felt nothing. *Nothing.*

Guess I prefer my males with multiple sets of limbs and eyes.

"Yeah, an alien," Ivy said with a soft smile.

Cole eased closer to her; the shift in his posture made the jumpsuit pull taut over his chest and shoulders. "Well, you're not alone anymore. I'll look out for you. There's nothing a little human muscle and brainpower can't overcome, right?"

Ivy's brows rose. "Oh. Uh, thank you, but that's—"

There was a familiar hiss, and Ivy's head whipped toward it —as did everyone else's—to find the chamber door open and a big, dark, inhuman shape standing in the blood red light of the corridor. Someone screamed, maybe more than one person, and the air was instantly bristling with tension and terror.

"What the fuck?" Cole said.

Ketahn stepped into the room, and his violet eyes met Ivy's.

She was about to take a step toward him when an arm banded around her waist and yanked her back. Cole drew Ivy against his side, turning his body toward Ketahn to shield her.

Mandibles spreading wide, Ketahn released a deep, rattling growl and strode forward, legs coming down heavily upon the floor. Several of the other humans scrambled away, their fearful cries lost to Ivy amidst the pounding of her own heart.

She pressed a hand against Cole's chest and tried to shove away from him, craning her neck to look at Ketahn around the man holding her. "Cole, stop! It's okay." She thrust her other hand at Ketahn. "Ketahn, no! Don't attack him."

Ketahn halted. Though they seemed directed at her, Ivy knew his eyes were focused entirely upon Cole.

"What is he doing to you?" Ketahn asked in gravelly, strongly accented English.

That drew fresh gasps from the others.

"Oh my God, did it just talk?" Ella whimpered.

"I-It looks like a spider," Ahmya stammered.

Cole's hold on Ivy tightened, and he dragged her farther back. "Will, grab that fucking flare gun!"

"Don't you dare!" Ivy snapped. Placing both palms on Cole's

chest, she pushed with all her might. It was enough to thrust herself out of his grip, but not without producing a sharp tear as his finger caught on her dress.

Ketahn's mandibles snapped together with a harsh clack, and he surged forward, the fine hairs on his legs bristling. Rage radiated from him in waves. Somehow, Ivy had set herself into motion a fraction of a second before him; though breaking free from Cole's grasp had thrown off her balance, she took advantage of her momentum, spinning and stumbling toward her mate.

She managed to insert herself between the two males just before Ketahn would've collided with Cole—meaning he collided with her instead.

Ivy was vaguely aware of his legs scrabbling over the floor as though he were skidding to a sudden stop. She was much more aware of the air being forced out of her lungs by the impact, but she wrapped her arms around Ketahn all the same.

All four of Ketahn's arms enveloped her, and he lifted her off the floor. His voice was low and frantic as he spoke to her, his words tumbling out in a blend of English and his native language that she understood without having to give it a second thought—most of which came down to *my mate, my heartsthread, are you all right? What have I done?*

One of his hands caught her chin and tipped her head back so she met his gaze, while another smoothed over her hair. Though fury still smoldered in his eyes, it was overpowered by concern.

"Oh fuck, fuck, fuck. It's going to eat her!" Callie cried.

He turned his face toward Callie and snarled, "Ketahn no eat Ivy!"

Though she felt as though she'd run into a concrete wall, Ivy's lips twitched into a smirk that she promptly tried to contain as she forced herself to glare up at Ketahn. "You were supposed to wait until I called for you."

Ketahn returned his attention to her and let out a soft huff. "Waited too long. I had to know you were safe."

This time, Ivy allowed herself to smile fully. "I'm safe."

"Why did that male have his arm around you?"

"He was trying to protect me. From you."

Subtly shifting his gaze, Ketahn glared at Cole. "I protect you. Not him."

"Yeah, well, I haven't had a chance to tell them much about you, and you just kind of barged in here all scary-like."

His mandibles drooped, and he hooked his thumb under her chin, grazing her skin with a claw. "You say I am not scary. I am sexy."

Ivy's skin flushed. "Um, yeah. To *me*."

"Wait. What the— Are you *fucking* that thing?" Cole demanded.

She stiffened. Cold crept down her spine. Drawing back from Ketahn, she looked at Cole. "That's none of your business. And he's not a thing."

Gently, Ketahn lowered Ivy to her feet, positioning himself so his body was blocking her from Cole. He didn't take his hands off her. "She is my mate."

"He's a giant…bug," Diego said.

Everyone stared at Ivy and Ketahn, their expressions etched with horror, disgust, awe, and uncertainty. Ivy hadn't even considered what the others might think about her interactions with Ketahn. But no matter what they thought of her in that instant, Ivy refused to feel ashamed of what she felt for Ketahn. They didn't know him like she did. They didn't know the things he'd done for her, the things he was willing to sacrifice. They didn't know the things he was willing to do for *them*.

She understood their fear, their repulsion. But she would not allow them to make her feel sinful.

"I am vrix," Ketahn said firmly. "And I will make you lessons to survive."

"This is the alien you talked about?" Callie asked.

"He is," Ivy said. "His name is Ketahn."

Callie's dark, rounded eyes ran over Ketahn's form. "When you said he was *different*, I never would have thought he'd be *this* different."

Ivy gave Ketahn a sidelong glance. "I didn't get a chance to prepare you for what you'd see."

"I don't know what you could've said that would've prepared us for...*this*," said Will. "I-I mean, for him."

Cole looked at the others, his brows furrowed. "Are you all seriously going to ignore the fact that she's fucking that thing? It's a damn spider!"

"Not spider," Ketahn growled, leaning toward Cole with his mandibles flaring. "Vrix."

Ivy made to step forward, but was held back by Ketahn, whose fingers flexed possessively around her waist. She sighed and pinched the bridge of her nose.

"Look"—she dropped her arm to her side—"what I do with Ketahn has nothing to do with our survival on this world. And it doesn't matter how different he looks, because he is the only one who can teach us how to survive here. To find a safe place to live. To thrive.

"Right now, there are...problems among Ketahn's people. So we all need to put aside whatever hang ups we might have and work together, because we don't have a lot of time before we need to be on the move."

"The hell do you mean?" Cole asked. Though he'd backed farther away, his eyes were fixed on Ketahn. "This place right here is our best bet. We have shelter and supplies here. We're not going anywhere, especially not with that thing."

"Your supplies are limited, and this place is going to be flooded soon."

"Flooded?" Diego asked.

"We're at the bottom of an impact crater right now," Ivy said.

"There are parts of the ship that are already flooded, and probably have been for years. And the rainy season is already starting. Even if the water doesn't reach all the way to this room, once it floods, it's going to be incredibly dangerous to get in and out of this ship."

"Then w-what are we going to do?" Lacey asked.

Ketahn drew in a deep breath, and there was a low, drawn-out rumbling in his chest. "You will make strength and be ready for travel. I will protect you until you can protect yourself."

Cole scowled. "I can take care of myself, thanks."

"Dude, will you just shut up already?" Callie said, glaring at Cole.

Diego shook his head. "We don't even know what's out there. Crazy as this is...Ketahn might be all we have right now."

"You're just going to trust that monster with your lives? Just like"—Cole snapped his fingers—"that?"

"Ivy looks like she's doing pretty damn good, so yeah," Callie said.

"You going to fuck a bug too?"

"You son of a—"

Will caught Callie by her shoulders, but that didn't stop the woman from pressing her lips together and shooting Cole a death glare.

"It isn't worth it," Will said quietly.

Callie stared at Cole a little longer before she huffed, nodded, and turned away, moving to sit against the wall.

"It is time for you to close your lips and be silent," Ketahn said in a measured but warning tone. "You will see what is outside this place soon. The jungle does not care about your big words. It does not care how far you traveled. It does not care that you come from the stars. All of you are small, and soft, and weak. Alone, you will not live."

"Is...this supposed to be a pep talk?" asked Lacey.

Ketahn turned his face down toward Ivy, tilting his head. "What does that mean, my *nyleea*?"

"Um, a pep talk is kind of like…trying to make someone feel brave and confident?" Ivy brushed a palm down his arm. "But I think you're just scaring them."

He grunted, mandibles dipping, before he looked back toward the others. "I…believe in you, humans."

Callie snort-laughed and covered her face with her hand. "Unbelievable."

Ivy caught her bottom lip with her teeth and tried to stop herself from smiling.

She failed.

Ketahn glanced between Callie and Ivy, a hint of uncertainty in his eyes. "What?"

"Nothing," Ivy said.

"Yeah, nothing," Cole grumbled. "I wish this was all a fucking joke."

Ignoring Cole, Ivy extracted herself from Ketahn's hold and made her way to the bags on the floor next to Ahmya. She crouched, stuffed the empty waterskins into the bags, and closed them.

Ahmya settled a trembling hand upon Ivy's forearm. "Are… are you really okay?"

Ivy looked at the woman, but Ahmya's dark, fearful eyes were focused on Ketahn. "Ahmya, look at me."

Ahmya slowly dragged her gaze to Ivy.

"Do I look hurt?" Ivy asked.

Ahmya shook her head. "No. It's just…just…" Her gaze flicked toward Ketahn. "He looks…"

"I know. He scared me in the beginning too. But I promise you, he is kind. He'd never hurt me."

Withdrawing her hand, Ahmya cradled it against her chest and looked down. "I'm terrified of spiders. E-even the tiny fuzzy ones with big eyes. And he's…"

"Big and scary?" Ivy suggested gently.

The dark-haired woman nodded. Her skin was pale but for blotches of color on her cheeks. These people hadn't been out of stasis for nearly long enough to be processing all this, but as always, it came down to time—and how little of it remained. Ketahn had intrigued the queen enough to earn eight days of respite. But by that eighth day, they needed to be far, far away from here.

"I know what he looks like, but really, Ahmya...he's not a spider, and he doesn't mean you or anyone else here any harm. It's asking a lot, but I need you to trust him. Or...at least trust me enough to follow him. I know we're not close friends or anything, that we hardly know each other, but me and Ketahn are just trying to help everyone."

Ketahn's stride was slow and heavy as he moved to Ivy; it was always a deliberate choice when he walked like that, because normally his steps were silent no matter how quick his pace. He stopped beside her—in front of Ahmya—and eased down, folding his legs to drop his underside onto the floor. Though that didn't mask his size, it put his head far closer to the level of Ivy's.

Ahmya sucked in a sharp breath and drew her legs to her chest.

"I do not want to scare," he said with gentleness in his deep voice, "only to protect. Ivy is my mate. You are her kind. So you are my kind, too."

The woman nodded.

Ivy smiled and handed Ketahn one of the bags. He accepted it and backed away, providing Ahmya some space.

Rising to her feet, Ivy slipped her arms through the straps of the other pack. "We'll be back, okay?"

"Wait, what are you doing?" Lacey asked, eyes rounding. "Are you leaving right now?"

"My mate dens with me," Ketahn rumbled, wrapping one of

his lower arms around Ivy's middle and drawing her close.

Cole curled his lip and turned away.

"You have some supplies here and plenty of food left over," Ivy said. "We'll...let you all rest and think everything over."

"So you just wake us up and leave?" Cole asked.

"Really, man, what is your problem?" demanded Callie. "Would you rather she left us in those pods to die?"

"Please," Ivy breathed, "please, let's not be at each other's throats. This is hard on all of us, okay? But I promise you, with Ketahn's help, we can all get through this. It's not the fresh start we all envisioned, but...but it's something, right? We're *alive*. All we can do is our best. We're going to make mistakes, but as long as we make them together, we'll be okay."

"Yeah, she says that as she leaves," Cole snapped.

"Why don't you go take a nap or something, man?" Diego said; he was still beside Ella's pod, once again checking her pulse. "You're acting like a cranky toddler."

Anger sparked in Cole's eyes, but he clenched his fists and seemed to swallow it down. He nodded repeatedly. "Yeah. Yeah, you're right. This is a lot. It's a fucking lot." He turned away from the others and stalked toward the far end of the room, where he sat with his back against the wall.

Ivy frowned. She hadn't expected any of this to be easy, and she'd never thought of herself as a leader in any capacity—especially not now—but she'd known that action needed to be taken. If things continued this way, though... The greatest threat to the humans would be each other.

"We all, um, internalize things like this differently," she offered, "and you guys are still foggy from stasis. Get some rest, cut each other some slack, and we'll discuss all this again when we're feeling better, okay?"

"Yeah," Will said, putting on a tired smile. "Thanks, Ivy."

"You'll be back soon?" Ahmya asked, flicking another uncertain glance at Ketahn.

Ivy's frown only deepened. "As soon as I can."

"Tomorrow," Ketahn said. "We will return tomorrow."

"Are we safe in here?" asked Lacey.

"Given the state of this room versus the amount of time that's passed, I'd say we're okay. It'd look a hell of a lot rougher otherwise," said Callie.

"The alien got in here," Cole called from the other side of the room.

"Nothing else will," Ketahn said, exchanging a brief, solemn glance with Ivy. "You are safe here."

The humans—minus Cole—said their goodbyes, and Ivy's attention lingered on Ella even as Ketahn led her to the door. For all the hope that had swelled in her heart knowing there were seven more survivors and that she had a chance to help them, there was a dark shadow cast there, too. She was determined to see these people through whatever ordeals awaited them. She was ready to face any hardships necessary to ensure their survival.

But even barely knowing them, Ivy wasn't sure if she could face the very real possibility that in a day, a week, a few months, there'd be fewer human faces on this planet. She'd awoken these people...could she bear it if she lost any of them?

She clung to Ketahn as they made their way off the *Somnium*, desperately shoving aside those dreaded what-ifs by focusing on his scent, his warmth, his solidness.

And she refused to acknowledge the most dreadful possibility of all—that she'd lose Ketahn before all this was done.

CHAPTER 10

WITH TOUGH, leathery skin, hard muscles, and a dense bone structure, vrix gave away very little with their bodies—and even less with their nearly unchangeable facial expressions. What clues they offered in body language were usually subtle. That had been Ivy's experience with Ketahn, at least.

But she'd spent enough time with him to learn some of his tiny tells.

As usual, Ivy was sitting astride his hindquarters with her arms around his torso as he traversed the boughs, heading home. Though the difference from the norm was miniscule, she recognized the extra tension in his muscles. She felt the hint of stiffness in his movements. And she couldn't ignore the low, faint growls that occasionally punctuated his exhalations, rumbling into her through his broad, solid back.

"You can talk to me," she said, smoothing a palm over the ridges of his abdomen. "You don't have to hold it all in."

Making a decidedly contemplative trill, Ketahn slowed his pace. The gloom was already thick in the jungle below, where the bioluminescent vegetation had been growing more visible by the minute, but up here there remained a few shreds of red-orange sunlight.

"You know all that troubles me, my heartsthread," he said after a few seconds. "The dangers we face. The...the bigness of this task."

"I do. But I also know there's something more now. Something new after meeting the other humans."

He grunted and extended his arms to grasp another thick branch, drawing himself up onto it.

"You're upset that they didn't call you spider man, right?" Ivy grinned. "I could let them know next time, if you want..."

Ketahn let out a short, sharp hiss as he moved along the branch. "No spider man. They...do not know me. Not yet. They are afraid and unsure."

Ivy frowned and tightened her embrace, resting her cheek against his shoulder. His long, violet-and-white-streaked black hair tickled her face. "They will know you. You just need to give them time. Then they will see you as I see you."

He purred gently and dropped a hand to cover hers. "That does not trouble me, my *nyleea*. I have you, and you will always be enough."

You will always be enough.

Ivy closed her eyes at the emotion that flooded her heart. For so long, she had hoped to hear that from her parents, to see it in their eyes. But she had never been enough—not for them, not for her ex, not for anyone she'd ever known. But to Ketahn...she would always be enough.

She blinked away her gathering tears and released a shaky breath. "What is it then?"

Ketahn huffed and shook his head. "That male. *Cole*."

"I know he came off really...rough, but we need to give him some time to adjust. It's not easy waking up only to discover your whole world has changed. To us, it's like getting up from a single night's rest to find everything we knew is...gone."

Ketahn growled and drew to a halt. "That does not matter, Ivy. He touched you."

Ivy's brows furrowed. Ketahn's body had tensed further, and the tiny hairs upon his legs were standing on end. She lifted her head and drew back to look at him, but he kept his mask-like face forward and his fists clenched at his sides.

Then it dawned on her.

"You're jealous," Ivy said.

"I do not know that word."

"You do not like other males touching me, or even the thought of it."

"Why would I like that?" he growled. "You are mine, Ivy. For him to touch you that way…it makes me feel as I never have. It wakes something inside me, like a beast in my hearts. I would have killed him if not for you."

Ivy pressed her palms to his back and slowly slid them up and over his shoulders until she could twine her arms around his neck. A shudder ran through him. She rose, pulling the silk rope binding them together taut, pressed herself flush against his back, and settled her cheek against his hair. "I've felt that way with you. Every time you've spoken of the queen touching you."

He loosely grasped her forearms in one big hand, absently stroking his thumb across her skin. "I do not want her. I have never wanted her."

"And I don't want Cole."

"He is human," Ketahn said in an uncharacteristically small, tight voice. "He has hair like yours, eyes like yours. Two arms and two legs."

"Looks do not always matter, Ketahn."

Tanner, her ex, had been a gorgeous man, and all it had done was blind her to the terrible person behind that handsome face. No, looks didn't mean a damn thing.

Ivy inhaled his earthy, mahogany-and-spice fragrance. It was like an aphrodisiac; it flowed through her, making her nipples harden and her core heat and clench. "I belong to you. Not Him."

"Yes," he rumbled, turning his face toward her. His eyes were fierce. "You are mine. And I will make sure none can question it. I will roar my claim to the entire jungle."

A giggle escaped her. "Don't you already do that?"

His gaze softened, and he chittered, dropping a hand to run along her calf. "Ah, my *nyleea*. I will do it again and again until the sky falls upon the jungle and this world is no more."

Badump-badump.

Ivy's heart quickened, and that inner warmth spread to encompass her entirely. How...how could this not be love?

She touched her forehead to the side of his and closed her eyes. "We should keep going."

He grunted his agreement, but it was several long, blissful seconds before he finally resumed their journey. Ivy sat back down and slipped her arms around his torso, keeping herself pressed firmly against him.

Some of the stiffness in his movements had faded, and some of the tension in his muscles had eased, but it was not all gone. Ivy feared it wouldn't be—not for a long, long time, anyway. Cole was just one of many sources of stress, and there was no telling if another day to recover and adjust would improve the man's demeanor at all.

She'd grown familiar enough with this part of the jungle— even up here, high in the trees—to know that they were less than a minute away from the den when Ketahn halted abruptly. His muscles went taut again, and he flattened a hand on a tree trunk to steady himself as he rose high on his long legs and turned his head.

Ivy's heart quickened for an entirely different reason now. She knew this posture—he'd heard something out of place.

Forcing herself to breathe as slowly and quietly as she could, she listened intently too.

It was only because the jungle's ambient sounds had become so normal to Ivy that she was able to pick out what had alerted him—voices from the direction of the den, barely audible over the rustling leaves and distant animal calls. Though too muted to make out any of the words, they were clearly speaking the vrix tongue.

"Is it them?" she asked quietly.

"Perhaps." Ketahn crept forward, his long limbs moving fluidly and silently, his barbed spear at the ready. His head moved side to side and up and down ceaselessly as he scanned the boughs all around.

Though she doubted she'd ever spot a threat before Ketahn, Ivy kept her eyes moving, too. For as often as she felt like she was in some tropical paradise with him, she could never forget the jungle's constant dangers.

The voices grew clearer as Ketahn climbed toward the den.

"...not here," said one vrix in a surprisingly smooth voice.

"We do not know until we go up and check," said another in a deeper, more gravelly tone.

"Were he in there, he would have heard you a full moon cycle ago. You stride as though you mean to break everything beneath you," the first replied.

"It is not like him to be late. All I am saying is we should go and check. What if he was hurt, and he lies there dying even now?"

"There is no blood scent," a third vrix said, his voice lower and raspier than the first two.

Ivy had to concentrate to follow their conversation; they spoke quickly, just as Ketahn had with his sister, which left her mind scrambling to untangle the alien syllables and find the recognizable words amongst them. That really made her appreciate how Ketahn always slowed his speech for her, giving each of his words space to breathe—and giving Ivy time to translate.

"How can you be sure from down here?" the second vrix asked.

"When was the last time you stalked the Tangle, Urkot?" asked the first.

Urkot grunted. "What does that matter, Rekosh?"

"You are not likely to smell anything through the stone *zirkeetahn* in your nose," Rekosh said.

Ketahn made a muffled sound that shook his chest. It took Ivy a moment to realize it was a suppressed chitter.

"Quiet," the third vrix snapped. The air grew tense in the ensuing silence, and even the jungle itself seemed to hold its breath. "Show yourself, or my spear will taste your blood."

By the sound of it, the other vrix were just on the other side of the nearest tree trunk—below the dangling nest that had become Ivy's home.

Drawing himself onto a thick branch jutting from that trunk, Ketahn let that chittering out fully.

"Ketahn," Urkot growled. "Show yourself so Telok can stab you for playing such a game."

"Be at ease," Ketahn called. "I must know if you were—"

"We were not followed," Telok said, "though a pair of Claws tried. They trailed us through Takarahl and into the Tangle, but we left them behind near the *Khalthai'ani Hak*."

"No simple matter with Urkot joining us," said Rekosh.

"As though you *vikar* a hundred words with each step is any better," Urkot replied.

"Have they been like this the entire journey?" Ketahn asked, his mandibles raised in what must've been a smile.

"Yes," Telok said with a huff. "All the skills I taught them, they have long since forgotten. They must have scared away every beast within ten *zekkan* segments."

"We were but doing our part in making the Tangle safer for us all," said Rekosh.

Ketahn raised a hand, tugging on his bound hair. "I am glad you have come, all the same."

"Have you called us here to play hunter-hider, or do you simply wish to spare our eyes the sight of you?" asked Urkot.

Ketahn's chitter was genuine, but it was short. He lowered his hand and bowed his head, releasing a quiet, unsteady breath. "No. I have something to show you."

"Then show us," said Rekosh.

Ivy curled her fingers and dug her nails into Ketahn's chest. She knew this was the plan, knew he'd asked his friends to come so they could meet her, but now that it was happening, anxiety prickled her skin. The humans had been shocked—and some disgusted—when they'd see Ketahn. How would these vrix react upon seeing her? Would they accept her?

Ketahn looked at her over his shoulder, his eyes soft and warm. "You are safe, my heartsthread."

Ivy took in a deep breath and relaxed her grip on him. She nodded. "I know. I trust you."

He dropped a hand to her thigh and gave it a reassuring squeeze. Then, keeping his spear in one hand, he climbed up the tree trunk and around to the branch upon which his friends were waiting.

"What is clinging to you, Ketahn?" asked Urkot as Ketahn settled on the wide bough—the same one upon which Ahnset had stood during her previous two visits.

Ivy didn't immediately see the other vrix, as Ketahn was facing them.

"She is a human." Ketahn unfastened the silk rope that bound he and Ivy together. Once he'd pulled it free, he reached back to offer her his hand.

Urkot grunted. "A *hyu-nin*?"

"What was that sound you made?" Rekosh asked. He

attempted to reproduce the *m* sound, failing just as thoroughly as Ketahn had when he'd first tried.

"There is much for me to tell you," Ketahn said.

Ivy hesitated briefly before placing her hand in Ketahn's, but he did not rush her. She peeked out from behind him at the three vrix standing before them. Her eyes flared. They shared Ketahn's spiderlike features, but each was so unique from the others.

One was nearly as tall as Ketahn, though he was more slender and graceful, if not a little sinister in appearance with his long, sharp claws and red eyes. He had crimson markings upon his hide with red and white streaks in his black hair to match. That hair was gathered in a thick, neat braid that was draped over his shoulder.

Next to him stood a shorter, bulkier vrix with blue and white markings. Dark, silky hair with bright blue streaks hung freely about his shoulders. His figure made her think of a body-builder—or perhaps more accurately a powerlifter. Though he was a good foot shorter than his nearest companion, he looked like he weighed twice as much, and all that weight was undoubtedly muscle. But what stood out most about him was his missing limb; there was only a patch of rough, scarred flesh where his lower left arm should have been.

The third vrix might have been able to pass for Ketahn from a distance if not for his green markings. He was of similar build to Ketahn, though a bit smaller, and held himself with similar confidence and ease. Though all three vrix bore visible scars—none so prominent as the missing arm—this one had the most. His green-and-white-streaked black hair was gathered in a topknot with a few loose strands dangling from it.

His intense, bright green eyes flicked toward Ivy, making her start. "What sort of creature is this, Ketahn? I have never seen its like."

Ivy swallowed thickly. Battling back her nervousness, she

shifted her weight and, using Ketahn's hand for support, swung her leg over his side to slide of his hindquarters. Her feet came down gently on the branch. Situating herself between two of his spindly legs, she swept her gaze over his friends.

"My name is Ivy," she said in the best vrix she could manage.

All three vrix recoiled, mandibles spreading and eyes flaring.

"It spoke," said the red vrix. "It spoke *words*, Ketahn."

"She," Ketahn corrected. "And how else would she speak, Rekosh?"

"All beasts have their calls," the green vrix said, "yet only vrix make words." His raspy voice marked him as Telok—which meant the bulky, blue-marked male was Urkot.

Ketahn chittered. "None but vrix and humans."

"That sound again." Urkot tilted his head, glancing briefly at Ketahn. "What... I do not understand. What is this, Ketahn? What is she?"

"I am a human." Ivy pressed her free hand to her chest. "And my name is Ivy."

"Not just words," Rekosh muttered as though he'd not heard anything that had been said since he'd made his statement a few moments before, "but *vrix* words." He eased closer; the movements of his long, spindly legs were as smooth as his voice.

"Vrix words?" Urkot tilted his head and folded his upper arms across his chest, bracing his lower right hand against his hip. "You can understand what she is saying? I would better understand a thorn skull than her."

Ivy tipped her head back to look up at Ketahn. "What does he mean? A...thorn skull?"

"Thornskulls are the vrix we battled in Zurvashi's war. They speak differently than us," Ketahn replied in a blend of English and his native language. "Many of their words are similar, but the way they say them are not the same. It can be difficult to understand what they are saying, and there are words that lose their meaning between us."

When Ivy lowered her gaze again, she found the other vrix all staring at Ketahn.

"Have you suffered a head wound?" Telok drew nearer, his mandibles twitching. "I could make out only one of every few words you spoke, Ketahn."

"He was speaking in my language," Ivy said, drawing Telok's attention to her again. His eyes were such a vibrant green, but they held so much of the predatory instinct she'd often seen in Ketahn's eyes that they nearly made her falter. "At least in part. And if you...slow your words, I could understand you better."

"What is she saying?" asked Urkot.

Rekosh let out a huff and glared at Urkot over his shoulder. "If you would *try* to listen, you would know. She said Ketahn was speaking her language and asked us to speak slowly."

He'd slowed his words for his reply to Urkot—but only relative to how quickly he'd been talking before.

Just like that, Ketahn's friends were staring at Ivy again. She felt like an animal in a zoo—one of the strange, rare creatures people would come to gawk at, odd enough to draw attention but too small and weak to instill fear.

This must have been how Ketahn had felt aboard the *Somnium* as the freshly awakened survivors stared at him, though the humans' reaction had been motivated more by fright than wonder. Ivy was a soft, pale, misshapen thing to the vrix, but her mate was a huge, monstrous predator to her kind.

Ketahn's friends moved closer still, and he shifted slightly, shielding more of her body with his. Ivy instinctually sought the cover he provided. Though these vrix were no more different from Ketahn than any of the human survivors were from Ivy, she didn't know them, and they could easily rip her apart if they decided to attack.

But why was she hiding? These were Ketahn's friends. If he trusted them enough to bring them here to meet her, she needed to trust them too. Ivy eased away from Ketahn, allowing the other vrix to see her fully.

"Is she a broodling?" Urkot asked. "She is so small."

"No," Ketahn replied. "She is full grown."

Ivy arched a brow at Urkot. "*She* is right here and can speak for herself."

Urkot blinked and tilted his head in the other direction. "A female in spirit, at least."

"A female in shape, also," Ivy replied. "Just not vrix shape."

Telok and Urkot chittered at that, but Rekosh's attention was otherwise occupied—his eyes were fixed on Ivy's body. He closed the distance between himself and Ivy in a single long stride, so quickly that Ivy's heart stuttered, and she gasped, retreating a few steps. But Ketahn placed himself in front of her before Rekosh's extended hand, with its long, razor-sharp claws, could reach her, halting the red-marked vrix.

"Do not touch," Ketahn snarled, his forelegs rising off the branch.

Though her view was largely obscured by Ketahn's body, she saw the others flinch back.

"Ketahn?" Telok's voice held a hint of uncertainty; something about his demeanor suggested such was not normal for him.

Ivy frowned. She hadn't meant to cause turmoil between them. She knew Ketahn's friends wouldn't hurt her, and she was sure Ketahn knew it as well, but he was acting purely on instinct now—the same instinct that had interpreted Cole grabbing her as a direct threat, a challenge.

Stepping forward, she placed a hand upon one of his arms. His muscles rippled beneath her palm. She tilted her head back to look up at him, but his eyes were focused on the other vrix.

"It's okay," she said in English. "He just startled me, Ketahn."

Ketahn's eyes flicked down to meet her gaze. His mandibles twitched. With a huff, he wound that arm around her middle, drew her forward so she was standing in front of him, and dropped his forelegs to either side of her. His lower arms wrapped around her waist, clutching her against his abdomen, and his claspers hooked her hips.

"Whatever Ivy is," he said, his voice low and rumbling, "know that she is my mate above all else."

Though their expressions could change only by a small degree, all three vrix were clearly stunned. Rekosh's mouth moved as though he meant to speak, but no sound came out; Telok's eyes shifted repeatedly between Ketahn and Ivy; Urkot's mandibles, dangling low, swayed as though in a gentle breeze.

It was Urkot who spoke first. "By the Eight. *Mate?*"

Hearing the vrix word for mate—*nyleea*—from someone other than Ketahn was strange. It didn't have nearly the same fire with which he instilled it, didn't have the same purr. And Urkot had spoken it with shock.

"This is what you have been hiding," Rekosh rasped. "*She* is what you have been hiding. The silk she is wearing…"

Ivy glanced down at her dress, the gift Ketahn had given her —a reminder of the night he had first claimed her as his. She touched the small tear at the waist where Cole's finger had snagged and frowned.

She met Rekosh's gaze. "Ketahn made this for me."

Something softened in Rekosh's eyes, and Ivy felt a spark of understanding—and she knew that she was now being looked at as a person, as an equal, and not some curiosity.

"Yes. He made it in my den. From suncrest to sunfall, he worked, *kitua* to finish it and leaving me to wonder why, after so long, he was weaving. And now I understand." He flicked his gaze to Ketahn. "And I was right."

Ketahn grunted. "About?"

"Your *lisiv* mate. I was right!"

"Yes," said Ketahn with a chitter of his own. "And so was I."

Rekosh chittered. "So you were. This certainly beats any *sythikar* I have ever heard in Takarahl, which is all of it."

"How long?" Telok asked, again shifting his attention between Ketahn and Ivy.

"I found her two moon cycles ago." Ketahn smoothed a palm down Ivy's hair. "The day I made my offering of mender roots to the queen."

Urkot thumped a leg on the branch, creating a vibration that even Ivy felt in her feet. "And you just...*mated* her?"

"No. I thought her a strange beast at first. A pet. I thought I had captured the rarest creature in the jungle, and my pride was such that I did not understand it was Ivy who had caught me."

"You made no mention of this when we spoke the following day," Telok said, eyes narrowing. "That is why you did not want me to join your hunt. You were hiding Ivy, even from me."

"From all of us," Rekosh added.

Ketahn huffed, banding another arm around Ivy's chest to pull her closer still. "My broodsister also. Ivy is mine, and even now I am *niktera* to share her."

Rekosh folded all four of his long arms across his chest. "Until you need aid."

"She is my mate. My heartsthread. Her safety is all that matters to me." There was a rawness in Ketahn's voice that Ivy had rarely heard—one part possessive, one part protective, one part aggressive. But there was vulnerability in it too.

Ivy turned slightly toward him and cradled his jaw in her hand, stroking it with her thumb.

Ketahn met her gaze and tucked her hair behind her ear, caressing the shell. He looked back to his friends. "It gave me no pleasure to keep *lisiv* from you, but I have done only what I thought best for her. And I will do so always."

Keep *lisiv*? They were talking about Ketahn hiding Ivy from everyone... So did *lisiv* mean secrets?

"So this *hyu-nin* is the reason you have at last decided to leave?" Urkot scratched his cheek; only then did Ivy notice that his fingers and claws were coated in pale dust.

"She is."

Rekosh chittered. "Thank you, Ivy, for making him finally see reason. Sometimes it seems Ketahn's head is fuller of rocks than Urkot's."

Ivy's brows furrowed.

"I would take that as praise, were I him," Urkot said.

"I am sure you would," Rekosh replied with a wave of his hand.

Telok scanned their surroundings with practiced care before returning his gaze to Ketahn and Ivy. "As welcome as your help would be in Takarahl, it is best you go. I do not know how you convinced the queen to let you walk away yesterday, but I would not see you risk another meeting with her."

"I told her I would return in an eightday, gifts in hand, to conquer her," Ketahn replied.

Though Ketahn had already told Ivy everything, she couldn't help but clench her jaw against the jealous fires in her belly. He wanted nothing to do with the queen, but just hearing him say those words, imagining him taking the queen as he had taken her, was almost more than Ivy could bear.

"You *what?*" demanded Rekosh.

"Shaper, unmake me," uttered Urkot.

"Of all the foolish things," rasped Telok.

Though all three had spoken simultaneously, Ivy had no difficulty understanding them—her response to Ketahn's news had been similar.

"It was the only way to earn time to prepare without Claws searching nearby," Ketahn said.

"The Queen's Claw has relaxed," said Telok, "but they have not withdrawn. More of them are back in Takarahl, but others still stalk the jungle as though in search."

Urkot grunted, absently reaching across his abdomen to

scratch the scar on his side. "And there were the two that tried to follow us today, out of all the vrix in the city."

"That was not by chance."

"We cannot ignore the whispers, either, that the Prime Claw is missing," said Rekosh. "Some go so far as to say the queen herself killed him in a rage while mating."

Telok's mandibles twitched. "Which matches her behavior during the High Claiming perfectly."

The tension within Ketahn increased further, and when he exhaled, a deep growl rolled in his chest. But his hold on Ivy remained steady—firm and secure but not painful. She caught her lower lip with her teeth as she glanced between his friends. Unease settled in her belly.

"The queen did not kill Durax," Ketahn said. "I did."

If Ketahn's friends were shocked by the revelation, they betrayed little of it in their reactions. Their moods seemed more contemplative than anything as far as Ivy could tell.

Telok cradled his spear along a forearm and folded his arms across his chest, angling his head down. "He found you."

"Yes. But not here."

"I always knew Durax would force it to such an end," Urkot grumbled.

"Even had he not forced a battle, I would have," Ketahn continued. "He found more than me. He found Ivy…and the rest of her kind."

Urkot's mandibles spread. "There are more like her?"

"Of course there are. They cannot very well hatch from nothingness." Rekosh cocked his head and looked at Ivy, his long braid brushing across his chest. "The better question is why have we never seen them before?"

"We came from the stars," Ivy said.

As one, Telok, Rekosh, and Urkot tipped their heads back to look skyward. Though the sky was darkening, it would still be a little while before the first stars were visible overhead—not that she could really point out the spot from which she'd come amidst all those glittering stars.

Ketahn combed his claws through her hair, producing a thrill along her scalp. Ivy knew it was more to comfort himself than her, but she appreciated it all the same.

"None but the Eight themselves can fly so high," Urkot said. "How could these *hyu-nins* come from there being so small and soft?"

"There is much to explain, and I understand little of it," Ketahn said, "but I will show you in two days. Bring what supplies you can gather to the pit that lies toward suncrest from this place."

Now Telok's mandibles rose, and he let out a low hiss. "That is a cursed place, Ketahn. Is the queen's fury not enough that you now seek to anger dark spirits?"

"Do you remember, Telok, when I told you I fell? That is where I fell. That is where I found Ivy."

The fine hairs on Telok's legs bristled, and he backed away. "Is that what her kind is then? *Hyu-nins* are spirits, *xinen* of the fire beast trapped down by the Eight?"

"She seems a bit too solid to be a spirit, does she not?" asked Rekosh.

"Spirits can confuse the senses," Urkot offered, though he didn't sound entirely convinced.

Ketahn growled. "She is flesh and blood and bone, and she is my mate."

Ivy gently pushed at one of Ketahn's arms. He held firm, turning his attention down to meet her gaze.

She offered him a smile. "Let me."

He tightened his embrace and flexed his fingers, pricking her skin with his claws, but finally he relinquished his hold.

She looked at the other vrix and stepped toward them. Despite living in a den far above the ground, despite traversing the branches and trees every day with Ketahn, walking along one on her own left her feeling off balance and uneasy. But she kept her attention forward, refusing to look down.

Ketahn's friends watched her approach. Telok remained wary, and Urkot was unreadable, but there was something different in Rekosh's eyes—at the very least, it was curiosity, but it might have bordered on excitement.

Stopping with a few feet between herself and the other vrix, Ivy lifted her hands, turning her palms up. "You can touch me."

"Remember that she is my mate," Ketahn growled from behind her.

Ivy's lips stretched into a grin. She found she quite liked his jealousy.

Rekosh chittered and stepped toward her without hesitation, lowering himself so his eyes were closer to her level. Moving slowly, he lifted a hand and pressed his fingers gently on her palm, keeping those long, razorlike claws away from her skin. Though his hand was rough, it wasn't as much so as Ketahn's, and his calluses were primarily at his fingertips.

"As you have heard by now, I am called Rekosh," he said in that smooth voice. "Should you desire truly *kirilka* silk, you need but ask. Ketahn is a clumsy weaver compared to me."

"She will wear no one's silk but mine," Ketahn said.

Ivy chuckled. "It is nice to meet you, Rekosh."

Rekosh's eyes dipped to her mouth, and his mandibles spread. "You bare your teeth at me. Why?"

"It is a smile." She smiled again. "It means I am happy."

Telok narrowed his eyes. "For any other creature, it would be a threat."

Urkot snorted. "Those teeth do not look threatening. She does not even have fangs." Easing closer, he peered down at her hands. He wrapped his thick fingers around her wrist, ignoring Ketahn's growl, and turned it to flip her hand over. "No claws either."

Though he was shorter than his friends, Urkot's hands were

TIFFANY ROBERTS

broader than Ketahn's, and his fingers were thick and blunt tipped compared to his companions'—not that Ivy doubted his dust-caked claws could do real damage when he needed them to. His hand engulfed more than half her forearm. He could have crushed her bones with a simple squeeze, but his grip was loose and careful.

"Soft, too," he continued. "And it is nice to meet someone with fewer arms than me for once."

Laughter burst from Ivy.

Rekosh and Urkot looked at her quizzically, the former going so far as to lean closer and stare at her mouth as though to puzzle out how she was making that sound.

Ivy sobered and leaned back. She knew they were curious—she'd gone through this once already with Ketahn—but she couldn't stop a resurgence of the feeling that she was on display like an oddity in a sideshow.

"It is called laughing," Ketahn said. "It is the same as chittering."

"A sound of amusement, then?" asked Rekosh.

"Yes. And it is louder when something is more amusing."

Urkot trilled and bumped a foreleg against Rekosh's. "She likes me better already!"

Telok grunted. "That is only because I have not introduced myself to her yet."

"It is not likely you will win her over after saying she must be a dark spirit come to work her curses upon us," said Rekosh, withdrawing his hand and easing back.

"There is no wrong in taking care," Telok replied. "This is new. She is new. And there are many things in the Tangle that appear harmless at a glance yet are anything but."

"I understand, Telok," Ivy said, meeting his gaze. "It took me a while to be at ease with Ketahn, and I still feel...out of place in this jungle. But he has all my trust now, and because he trusts you, so do I."

116

Telok's eyes lingered on her for a few more heartbeats. Then he brought his forearms together and bowed; she knew from Ketahn it was a gesture of apology. "I do not know every word you say, Ivy, but I know your meaning."

"She cannot make the sounds we do, but full understanding will come in time." Ketahn stepped into place behind Ivy, placing one pair of hands on her shoulders and the other on her hips. "If you are still willing to help. I did not ask it of you before, but I would have the three of you come with us when we leave this part of the Tangle."

"To leave behind Takarahl and everything we have known?" Urkot asked. "How would Rekosh survive without his *sythikar*?"

"I suppose I would have to learn to speak with trees and rocks like the rest of you," Rekosh said with what seemed an exaggerated exhalation. "But we must understand that, with Ketahn gone, Takarahl will be far less welcoming to any of us in the queen's fury. She has spared the three of us thus far, but she certainly knows of us."

"She has threatened all of you, and my broodsister, to get at me," Ketahn said, his deep voice rumbling into Ivy. "I never meant to put you in danger, but my wants cannot deter her."

Telok glanced around again, drawing in a deep breath. "I have at times envied your life in the Tangle, Ketahn. But this is…it is much to think upon."

"I know. You three have done much for me, and I have asked much more than I have any right to. Think on it. The humans need my aid if they are to survive…and I need yours if I am to help them."

"You will have it, Ketahn," Rekosh said, striding forward and touching one of his forelegs to Ketahn's. "You can trust us."

CHAPTER 11

DESPITE THE DISTINCT scent of spinewood sap fires and the fragrant smoke of burning herbs, these tunnels and chambers smelled of death. Old death. It was the sort of odor that sank into every crack and crevice, that seeped into every stone, that prowled in the shadows of every depression and alcove, that lingered as a reminder—*all things must die eventually.*

Ketahn had no need for such a reminder. He'd long understood that fact and had long since accepted it. But for the first time in years, he had something truly worth living for. Everything he held dear was dangling from a single overburdened thread surrounded by merciless claws. Those claws would sever that strand the instant his guard faltered.

Frustration, impatience, and helplessness flared in him, constricting his chest. Takarahl was the last place he wanted to be, now more than ever—because he'd left Ivy on the ship with the other humans.

Through the entryway before him, which had its huge stone doors open wide, he watched Archspeaker Valkai lead seven spiritspeakers through a ritual of offering. Their silk-clad forms were deeply shadowed and otherworldly in the dancing blue-green firelight. All eight speakers—one for each god—stood in a circle at the center of the chamber, which was so large it made even those females look small and meek. But that was the purpose of the Queens' Tomb, was it not?

Everyone was meant to feel small in the face of Queen Takari's legacy. Was it any wonder why Zurvashi had chosen to end that bloodline and take the glory for herself?

The spiritspeakers waved smoldering bundles of herbs and raised baskets filled with offerings off the altars before which they stood, invoking the Eight one by one as they did so. Their chanting was a low hum that made the swirling smoke seem even more surreal.

It wouldn't have been difficult to believe the veil between the living realm and the hazy spirit realm had been pierced in that chamber.

But Ketahn had no interest in such matters. He'd come here for a specific purpose, and even that had been difficult to focus upon...because Ivy was on that ship with seven humans Ketahn neither knew nor trusted.

She was on that ship with *Cole*.

Barely holding in a growl, he turned away from the chamber and paced toward the far wall. His hide prickled under the gazes upon him—those of the pair of Fangs guarding the entryway and the pair of Claws standing several segments down the tunnel. The latter had followed Ketahn since his arrival in Takarahl this morning.

He shouldn't have come here. Not because it was foolish—which it was—but because he'd left Ivy with the other humans. What protection did she have from them? What protection did she have from Cole? Fire blasted through Ketahn's veins as he saw Cole grabbing Ivy in his mind's eye. The human male's words yesterday had been unimportant, but his actions...

They were unacceptable.

Ketahn clenched his fists. The bite of his claws against his palms offered no distraction.

Only he was meant to touch Ivy. She was his mate, his purpose, his everything. Cole's intentions made no difference; he'd touched Ivy as though she belonged to him. He'd *grabbed* her. There was no justification for that.

Ketahn's fine hairs bristled, and a growl rumbled in his chest.

"The ritual is nearly through," said one of the Fangs, her voice echoing in the corridor despite being so low.

"Impatience does not befit a hunter," said one of the Claws.

Ketahn snapped his gaze to the two males. "Nor does being dead."

The Claws were standing with their shoulders leaned against the tunnel wall, grasping at an appearance of nonchalance. But the way each kept a hand upon the axe dangling from his belt, the way their fingers and mandibles twitched, and their fine hairs were often standing on end, spoke of their unease.

Killing them wouldn't bring Ketahn satisfaction. It would only cause more problems, as bloodshed always did. And yet, though he could resist those urges, he could not silence them.

Ketahn stopped at the wall, leaned his shoulder against it, and returned his attention to the speakers performing the ritual in the Queens' Tomb.

Archspeaker Valkai was holding an offering basket overhead and speaking. He believed she was asking the Eight and the spirits of the past queens to continue watching over Takarahl; her words were difficult to make out. This deep understone, especially in these winding tunnels and dark burial chambers, the pervading quiet had a way of amplifying even the smallest sounds. The rasp of a single hair against stone could be heard from several segments away, and every noise created long, distorted echoes. But sound was not carrying so easily out of the Queens' Tomb.

It was like the chamber devoured the voices of those within.

Ketahn shifted his gaze to the two other figures inside the chamber—another pair of Fangs, their features largely lost in the flickering light but their gold and gemstone adornments glinting. They stood in rigid stances behind and to either side of the Archspeaker. One of them was Ahnset, though Ketahn didn't know which.

Forcing himself to be still, Ketahn watched the ritual to its conclusion. The smoke from the burned herbs curled and dissipated, carried away on the gentle air flow that permeated Takarahl, even down here.

One at a time, the spiritspeakers placed their offerings atop their respective altars, backed away, and strode toward the doorway with their silk coverings flowing around their bodies. As they entered the tunnel, they split apart smoothly, alternating between turning left and right to follow the path onward.

The burial chambers were maintained solely by the spiritspeakers. They were responsible even for the bowls of spinewood sap that provided the only light, a task fulfilled by lightkeepers throughout the rest of the city.

Thought of the speakers' duties only reminded Ketahn of his duties to his mate, and how he was currently failing to fulfill them. How he wasn't there to guard her.

Inside the Queens' Tomb, the Fangs had moved closer to the Archspeaker, and the three were now engaged in quiet conversation. Their new positions placed them in just enough light for Ketahn to identify them—Ahnset was with Prime Fang Korahla. Their hushed tones would've made their words difficult to hear even were they not in a chamber that swallowed sound.

Ahnset and Korahla looked at one another for several heartbeats. When they returned their gazes to Archspeaker Valkai, she slid her forelegs forward, freeing them of her silk covering, and brushed them against the Fangs' forelegs. She sank into the crossed forearms gesture of the Eight.

Korahla and Ahnset turned toward each other.

Ketahn tilted his head and pushed away from the wall, arms falling to hang at his sides. One of the Claws tapped his fingers against the blackrock head of his axe. The clinking sounds rose over the fading noise of the spiritspeakers' departure, thrumming along the mental thread that was fastened directly to Ketahn's irritation.

Had he been holding his spear at that moment, he would have thrown it at the Claw without hesitation—and without looking away from his broodsister and the Prime Fang.

Ahnset and Korahla leaned closer to one another and tipped their headcrests together. As they held that intimate, trusting pose, their forelegs gently brushed together.

The Claws were too far to the side of the entryway to see into the chamber, and the Fangs guarding the doors were facing the wrong direction. Ketahn was grateful for that. What Ahnset and Korahla were doing... Word of it did not need to spread, especially not through the Queen's Claw.

The Prime Fang and Ahnset withdrew from each other slowly, their forelegs remaining in contact for as long as possible. They turned back to the Archspeaker, and Korahla gestured for Valkai to walk.

With the Fangs at her back, Archspeaker Valkai strode toward the door, her long, white silks swishing around her. Her blue eyes met Ketahn's, and she slowed to a halt several segments before reaching the doorway.

"Ketahn." She lifted a hand to beckon him. "I would speak with you, if you might spare a few moments."

He crossed his forearms and bowed, biting back a flare of impatience. He'd been gone for much too long already—not that he should've left Ivy to begin with, not with those humans. She would have been safer alone in the den; he would have been more at ease were she alone in the den. And now that he was so close to achieving his purpose for coming to Takarahl, the thought of even a few more moments' delay was maddening.

Yes, Ketahn's open return to the city would show Zurvashi that he'd not fled Takarahl during the eightday she'd granted him. Not yet. But he'd come for a singular reason—he needed to speak to his broodsister, face to face. He needed to look into her eyes before he asked her to venture into the jungle and become entangled in something she would never forget. Before he asked her to betray the queen she'd served for years.

"Always for you, Archspeaker," Ketahn said as he straightened and strode forward.

The Claws pushed away from the wall and moved to follow him.

"Are you training these broodlings, Ketahn?" asked one of the door guards.

"No. Some are beyond learning." He passed between the Fangs, and the *thunks* of spear butts being planted on the floor behind him made Ketahn glance over his shoulder.

The guards had moved to block the Claws, crossing the shafts of their spears in the space between them.

"We have been ordered to follow him," one of the Claws growled.

"And we have been ordered to allow no one into the Queens' Tomb without word from either the Archspeaker or the Prime Fang."

"Our orders come directly from the Queen!"

Korahla stormed toward the doorway, making the floor vibrate with her heavy steps. Ketahn moved out of her path without hesitation.

"And from where do you think our orders come?" the Prime Fang demanded.

The Claws shrank back from her advance, but only a few steps.

"We are to keep Ketahn tes Ishuun'ani Ir'okari in sight at all times, and by the Hunter's grace, that is what we mean to do." The male who'd spoken stood up straighter and squared his shoulders as though to draw attention to the black fur slung over his shoulder that marked him as a Queen's Claw.

Ketahn clenched his fists, again digging his claws into his palms, and gnashed his mandibles. All he wanted was a peaceful life with his mate. Zurvashi could have everything else for all he cared; he needed only Ivy.

"Such as you have never known the Hunter's grace," Ketahn said in a low, raw voice. "You are not Claws. You are no different than the recordkeepers, save you watch the comings and goings of your fellow vrix rather than that of food and materials."

"You grub bellied jung—"

Korahla slammed a leg down, prompting the Claw to snap his mouth shut. "Enough. This chamber has but one entrance. Your quarry will not elude you here."

"We will not allow him to slip through our web," the other Claw said. "Not like your Fangs did the other day."

Korahla stiffened, her hands tightening on her war spear. She was more than strong enough to run that spearhead clear through both Claws at once with a single thrust. Ketahn wondered if she meant to do just that as she stalked closer to the males.

In a hard, growling voice, she said to the entryway guards, "Escort these two out of the burial chambers, and ensure they go nowhere until I come to fetch them."

"We have orders from the queen," repeated one of the males.

"The Prime Claw will hear of this," snarled the other.

The door guards stepped forward, and the Claws retreated before them.

"You are welcome to tell Durax anything you like," Korahla

said, reverting to her usual stony calm, "should you ever discover where he crept off to."

As Ketahn watched the two Fangs guide the Claws away, Ahnset and the Archspeaker walked over to him; the former's stride was marked by the clanging of golden adornments and beads, the latter's by the soft rustling of cloth.

"Your exploits are the talk of Takarahl lately," the Archspeaker said. "I had not expected to see you for several more days."

Ketahn turned to face the females, bowed, and gestured apologetically; he didn't miss the disappointment in Ahnset's eyes before doing so. "I did not mean to cause trouble, Archspeaker."

Archspeaker Valkai chittered and extended a foreleg, tapping it against Ketahn's. "Your actions might say otherwise, Ketahn. Some say you are overly bold. Others that you are a reckless fool."

The strong smell of herb smoke clung to her, layered over a softer, more feminine scent. Perhaps at another time in his life, Ketahn might have found it appealing, but all he wanted now was for Ivy's fragrance to wash all the others away.

Ahnset grunted her agreement with the Archspeaker's words.

Ketahn straightened. Like all full-grown females, Valkai towered over him, but she did not loom. Despite being nearly as large as Ahnset, she was unthreatening. It might have been an effect of the swaths of white silk shrouding her body. It might also have been the result of her gentle demeanor, or her easy posture.

"I believe there is truth in both," he said.

With a huff, Ahnset thumped a leg on the floor. Her mandibles twitched, and her eyes seemed full to bursting with emotion, but she did not speak.

The Archspeaker chittered again, the sound soft and warm.

Ketahn was torn; she was kind, and that made him ashamed of his impatience, but he would not let that impatience go. His place was at Ivy's side. Her laughter was what he longed to hear.

"I would guess the truth is far more complicated," Valkai said.

"We but cling to the tangled webs the Eight have spun, clawing toward our fates," Ketahn replied. Spiritspeakers often said such things, but he'd never put much thought into such words. He was certain of one thing now, however—no matter which strand of fate he followed, it would lead him to Ivy. He'd accept nothing else.

"So have we been taught. And yet, I wonder…"

Archspeaker Valkai lifted her gaze, sweeping it about the chamber slowly. Ketahn followed the path of her eyes with his own.

He'd never been inside this chamber before. The doors were usually sealed, opened only when the speakers performed their offering rituals or when the remains of a queen were put to rest. The chamber was large enough that the blue-green firelight didn't touch the ceiling, which was supported by huge stone columns standing at regular intervals. A ring of altars stood at the center of the space. Square slabs lined the two walls perpendicular to the entrance. Many of those slabs were blank; many more bore carvings that depicted the likenesses and names of past queens.

At the far end of the chamber, opposite the entrance, was a raised stone dais upon which rested a large blackrock sarcophagus. It held Queen Takari herself, founder of Takarahl, mother to a line of queens who'd ruled for generation after generation. It was there that both Valkai and Ketahn's gazes paused.

He was stricken again by a sense of being tiny and insignificant in the face of all this, as though no vrix could ever hope to compare to what the city's first queen had wrought. As though all their struggles mattered not, for only queens were worthy of remembrance.

Had Ivy and the other humans ever experienced similar sensations on their world? Did powerful humans go out of their way to make those they ruled feel weak, small, and pointless? Had it played a part in their choice to leave?

Perhaps Zurvashi had tainted his view of all queens. She'd slain her predecessor and ascended to rule Takarahl while Ketahn was still a broodling, and he recalled little of the previous queen. Many of the vrix seemed to revere Takarahl's descendants, praising them as benevolent, just, wise rulers—albeit quietly, lest those whispers find their way to the center of the Zurvashi's web.

Ketahn had trouble believing Takari's descendants had been so selfless.

Korahla's heavy steps drew near. The Prime Fang took position beside Ahnset, making the gold band on her right mandible line up with the matching band on Ahnset's left mandible. "What is it, Archspeaker?"

"You must forgive me," Archspeaker Valkai said. "As of late, my thoughts wander as much as the threads of a broodling's first web. I wondered if fate is truly determined by the Eight, or if we vrix have the power to shape it ourselves."

Her eyes returned to Ketahn, her stare suddenly heavier. For a moment, it felt as though she were staring directly into him. As though his thoughts, his emotions, his secrets, his very spirit were laid bare to her.

But he refused to let her see his heartsthread; that belonged to Ketahn alone.

Ivy belonged to him alone.

CHAPTER 12

"A QUESTION BEYOND ME," Prime Fang Korahla said. "The place of the Fangs is to enact the will of the queen. Our fates are always tied to another, be they to her or the gods."

"And yet our queen was once a Fang herself." The Archspeaker kept her thoughtful, piercing eyes on Ketahn. "Was she chosen by the Eight to become queen, or did she shape her own fate?"

Ketahn did not look away from her even as her gaze sharpened and gleamed with a strange light.

"I will leave such questions to you and your sisters, Archspeaker," Korahla said. "To me it matters little. I am sworn to defend the queen. It is no more nor less complex than that."

"As was Zurvashi, once," Ketahn said.

Ahnset and Korahla snapped their attention to her, mandibles twitching.

"My broodbrother is a fool," Ahnset rumbled, tightening her hold on her war spear. "His mind has been addled by the Tangle."

Ketahn stared into Ahnset's eyes. He recognized much of what he saw there, recognized her, but more than ever he was aware that he and his sister had spent so much time apart that they simply couldn't know each other as well as they once had. The lives they'd led had drifted apart, like two strands in a web that had been disintegrating over the years, left connected by only a few thin, worn bits of silk.

"Such things should not be discussed," Korahla said in a low, tight voice.

"I have but spoken the truth," Ketahn replied, turning his palms toward the shadow-shrouded ceiling.

"If you are so dedicated to the truth"—Ahnset leaned toward him, clacking her mandible fangs—"open your eyes to the truth of your situation, Ketahn."

"I have, broodsister. More than you know."

"And yet you pursue whatever you desire and ignore what will keep you safe and alive?"

"All spirits yearn for something," Archspeaker Valkai said, her relatively soft voice commanding attention. "For most, survival is enough. But for others, it may be change, power, peace, companionship, or any number of things. Only rarely can we know what comprises the heartsthread of another. But in those mysteries, I think, may lie the answers to the questions I have posed."

Silence followed her words, seizing the chamber for the space of several heartbeats—during which time Ketahn did not miss the prolonged eye contact between Ahnset and Korahla.

A low buzz sounded in Korahla's chest. "Come, Archspeaker. We shall see you through your remaining duties." She gestured toward the open entryway.

"Very well, Prime Fang," Valkai replied.

"May my broodsister be excused from her duties briefly?" Ketahn asked.

Korahla grunted, narrowing her eyes at Ketahn. "So long as she and Archspeaker Valkai consent."

"It is not my place to disrupt the sacred bond between brood siblings," Valkai said.

Ahnset thumped the butt of her spear on the floor and bowed her head. The band on her mandible glinted in the firelight. "I shall not be long behind, Prime Fang."

"All is well in hand." Korahla brushed a foreleg against Ahnset's. "We shall see you soon."

The Prime Fang strode toward the entryway, but the Archspeaker lingered, glancing between Ketahn and Ahnset. She leaned close, her silk coverings whispering on the floor. "Behind Queen Takari's sarcophagus, sound does not carry far. You will have as much privacy there as Takarahl can offer."

After gracefully making the sign of the Eight, she turned and followed Korahla. The Prime Fang paused long enough to glance over her shoulder at Ahnset before exiting the chamber and turning into the tunnel beyond. The Archspeaker kept close behind her.

Wordlessly, Ahnset stalked toward the rear of the Queens' Tomb, her heavy steps oddly muted in the space. Ketahn followed, studying his surroundings. The elaborateness of this chamber, the crafting skill on display here, made the other burial chambers seem little more than crude, clumsy efforts.

This made the place his mother had been laid to rest seem like a burrow clawed out by a blind subterranean beast.

Ahnset mounted the dais and, giving the sarcophagus respectful space, walked to the back wall, where old silk banners hung. Their crimson dye was surprisingly vibrant despite their apparent age. Ketahn paid neither the sarcophagus nor the silk much attention as he joined his broodsister; her posture was stiff, her fine hairs standing, and her breaths deep and heavy.

"You eightfold-cursed fool," she growled. "Sneaking into the queen's sanctum like a killer prowling the shadows? Are you truly so eager to meet your own death?"

131

"I sought only to speak with her," he replied as steadily as he could.

Ahnset spun to face him, throwing her arms out to the sides. "I would have taken you to her! Kora—the Prime Fang would have taken you."

"To my death. Zurvashi wants a worthy male. To prove my worth, I had to accomplish something no other could." Ketahn's insides twisted at his own words. All he'd done had been for *Ivy*, and even pretending that he'd taken those risks for Zurvashi was sickening.

Ahnset dropped her arms and closed the distance between them in one step, forcing Ketahn to tilt his head back farther to hold her gaze.

"Had you gone in peace, she would have listened. But the way you went to her, broodbrother... It is a wonder she spared your life."

Ketahn's mandibles twitched. "I know what intrigues her. I took a chance to regain her favor."

Releasing a sound that was half growl, half snort, Ahnset curled her hands into fists. "That chance was as small as a single leaf compared to the whole of the Tangle. That is no reason to be confident."

Clenching his jaw, Ketahn huffed. Heat skittered beneath the surface of his hide. Anger; frustration; impatience. The same as he'd felt since he'd left the pit this morning, since he'd left his mate behind.

"I am not your broodling, Ahnset," he said, his voice harsher than he'd intended.

"Yet you insist upon acting like one."

A thought darted through his mind—*should not have come here*—and vanished as quickly as it had come, but it was enough to stab him with a jagged shard of guilt. Again, he felt the distance that had grown between them. He refused to let it remain.

"Do you remember how we would sneak into these tunnels when we were young?" he asked, gentling his tone.

Ahnset averted her gaze. "Yes. The echoes were so much louder down here, and we always used to argue about why."

"Urkot thought they were spirits mocking us, that they would make the dead walk if we were too noisy. Telok said they were monsters hiding in the darkness, trying to draw us close enough to attack. Rekosh always tried to get them to say something different than what he had."

Ahnset's chitter was small and a bit sorrowful. "He succeeded only in insulting himself. And all the while, you and I would chase those echoes to every shadowed chamber, eager to defend our friends."

"And we succeeded only in bruising our broodbrother."

She chittered again; it was warmer than the first time, yet even sadder. "Ishkal feared no shadows. It was like they embraced him. Even full grown vrix could not find him if he did not want to be found."

Ketahn's mandibles crept into a smile. "And though we knew it was always Ishkal lurking in the shadows waiting to startle us, he managed to give us a fright every time."

"He never stopped, even knowing how we would react."

"Oh, he earned those bruises. He wore them with pride." Ketahn's gaze dipped briefly, running over the many scars on his hide. Vrix believed such marks were an honor to carry.

He would gladly have traded that honor to have his broodbrother at his side again.

After a long silence, Ahnset said, "He would always have become a Claw, whether the war had happened or not."

An old, gnarled, bitter emotion twisted in Ketahn's gut. "Yes. It was natural for him, and there were none who matched him in the Tangle."

"What fools were we to have thought ourselves warriors as broodlings?"

"We were not fools. We simply did not know."

"How foolish we must have looked, regardless."

"You with the stick you imagined a spear."

"And you with your bone needles and little knife, ready to poke even the most fearsome beast to death."

Ketahn chittered and folded his arms across his chest. "I would have tried to stitch the monster's eyes and mouth shut first, that it could not see or bite us."

"You have never been that cruel, Ketahn."

"*You* have never been that cruel, Ahnset. I…served in the Queen's Claw against Kaldarak. I had to learn cruelty to survive."

She sighed, and her posture sagged. "For seven years and more, we have but rarely seen each other. It is no wonder we know so little about one another."

"Ah, my sister," Ketahn rumbled, brushing a foreleg against hers. There were several smells clinging to Ahnset—the fragrant herb smoke, her familiar fragrance, and, stronger than seemed possible after so brief a bit of contact, Korahla's scent. "You speak true, but I would not have it remain so. I have kept secrets, but I no longer wish for them to be an invisible wall between us."

"You are not alone in keeping secrets, broodbrother." She lifted a hand to tap the gold band on her mandible. "I have long hidden the truth of my heartsthread, even from you."

"Korahla," he said gently.

Ahnset turned her palms toward the ceiling. "What else could we have done but kept silent? Fangs rarely have time to satisfy their urges with males, especially when the queen expects us to take only the finest mates lest it reflect poorly upon her. Many of my spear sisters find release with one another from time to time."

A low, unhappy buzz vibrated in her chest. "Sharing pleasure with the Prime Fang is acceptable. Sharing more…"

Something in Ketahn's chest constricted, squeezing his hearts and making his lungs burn. Had he been concerned only with himself for so long that he'd missed the signs that must have been there? Had he so easily forgotten that his broodsister was a vrix with her own wants, her own yearnings, her own heartsthread? His thoughts these past two moon cycles had been only of Ivy and how he might be with her, and he'd been willing to forsake everything else in that pursuit.

Even knowing this, he was still willing to forsake all else. But he didn't want it to come to that.

He could not blame his broodsister for hiding this from him, especially not when he'd kept his own mate a secret. All he could do was hope this would help Ahnset understand what he'd done and what he meant to do.

"To protect what you share with her, you must hide it," Ketahn said, pressing his other foreleg against hers. He reached up, hooked a hand behind her neck, and drew her down to touch his headcrest to hers. "I understand, broodsister."

"How could you, Ketahn?" Her voice was soft and small, run through with pain but holding no trace of accusation, anger, or bitterness. "You left everything behind, everyone, to be alone."

"I did. I forsook everything to seize my freedom...to escape her."

"And she drags you back with more ferocity each time you pull away. All I have done is encourage you to submit." She closed her eyes and clamped a hand on his shoulder. "Now...you must fulfill your word to her, or you will die. Because I bade you go to her."

"It is not your doing, broodsister." The next words he spoke came out unbidden, emerging in a rasp that thickened the air. "I have a mate."

Ahnset stiffened, and her grip on his shoulder became crushing. "Ketahn..."

"I came to Takarahl today to speak with you," he said. His

heartsthread was taut and thrumming, stretched to its limits, and this was it; this was the moment when he had to give voice to the decision he'd made, when he had to make it all real.

"I must do all in my power to protect her," he continued, "and that means I must leave Takarahl far behind."

Ahnset opened her eyes and straightened her back, lifting her head to stare down at Ketahn with a mixture of confusion and alarm.

He held her gaze. Each word he spoke lifted a little of the burden off him and eased the pressure on his hearts. "This is my final visit to the city. I shall never walk these tunnels again."

"You... Ketahn, you cannot mean this. You..." Her grip strengthened further. "Her fury will burn the Tangle to cinder. Every Claw, every Fang, will be ordered to slay you the moment you are found. I... I will be ordered to slay you."

"I came here openly only so she would think I have not yet fled. So she would think I am sincere. But once I am gone, I will not be found. She will never see me again, Ahnset."

"And I shall never see you again, either." Ahnset's mandibles drooped.

"Knowing what you have found here, broodsister, I cannot ask you to leave with me, though I long to do so. This situation is far more complicated than I can explain."

"Try, at least."

Ketahn chittered humorlessly and shook his head, though she couldn't have known what the gesture meant. "Truly, I cannot. You would not believe me even if I found the right words."

She bent down, drawing her face closer to his. "Broodbrother, you must tell me. Your life dangles from a single thread."

"And that thread is fraying," Ketahn said. Considering Ahnset's position as a Fang and her relationship with Korahla, she was already far too involved in his affairs to keep her safe—

and he had no desire to place her in even greater danger. He had no intention of threatening her way of life.

But neither could he leave her questioning why he'd left or what he would do for the rest of his days, never to know the answers because he'd vanished into the Tangle.

She deserved to know. And Ketahn could not deny that he wanted the pride of introducing his mate to his broodsister, even if the two only met once.

"Can you leave Takarahl tonight?" he asked.

Her mandibles twitched, and a shudder wracked her, making her adornments jingle. "I cannot turn my back on Takarahl, on my duties, on my…my mate."

Ketahn bumped her leg with his. "I am not asking you to, Ahnset. All I want is for you to come to my den so you may meet my mate. So I might explain what I can before I must go."

"What you ask…does it mean betraying the queen?"

"In her eyes, surely. But for you, only in that I beg you to never speak to her of any of it."

Ahnset drew in a deep breath. When she spoke, her voice had regained much of its usual confidence. "The Prime Fang will grant me leave should I ask it of her."

A satisfied trill sounded in Ketahn's chest. "Good. Then we shall see one another again under the light of the moons, as nothing more than brother and sister."

She squeezed his shoulder again, heightening that flicker of pain. "It is not too late for you to renounce all this, broodbrother. To…become the queen's and avoid all the risk."

"Ahnset." Ketahn reached across his chest to place his hand atop hers, easing her hold on his shoulder but not breaking it. "You know me well enough to understand that it has always been too late for that."

"If you have found a mate… Yes, I know all too well." With a last, affectionate squeeze, Ahnset withdrew her hand and stepped back. "I have long been torn between wishing to see you safe and wishing to see you happy, Ketahn. Perhaps it was foolish of me to hope you could have both...but the queen will never allow it."

"It is possible, broodsister. Just not in her shadow."

Ahnset stood up straight, squaring her shoulders; that sudden shift from sister to Fang right before his eyes, one last time. "I must return to my duties. The Prime Fang and the Archspeaker must surely think me negligent by now."

Ketahn sketched an apologetic gesture. "My fault, as ever. Forgive me."

She chittered, deep and a little rough. "Get moving, that I may seal the chamber. Until tonight. Protector, shield you."

"And you, Ahnset."

Ketahn turned away from her, descended from the dais, and strode out of the Queens' Tomb without looking it over again. Queen Takari had left an immense legacy behind, but it had been ended by a single challenge. What difference did it make if Takari's heirs had been wise and just if they'd fallen to Zurvashi's unrestrained strength and cruelty?

He did not look back as he moved in the direction of the spiraling ramp that led to Takarahl's higher levels. Ahnset's heavy, clanking steps echoed behind him, fainter with each moment.

There was a future to look toward, one that could be informed by the past but didn't need to be overshadowed by it. One that he could share with his mate, his Ivy, no matter how far from Takarahl they had to journey.

But first, he had to return to her. And he'd not forgotten where she was now—or who she was there with.

Ivy had assured Ketahn that she belonged to him. He did not doubt her, but all the same he could not stop the thoughts from coming. What if she wanted broodlings—*babies*? What if she wanted to be a mother? She could only bear young if she mated with one of her kind. He could never fulfill that desire, should she have it.

His fingers flexed, muscles tight, and his leg claws raked the floor.

The thought of her being with another male—touching, kissing, mating—lit a fire in his chest that made his body tremble with rage. He clenched his jaw and let out a huff. This was jealousy, ravenous and aggressive, flowing to his core like rainwater along the strands of a web.

And what would it gain him? What male could he direct this fury toward, who would serve as a rightful target of it? It was useless. It was draining.

It was woefully persistent.

Ketahn quickened his pace, ignoring the dark, silent chambers he strode past, ignoring the cloying stench of death that wafted from the very stone, ignoring Ahnset's fading steps. All he saw in his mind's eye was Ivy.

She was all he wanted. All he needed. All he craved. Soon, they would carve out the sort of life they wanted to share, and the Tangle could take anyone who stood in their way.

But he couldn't ignore the new sound that pierced his thoughts much too late—several sets of heavy steps, thumping and jingling, from ahead.

The newcomers rounded the next bend before Ketahn could duck into one of the nearby burial chambers to hide. Queen Zurvashi was at the head of the pack, unmistakable even in the flickering light, stalking toward Ketahn with her purple silk wrappings billowing around her and her adornments gleaming. Two Fangs marched in step behind her, and three Claws behind them—the pair Korahla had ordered away from the Queens' Tomb and their companion, who'd broken away from the others shortly after Ketahn had entered Takarahl.

Ketahn's instincts roared, dumping further heat into his veins. Dread and rage swirled inside him with equal strength and ferocity. Encountering the queen was always a possibility when he returned to Takarahl. He'd been a fool to hope that his open presence would keep her away, that it would intensify her anticipation and convince her to wait until the day he was meant to deliver on his promises.

Apparently, he should have counted himself amongst those who were beyond learning.

Without slowing his pace, Ketahn stood taller, squared his shoulders, and tipped his chin up. Zurvashi's predatory gaze was upon him, cold and calculating, and her stride maintained its speed. Ketahn drew in a slow, deep breath. Already, he could scent her; her fragrance was sickeningly complemented by the underlying stench of death.

As they drew near to one another, Ketahn said, "My queen, I did not—"

Zurvashi lunged, clamping a hand around Ketahn's neck. Her hold made Ahnset's bruising grasp seem tender and careful. He caught her wrist in two hands, clutching it with flaring panic as she heaved him up and swung him to the side.

Darkness swallowed Ketahn as the queen strode forward, but it wasn't due to lack of air—he felt too much pain to be losing consciousness. Beyond the huge, imposing form of Zurvashi, he glimpsed blue-green light dancing in an entryway surrounded by shadows. She'd forced him into a burial chamber. Out in the corridor, the Claws chittered; the sounds of their smug amusement echoed along the tunnel, warping into the otherworldly chittering of spiteful spirits.

Ketahn's legs skittered for purchase, but the queen only lifted him higher. Her claws bit into the sides of his neck.

His chest was ablaze with want for air, and his neck was pulsing with agony. He felt the strength draining from his muscles. Darkness encroached on the edges of his mind, dulling his thoughts.

He would not allow Zurvashi an uncontested victory.

Ketahn would do all he could to get back to Ivy, to hold her in his arms again, to claim the future he had come to yearn for so wholly.

Ketahn reached for the knife he'd strapped to the upper segment of his rear leg. Against the queen, it would do little better than a bone needle would have against the imagined monsters of his youth, but she would not slay him without some of her own blood being spilled.

His fingers closed around the knife handle.

Zurvashi growled and slammed Ketahn down on his back. The combination of his weight and her strength made it feel as though he'd fallen hundreds of segments onto solid stone. The knife slipped from his grasp, stuck in its binding.

The pain was stunning, blasting into his bones.

She came down atop him, catching his upper arms in one hand and forcing them over his head; she caught his lower arms with her remaining pair of hands and spread them to the sides. Her weight only made his uncomfortable position more agonizing—his back and hindquarters were pressed flat on the floor, putting unbearable pressure on his spine.

Her pelvis pressed against his. Her hide radiated heat, all centered on her slit. Ketahn spread his mandibles and snarled as her large, thick legs rubbed against his, smearing her heady scent across his fine hairs.

"You have denied my cravings for too long." Her voice vibrated around him, into him, as invasive and insistent as her smell.

Zurvashi ground her slit against his, forcing him even more firmly against the floor. The cold stone bit into his hide. When he opened his mouth to speak, she tightened her hold on his neck and forced his chin up.

"Is this my mighty conqueror? Is this the male I thought worthy of me, who declared that worth himself?" she asked, leaning her head down.

The faintest glow highlighted the edges of her outermost adornments, and pinpoints of chilled gold glinted in her eyes. She brushed a thumb over his mandible. Ketahn snapped those mandibles together, but she was out of his reach.

And still her legs brushed against his, still her scent and heat assailed him.

Ketahn's insides twisted into knots, and his hide felt on the verge of leaping off his body to flee deeper into the shadows. But was there truly anywhere to hide from her?

The queen rose slightly only to slam her pelvis atop his again, triggering a deep ache in his bones. He kept his claspers tightly drawn in; he refused to let his slit part even a thread's width. Her scent, thickening with each heartbeat, filled his senses like a cloying fog.

He would not betray his mate. Not for Zurvashi or anyone else. Not even to save his own life.

"Why should I wait?" the queen snarled. As she gyrated her pelvis, her slit parted against Ketahn's hide, baring the smoother, softer flesh within. "Who are you to deny me what I desire? I take what I want. I will be denied *nothing*."

She leaned her torso further over him, increasing the pressure on his arms and altering the angle of her gyrations. The new angle threatened to pry his slit open. "I am the conqueror. I am the queen, and you are mine until I have tired of you—or broken you beyond repair."

Zurvashi dipped her face closer still, bracing her mandibles against the insides of his—making it impossible for him to shut them.

"Now, Ketahn, my claim is—"

Ketahn snapped his head up, hammering his headcrest into the queen's face. With a startled grunt, she reeled back, but the sound gave way to a chitter. There was no time to contemplate the change; his chance to act would not survive even the slightest hesitation.

Her altered position removed some of the weight that had been pinning his upper arms to the floor. Ketahn twisted them free of her grasp, laced the fingers of both hands together, and swung them like a club. His fists struck the inside of her elbow, making her arm buckle and breaking her hold on his throat.

The queen trilled and fixed her eyes upon him again. Even in the meager light, he could not miss the lustful, excited gleam in her gaze.

She threw her torso forward, driving her upper left elbow down toward his face. He tilted his head sharply aside. Her huge arm hit the floor less than a finger's breadth from his face with a heavy *thwap*. The shift in stance placed her chest directly over Ketahn's eyes; though her elbow had missed, her dangling beads, pendants, and gold adornments fell to dully strike his face and obscure his view.

His sense of smell was likewise obstructed. Zurvashi's scent was battering his senses with more strength than ever. He was kept alert only by pain, centered now on his lower forearms, which were still trapped beneath her lower hands and bore the majority of her weight.

He latched onto that pain, willing it to course through him and anchor him like the roots of a tree, hoping it would be enough to hold him through this raging storm. He would not allow her scent to break through. He would not allow it to affect him.

Bracing one pair of legs against the floor, he wrapped the rest around the queen's lower half, drawing his hindquarters snugly against hers. She pulsed with warmth and made an unsettlingly hungry buzz.

With a growl, Ketahn twisted his hips and heaved. Every muscle in his body strained and screamed. Thankfully, the struggle was brief; the queen's balance had already been disrupted. She tumbled onto her side with a grunt and the clanging of many pieces of metal against stone, but she didn't release his arms, and two of his legs were now stuck between her hindquarters and the floor.

Though He heard heavy steps and voices somewhere behind him, saw the scant light broken by large shadows, yet he could not afford to remove his attention from the queen for even the space of a heartbeat. She was too dangerous.

Zurvashi carried her momentum into a roll, dragging Ketahn along with her. He threw his free legs wide and planted them on the floor, using all his strength to halt that roll as she came down on her back and preventing her from following through to tumble him beneath him again.

Her upper hands darted up toward his neck. Ketahn bent his left arm, catching her thrusting hands with his forearm and leaning his weight against them. His limb shuddered against the terrible strength she exerted. Panic threatened to explode inside him; he knew this was but a sliver of her might. She'd win this contest of strength the instant she chose to do so.

Ketahn reached back with his right arm and tore the knife free from his leg. Quick as a lightning strike, he had the blade against Zurvashi's throat.

The queen's amber eyes flared, and she spread her mandibles. The countless braids of her hair were strewn around her head in wild tendrils, her many adornments were in disarray, and a trickle of blood glistened at the corner of her mouth, likely the result of the blow inflicted by his headcrest.

Slowly, she opened her mouth, and her long, yellow tongue slipped out to lick away the blood.

The queen chittered again. It echoed in the chamber, building into something impossibly more twisted than usual. "Ah, dear little Ketahn."

He snarled and threw his weight onto the knife—but it had not yet bit into flesh when powerful hands grabbed all four of his arms and ripped him away from Zurvashi, who finally released her hold on him.

Though he could now see the Fangs who'd accompanied the queen on either side of him, his crimson-tinted vision remained on Zurvashi. His legs skittered across the floor, claws scraping stone in his desperation to get back to her and finish what she had begun.

To finish her.

One of the Fangs wrenched his arm, breaking his hold on the knife. The weapon fell to clatter on the floor. Then he was dragged to the rear of the chamber, spun about to face the entrance, and slammed against the wall. His back struck cold, hard stone. His hindquarters scraped roughhewn rock and bumped into something wrapped in thick silk; it had slipped into one of the burial holes.

Zurvashi was already standing. She straightened her attire nonchalantly, reclaiming her queenly composure a little at a time.

"What is this?" Prime Fang Korahla demanded from the corridor.

There were more steps rushing to the chamber, more figures charging in through the entrance. But Ketahn's attention was fixed on the queen, who was a towering, shadowy shape before him.

"So, there is some merit to your boasts," Zurvashi said, stepping toward Ketahn.

Ivy...I am sorry.

"Six days, Ketahn." The queen slowly trailed a foreleg along the side of his, forcing more of her scent onto him. That sickening hunger still gleamed in her eyes, though there was something terrifyingly tender in them now also, and her voice became a purr. "I am hopeful after this display. Next time, I will not hold back...and I expect you will impress me with your claiming."

She turned and strode toward the exit as Korahla and Ahnset entered the chamber, their eyes unreadable in the shadows.

Zurvashi shoved past them and waved a hand in the air. "Release my little hunter. He has much to do in the days to come."

The queen paused in the entryway and glanced over her shoulder as the Fangs let go of Ketahn. "And tell that fool Durax to report to me immediately should you happen across him out there. He has exhausted my good grace."

And then Zurvashi was gone, the two Fangs hurrying after her.

Ketahn's legs nearly buckled as weakness coursed through him like floodwater from an overfed stream. The queen's smell clung to him, overpowering every other scent. His hide thrummed, crawling with sickening heat, and pain throbbed in more places than he could count.

He was fiercely brushing at his legs with all four hands, desperate to wipe away that scent, that taste, when Ahnset grasped his shoulder.

But the queen's smell wouldn't fade. She had buried it into his very hide.

"Easy," someone said; it might have been his sister, but might also have been Korahla.

Ketahn struggled against the hand on his shoulder. "I must go. Must return to…"

To Ivy. Only she could fix this. Only she could make it better. Only she could make him forget the taint the queen had left upon him.

CHAPTER 13

"HOW'S THIS?" Ella asked, holding up the basket she was making.

Ivy looked up from her own basket to look over Ella's. The wide, green blades of grass were tightly woven, and Ivy could already tell that it would turn out much better than any of her own early attempts. "That looks great!"

Ella lowered the basket into her lap. Her trembling fingers resumed their work, threading another long, thick blade. "When I was a kid, I used to make friendship bracelets during recess in school. I didn't have much time to make them at home because there were always so many chores to do on the farm when I wasn't doing homework. But all my classmates loved them and always asked if I could make them some. I loved making them. This reminds me of that."

Ivy smiled. She had come up with the idea of teaching the other survivors to weave baskets early this morning before Ketahn had left to visit his sister, and he'd helped her gather the grass and lash it together with a silk rope on their way to the pit. Not only had she hoped to occupy her mind and stop herself from thinking about all the horrible things that could happen to Ketahn during his return to Takarahl, but she'd also wanted to give the other humans a way to pass their time more pleasantly.

Idle hands are the devil's tools, as her mother had been fond of saying.

Ugh, don't go there, Ivy.

Most of the others had taken to the task eagerly, grateful for something to do. Hearing Ella's fond reminiscences made Ivy's heart swell. She was glad she'd been able to bring the woman a little joy despite the circumstances.

Ivy ran her gaze over Ella, and her smile faded. Ella's condition hadn't improved. If anything, she looked worse than she had the day before. The woman's gray pallor and the dark circles under her eyes were more prominent, and Diego was worried—though he'd been careful not show it around Ella. At least Ella had mustered enough energy to slip out of her cryochamber and move about the room today, but even that had taken a lot out of her.

Fortunately, sitting on the floor weaving baskets was something she could manage without overtaxing herself.

Time, Ivy. Ella just needs time to recover.

But time was something they didn't have.

Ivy glanced at the door as though it would open that very moment to reveal Ketahn. As much as she liked being around other humans, she missed him and longed for his presence, for the loving caress of his hands, for the gentle scrape of his claws over her skin and through her hair. She'd lived so long without physical touch—without intimate, loving, physical touch—but Ketahn gave it to her in abundance, and she loved every bit of it. She'd come to crave it.

He hadn't relished the idea of leaving Ivy in this place of death among people he didn't trust, and he'd been particularly agitated after what had happened with Cole yesterday. When Ketahn had brought her here this morning, his eyes had immediately locked on to Cole; his mandibles had spread wide, his fine hairs had bristled, and he'd held himself taller, wider, somehow becoming even more imposing than normal. Thankfully, Ivy had been the only one close enough to hear his displeased growl.

Her eyes wandered, drifting over the cryochambers lined up along the walls. Most of them were covered now; the others had used blankets from the emergency caches to do so. Unfortunately, that was the most respectful—and practical—way to deal with the dead.

It only helped a little in pretending that there weren't twelve corpses sharing this space with the survivors.

"So you worked on a farm, Ella?" Ahmya asked, bringing Ivy's attention back to the conversation.

"Yeah, my family's farm," Ella replied. "We had some dairy cows, a few pigs, a whole mess of chickens, and two hundred acres of crops."

Callie chuckled. "I didn't realize there were still family farms like that. I thought everything was automated nowadays."

"A lot of places have gone under or been bought out over the years, yeah, but my family's had that land for a long, long time. My parents didn't want to give it up, and there was just enough of a local market for fresh produce to keep us going. My brother is set up to inherit it after they..." Ella dropped her gaze, but not before Ivy caught sight of tears gathering in her eyes. "Well, I guess he would have taken over a long time ago, huh?"

"I know it's hard to come to terms with," Ivy said gently, "but we'll always have the memories of what we left behind."

For better or worse, right? Even if we'd rather forget...

"I had a small apiary and raised a couple goats," Lacey said, tilting her head as she worked a strand of grass between the other blades. "I ran a small business selling homemade goatmilk soap, bath bombs and salts, and fresh honey. I'd sometimes get calls about beehives in people's homes or other random places, and I'd drive out to extract them and bring back home."

"You girls grew up running around in the county, and here I am, born and raised in New York City," Callie said with a smirk.

"What'd you do, Callie?" Ivy asked.

"I'd just graduated college with my master's degree in chemistry when I was approached about joining the Homeworld Initiative."

"Wow," Ella said. "They approached you?"

"Yeah. I think they were recruiting experts pretty zealously for this trip, and they offered me a chance to *expand the width and breadth of human knowledge* by joining the mission and working with all the alien compounds on Xolea. They really knew how to get to a young science nerd's heart, you know?" She lifted her shabbily made basket up and studied it with displeasure. "Not that I'll be doing much of that now." She flicked her gaze to Ivy. "What about you?"

Ivy rubbed her arm as a flare of embarrassment rushed through her. Everyone else's lives sounded so nice compared to her own. "When I was in high school, my plan was to become a teacher. But… well, I made some poor choices and ended up working as a cashier."

Ahmya nudged Ivy's arm, offering her a small, encouraging smile. "Life doesn't always go according to plan."

Lacey snickered and waved a hand around her. "You got that right."

"What'd you do, Ahmya?" Ivy asked.

"I was a florist," Ahmya said, looking down at the basket in her lap. Hers was nearly halfway done and by far the best of anyone's. "I thought about going to college for botany but…I kind of suck at math."

Ella chuckled. "Me too."

Ahmya smiled. "But it's okay. I got to spend every day working with beautiful flowers."

Cole dropped down on the floor next to them and drew up his legs, dangling his hands off his knees. "You're all over here playing with grass and talking about flowers like we're on some vacation."

"Is making a basket too hard for Mr. Construction Worker?" Diego asked without looking up from his clumsy attempt at basket weaving. He'd closed his cryochamber and was sitting atop it, legs hanging off the side. "Good thing I never hired you to build me a deck or anything."

"Tch. Making baskets is a totally different set of skills," Cole said with a smirk. His mood had been better today—at least since Ketahn had left.

Callie tossed her basket—which had started to come apart—onto the floor in front of her. "And what kinds of *skills* do you have?"

"Well, I *can* build a pretty damn good-looking deck for one thing."

Ivy smiled. "That could come in handy. There's definitely plenty of wood out there."

He grinned at her, flashing his straight white teeth. "I'm very good at handling wood."

"Really, Cole?" Will shook his head. He hadn't taken part in the basket weaving lesson and had instead watched quietly from his position sitting against the wall. His fingertips were a bit tender after he and a few of the others had gone into the nearby chambers yesterday to scrounge for extra supplies—an electric panel had shorted while he was accessing it, and he'd suffered some minor burns. "I thought those kinds of lines died off like two hundred years ago."

"And for good reason," Callie said.

"Oh, come on." Cole threw his hands up in mock exasperation. "Just trying to have a little fun."

Diego pinched his finger and thumb together until there was

but an inch of space between them. "Little being the key word, right?"

Callie hissed. "Ooo, that's a burn."

"Harsh, man. Harsh," Cole said. "I bring a very valuable and practical skillset to this...team, or whatever we want to call it. Who do you think is going to build us a shelter out there?"

"The spider guy," said Lacey.

"Vrix," Ivy corrected with a quiet snicker.

Lacey arched a brow. "What kind of homes do they live in anyway?"

"Well, Ketahn's people live underground, but he made his nest high up in the trees. It's safer to be off the ground."

"Up in the trees? You're not going to tell us he lives on a web or something, are you?" Cole asked.

"He...kind of does. His nest is built out of branches, vines, and silk, and it's suspended by a giant web that's kind of woven into the nearby branches and anchored to the tree trunks."

Ahmya's eyes widened. "And you...you live there too? With him?"

Warmth flooded Ivy's cheeks. They already knew Ketahn was her mate, and Cole had outright asked—no, he'd demanded—if she was fucking Ketahn, so she could only imagine what they thought of her. For an instant, the heat burning under her skin was that old shame she'd felt under the judgmental stares of her parents, but she swiftly shoved that feeling away.

"Yeah. It took a lot of getting used to," Ivy said, lowering her basket to her lap. "Honestly, I'm still not used to being up so high, but I trust Ketahn with my life."

"What's the plan for when we get out of here?" Will asked.

Ivy shook her head. "I don't know yet."

"*When* are we leaving, anyway?" Cole shoved himself to his feet and walked toward their pile of supplies. He snatched up one of the hydration packets. "I don't want to be the one to complain, but I don't think I can get through a week of staring at these walls with nothing to do." Biting open the packet, he tipped his head back and drank.

"Soon," Ivy said, wishing she could give a better answer. "Ketahn is going to need help carrying everyone and all these supplies out of here, but he also needs help keeping everyone safe, teaching us, and providing fresh food for us. He has to be careful arranging all that."

"So there's going to be more of them? More vrix?" asked Diego.

Cole waved a palm at Ivy. "Hold on a sec now. One of those things is big enough to eat all of us for breakfast in one sitting, and now you're telling me there'll be more soon? We have everything we need right here. We can figure it out, can't we? There's no reason to invite more of them along."

"We don't have the knowledge we need about this planet. About its flora and fauna, about the landscape we're in," Callie said.

"We don't have all the tools we'll need to survive out there. There's no way we'd even be able to climb out of this crater," Ivy added.

Cole gestured to the supplies stacked before him. "We have tools."

Will ran a hand over his short hair. "Survival knives and chem scanners, mostly. A couple fire starters and flare guns. What we have is a start, but it's not exactly an all-in-one kit for easy jungle living, man. And we don't know what else is out there."

Ivy caught her lower lip between her teeth. She'd never been a leader, had never had any knack for the required skills, and she was surrounded by people who, for the most part, were far more qualified to talk about all this than her, the former cashier.

But she could not lose sight of what was necessary. These people needed to be ready to move as soon as possible, and they needed to do it together, as a unit.

"I know it's a lot, but I'm asking you to trust Ketahn and his friends," Ivy said. "They want to help us. And in this situation, we need all the help we can get."

Will sighed. "I agree. There are only eight of us, and if what Ivy said was true, we'll be flooded out of here before long. Everything we were meant to use to establish the colony on Xolea is gone. All that equipment, all that food, the starter seeds for crops, the meds, the prefab buildings, it's all gone."

"And who better to teach us how to adapt to this world than the natives?" asked Lacey.

"So just like that we're going back to the stone age?" Cole shook his head. "No, there's gotta be a way to make use of all this tech we're sitting on. Come on, Will. There's something you can do, right?"

With a humorless chuckle, Will turned his palms toward the ceiling. "Give me a few weeks and I can probably clear about half the errors out of the computer system. Might even be able to squeeze a few more days' worth of power out of the backup reactors by shutting down systems that are needlessly draining power. But that doesn't really do us any good if we need to get out of here."

"Which we really do." Callie gestured toward the door. "We all saw the flood line in the corridor. And these rations will only go so far. It's either get out of here and rough it in the wilds, or get trapped in here and die."

"It…could be like those survivalist shows," Ella said with a smile. "But we'll have guides who can help us."

Lacey chuckled. "Too bad we won't have the producers just off camera to take us back to civilization if we want to tap out."

"It's hard work and sometimes dangerous, but it's not all bad." Ivy set her basket on the floor and unfolded her legs. "And it'll be easier with all of us working together."

Cole crossed his arms over his chest. "You mean working

with those spider things. Are we all going to have to bend over and get fucked in exchange for their help?"

Ivy glared at him.

"I'm all for it if it'll calm you the fuck down, man," Diego said, shooting a glare of his own at Cole. "I don't even know why it needs to be said, but what she does with her body"—he nodded toward Ivy—"isn't any of your business. It's not anyone's business but hers."

Something within Ivy softened toward Diego even as her respect for him solidified. It…was not often that anyone stood up for her.

Cole's lips peeled back. "It's just disgusting."

Angry fire sparked within Ivy's chest, burning her throat. She swallowed it down. They didn't need this. They didn't need the bickering, the fighting, the animosity.

Pushing herself to her feet, she faced Cole. "As Diego said, what I do is *none* of your business, so I would appreciate it if you stopped making unwanted comments. And no, Ketahn isn't asking anything of you other than for you to do your part. He doesn't have to do this at all. He has no obligation to any of you. But despite the risk to his own life, he's helping you because it's the right thing to do."

Ivy approached Cole and stopped directly in front of him. "You are more than welcome to do this on your own if that's what you want. We're not going to force you to follow us. That is your choice."

Cole stared down at her, his eyes gleaming—but she couldn't tell if that gleam was due to shame or anger. He looked away abruptly. "I'll stay with the group," he muttered. "Humans need to stick together."

"The vrix are not our enemies, Cole."

"Nothing wrong with being on my guard."

Ivy nodded. "I understand that." She reached out and touched his arm, wanting to show him there were no hard feelings, that she could forgive. "I just hope you'll come to see them as people instead of monsters."

There was a faint hiss as the pressurization system released air, and then the door opened with a *swoosh*. Having been focused on the conversation, several of the others gasped or started. Everyone's eyes darted toward the now open door, which Ketahn was already stepping through, his hair and hide dripping with water.

His mandibles were spread, and they widened more when his eyes—which held a sharp, heated glint—fell upon Ivy.

Whose hand was still on Cole's arm.

Oh, for God's sake.

As happy as she was to see him…

Worst timing ever.

She swiftly withdrew her hand and stepped away from Cole. A smile touched her lips, but it dropped when Ketahn stalked toward her, leg hairs bristling and posture stiff. He commanded so much of her attention that she was only vaguely aware of a couple of the others shrinking back as he passed them.

Ivy's brows furrowed. "Ketahn, are you—"

Ketahn turned toward Cole and hissed, curling his fingers to brandish his claws. Cole spat a curse and stumbled backward. His feet bumped into the neatly stacked supplies, knocking rations and medkits onto the floor with a jarring clatter.

"Ketahn, stop!" She placed her hand on one of his forearms, pushing it down. "That's not helping."

With a snarl, Ketahn spun to face her. Before she could even meet his gaze, he had all his arms around her. He lifted her off her feet, and his lower hands guided her legs around his waist as his claspers hooked around her hips, locking her against him.

Another turn, and he carried her out of the room. If anyone said anything, Ivy didn't hear—Ketahn was again her whole world.

His stride was fast, almost violent, and his body was thrumming with tension and restless energy, making the air seem charged—like he was a gathering thunderstorm about to burst. Heat pulsed from his skin, and his spicy scent enveloped her. The red light in the corridor was more fitting than ever in that moment.

Red for blood. Red for fury. Red for passion. Red for unbridled, consuming desire.

Ivy clutched him as he exited the *Somnium*. A light rain was falling, filtered into heavy, erratic droplets through the tangled plant growth overhead. Ketahn snatched up his spear from where he'd leaned it against the ship's hull and stalked forward. His pace only sped now that they were outside, his long legs devouring the distance as he crossed the damp, debris strewn ground.

She frowned. Something was wrong. Something had happened while he was in Takarahl.

She clung tighter still when he reached the crater wall, shoved the shaft of his spear between his back and his backpack, and began climbing. His limbs worked furiously, dragging them higher and higher, faster than she'd ever seen him go even though he was only using two arms. The thick strands of silk he'd anchored on jutting roots and deep in the dirt aided him, but most of his speed seemed born of desperation. Bits of dirt and pebbles slid free and tumbled down to land in the standing water below. And regardless of his speed, regardless of this frenzy that had overcome him, his body was as solid and stable as ever.

Ivy remained silent. They'd talk once they were out of the pit and work through what was bothering him. Seeing her touching Cole had undoubtedly added to his agitation, but there was definitely more to it. A lot more.

The rain, no longer blocked by the tangled growth, fell upon them freely, slickening Ivy's skin and wetting her hair. She smoothed her hands up and down his back as he climbed, doing her best to ease him, to comfort him, but his tension only strengthened. His fingers flexed on her ass, prickling her with his claws. Despite everything, the sensation tingled across her skin and sparked Ivy's desire, pooling heat into her core. He pressed her sex more firmly against his abdomen.

Ketahn climbed up and over the edge, scaling a boulder and coming down on a patch of jungle floor that was blanketed with moss, fern-like plants, and tufts of thin, soft grass. It was there that he stopped, chest heaving, breath ragged.

Ivy lifted her head and drew back to look at him as he tugged his spear free and tossed it aside.

His eyes locked with hers for but a moment before he spun her around and forced her face down onto the mossy ground. She gasped, stunned, and flattened her hands on the ground. The grass tickled her palms.

Ketahn's rough palms trailed up her thighs and lifted her skirt, baring her ass to the rainfall. She shivered at the sensation. The cloying scents of damp earth, vegetation, and rain filled her senses.

Ivy turned her head, her vision obstructed by strands of wet hair. Ketahn leaned over her, bracing his upper arms to either side of her shoulders and curling his claws into the ground. His pelvis pressed against her ass, radiating maddening heat, and she felt his slit part as his claspers snaked around her hips again.

Her breath quickened, and her sex clenched in response. "Ketahn."

He touched his forehead to the back of her head and inhaled deeply. When he exhaled, she felt his warm breath on her neck through her hair.

He growled, *"Kir telenas kess, kir'ani nyleea."*

I need you, my mate.

CHAPTER 14

Ivy QUIVERED at the raw edge in his voice, at the depth and honesty of those simple words, at the knowledge that he *needed* her as much as he needed air, food, and water.

And she needed him just as much.

The instant the word *nyleea* had come out of his mouth, Ketahn was in motion. He grabbed her arm and lashed a silk strand around it, the beginning of something far more elaborate. His hands, fast but ever gentle even in his desperation, manipulated her body deftly as he ran that strand under her chest, cradling her breasts, and around her back. He caught her other arm with it, his twists and knots forming a crude but effective harness around her upper body.

When he pulled back on the rope, Ivy's elbows rose behind her and her chest lifted off the ground. She braced her hands on the moss; he allowed her no more space to move than that.

His hands rasped across her skin, weaving the bindings around her abdomen, thighs, and pelvis as his cock—hot, slick, and throbbing—emerged from his slit to nestle between her ass cheeks. He groaned and looped the silk around her ankles.

Shivering with anticipation, Ivy whispered his name again,

and he rumbled hers, his voice more bestial than ever. He lifted her legs, angling her backside up toward him, and Ivy moaned as a knot rubbed her clit. Ketahn slid his bent forelegs beneath her for support. She felt him trembling with each brush of her skin against his shaft. His hearts quickened, his pulse pounded all around her, and his breath shook.

Holding the silk strand taut, Ketahn grasped her waist with his lower hands and drew his hips back. Despite the humidity, the rainy air was chill against her bared pussy. Being tied like this, trapped and vulnerable, aroused her more than she ever could have imagined. The ache within her core intensified. Ivy strained toward him, arching her ass higher as she caught her bottom lip between her teeth.

Then she felt his tip poised at her entrance.

With a single hard thrust, Ketahn plunged his cock fully inside her.

Ivy cried out. Body stiffening, she squeezed her eyes shut and curled her fingers into the wet, mossy ground. As aroused as she had been, their combined slick had not been enough to ease his sudden entry. The pain was startling, breathtaking, and immense, but it was nothing compared to the stretch and fullness caused by his sheer size. And in this position, she felt *everything*.

Ketahn hissed. His fingers clenched her hips, creating thrilling tingles where his claws pricked her flesh. His claspers curled around her backside and latched on. Slowly, he drew back his pelvis. The slide of his cock rocked her with pleasure, and her sex clamped down on him as though loath to let him go.

Just as it seemed he'd withdraw from her completely, he surged forward again, burying himself even deeper and jolting her whole body with the force. Ivy gasped.

She had no time to recover; he set a frantic pace, pumping with brutal speed, using his hands to keep her close and the ropes to control the angle of his entry, slamming into her harder and harder, faster and faster. Soon, his every breath was punctuated by a snarl.

Ivy moaned as pleasure unfurled within her, flooding her with heat. That heat pooled in her core and dripped down her thighs. The cold rain fell heavier, pouring down upon their connected bodies, but Ivy was barely aware of it. She was burning up inside, seared by Ketahn's scalding shaft.

She tried to spread her thighs wider, tried to reach her hand back and touch him, but she was restrained. All she could do was take what he gave—*all* of it. Every thrust rocked her clit against that silken knot, making her whimper.

"Need you," he rasped. "Need that scent. Your scent." One of his hands slid under her, brushing across her belly and the coils of rope, and then he ran his fingers over her sex and along her inner thighs, gathering her slick.

He increased the pressure of his fingers, kneading her flesh. "I am for you. You. No other, never another."

Something in his voice broke through the fog of her pleasure. Ivy opened her eyes and turned her head. She could see just enough of him to watch as he withdrew that hand and brushed it along his leg, rubbing her essence onto his fine hairs. A shudder wracked him; it pulsed through his body and straight into her, only heightening the sensations, lifting her closer still to her peak.

"Never her." Ketahn's thrusts became more forceful, more demanding. He growled, "There is only you. My Ivy."

Pleasure coalesced within Ivy, growing heavier with each beat of her heart, winding tighter and tighter around her core, threatening to tear her asunder.

Ketahn caught a fistful of her hair, pulling back on it and the silk strand with which she was bound to drive himself impossibly deeper. His cock pounded into her at a new angle, stroking her clit, and Ivy came apart. Her breath hitched. Body seizing, she squeezed her eyes shut as ecstasy burst through her.

But Ketahn was in control, and he continued to slam into her mercilessly. Every thrust triggered a burst of starlight behind her eyelids and sent a fresh wave of pleasure through her, each of which was stronger than the last. Her cries escalated; breathless moans and gasps became primal screams of overwhelming, unrelenting bliss.

Harsh, feral sounds escaped Ketahn. His fingers curled tighter, pressing those wicked claws into her skin and producing small flares of pain, and still he kept those hips moving ever faster, his breaths nothing more than savage grunts and growls as he ravaged her body.

He came with a roar. His claspers clutched her against him, his muscles locked around her, and his cock grew for an instant before his seed blasted hot and forceful inside her. That familiar fluttering sensation came next, vibrating and stimulating her cervix; it sent her to another peak that had her near crying. Her core contracted, and her sex squeezed Ketahn's cock tight, milking him for everything he had and more.

When her pleasure finally began to ebb, Ivy's body slackened in the silk binding. Ketahn released the tension on the strand, and though she remained bound, her limbs were granted the leeway to relax. She laid her head down upon the moss. He released his grip on her hair and smoothed his palm over her head, sweeping the wet, tousled strands out of her face. His cock pulsed, and Ketahn shuddered again as more seed filled her.

He leaned forward, sagging atop her with his arms planted on the ground to both sides of her. Once, she might've thought of it as him caging her in, but she saw it differently now—he was sheltering her. Their chests heaved with ragged breaths as they lay like that in the rain. His heartbeats, though gradually slowing, served as a steady, dependable counter to the more erratic rhythm of the rainfall.

"What happened?" Ivy asked softly, breaking their silence.

Ketahn tensed, the claws of one hand sinking into the moss. "The queen tried to make me hers."

Nausea roiled in Ivy's belly, sobering her and souring the pleasure still thrumming through her.

Need you. Need that scent. Your scent.

I am for you. You. No other, never another.

Never her. There is only you. My Ivy.

Oh God. What had the queen done? Ivy had forgotten that however big Ketahn was, vrix females were even larger and stronger. She knew what it felt like to be so vulnerable, knew what it felt like to be powerless, and she hated that Ketahn, so strong and virile, had had to experience it.

She swallowed thickly as tears stung her eyes. "Did she…?"

"She failed." His voice was low, raw. "But she left her scent on me, and it would not wash away."

Ivy closed her eyes and turned her face more toward the ground, relieved that it hadn't been worse, but the tears fell anyway, mingling with the rainwater on her cheeks. Her chest constricted with the words she spoke next. "Is…is this wrong? What we're doing? Y-you and me?"

He flinched, and more of his weight pressed down on her for a fleeting moment before he recovered himself and growled, "No, Ivy. Not wrong. Never wrong. You are the only thing right."

A sob wracked her, and she clutched at the moss beneath her palms. "If you hadn't found me, none of this would be happening."

"Ivy…"

"I don't want you to get hurt, Ketahn. *I'm* the reason you're suffering now." She pressed her forehead to the ground. "This is all because of me."

Ketahn shoved himself up with a grunt, sliding his forelegs out from beneath Ivy and lifting his body off her. He withdrew his cock abruptly, the shaft still pulsing dully even as it slid out of her, leaving her bereft as his seed spilled from her sex and ran down her inner thighs.

The silk rope binding her pulled taut as he grabbed it again, but that only lasted for an instant before his claws sliced through it in several places. There was a hint of that frantic energy in his movements again as he tore the strands away and freed her limbs. Then his hands were on her, picking her up off the ground and gathering her in his arms, clutching her to his chest.

Ivy wrapped an arm around his neck and buried her face against him. "I'm sorry. For all this."

"She is not cruel because of you," Ketahn rumbled as he petted her hair. "She only knows how to spread suffering." Releasing Ivy with one hand, he caught her chin and turned her face up, forcing her to meet his eyes. His hair hung around his shoulders, dripping with water. "That is not your fault, my *nyleea*. You did not lead me to the queen's cruelty. Her cruelty led me to you."

Ivy blinked tears and raindrops from her eyes as her lower lip quivered. "If it weren't for me, you wouldn't be stuck here. You wouldn't have had to go back there to…to her."

"And she and her Claws would be hunting me all the same. She was not going to let me go easily, Ivy." He hunched down to tip his headcrest against her forehead. "Even had I known what would come, I would change nothing. I would choose to wake you. I would choose to take you as mine.

"That you are small, soft, and human does not matter. That I am big, hard, and vrix does not matter." Ketahn brushed his rough knuckles across her cheek. "Our heartsthreads, our spirits, are all that matter, and they are bound. Fate brought me to you, my heartsthread, and even if it tried to turn me away, I would defy it. *Nothing* will come between us. So long as the sun, moons, and stars make their treks across the sky, you will be mine, Ivy."

CHAPTER 15

Ivy CLUTCHED Ketahn as she rode on his hindquarters, her chest pressed to his back, legs locked around his body, and fingers curled against his chest. She tried to ignore the way her stomach flipped at his every jump, swing, and dip as he climbed through the trees with his spear in one hand. Though the rain had persisted, the boughs and leaves overhead offered some shelter. Only irregular drops filtered down to hit Ketahn and Ivy save for when he crossed beneath the sparse open patches—not that it mattered, as they had been soaked well before they began this journey. Her silk dress stuck to her like a second skin.

Though she wasn't a fan of storms, Ivy found the jungle rain soothing. Everything else went quiet when it rained, leaving only the constant, gentle sounds of water falling on leaves and trickling along the networks of vines and branches.

The skies had darkened since she and Ketahn had left the *Somnium*, and not just because of the rain clouds. Night was approaching. That was a little disorienting. The morning sun had been bright when Ivy had entered the ship today, and it hadn't felt like she'd spent the entire day inside—perhaps because the company had helped the time pass so smoothly.

But with the rain and approaching nightfall came the cold. It kissed her bare skin and clung to her wet clothing and hair, making her skin prickle with goosebumps. She shivered. All she wanted in that moment was to be home, dry and warm, tucked against Ketahn upon their bed of silk fluff.

I wouldn't say no to a steaming hot bath either...

She was mentally and physically exhausted. Her eyes were swollen and tired after crying, and as much as she'd enjoyed mating with Ketahn, it had left her weak and sore—albeit a good sore. Her sex still pulsed in reminder of what they'd shared. Rough or gentle, Ivy loved and craved everything Ketahn gave her. It didn't matter that he was a vrix. Her body recognized his touch as the only one it wanted.

Ivy smoothed her hands up Ketahn's chest and hugged him tighter. "Are we almost home?"

Ketahn dropped onto a thick branch and covered her hand with one of his. "Yes, my *nyleea*."

However familiar she'd been growing with the surrounding jungle, everything changed in the darkness. The thickening shadows made any landmarks she might have used to guide her look twisted and alien.

Well, more alien, anyway.

He continued along the massive boughs with a subtle but noticeable hesitance. Ivy could guess where it was coming from —partly caution, as the rain had made every surface slippery; partly the lingering stiffness of his agitation; partly some soreness of his own.

Gentle was clearly not part of the queen's vocabulary. It filled Ivy with anger to see her big, powerful mate battered and aching, and that anger only fed into her sorrow thanks to its impotence. All she could do to protect him from more abuse was get the other survivors ready to move as soon as possible… and that wasn't nearly enough.

For now, she just held on to him, determined to never let go.

Ketahn climbed onto another branch, took a step forward, and halted. Ivy glanced up. The web was overhead, coated in countless droplets of water that she could make out only because they reflected pinpoints of faint gray light, the last shreds of daylight that were barely visible in the sky.

"Shaper, unmake me," Ketahn rasped, posture becoming more rigid.

Ivy lowered her eyes to find him looking ahead along the branch.

Bracing her hands on his shoulders, Ivy rose slightly to peek past him.

A huge figure stood no more than fifty feet in front of them, directly beneath the dangling nest. That distance did nothing to cushion the shock of seeing a female vrix head on—she was huge. The pieces of gold the female was wearing had a dull luster in the dying light, giving her a ghostly cast.

Nails involuntarily digging into Ketahn's flesh, Ivy shrank back, making herself as small as possible behind him.

"Have I come early, or you late?" the female asked.

Ivy recognized her voice. She was Ahnset, Ketahn's sister. A little of Ivy's tension eased, and she loosened her grip on Ketahn.

"Both, perhaps," Ketahn replied. There was an unsettled edge in his tone, sharp but razor thin. "So long as we are all here, it matters not."

"You didn't tell me you asked your sister to come here," Ivy whispered.

Ketahn looked at Ivy over his shoulder. His violet eyes gleamed softly. "I am sorry, Ivy. My mind was…occupied with many things."

She snorted, a smirk playing upon her lips. "So you let your cock take over thinking for a little while?"

He chittered gently but sorrowfully. "I meant to tell you."

Ivy's smile faded, and she reached up to stroke his jaw. "It's okay. I understand."

The branch rumbled with movement. Another peek around Ketahn revealed that Ahnset was coming closer, head tilted to the side and eyes fixed on Ketahn. Her weight sent tremors through the wood.

"Who are you speaking to, Ketahn?" Ahnset asked. "And what… Is there something on your back?"

"Someone," he replied, facing his sister. "Someone I would like you to meet."

The silk rope securing Ivy to Ketahn went taut for a moment before it loosened and dropped away.

Catching her bottom lip with her teeth, Ivy took a deep breath, trying to push away her nervousness. She'd already met three of Ketahn's friends, vrix who he trusted. This was his sister. Ivy had seen Ahnset twice from the den, had witnessed their interactions, had heard them speak to one another with affection.

Swinging a leg over Ketahn, Ivy slid off his hindquarters, landing lightly on the branch. She cringed when she felt Ketahn's warm seed trickle down her inner thigh.

Perfect. Meeting my sister-in-law with cum running down my leg.

Ivy turned toward Ahnset and was once more struck by the sheer size of her. The female vrix had to be at least ten feet tall, and the spear she clutched in one of her massive hands looked nearly as long.

Ketahn passed his spear to his left hand and extended his right arms, holding them in front of Ivy—perhaps to shield her, perhaps to offer support. Likely both.

As for Ahnset, she'd leaned back slightly, eyes flared as though in shock. Her mandibles drew together, twitched, and spread again before falling limp. "What manner of creature is this, Ketahn?"

"She is a human." He lowered his arms with unmasked reluctance. "Her name is Ivy."

"You have named it?" Ahnset shifted closer, leaving only a few feet between them—far too close for a being that could close her hand around Ivy's whole head. "Is it some sort of pet?"

"I am not a pet," Ivy said carefully in vrix with a small smile. She'd grown used to tilting her head back to meet Ketahn's gaze over the last couple months, but looking up at Ahnset was a new extreme.

Despite her size and obvious strength, Ahnset reared back with a glint of fear in her eyes. She brought her spear forward almost faster than Ivy could register, taking it in a defensive, two-handed grip. Ketahn moved even faster, sweeping Ivy behind him with his right arms and placing his body between her and his sister. He held the shaft of his spear up, but kept the head pointed down.

"Back away, Ahnset," he growled.

Ivy's heart pounded against her ribs as she clung to Ketahn's arm in a death grip. He was the only thing keeping her upright.

Okay, so cum is the least of my worries.

"Only two things speak, Ketahn," Ahnset said, her voice low and deep. "Vrix and spirits. This creature is not vrix."

"Nor is she a spirit," he replied. "Humans also speak, and Ivy is a human."

"Ketahn, this—"

"Lower your spear. I will allow no threat to Ivy, not even from you."

Ahnset stared at him. She remained still but for the twitching of her mandibles. Finally, she eased her grip and lowered her spear. "You have never raised a weapon to me in threat before, broodbrother."

Ketahn didn't lower his spear, which was still angled downward, and his stance did not relax. "And I have not done so now, broodsister. There is no threat from me. But I will defend her with my life from anyone who means her harm."

Ivy gently pushed his arm down. "It is okay, Ketahn. This is new to her—*I* am new to her." Ivy looked back at Ahnset. "I do not think she will hurt me."

He glanced at Ivy over his shoulder, released a long, heavy breath, and finally lowered his spear, letting the head fall to rest on the branch.

"How does it speak our tongue?" Ahnset asked.

"She," Ketahn corrected. "She is learning from me. By showing, by speaking, by working together. By living together."

Mandibles falling, Ahnset eased closer, sinking down and dipping her head so she could look at Ivy directly. "Why have we never seen such creatures before? Where did you find her?"

There was just enough light for Ivy to see that Ahnset's eyes were the same purple as Ketahn's, and that they held a glimmer of the same curiosity he'd often exhibited. Ivy's heart was still pounding, but it slowed just a bit. "Because we are from another world. A place in the stars."

"The stars?" Ahnset tilted her head back and looked up, mandibles twitching, before returning her gaze to Ivy. "How is that possible?"

"They came from the sky in a ship," Ketahn said, that last word in English. "It fell in the pit, the one legend says holds a fiery beast defeated by the Eight."

"It did not fall into the pit," Ivy said gently, speaking slowly to make the vrix words clear enough for Ahnset to understand. "It crashed and *made* the pit."

"A...*shit*," Ahnset said with equal care, unsurprisingly failing to pronounce the *p* sound.

"A shit is a very different thing, broodsister," Ketahn said with a chitter.

Ivy elbowed him and said in English, "I can recall a certain spider man having a problem with *p*—in more ways than one."

"And one of those was made by a little human," he replied in his heavily accented English with humor in his voice.

Ivy rolled her eyes. "It wasn't my fault."

"What did she do with her eyes?" Ahnset asked. "And what did you both say?"

Ketahn looked back at Ivy again. Their gentle teasing had apparently relaxed him, as he finally shifted so his body wasn't planted between Ivy and Ahnset like a shield wall. He switched back into his native tongue smoothly. "She only moved them. Human eyes are...different, but the sight of them becomes less unsettling over time. As for what she said..."

"I told him he had trouble saying human words too," Ivy said.

"So this...sh...shi..." Ahnset tilted her head.

"Ship," Ivy offered.

"That. It fell from the sky"—Ahnset looked up again, as though she'd see a flaming spacecraft plummeting from the heavens even now—"and made the pit. That...I do not understand. Is the...the *shit* the beast, or was it there when the beast was defeated?" She raised a hand and tugged on one of her braids; it was reminiscent of the gesture Ketahn made when he was deep in thought or particularly troubled. "But the Eight made the pit, and the plants that trap the beast..."

"I think the ship was the beast. Your...your... The vrix who lived before you must have seen it fall and did not understand what it really was. But it is not a living thing."

"That was long ago. Why do you appear now?"

"I was sleeping." Ivy tucked a strand of hair behind her ear, brows furrowing. She had a much easier time communicating with Ketahn because she could use English to fill in for vrix words she didn't know or couldn't properly pronounce. "I was in something like a...a...cocoon." She cupped her hands together, one on atop the other, and lifted the top like the lid of a cryochamber. "Ketahn found me inside and woke me."

Ahnset lowered her eyes to Ivy, and a thoughtful trill sounded in her chest. "I…do not know what to say. What to think. This is…"

"Madness," Ketahn said softly. "It seems like madness."

"Yes." Ahnset thumped a leg on the branch, sending a deep vibration through the wood under Ivy's feet. "And it goes against so much of what we know, Ketahn. If the Eight truly did not create that pit to trap a terrible beast, what else is wrong? What else is…untrue?"

"I have spent much time thinking on such questions, brood-sister. All I can say is this—there is no beast in that pit, and I have seen no sign that there ever was, apart from the creatures that have fallen in and died."

Ahnset stared at Ivy. "She is…so different. Small. Soft. *Hyunin* males must be small enough to hold in hand." To demonstrate, she raised one of her hands, palm up.

Ivy half suspected she could sit on that hand and Ahnset wouldn't have any trouble supporting her weight.

"Our males are usually bigger than our females," Ivy said.

Ahnset moved closer and extended her hand toward Ivy. The claws upon it were just as sharp as Ketahn's, but far larger. Lethal. One of Ketahn's hands darted out, catching Ahnset's arm by the wrist and halting it.

The huge female looked at her brother questioningly, her mandibles twitching and rising. "I will not hurt her, brother."

"I trust that you will not." He hesitated, holding his sister's stare before releasing her.

With great care, Ahnset touched the pads of her fingers to Ivy's bare arm. She shuddered but pressed harder. "She is so soft. It is like touching fresh meat."

Ivy wrinkled her nose at that comparison.

"We are all made of meat, Ahnset," Ketahn rumbled, his eyes intent upon his sister's hand.

"She has no hide, no armor, no fur." Ashnet picked up one of

Ivy's hands and inspected her fingers. "No claws. How does she survive?"

One of Ketahn's legs slid behind Ivy and brushed along the backs of her calves, sending a thrill through her. "Her kind is far stronger than they appear, and they are intelligent. They have built things beyond vrix imagining."

"She just looks so...*weak*. And her scent..." Ahnset tipped her face closer and inhaled deeply. Suddenly, her entire body went rigid, and her hold on Ivy's hand tightened to the point of pain.

Ivy flinched, hissing through her teeth as she tried to pull her hand back.

Again, Ketahn grabbed his sister's wrist, this time moving his body in front of her. "Release your hold, Ahnset," he growled. "You are hurting her."

Ahnset let go, and Ivy brought her hand to her chest, rubbing it soothingly. The larger vrix hadn't done any real damage, but Ivy knew it wouldn't have taken much more for Ahnset to have crushed her hand entirely.

"Why does she smell like you, Ketahn?" Ahnset asked, looking at her brother. "Why does she smell like...like *seed*?"

Ketahn stood up straight, squared his shoulders, and gave Ivy a little bump with his rear leg to guide her closer so he could band his arms around her waist and shoulders. His chin notched up. "She is my mate."

Ahnset recoiled, scrambling backward a few steps and shaking the branch in the process. One of her thick legs slipped off the edge of the branch, and she nearly lost her balance; Ivy could only assume it was Ahnset's unimaginable physical strength alone that prevented her from falling.

"You...you mated...*that*?" Ahnset's voice was raw and thin, seeming for a moment as though it couldn't possibly have come from that powerful body.

"Were my words unclear?" Ketahn's voice, in contrast, was strong and unyielding, solid as deep-rooted stone.

"She is a beast, Ketahn! She is not vrix. It is…it is vile!"

Ivy clenched her fists, briefly closing her eyes against the pang of hurt those words invoked in her heart.

Ketahn's hold on Ivy tightened, and something dangerous rumbled in his chest. "Ivy is no more beast than you or me, broodsister. Her kind is like ours. They seek only to survive and find their place in the Tangle."

"There are more of them?" Ahnset dipped her chin toward Ivy. "More of these pale, weak things who you claim have *vrakas* like the Eight?"

"There are more, yes, but they do not have *vrakas*. They had…tools. Now they have nothing, and I am helping them."

"Helping these creatures is one thing, but you *mated* with one, brother. Your scent clings to her."

Ivy pressed her thighs together, which were slick and sticky with Ketahn's seed. It was a reminder of what they'd done right before this meeting. Once again, she pushed away the shame that lingered on the edges of her consciousness.

Ketahn's fingers flexed upon Ivy. "As Korahla's scent clings to you, sister."

"It is not the same."

"Because she is vrix, but Ivy is not?" He turned his head to look down at Ivy, catching her eyes with his own. "My mate has a spirit, the strongest I have known. She learns and speaks, she overcomes problems, she is free with her humor, and she sees wonder in this jungle to which I had almost blinded myself. More than all that, her heart swells with compassion."

In that moment, Ivy's heart did swell; his words stole her breath and brought tears to her eyes. Love. It had to be love. Otherwise, how could it be this powerful? This painful? This…wonderful?

Ketahn's eyes softened. He brushed a strand of hair from Ivy's face and caressed her cheek with his rough fingers before looking at his sister again. "That reminds me of another female I know. And as much as I long to see it as a weakness, it is a strength I cannot deny…and which I cannot help but be drawn to. Her body is different, but she is woven into my heartsthread all the same. She is my mate, Ahnset. Forever."

Ahnset was silent as she looked between the two of them. She opened her mouth, snapped it closed, and huffed. With a long, tired sigh, she ran a hand over her headcrest and down her braided hair, wiping water away from the beads and gold twined into the strands. "You are always so difficult, broodbrother. You insist on spinning whole webs when a single strand would do."

"All I have left are strands," he replied. "I am struggling to make a web of them."

The female vrix met Ivy's gaze. "The queen should know of these…*hyu-nins*."

"No," Ketahn snarled.

"We cannot keep them a secret, Ketahn. We do not know these creatures, or what threat they might pose to Takarahl."

Ketahn released his hold on Ivy and strode forward until he was immediately in front of his sister, straightening his legs to raise himself to her level. Though he was physically smaller, he cut an intimidating figure, even in comparison—simply by the strength of his presence.

"She must *never* know," he said in a low, dark voice. "Especially about Ivy."

"It is not only the queen we must think about. What of all the others who dwell in Takarahl? Zurvashi is but one in an entire city, Ketahn." There was an almost pleading note in Ahnset's words.

"We are not a threat, Ahnset," Ivy said gently. "We do not have the weapons, skill, or…or the want to do harm to the vrix. There are only eight of us left in this world."

"Eight?" Ashnet asked softly.

"Whether by chance or fate, yes. There are eight humans,"

Ketahn said. "And I mean for there to remain eight humans so long as I draw breath."

"Eight, Ketahn," Ahnset muttered, her eyes still on Ivy. "Is it a sign?"

"It does not matter if it is a sign, broodsister. Ivy is my heartsthread, and I am trusting you with this secret." He extended a foreleg and brushed it against his sister's. "Do not betray me."

Ahnset flinched, but she did not retreat from his touch. She exhaled and shifted closer, spreading her mandibles wide as she pressed her headcrest to Ketahn's. "I am bound to serve our queen. But I could not betray you, broodbrother. You and your mate will have my help if you need it."

"It will be welcome, Ahnset, but I cannot ask you to betray the queen to aid me. I only wanted you to know why I must leave. And I wanted you to meet my mate."

"Thank you. But I would do what I can, so that I may rest well knowing my only sibling is alive and well somewhere out here." Ahnset drew back and lifted her head to look at Ivy. "Welcome, sister."

Ivy smiled and placed a hand on Ketahn's hindquarters, gently guiding him aside. He obeyed with that hint of reluctance she'd come to expect, clearing the space between Ivy and Ahnset. The huge female held Ivy's gaze, and Ivy tilted her head back as she stepped forward.

"Can you…come down?" Ivy asked.

Ahnset cocked her head and sent a questioning glance at Ketahn before lowering herself, spreading her legs and bending them slowly so as not to lose her footing. Even with her underside flat on the branch, she was much taller than Ivy, but she bent forward to draw nearer to Ivy's eye level.

Trying to ignore the fact that Ahnset's mandibles looked as big as her own forearms, Ivy tentatively reached forward and placed her hands on either side of Ahnset's face. Ahnset stiffened, but she did not pull back, and when Ivy angled Ahnset's head down, the vrix did not resist.

Ivy tipped her forehead against Ahnset's headcrest. "Thank you, sister."

Ahnset's mandibles twitched as though with uncertainty, and then fell. A soft trill sounded in her chest. She closed her eyes and released a long, shallow breath. "It...has been too long since I have had a sister. I am glad to call you one now, *Ay-vee*."

CHAPTER 16

DIEGO CLOSED his eyes and moaned as he chewed. "This is *so* good."

Lacey made a similar sound and swallowed her mouthful. "Understatement of the year. Feel like it's been forever since I ate real meat."

"Well"—Callie sucked the meat juices from her fingertips—"I don't know about forever, but it has been at least one hundred and sixty-eight years."

A few of the humans laughed. Ketahn thought there was a hint of sadness in that laughter, but he couldn't have expected otherwise knowing their situation.

"It's almost good enough to make me forget how bad it stinks out here," said Will as he finished off what must've been his third or fourth helping of meat.

"Sorry," Cole said, "That's on me. Been a while since I had a shower."

This time, the human laughter was a bit less troubled.

Ketahn looked down at Ivy, who was sitting beside him, to find her smiling. Her blue eyes glittered in the firelight, bright as ever, and were filled with contentment. Though he remained uncertain of these other humans, he couldn't deny that their presence bolstered her already strong spirit.

Reaching forward, Ketahn tore a piece off the chunk of meat that was roasting over the flames and let it dangle, pinched between the claws of his forefinger and thumb, to cool. As he waited, he studied the other humans.

Though the morning sun was bathing the Tangle above with its golden rays, night clung to this pit, unwilling to relinquish its grasp. Little of the light from overhead reached this deep, leaving only the fire to provide illumination—the fire and the slowly pulsing glow cast by the ship.

In the warm, flickering firelight, the humans looked more... real. More alive. The pure white lights inside the stasis chamber, though amazing in their intensity and constancy, always felt wrong. Unnatural. Mildly unsettling in the same manner as pockets of persistent, impenetrable darkness. Yet soon enough, the ship and its strangeness would be left behind.

But these small, soft beings would remain with Ketahn, and he had no doubt they'd eventually look as much like they belonged in the Tangle as any vrix.

His eyes stopped on the female called Ella. She'd set her portion of meat on a broad leaf, which she'd placed on the stone before her. She hadn't eaten more than a few bites of it. The others, in contrast—particularly Cole and Will—had devoured theirs. Ella's pale skin looked sickly, and the sheen of sweat upon it was heavier than that worn by any of the others. Her hair was damp and limp, making her look like she'd just emerged from a pool of water.

Ketahn's knowledge of humans remained limited, but Ella reminded him of the way Ivy had looked when she'd fallen terribly ill...and Ella seemed to be worsening day by day.

Traveling through the Tangle with eight humans would be difficult and dangerous enough already, but with one of them sick...

Ivy placed a hand on the upper segment of Ketahn's foreleg and brushed her fingertips over his hide, rousing him from his thoughts. When he looked at her again, she smiled. He offered his version of the expression before holding up the piece of meat to her mouth.

"Eat more, my heartsthread," he said. "You need strength for what is to come."

Ivy parted her lips, and her tongue flicked out to draw the meat into her mouth, her lips brushing his finger in the process.

Desire sparked within him, and he stared at her mouth as she chewed. His hearts quickened and searing heat suffused him when her little pink tongue reemerged to lick her lips clean. He'd felt those lips upon his mouth many times since she'd first kissed him, had relished their softness, and he craved ever more of them and their clever, caressing movements.

He'd always enjoyed those quiet moments alone with his mate, exploring one another's bodies and spirits, but he feared they would be woefully few in the times to come. The plan to lead the humans to a new home, far away from Takarahl, was in motion now, and Ketahn would not deviate from it. That meant he and Ivy had already said goodbye to their den; they'd be staying with the humans from now on. They didn't have time to waste traveling to and from the pit every day.

"What exactly is to come?" Will asked, rubbing his chin with the back of his hand.

"A long walk in the jungle," Ketahn replied, "and many lessons on the way."

"What kind of lessons? Like *boi skowt* shit?" Cole asked.

Ketahn glanced at Ivy and tilted his head in question.

Ivy shrugged. "If *boi skowts* go camping in jungles full of things that want to eat them, then yeah. *Boi skowt* stuff."

"That's...not encouraging," said Ella.

"I know." Ivy sighed, held her hands out in front of her,

palms up, and furrowed her brow as she looked down at them. "I'd like to say it'll be easy, but I can't."

"As shitty as it is, I think I prefer the truth," Lacey said, tossing a bone into the fire.

"Me too," said Ahmya, who was staring at the half-eaten piece of meat in her hands.

"I don't know," Will said. "If there's stuff that looks *freekee-ur* than the animal Ketahn brought for breakfast, do we really want to know what else is out there?"

Ketahn huffed and lifted a hand, grasping the bundled hair at the back of his head and tugging it absently. "The jungle is death. That is truth. But it is life, also. Much beauty, much danger. We vrix will show you to live. We will show you to make your home in the jungle. But you must hear us, and you must obey."

"So, do your, uh, friends speak English, too?" asked Diego.

"No."

Cole released a humorless laugh. "Kinda hard to hear and obey then, don't you think?"

"You will just have to try more hard to understand," Ketahn said, mimicking Ivy's shrug.

Diego narrowed his eyes and leaned forward, resting his arms on his knees as he glanced at Ivy. "Is he joking? That almost seemed like he was being funny."

Ivy chuckled. "He's kind of a smart ass."

Ketahn snapped his gaze to Ivy and clicked his mandible fangs together. "I told you do not call me what poop comes from, female."

Callie choked and coughed, spitting out a small chunk of food she must have inhaled. "*What?*"

Ivy grinned. "Lost in translation kind of thing."

Before Ketahn could comment further, a sound caught his attention—Telok's signature blackrock clacking from somewhere above the pit. The humans fell quiet, their eyes suddenly wide and searching. That was a good sign; they were alert despite their generally relaxed demeanors. He hoped that would continue even after they were more familiar with the Tangle.

The easiest mistake one could make out here was becoming too complacent.

Ketahn twisted aside to pick up his spear and draw the knife he'd strapped to his leg. He tapped the blackrock blades together in an answering beat. Telok made a response, which slowly broke apart into nothingness as it echoed between the trees and down into the pit.

"The others have come," Ketahn said. He plucked the spitted meat away from the fire, passed the stick to Ivy, and rose, turning his attention to the side of the pit where he'd anchored silk ropes to aid in climbing.

Soon enough, the sounds of a group moving through the undergrowth above drifted to the bottom of the pit. Those sounds were surprisingly hushed, given how long it had been since Urkot and Rekosh had ventured this deep into the Tangle, and that further reinforced Ketahn's hope. They were on the edge of a new life, a new future. Just a little more…

"Stay here," Ketahn said to the humans. He strode toward the wall, his legs dipping into the standing water far sooner than they would have an eightday ago; the recent rains had been steadily filling the pit, and the waters had already risen to cover almost half the ground that had been exposed when Ketahn first fell into this place.

As he neared the wall—where he had to straighten his legs slightly to keep the water from touching his underside—he tipped his head back. He'd cleared a wide portion of the plant growth overhead to allow for easy passage, and it was the only spot in the pit with a clear view to the world above.

A vrix's head popped out over the edge of the pit, his bright red markings standing out amidst all the green, purple, and gray. Rekosh looked across the pit, his eyes slowly sweeping it, until finally he looked down at Ketahn.

Rekosh chittered. "Still hiding in that hole, Ketahn?"

"I have been keeping it warm for you, my friend," Ketahn replied, slipping back into his native tongue.

"Are you climbing up," Urkot called from out of sight, "or are you going to make us climb down?"

Rekosh's mandibles twitched as he glanced over his shoulder. "As though you do not spend your days delving into dark holes, Urkot."

"I was led to believe this would be a change for me, Rekosh. And yet here I am, about to do the same thing as always."

"No matter how many years pass, the two of you never change," said Ahnset with a chitter.

Ketahn's fine hairs bristled, and his mandibles flared wide in surprise. He'd told his friends to come two days before, but he had not expected his broodsister.

Shaking off the surprise of Ahnset's presence, Ketahn said, "Come down."

Telok leaned over the edge to peer down. His mandibles twitched fiercely as he scanned the pit, and his voice was a touch unsteady when he spoke. "What of the supplies, Ketahn?"

Ketahn glanced back at the humans. They were huddled atop a relatively flat patch of stone that Ketahn had swept clean of muck and debris as best he could, reflected firelight gleaming in their rounded eyes. They looked like fragile, skittish creatures huddled in the dark, waiting for some ravenous beast to determine whether it would eat them or not.

But he recalled what Ivy had said, what he knew to be true—humans were not nearly as weak as he'd thought. They were not nearly as incapable as they appeared. All they needed was guidance and aid.

Ketahn returned his attention to his friends. "Bring everything down. We will have to haul it up again soon enough, but it is best we leave nothing to the mercy of the Tangle for now."

Using long ropes, the vrix lowered the supplies they'd carried through the jungle a little at a time. Ketahn called the humans over to help carry those supplies back to the ship. Only Ella remained behind—though she did attempt to rise and lend her assistance.

Diego was the first to tell her not to, but she seemed ready to persist until Ketahn strode over and sank down in front of her.

Tears filled Ella's eyes. "I'm sorry. I'm not usually this weak, I swear. I…I want to help." She gave a little laugh as she wiped an escaped tear off her cheek. "My dad would be chewing me out about how lazy I'm being right now."

"It is okay, Ella," Ketahn said slowly, wanting to make sure he got the words right. "When one is not well, the others will help. We are all"—he locked the fingers of his upper hands— "together. As one. Another day, you will help when one of us is not well."

Her gaze flicked over Ketahn as she drew her lips into her mouth. Finally, she nodded. "Thank you, Ketahn."

"Sit, Ella. Rest."

"Okay."

Diego helped her settle back down upon the rock. "The stasis affects everyone differently. Just give it some more time, Ella."

Ketahn relaxed his mandibles and turned away. Perhaps he did not know these humans, perhaps he did not fully trust them, but his time with Ivy made it impossible not to see them the same way he would any vrix. And he feared for Ella—because her illness would make the journey to come harder on her than on anyone else.

He sought out Ivy, who stood knee deep in the water with the other humans. Her gaze met his, and he saw familiar worry in her eyes as she glanced at Ella.

Though he had no intention of leaving any of these humans behind, Ketahn could not deny reality. There was a chance their group would be smaller before they reached wherever they choose to settle down and make their new lives.

As they received the last of the supplies—the humans with their eyes watering and noses scrunched because, in Cole's words, it smelled *'like hot shit and death'*—Rekosh began his descent, demonstrating that effortless agility with which he always carried himself.

His legs touched down in the murky water, and he stepped away from the wall. "I would be lying if I were to say I have smelled worse than this."

Ketahn chittered. "I think the humans feel the same."

Rekosh lifted a leg out of the water, glanced down at the muck clinging to his hide, and shuddered. He flicked the muck away; it landed with a splash near Will and Lacey.

Will recoiled. "Come on! This stuff is gross!"

"Covered in it already," Lacey said with a frown. "What difference does a little more make?"

Ivy chuckled as she pinched at the material of the human clothing—she called it a *jumpsuit*—she'd dressed in and tugged it away from her body. "Least it's waterproof."

Ketahn wasn't sure how he felt seeing her in the jumpsuit and the foot coverings she said were *boots*. Yes, the human garments offered her delicate skin more protection than the dress, but he preferred seeing her in his silk—and he liked having an unhindered view of her little feet and shapely legs.

"Doesn't stop it from stinking to high *heh-ven*," Cole muttered.

Rekosh tilted his head as he regarded the humans. "What are they saying?"

"They are very glad for the stink," Ketahn replied, smiling.

"Do not lie, Ketahn," Ivy said in vrix with a smirk, crossing her arms over her chest.

Chittering, Rekosh thumped a mucky leg against one of Ketahn's. "Always interesting with you."

"What is that sound they make?" Ahmya asked as she stepped up beside Ivy.

Ivy was a tiny female, but Ahmya was even smaller. The dark-haired human looked like a broodling compared to the others, Ivy included, and even now Ketahn had trouble remembering that she was full-grown.

Rekosh's red eyes fell upon Ahmya. Realizing she was being stared at, the small female looked up at him, her own dark eyes going wide. A soft, strange trill rolled in Rekosh's chest. He glided forward slowly, barely disturbing the water's surface.

"They all look…so different," Rekosh said distractedly. "But this one… Another female?"

"Yes," Ketahn replied.

Ahmya shied back from the approaching vrix, but she did not retreat fully; she grasped Ivy's arm and almost seemed to hide behind her.

Pressing his forearms together, Rekosh bowed, his long braid falling over his shoulder. "Forgive me for being unable to understand your words. I am called Rekosh."

Ahmya swallowed audibly and looked up at Ivy, whispering something Ketahn didn't hear.

Ivy smiled and replied in English. "He's introducing himself. He's sorry he can't speak our language. His name is Rekosh."

"Rekosh," Ahmya repeated breathlessly.

Another trill from Rekosh, who lifted his head but did not rise from his bow. "Will she tell me her name?" he asked Ivy without looking away from Ahmya.

Ivy translated.

Tentatively, the dark-haired female extended her right hand. She halted it after a moment, fingers curling, and seemed about to pull back when Rekosh put out a hand of his own. She stiffened as he bent a single finger and hooked it beneath hers, lifting her tiny hand slightly. The pad of his thumb brushed her knuckles.

"Ahmya," she said quietly.

"*Ahnya*," Rekosh purred. "So delicate and soft."

Brow creased, Ahmya shifted her gaze between Rekosh and Ivy.

"What's that one doing?" Cole asked, stopping behind Ivy. "More spiders looking to steal and fuck our women?"

Ketahn strode toward them, leg hairs bristling with a flare of instinctual rage. The way Cole had said that—*our women*—could not be ignored, and it was difficult not to take it as a challenge.

Ivy belonged to no one but Ketahn.

Ahmya gasped, yanked her hand away from Rekosh, and cradled it against her chest, her cheeks turning bright red. "H-He was just telling me his name."

"Dude, you really need to learn when to keep your mouth shut," Diego said to Cole, though his eyes were fixed on Ketahn.

"Can't really blame them if they don't know what a hand-shake is, Cole," Will said carefully.

Ahmya glanced at Ivy again, her cheeks somehow darkening further. "Um…he is a he, right?"

"Yes," Ketahn rumbled, moving past Ivy to place himself between her and Cole. "Rekosh is male. As are Telok and Urkot."

Cole raised his hands and took a step back. "All I'm saying is that the red one was looking a little too cozy with Ahmya." He looked to the other humans as though searching for support. "How are we supposed to colonize if all our females are taken by spiders?"

"That's enough, Cole," Ivy said.

He dropped his hands. "Just saying. Do the *math*. Five women and three men. And I doubt Ivy will be popping out any babies."

"I said that's enough," Ivy said, voice tight.

"What? Just voicing what we're all thinking. Eight people,

Ivy. That's all that's left of us. How long before every single one of us is gone? We might have a chance at creating something here, but not if you spread your legs for one of—"

Ketahn snapped his mandible fangs together and leaned closer to Cole, a growl rattling in his chest. *"Be silent, human!"*

Cole stumbled back but caught his balance quickly. Combing his hands through his hair to smooth it out of his face, he pressed his lips together and glared up at Ketahn.

"Jeezus, you really need to learn when to shut up," Callie said.

Rekosh, still standing in front of Ahmya, trilled thoughtfully. "Has that one been causing trouble?"

Ketahn's leg hairs bristled, and it took considerable effort to keep from gnashing his mandibles again. He clenched his fists tightly enough that they trembled as he replied to Rekosh in the vrix tongue. "Some. He carries much anger and fear, and often lets them be his master."

"Here," Will said, thrusting a bulging yatin hide bag against Cole's chest. "Take this inside. Cool off."

Cole wrapped his hands around the bag and stared at Ketahn for a heated moment before turning and stalking toward the ship.

The lingering tension was broken unexpectedly by a large splash near the wall. Ketahn and the others turned toward the disturbance to see Urkot standing in the water, specks of muck having splattered him in his landing.

"You left the last rope too high, Ketahn," he grumbled, shaking the dark sludge off his arms.

Rekosh chittered. "Or the Eight left you too low, Urkot."

Urkot chittered also as he trudged toward Rekosh. "Not so low that I cannot drag you down here with me, my friend."

With his usual grace, Rekosh skittered clear of Urkot, who— likely realizing he couldn't hope to catch the taller male—bent down to scoop up a handful of mud. He threw it at Rekosh with a grunt.

Rekosh shifted aside to dodge the bulk of the muck; only a few drops spattered his arm and one of his legs. But the wad of filth did find a target—the chest of Ahmya's jumpsuit.

Ahmya gasped, her hands flying up to shield her from the muck, but it was too late. Droplets speckled her face and hair as the wad broke apart on her clothing. She flinched, turning her face up, scrunching her nose, and squeezing her eyes shut.

Ivy stared at Ahmya, mouth agape and eyes rounded.

Rekosh stilled, his crimson stare fixed on the tiny human and the muck dripping down her front. He was speechless—something that had occurred only a few times during Ketahn's lifelong friendship with him.

"So…is that how they greet each other or something?" Callie asked, nose wrinkled.

Ahmya opened her eyes and looked down. She shuddered and gagged before wiping the thick muck off her chest. "Oh, that's so gross."

Urkot offered words and a deep, sincere gesture in apology. Several segments behind him, Telok reached the base of the wall, smoothly stepped down into the water, and glanced about with wary eyes.

As though he'd been bound by an invisible strand that suddenly snapped, Rekosh set into motion, swinging his bag off his back and opening it with uncharacteristically hurried, jerky movements. He removed a swath of cloth and a bulging waterskin from within and stepped closer to Ahmya. "Please, allow me to help."

Ahmya's breath hitched, and she cringed back from Rekosh.

His posture crumbled in a way Ketahn had never seen. Rekosh had always had his bouts of passion and excitement, but he'd rarely let anything else slip through.

Ivy offered Rekosh a smile. "Give her time to get used to you," she said in vrix before turning to Ahmya and placing a hand on her shoulder. She switched back to English. "Let's go inside and get changed and cleaned up."

Ketahn watched as his mate led Ahmya back to the ship. His legs twitched, eager to follow, to keep his mate in sight, but it fell on him now to act as sole translator while she was away. He had a feeling his new responsibilities would clash with his desires and instincts a great deal in the coming moon cycles.

Rekosh bowed his head, mandibles twitching as though trying—and failing—to come together.

"Making use of your charms again, Rekosh?" Telok asked, but his voice was decidedly distracted as he advanced, and his eyes were scanning the pit as though something would leap out and attack at any moment.

Rekosh stiffened at that, back straightening. He spun about and jabbed a long-clawed finger toward Urkot. "It is his doing. Acting like a broodling when we need to make a good impression on these creatures."

Urkot snorted and folded his arms across his chest, apparently unconcerned that one of his hands was still covered in muck. "You are the one who refused to face your fate with courage."

"And what courage is there in throwing filth?"

"Is it that you have already taken a liking to the tiny one?" Urkot tilted his head.

"I am simply trying to be friendly," Rekosh said with a hiss, striding to Urkot. "If you have forgotten, these *hyu-nins* are going to be our companions for the foreseeable future."

Lacey stepped closer to Ketahn, though he didn't miss her hesitance. "Are they…arguing?"

Telok's gaze had finally stopped roving—it was settled on Lacey, and there was an odd gleam within it.

Ketahn chittered. "They are being friends."

"Oh. Strange way to show it," she said.

"I think it's pretty normal for guys, actually," Will said. "I mean, I assume they're insulting each other, right?"

Ketahn lifted his mandibles in a smile. "Yes."

Will chuckled. "Guess you're not so different from humans, after all."

Diego smirked, and there was humor in his voice as he said, "I can think of a few ways they're pretty different."

"Well, if they're going to start chucking more of that nasty shit, give us some warning, okay?" Lacey said.

Rekosh and Urkot were both looking at the humans questioningly.

"Are they talking about us?" Rekosh asked.

"Of course, they are," said Urkot, reaching forward to slap Rekosh on the shoulder—with his muddy hand. "Look at us. Acting like a couple broodlings."

With a low growl, Rekosh glanced down at Urkot's hand. Urkot chittered and withdrew it, but not before smearing more of the muck on Rekosh's hide.

Seemingly oblivious to everything else, Telok walked toward Lacey, never once looking away from her.

"Are they about to start…" Lacey's words trailed off as she realized Telok was approaching her, and she turned her attention to him.

He stopped a full segment in front of her, his green eyes sharp as he studied her.

Looking uncertain, she raised her hand and waved. "Um…hi?"

Telok's eyes flicked to Ketahn.

"She said hello," Ketahn said.

Telok lifted a hand to copy her gesture. "*Uh hi.*"

"He's just staring at me," Lacey said from the side of her mouth. "I don't know what to do."

"Tell him your name maybe?" Ella called from her place near the fire.

Lacey let out a puff of air that sent strands of her red hair to the side. She studied Telok's scarred hide. "Jeez, he's scary." Pressing a hand to her chest, she said, "Lacey. My name is Lacey."

Again, Telok mimicked her gesture, pressing his hand to his own chest. "Telok."

"Great. Now that we estab—"

Telok extended an arm, hooked a lock of her hair with his fingers, and lifted it. "She is so colorful. Unlike any female I have seen."

Lacey stilled, staring at Telok with wide eyes. "W-what's he doing?"

Will snickered. "He looks pretty fascinated."

"Female vrix do not have colors such as yours," Ketahn replied.

"Ah, well"—Lacey reached up and plucked her hair out of Telok's fingers—"human females come in all different colors. Males too."

Ketahn relayed her meaning to Telok, who only tilted his head and said, "Yet there are none such as her among these ones. There are none like her in all the Tangle."

"In all the world," Rekosh suggested.

Before the discussion could continue, the final vrix reached the bottom of the pit. All eyes turned toward Ahnset.

Despite her size and weight, she lowered herself gently into the water. She had forgone many of her usual adornments, keeping the leather and gold neck piece, the bands around her arms and wrists, and the gold ring on her mandible. There were still beads and gold woven into her braided hair, but Ketahn knew those would've been more tedious to remove. Her belt was thick leather without decoration.

A few of the humans gasped as Ahnset turned toward them and joined the other vrix, which put her size in perspective.

"Holy shit," Will muttered.

"Damn," breathed Diego.

"How…how could there possibly be even bigger ones?" asked Callie.

Ketahn strode forward until he was before his sister. She bent down, and they tipped their headcrests together.

"I did not expect you to come today, broodsister," he said.

"I have been released from my duties for several days," she replied in a low voice. "I told Korahla I wanted to assist you. She agreed and sent me off. She will tell any who ask that I am on a secret assignment for the Fang. I will aid you in all ways I can, broodbrother…but I cannot accompany you on your journey like the others."

"Like the others?" Ketahn withdrew from her and looked over his shoulder at his friends, all three of whom were turned toward him.

"We have chosen," Rekosh said. "When you leave, we will be with you."

"To whatever end this reaches," Urkot added.

"I hope you are prepared to have these two bickering beside you for the rest of your days, Ketahn." Telok chittered. "Your peaceful solitude is at an end. Now you must share in the burden I have carried all these years."

"Thank you, my friends," Ketahn said through a growing tightness in his chest. It was more than he'd wanted to ask, more than he'd dared to hope. But it meant everything to him. He looked past his friends to see the humans beyond them, having clumped together in a loose group.

Uncertainty was plain in their expressions, and their eyes repeatedly darted toward Ahnset and away again.

It was Lacey who broke their silence. "Ketahn…that one is…"

"Big," Diego offered.

"Yeah." Lacey nodded rapidly. "Big. And, um…"

Ketahn stepped aside, offering them full view of Ahnset. He gestured to her. "She has come to help, like the others."

"*She?*" Callie asked incredulously.

"Yes. This is my sister. She is called Ahnset."

"Is she your...your older sister?" Will asked. "Are you not even full grown yet?"

Ketahn chittered and shook his head. "We hatched together in the same brood. And I am the most big male in Takarahl."

"It makes sense," Lacey said, reclaiming her composure. "For a lot of insects and spiders, females are larger and stronger."

Reflex nearly had Ketahn insisting that he was not a spider, but he held the retort back. "Now that my friends have come, you humans must prepare to move. We must choose."

"Choose what?" Callie asked, one eyebrow arched.

Ketahn pointed toward the top of the pit. "Which vrix will carry which humans."

"Oh, hell no," Will said, shaking his head.

"How else did you expect to get out of here?" Lacey asked, waving a hand toward the pit wall. "Not like there are *stairz*, and I'm pretty sure the *eleh vayder* is out of order."

Rekosh asked what the humans were saying. Ketahn explained the situation briefly—though he didn't know some of Lacey's words—and Rekosh gave a chittering response.

"What'd he say?" Diego asked.

Ketahn smiled. "We can hug you in silk cocoons so you feel safe as we climb."

Callie's dark eyes flared wide. "You're kidding. Please tell me you're kidding."

Diego chuckled and grinned. "Guess we're ending up as spider food after all."

"Not spider," Ketahn corrected. "Vrix."

His clarification didn't seem to offer the humans any comfort.

CHAPTER 17

KETAHN SWEPT his gaze over the surrounding jungle, watching, as ever, for threats. Of course, his attention was split today—he had to watch the humans as closely as he watched the Tangle. Otherwise, all this served no purpose.

One and all, the humans were damp with sweat. A few had pulled down the upper portions of their jumpsuits to reveal the thinner white garments beneath, which were identical to what Ivy had been wearing when he first found her.

Cole had removed his shirt. The toned muscles of his torso were fascinating to Ketahn, vaguely reminiscent of vrix muscles but also utterly alien. They were also irritating; Ketahn couldn't be certain, but he had the sense that there was something calculating about the human male removing his covering when the others seemed so insistent upon wearing clothing as often as possible.

Was Cole attempting to attract a mate?

Ketahn ground his teeth.

Though he had no problem with these humans mating amongst themselves, he would not tolerate anyone trying to

TIFFANY ROBERTS

take his mate—and Cole had certainly cast heavy glances at Ivy throughout the day.

Gnashing his mandible fangs and curling a hand into a useless fist, Ketahn looked at Ivy. She was walking along the jungle floor several segments below him as she told Diego about the time she'd eaten sweetfang root and fallen ill. They mentioned *injek shuns* having likely saved her. Ketahn bit back a resurgence of helplessness. He refused to fall into that torturous feeling again.

Today was not about helplessness. It was about discovering limits, teaching, and ensuring that everyone was prepared to face the many challenges that awaited—at least as prepared as they could possibly become in a few days' time.

Ketahn's eyes fell upon flecks of yellow against a dark tree trunk. "Ivy."

She glanced up at him, following his gesture with her eyes as he pointed toward the yellow.

"Goldcrests," he said. "Show the others."

Lips curling into a smile, she nodded and called the other humans over to the cluster of goldcrests. Ahnset strode to join them and sank low to allow her rider down.

Ella slipped off Ahnset unsteadily. Callie caught one of her arms to provide her support, Ahnset the other.

There'd been some debate as to whether they should bring Ella along. Diego had gently explained that she needed rest more than anything. She'd shown impressive strength of will in her desire to come, but she'd admitted that Diego was right, and had said she didn't want to slow everyone down.

Though Ahnset had been uncertain about doing so, she'd offered to carry Ella and ensure the human did not fall behind. Ketahn guessed it was the disparity in their sizes that caused his broodsister's hesitance more than the strangeness of the humans; Ahnset would have to take great care in handling Ella to avoid doing her any harm.

But Ahnset had kept true to her word, demonstrating immense consideration and gentleness. More, Ella's presence seemed to encourage the others—human and vrix alike. Ella had shown little unease around the vrix from the start. While traveling with Ahnset, she'd smiled often, and had even made clumsy but determined attempts to learn and pronounce vrix words.

Ahnset seemed just as taken by the human female. Their mutual curiosity was heartening to observe.

"Your thoughts?" Telok asked as he climbed onto the fallen tree upon which Ketahn was perched. He looked down at the humans, who were watching as Ivy gathered the goldcrests and passed them out.

"Stronger than I expected, as my mate said," Ketahn replied. "But they are not yet fully recovered from their slumber."

"They are loud." Telok's mandibles sagged and twitched back upward. "Small as they are, they make Ahnset and Urkot seem quiet in comparison."

Ketahn released a thoughtful trill. "An impressive accomplishment."

Telok chittered.

Ivy encouraged the other humans to taste the goldcrests. Beyond them, Urkot and Rekosh had taken elevated positions to scan the jungle—though Urkot cast the occasional longing glance back at the humans.

For all his complaints about being forced to eat only roots and mushrooms, Urkot had always been fond of both.

"They must learn to walk the Tangle before they can do so quietly," said Ketahn.

Telok grunted, folded his upper arms across his chest, and glanced skyward. Late day sunlight streamed through gaps in the canopy, casting indistinct, dancing shadows on everything below.

"How long do you mean to keep them out here, Ketahn?"

"Until after dark."

Telok thumped a leg on the log in a slow, soft beat. "Most of them will be exhausted well before sunfall."

Below, Lacey gathered her red hair and lifted it away from her neck, twisting it into a crude bundle. The back of her neck glistened with sweat. Telok's attention fell upon her and remained there.

"We must know," Ketahn said.

Ivy divided the remaining goldcrests and passed them out to the others, leaving none for herself. Despite the tension that caused in Ketahn's jaw, he continued.

"We must find their limits and push beyond them. The Claws, for all their cowardice, will not rest as they search."

"It will help us little if these *hyu-nins* cannot even remain upright by the time we return." Telok turned his head to look at Ketahn. "We brought them out here to teach them."

"And to learn, my friend." Ketahn met Telok's gaze. "We have as much to learn as they do."

Once the last piece of goldcrest had been handed out—to Ella, who closed a shaky hand around it—Ketahn called for them to continue. He and Telok remained high, covering the flanks. Rekosh and Urkot returned to the ground, the former taking up the formation's rear, the latter its head. Ahnset, with Ella back in place on her hindquarters, strode at the center, the towering heart of the group.

Such had been a standard arrangement for vrix hunting parties for generations. The lead tracker out front, all angles watched, all sides protected.

Of course, all the members of a vrix hunting party carried spears, and these humans were armed only with the small metal knives they'd found in the ship except for Ivy, who carried the spear she'd crafted. That would have to be remedied soon. Fortunately, Urkot had brought some chunks of blackrock that would work well as spear heads.

The lessons continued as they had all morning—both the vrix and Ivy pointing out notable plants, animal tracks, and hazards, and the group stopping occasionally so Ketahn could show them things with greater detail.

When he brought them to a grub infested tree, indicated the signs of the infestation, and demonstrated how to pry up the bark to get at the plump grubs beneath, a few of the humans paled.

Ketahn plucked out a squirming grub, tossed it into his mouth, and bit down. There was an audible *pop* as it burst between his teeth.

Most of the humans looked ill after that.

"Somehow that's worse to watch the second time around," Ivy muttered, turning away.

Ketahn wasn't surprised by her reaction, and thus he was not surprised that the others reacted similarly. But he was caught off guard when both Lacey and Will stepped forward and said they would taste the grubs. Cole volunteered immediately after Will, again giving Ketahn the impression of some underlying mating ritual—as though Cole thought himself in competition with the other males.

All three humans made uncertain faces as they slipped wriggling grubs into their mouths—lips downturned, brows creased, and noses scrunched.

Ketahn didn't miss the oddly prideful gleam in Telok's eyes, which were again fixed upon Lacey.

"Oh, God, that's weird," Lacey said after she'd chewed and swallowed. A shudder wracked her. "Ugh, why did I do that?"

"Yeah." Will drank from one of the waterskins, doing that strange human thing in which he swished the liquid around in his mouth, making his cheeks puff out from side to side, before spitting it onto the ground. "That taste just doesn't fit with the texture."

Cole swallowed, and the corners of his mouth peeled back,

making the cords of his neck stand out briefly. He released a harsh breath and shook his head. "Not bad."

Lacey stuck out her tongue and scrunched her nose. "It's like nuts and wood ground into a squishy pulp."

Will nodded, staring at Cole from the corner of his eye before taking another long drink of water.

No one else wanted to try a grub despite Ketahn's coaxing.

Ivy chuckled and bumped Ketahn's leg with her hip. "See? It's not just me."

Ketahn chittered, and the group resumed their journey. Though the humans were displaying signs of tiredness, he pushed them a little faster, guiding them up a broad root that led higher into the trees. They fared about as well traveling such paths as he'd expected—poorly.

Ivy managed all right, though her pace was slower than normal, but the others were unsteady and even slower than her.

Telok and Ketahn glanced at each other as the humans were attempting to cross from the root to a low branch.

Understanding passed between the two vrix. Their real journey, their flight from Takarahl, would be slow, difficult, and extremely dangerous—especially because they'd have to make it almost entirely on the ground.

And yet, Ketahn was encouraged. The humans had offered little complaint despite their obvious discomfort. They'd been attentive, and he'd seen them helping one another in small ways throughout the day. They were far from experienced, and it would be a while before they worked together like it was instinctual, but there was potential.

As the first orange hints of approaching sunfall crept into the sky, Urkot happened across a nurunal, which he killed with a throw of his spear. While Urkot collected the lean, furred animal and slung it over his shoulder, still impaled on the spear, Telok guided the group to a nearby clearing.

Ahmya, who'd been so quiet thus far that it would've been

easy to forget the little human was even there, sucked in a sharp breath.

Ketahn tensed, raised his spear, and spun toward her; such a sound surely meant danger. At the edge of his vision, Rekosh was already moving toward the female, who'd gone to the edge of the clearing. She stood in front of a plant with broad leaves and long-stemmed flowers.

Ketahn's fine hairs stood on end. His eyes raked the jungle growth around Ahmya, and he drew in a deep breath through his nostrils, seeking any signs of nearby predators.

"What is it, Ahmya?" asked Ivy, taking a step toward the dark-haired human.

Ketahn hurried to place himself between Ivy and Ahmya. If there was an unseen threat, he would not leave his mate exposed to it.

"These flowers," Ahmya replied, shaking her head slowly. "They're *amazing.*"

"Scaring everyone because you saw some damned flowers? What the hell?" Cole grumbled.

"How many species of alien flowers have you seen?" Ahmya replied distractedly. She reached toward the nearest blossom.

Its petals were long and thin, flaring out and tapering sharply at their ends. They were deep, vibrant blue—though with a turn of one's head, they could just as easily look purple—with crimson streaks leading toward their centers. The long tendrils that grew from those centers had small red clusters on their ends.

Ahmya's hand stopped in midair. She glanced at Ketahn and Ivy over her shoulder. "Are they safe to touch?"

Ketahn nodded. Ahmya grinned and returned her attention to the flower. With unimaginable delicacy, she brushed her fingertips over a petal. The slight movement caused by her touch made the petal shimmer between blue and purple.

"Do I get to stand around and smell the *rohzez*, too?" Cole asked.

"Go make fire," Ketahn said in English. "There is meat to tend."

Cole made a sound that was equally bitter and amused and walked away.

Ketahn didn't look at the human male; he was too interest in what was going on ahead of him.

Rekosh approached Ahmya slowly, head tilted and eyes intent upon her. "They are called spearblossoms."

Ahmya started, her attention snapping toward Rekosh. "I, uh... I..."

"Do you find them beautiful?" Rekosh asked gently.

"He says they are spearblossoms," Ketahn said in English, "and asks if they are beautiful."

The small woman's expression eased, leaving only a joyous light in her eyes. She smiled at Rekosh and nodded. "Some of the most beautiful I have ever seen."

After Ketahn translated her words, Rekosh purred. He glanced at the flowers briefly. "For the vrix, they are signs of remembrance. The petals are spears of hunters, of warriors, and the red is the blood that has been shed to allow our kind to survive. Spearblossoms are memories of all those who have been lost... But they are a hope for the future, also. They mean suffering and pain, but they also mean *life*."

Ivy had stepped up beside Ketahn as Rekosh spoke. She caught hold of Ketahn's fingers and gave them an affectionate squeeze. He gently closed his hand around hers and relayed Rekosh's words to Ahmya.

Ahmya's smile softened, as did something in her gaze.

Leaving the two to their flowers, Ketahn and Ivy turned back to the rest of the group. The humans had a small fire already burning. Ketahn felt a small pang of regret at that; he was fascinated by the little tool they used to light the kindling. It was faster and more efficient than even the best methods practiced by the vrix, and he wanted to see it in use again.

Once the fire was built up more, Rekosh, Urkot, and Telok formed a loose ring around the group. Ketahn and Ivy joined the humans and his sister near the fire, and he explained how to skin the nurunal, which Will said looked a bit like something called a *poss-uhm*. He was surprised again when Ella asked to try. Despite her illness, she kept her hand steady, and used her knife with familiarity and confidence.

She required little instruction to skin the animal, though Cole did help her move the carcass and peel back the skin when it proved too much for her diminished strength.

Ella let Cole finish removing the creature's hide and sat back, cleaning her knife with a leaf. "Used to have to do that on the farm sometimes," she said, offering a smile as Ivy uncorked a waterskin and rinsed Ella's hands. "I didn't care for it much at first, but after a while, you just…get used to it."

"It's just meat, right?" asked Will, voice a little unsteady.

"We're all just meat," Cole said.

Ketahn nearly chittered at that; he'd said the same to Ahnset not long ago. He dipped his chin toward Cole. "A good lesson. There is always something more big in the Tangle that thinks we are food."

"I never thought we'd be shoved down to the bottom of the food chain," said Callie.

Cole drew his own knife, poising it over the skinned nurunal. "Just going to have to claw our way back up."

Ketahn showed him how to carve the animal, and they soon had meat roasting over the flames. The savory aroma filled the air, sparking hungry gleams in the humans' eyes, and the group settled around the fire, finally letting themselves rest.

It had been a long while since Ketahn had joined a hunting party. His treks through the Tangle had mostly been made in solitude until he found Ivy, and her companionship was so natural, so effortless, that nothing felt right without her. It would take time to adjust to this, but it felt good to have his friends with him again. It felt good to have a group formed around him and Ivy. To have...a tribe.

He lowered himself to the ground a couple segments away from the fire, and Ivy sat in the cradle of his forelegs, her shoulder against his chest.

"Are we heading back after this?" she asked.

Ketahn glanced skyward. "Yes, but we will follow a different path. There is far more to show and too little time for it." When he lowered his gaze, he found Ivy idly toying with the material of her jumpsuit with restless fingers, head bowed.

"This has been good, right?" she asked in a small, soft voice. "I...I'm trying to help, but there is still so much I don't know, and I..."

Cupping the underside of her jaw, Ketahn tilted Ivy's chin up, forcing her to look at him. The uncertainty in her eyes, even if it was but a hint, tore at his heartsthread.

He bent down until his face was close to hers. "You did well, my Ivy. As always, you have made my chest swell."

She stared up at him for several heartbeats, searching for something, before a light sparked in her eyes. Throwing an arm around his neck, she pulled him down the rest of the way, pressed those soft, soft lips to his mouth, and delicately flicked her tongue against his. With a purr, Ketahn slipped his fingers into her hair to cradle the back of her head and wrapped his lower arms around her, wanting—*needing*—more of her.

A blissful eternity later, she withdrew. Her eyes were bright with passion, her cheeks were stained pink, and her lips were slanted in a smirk. "I bet that is not the only thing I can make swell," she whispered.

The sound that rumbled in Ketahn's chest was half growl, half trill, wholly primal. "Ah, my heartsthread... My sweet little *nyleea*..." His claspers extended to lock around her hips.

The heat of the jungle air was nothing compared to the heat she awoke under his hide.

Ivy chuckled with delightful wickedness and caught hold of his bound hair. "But not now, spider man."

Ketahn grunted. "Not even if I pretend you did not call me that?"

"We're right fucking here," Cole said. "The rest of us don't need to see that lovey-dovey shit."

The heat within Ketahn shifted from passion to rage that quickly. His muscles tensed, his fingers curled, and his mandibles opened. But that fury was halted when Ivy twirled his hair around her fingers and stretched her smirk into a grin; she gave no other acknowledgement to Cole.

"Wouldn't hurt you to get in touch with your more sensitive side for once, man," Diego said in a calm, easy tone. "Not doing you any favors being so high strung all the time."

He and Will were sitting near Ella, who was leaning against Ahnset's hindquarters with her eyes closed.

"Yeah, well...stress builds strength," Cole replied. "That's human *ehvo looshun*."

"To some *duhgree*," Callie said. "We're *wyurd* to deal with certain levels of stress as a survival *mekuh nizm*, but..."

Ivy turned her head to look at the others, and Ketahn lowered his hand from her chin, wrapping that arm around her.

"Constant stress is *detruh men tull* to your health," Diego finished.

"I just..." Cole sighed heavily and ran his gaze over the group, his expression difficult to read. "Don't need everyone ganging up on me all the time, you know?"

"We're not," Ivy said gently.

Will stretched his legs out in front of him and brushed some dirt off the leg of his jumpsuit. "Everyone is coping in their own way, but we're all in this together. We just...just need to cut each other some slack, yeah?"

Cole nodded and combed his fingers through his hair, settling his eyes on Ivy. "Yeah. Yeah, I get it."

Ivy's smile was genuine and soft; Ketahn nearly growled at seeing her gift it to Cole. She was Ketahn's mate, and only Ketahn should have received such looks from her. His hold on her grew more possessive, and he narrowed his eyes at Cole.

"What are they saying, Ketahn?" Ahnset asked.

She'd been surrounded by beings she could not understand all day. Ketahn was familiar with such frustration. He'd had enough trouble when it was just Ivy talking to him in a language of which he couldn't make sense.

Ketahn stomped down his ire and gave himself a few moments to craft a response. "These humans are not bound by blood, and they did not know one another before waking from their sleep. They are still building bonds with one another. Weaving the threads between them."

"Things will be hard, but we *are* in this together," Callie said. "We're all important."

Ketahn's claspers squeezed Ivy's hips, and in a low, rumbling voice—and his native tongue—he said, "None as much as you, my *nyleea*."

She nestled against him, nuzzling his chest with her cheek.

"Cole especially," Will said. "Don't see how we're going to make a new home here without an awesome *dek* to *louwnge* on."

The humans laughed, and the vrix exchanged confused glances with each other. Ketahn didn't bother explaining; he wasn't sure what Will meant either.

Fortunately, the laughter seemed to break the tension. Telok, Urkot, and Rekosh drifted closer, and the humans and vrix were soon trying to teach each other words in their respective languages. Ivy translated, smiling and laughing along with everyone else as they stumbled over pronunciations —or as Rekosh, with exaggerated seriousness, struggled to produce the human *mmm* sound. Though Rekosh didn't explain why he was so determined, Ketahn could guess his friend's reason.

Ahmya's name had that sound in it.

Ketahn remained largely quiet; he was content to simply enjoy his mate's nearness.

So much had happened over the last several days, and he'd lost so much time with Ivy. At least he would face the days to come with her by his side. That meant everything, no matter what challenges awaited.

"They are like broodlings," Ahnset said, calling Ketahn's attention to her. She was in a lowered position, forelegs bent and tucked partially beneath her, staring at Ella. She'd planted her war spear in the ground beside her; its shaft towered high over everyone present.

"But they are not broodlings," Ketahn replied gently, "and we cannot treat them as such."

"I know, broodbrother." Ahnset lifted a hand, fingers splayed, and gestured to her face. "It is in their eyes. They are lost, confused, afraid, sorrowful...but they are not broodlings. There is a fire in their eyes."

"Yes," Rekosh said with a click of his mandibles. He was turned away from the group, watching the jungle. "After all, what broodlings could have created a means to travel between the stars and sleep for hundreds of years without dying?"

"We are not broodlings," Ivy said with a smirk, carefully pronouncing the vrix words, "but for all the wonders we have made, we often act like children."

At Ahnset's questioning glance, Ketahn explained the meaning of the human word *children*. She grunted, settled her lower hands on her forelegs, and returned her attention to Ella.

Ahnset had always been a protector, even before she'd become a Fang. She had taken on Ella as her charge, at least for now—and no one, human or vrix, could ask for a more capable protector than Ahnset tes Ishuun'ani Ir'okari.

He wished they did not have to part in a few short days; he'd miss his broodsister immensely.

Telok tended the roasting meat while Urkot and Rekosh kept close to the group, both standing upright to keep watch—though their attention often turned toward to humans.

This had been a good day of teaching and learning, of coming together despite differences in appearance and language. But the day was not done. If they took a meandering path on their return journey, they'd near the pit around night-fall, just as Ketahn planned—he wanted them to have a taste of the Tangle in the dark.

Unfortunately, the jungle—much like Queen Zurvashi—cared nothing for Ketahn's plans.

A roar echoed through the boughs, guttural and undulating.

Ketahn's hearts quickened, and his fine hairs bristled as he turned his head toward the roar. Everyone else had done the same.

"What was that?" Ahmya whispered.

"The *bass terd* child of a *lyun* and a *wolruss*," Cole replied without a hint of unsteadiness in his voice.

"Yatin," Ketahn said, standing up and helping Ivy to her feet.

"Three hundred segments," Telok rasped, "perhaps a little more."

Urkot thumped a leg on the ground. "Or a little less."

"I take it that sound is bad?" asked Will.

A second roar sounded from a different direction, deeper and rougher than the first and only slightly farther away.

"Everyone up," Ketahn said in English, snatching the pair of spears off the ground. He handed Ivy her weapon. "Gather all things. Fast."

"Are there more than one of those things?" Lacey asked as she collected the waterskins that had been set out for the meal.

"Two males." Ketahn strode to Ahnset and Ella, picked up the sickly human, and placed her atop his broodsister's hindquarters. "They make challenge to each other, to win this ground."

"A *terih toree ul dizpute?*" Diego swung a bag over his shoulder as he rose. "Can't we just let them fight it out?"

Ketahn helped Ahnset and Ella fasten their torsos together with a rope and shook his head. Rekosh, Urkot, and Telok had already taken positions around the group, their spears at the ready, and Ahnset had plucked her mighty war spear from the ground.

Extending an arm, Ketahn pointed in the direction of the pit even as he furiously kicked damp dirt over the fire. "Fast."

Somewhere distant, wood cracked like a peal of thunder. Whether it had just been branches or an entire tree, it meant one of the yatins was on the move.

"Now," Ketahn snarled at the wide-eyed humans.

The group set into motion. Ivy, carrying her little spear in one clenched fist, was at their rear, just ahead of Ketahn—who'd placed himself in the back deliberately. He'd led this journey. He would be the first shield between his companions and any threat.

Despite their weariness, the humans traveled at a decent pace, helping each other navigate the unavoidable obstacles strewn about the jungle floor.

"Are those things *karnih vorz* or *errbih vorz?*" Callie asked breathlessly.

Ketahn glanced at Ivy's back; anticipating his lack of understanding, she provided a simple translation. Had the situation not been so dire, he would have asked why humans needed such odd words to say if animals at meats or plants.

"Yatins eat plants," he said.

The first yatin called again, from much closer than before.

"Shaper, unmake me," Urkot grumbled.

"Protector, shield us," Ahnset intoned.

"What the hell does it matter what they eat?" demanded

Cole. He held his metal knife in one hand, blade angled down. The weapon would pierce a yatin's hide, but it was unlikely to inflict significant wounds on such a beast.

"It does not matter," said Ketahn, watching Ivy's golden hair bounce and sway with her every step.

"I just wanted to know if we're about to be trampled or eaten," Callie said.

The second yatin made its call of challenge; it too was uncomfortably closer.

"They must have our scent," Telok said over his shoulder.

"We need to get off the ground," Ahnset said.

"We cannot move all the humans fast enough. Two of them on your back would impede even you as you climbed, Ahnset," said Rekosh.

Ketahn growled, fighting the urge to close the distance between himself and Ivy so he could scoop her up and race to safety. "The thorn snarl we passed earlier. That is our aim, Telok."

Urkot snapped his mandibles. "Will that be enough?"

"It must be." Ketahn's fine hairs were still standing on end, and his hearts beat rapidly. Heat skittered just beneath his hide. He knew this feeling, recognized it; these were the moments before battle, when everything took on stunning, cold clarity.

The humans were breathing heavily, several of them sweating more than before, but none flagged or fell behind. Ivy had given Ketahn a glimpse of human willpower; perhaps it was even stronger than he'd guessed.

"Why are they chasing us?" Lacey asked between panting breaths.

"Yatin can smell from far," Ketahn replied. "And they smell us on their ground."

"They sound huge." Will glanced over his shoulder, nearly tripping on an exposed root when a yatin roared again. "Why would they treat us as a threat?"

"They smell vrix and know we are hunters." Ketahn adjusted his hold on his spear and readied the coil of silk rope attached to it. Through his legs, he felt the vibrations of the yatins plodding ever nearer. "They smell humans, and do not know you at all. Both are threats."

"Fuck," Cole spat.

Despite everything, Ketahn couldn't help but admire the versatility of that word.

"There," Telok called.

The thorn snarl came into Ketahn's view as he crossed over a hollowed, rotting log, having helped Ivy over a moment before —not because she couldn't do so on her own, but because the yatins were so close that he could hear their furious, snorting breaths.

Tangled vines, some as thick as tree roots, rose from the jungle floor ahead, creating an expanse of dense, thorny growth fraught with knifevines and grappler plants. In the failing sunlight, the shadows amidst the thorn snarl were deeper and fuller than those anywhere else.

"Is *that* where we're going?" Diego asked in disbelief.

"Go," Ketahn growled. He'd only made it twenty segments away from the log when it shattered with a bone-rattling crunch behind him.

The humans gasped and screamed, looking over their shoulders in terror—and some of them stumbled or slowed their paces in doing so.

Ketahn might've roared himself, but he could not afford to waste the time and effort it would've required. He'd wanted the humans to learn how dangerous the Tangle could be. Well, this was a perfect demonstration—male yatins battling over territory was amongst the most frightening, violent sights to behold beneath the jungle canopy.

The vrix hunted yatins, yes, but always in large groups and always from above.

"Urkot, Ahnset," Ketahn shouted over the thunder of hooves, "take the humans in!"

Without missing a stride, Urkot waved the humans on and raced for the snarl. Telok and Rekosh fell back to join Ketahn, taking the silk ropes tied to theirs spears in hand. Ahnset clacked her mandible fangs and hurried along with the humans.

Ivy glanced back as she neared the opening at the edge of the snarl, brow creased, blue eyes gleaming with worry. Those eyes rounded as she glanced past Ketahn; in her time here, she'd seen many creatures, but yatins were new to her.

Ketahn hoped his eyes conveyed the message thrumming along his heartsthread when he met his mate's gaze.

He would be with her soon.

Raising his spear, he spun to face the charging yatin.

CHAPTER 18

THE YATIN WAS a nightmarish amalgamation of beasts. Ivy's brain couldn't decide which Earth creature it resembled more; there were hints of boar, moose, bull, and elephant, and it was larger than all those animals. Even Ahnset would look small beside the yatin, which had to stand at least fifteen feet tall at its hulking, powerful shoulders—and it was likely twice that in length.

Ivy wasn't sure whether to call the massive bony protrusions on the sides of its head antlers or horns. They were terrifying either way, broad and flat like moose antlers in some places but flaring into wicked points. A pair of thick, stained tusks jutted from its mouth, curving upward into blunt but deadly hooks. Its body was bulging muscle beneath a scarred, light brown hide, with a large patch of shaggy fur at the top of its thick neck that swept back past its massive shoulders.

Before now, the only thing she'd known about yatins was that the vrix used their hides to make leather.

Even the supplest leather isn't worth facing that.

And Ketahn, Rekosh, and Telok had turned to battle the beast.

"Come! Hurry, *hyu-nins*," Urkot bellowed in vrix, waving for the humans to pass beneath an arch-shaped vine studded with inches-long thorns.

Ahnset skidded to a halt, her thick legs gouging the ground, and spun to face the yatin and the other males. Ella was clinging to Ahnset's hindquarters with desperate strength that belied her condition.

With an ear-splitting roar, a second yatin just as large as the first burst out of the undergrowth from a different direction, its huge hooves tearing a path of destruction. It slammed into the first beast. Hide and muscle rippled with the impact. Horns and tusks clashed with sharp, echoing clacks of bone against bone.

"Take Ella," Ahnset called.

Ivy looked at her to see the female vrix working at the rope that kept Ella securely atop her; Ahnset's large fingers were fumbling with the knot. Before any more time was lost, Ahnset hooked a claw under the rope and sliced it apart.

Rushing to Ahnset's side, Ivy reached up and helped Ella down. The sick woman slumped over with a gasp, her full weight coming down on Ivy. Fortunately, Diego had also hurried over, and he helped catch Ella before she and Ivy could fall.

Throwing Ella's arms over their shoulders to support her weight, Ivy and Diego carried her to the archway, ducking their heads to pass beneath.

"Come, Ahnset," said Urkot.

"I will not fit," Ahnset replied, taking her spear in her right hands and tugging the club studded with blackrock shards off her belt with her upper left hand. "Bring them in deeper."

"Quickly, *hyu-nins*," Urkot growled. Hunched low, he pushed ahead of the others and delved into the thorny vines, moving along an oddly tunnel-like opening.

Roars and crashing vegetation from behind made Ivy glance backward as she and Diego followed the others.

She couldn't see Ketahn or the other males. Only Ahnset, standing firm before the low opening, and the second yatin beyond her. It had broken away from the first beast—and it was charging at the female vrix.

Ivy's stomach twisted into knots, and ice formed in her blood. Her legs felt like they weighed a thousand pounds.

Ahnset leapt aside at the last moment. Ivy thought she saw the vrix's spear plunge into the beast's ribs just before the yatin crashed headfirst into the mass of thorny vines.

There were screams from the other humans as the vegetation broke and shook with the yatin's thrashing, and bits of wood and thorns sprayed inward. Ivy didn't know if her own voice was amongst the screams—or if she'd made any sound at all.

Though she couldn't look away from the beast and its tusks, each of which looked nearly as long as she was tall, she somehow kept her legs moving.

Nostrils flaring with great, snorting breaths, the yatin shoved its head deeper into the thorns. Just enough light broke through the crumbling vegetation for Ivy to see dark blood glistening all over the beast's snout.

With a series of pained huffs and grunts, the yatin dragged itself free of the thorns.

Urkot shouted in his deep, rumbling voice for them to move; his tone was enough to shatter the language barrier, as all the humans hurried to join him. Ivy's breath sawed in and out of her lungs, and every muscle in her body burned, even with that cold fear in her blood. Somehow, she'd held onto her spear through all this. She doubted it would do any good against such monstrous animals, but it was *something*.

The group delved deeper still, ducking and twisting as thorns snagged at their hair and clothing. Ivy felt a few of those thorns bite hard enough to break her skin, but the pain didn't come. Adrenaline was taking care of her.

At least for now.

The noise from outside the bramble was barely diminished; it sounded like a herd of stampeding beasts was knocking down the entire jungle. Roars, growls, and snorts filled the air, some aggressive, some pained.

But she did not hear the other male vrix.

Please be okay, Ketahn. All of you, please be okay.

"Careful through here," Diego said, drawing Ivy's attention forward again.

Urkot and the others had gone through a wide, low space—he must've crawled on his belly to fit—and now it was Ivy, Diego, and Ella's turn. Thankfully, Ella had strength enough to move her legs while they were crouched. After a lot of struggling and battling countless grabbing thorns, they emerged in a surprisingly open area where it looked like the plants and vines had been deliberately cleared away. Urkot and the others stood in the center, their forms shadowed and grim in the gloom.

"Ready your spear, Ivy," Urkot said in a tight voice that barely carried above the din of the battle outside. His legs were spread in a wide, solid stance, and his gaze was fixed on the far side of the clearing, where there were several more paths through the vegetation just like the one through which they'd just come. They were like tunnels bored into to the bramble, and Ivy was not eager to find out what had made them.

"Um, can you manage alone, Diego?" Ivy asked. The knots in her stomach were doubling, tripling, growing impossibly heavy and sinking lower and lower.

"I'll help." Ahmya stepped over to them.

Ivy traded spots with Ahmya, draping Ella's arm over the smaller woman's shoulders. Ella slumped a little more to that side, and Diego stooped slightly to compensate.

"Got her," Diego said. "You doing okay, Ella?"

Ella offered a shallow nod. "Mhmm."

The trio joined the others. Ivy grasped her spear in both

hands and walked around the group. Her boot bumped into something small and hard, and she looked down.

The ground was covered with dried grass, leaves, and debris that was thickest at the center. Some of that debris was twigs, branches, and crumbling bits of vines. But despite the poor lighting, she knew some of it was clearly...bone.

This is a nest.

"Shit." Cole kicked a piece of bone away with the toe of his boot, having apparently reached the same conclusion.

Swallowing thickly, Ivy assumed a wide stance beside Urkot. She wished there'd been more time for Ketahn to teach her how to use her spear, that there'd been more time to practice. She wished that they weren't in a situation in which people's lives might depend upon her ability to use the weapon.

Most of all, she wished Ketahn was at her side, safe and sound.

He's a hunter, Ivy. A warrior. He'll be fine. Right now, you need to focus on getting your own ass out of this alive.

Something moved within the tangled plant growth ahead, and Ivy set aside her wishes to face reality, adjusting the positions of her clammy hands on the spear.

Someone moved into her peripheral vision, and she glanced over to see Will and Cole standing beside her, each holding a survival knife. Both wore sheens of sweat like face masks in the dull light.

"Xiskals," Urkot said, mandibles twitching, "and we are in their nest."

For all the noise of the raging fight beyond the thorns, this clearing—this nest—was deathly silent. Ivy was certain everyone else could hear her pounding heart, which seemed likely to hammer straight out of her chest at any moment.

Urkot released a low, rumbling growl. "Tell them. Close together. Tight group."

Nodding, Ivy relayed the message. The humans packed

closer together; Lacey and Callie, knives in hand, joined Will and Cole in a small defensive ring with Ella at the center, still supported by Diego and Ahmya. Just as their group formed, all hell broke loose.

Something shrieked ahead—the call was reminiscent of a bird of prey. It was answered by similar calls from all around. The sounds built into a menacing chorus.

Someone cried out; it sounded like Callie.

Urkot was in motion before Ivy could even register what was happening. He lunged to the side, right arms darting out with his spear as a black shape leapt at Callie from one of the openings in the thorny vines.

The creature yelped in pain as the head of Urkot's spear met it in midair, abruptly reversing its momentum and slamming it to the ground. It was writhing on the end of that spear, pinned down, when two more of the things rushed out of other tunnel like paths.

All at once, the surrounding bramble came alive with hisses, growls, and shrieks. Ivy saw Urkot tug on his spear, which seemed to be stuck on the first xiskal, before hefting the weapon like a club and using the flailing beast to beat away its companions.

Another xiskal emerged closer to Ivy. Her heart leapt into her throat; her glimpse of the creature was brief, but it was enough to etch its visage forever into her mind. Four gleaming eyes, a leathery, mottled hide, long, hooked claws, and a row of spikes along its spine.

She thrust her spear hard before fear could paralyze her. The blackrock head struck the creature's forward shoulder, jolted against what must have been bone, and glanced aside, leaving a trail of blood in its wake.

More of the beasts came. Ivy's thrusts were fast, wild, and not especially accurate, but she fought with her all, creating a wall of thrashing blackrock to shield her companions. She was aware of human shouts, screams, and curses mingling with the beasts' shrieks, yelps, and hisses, mingling with the thunder of plodding hooves and the crashes of shattering vegetation beyond the bramble. She was aware of Urkot, his spear broken in two, using both halves of the shaft and his claws to fight the swarming beasts.

But more than anything, she was aware of the people— human and vrix alike—who she was desperate to protect, who she already cared about.

She was aware of the male she loved, who was battling to save her even now. No matter how scared or worried she was, she would not let his effort, his risk, be in vain.

Ivy screamed, pouring all her tightly wound emotion into it, and plunged her spear into a xiskal's chest.

CHAPTER 19

Even the deafening noise of the rampaging yatins could not stop Ketahn from hearing Ivy's scream. It sliced through all the other sound and pierced to his core, wrapping around his heartsthread and sparking terrible fire within him.

He felt the fear in her cry. He felt the defiance, the anger, the passion, the selflessness. And he felt his failure.

My mate.

He'd sent her ahead with Urkot and the others to keep her safe. But now he could not get to her. Now he could not be at her side to protect her.

No.

The word rumbled from the depths of his spirit, thrumming with power.

His mate needed him. Whether it was an enraged yatin, a hungry mire, or Zurvashi herself with every warrior in Takarahl at her command, no obstacle would keep Ketahn from Ivy.

The ground shook beneath him as the yatin he and Telok were battling charged. Ketahn embraced the flames in his chest, willing them hotter still and welcoming their heat into his limbs. His muscles swelled with desperate, bristling energy. This beast was not just an obstacle keeping him from Ivy—it was a direct threat to her.

Ketahn ran toward the beast, his hearts beating faster than the frantic pounding of legs over the battered ground. The yatin snorted and dipped its head, angling its huge, stained tusks toward him.

He would be with Ivy soon.

Ketahn dove forward, stretching his body to pass through the space between the yatin's curved tusk and its broad horn. The beast snapped its head aside as though to catch him. The hard bone of a tusk struck Ketahn's legs with enough force to disrupt his arc, but there was no pain—not until he landed.

His left upper shoulder took the brunt of the impact as he came down. Agony burst through it, echoes of the damage Zurvashi had inflicted recently. But he twisted as he fell and threw out a right hand, slapping it down on the shaft of his fallen spear. His fingers closed around the weapon and, using the momentum of his fall, he rolled until his legs were again beneath him.

Xiskals shrieked in the thorn snarl, and humans shouted in panicked voices. Something powerful clutched Ketahn's heartsthread and pulled it hard toward the sounds. But his vision focused on the yatin.

The beast skidded to a stumbling halt that whipped its hindquarters around into a nearby tree trunk. Bark splintered, cracked, and showered the ground. A spear shaft—Telok's spear —bounced and shook on the yatin's flank, the head buried too deep for it to be shaken free. A dozen other wounds made the creature's hide glisten with dark blood, but Ketahn knew none of those wounds were deadly. The hunters' efforts had yet to so much as slow the beast down.

Now, Ketahn charged at the momentarily disadvantaged creature. His limbs burned with the fires of his fury and desperation. The yatin threw its weight aside, turning its bulky body to settle its small, dark eyes upon Ketahn. It roared.

Ketahn roared back, the harsh sound tearing out of his throat. His lower hands worked furiously to coil the long silk rope trailing from his spear, but their work was not yet done by the time he jumped.

The yatin swung its head upward, anticipating Ketahn's path through the air. He threw out his arms and legs and latched onto the beast's head as he came down, grasping horns, tusks, and hide. The air fled his lungs at the impact, and his stomach lurched; for an instant, it seemed as though the beast would fling him off, but he held fast.

The yatin snorted and shook its head furiously. Its hooves tore up clumps of damp dirt and moss and crushed undergrowth, enhancing the jolts assaulting Ketahn's body. His lower hands worked deftly, lashing the silk rope around the yatin's horns.

The jungle whirled around Ketahn as the yatin spun. Though he did not see it, he felt a solid, towering object looming behind him, and heat crackled along his back. The yatin lunged forward. Ketahn tightened his hold on the rope's slack and threw himself up and over the beast's horns.

The yatin's downturned head crashed into the tree with immense force that resonated through every thread of Ketahn's being, but he was clear of the blow. The rope went taut and cinched around Ketahn's hand. His body jerked, falling to the side of the yatin's thick neck; his weight tugged on the horns around which the rope was tangled, twisting the beast's great head aside.

With a stunned groan, the yatin staggered back from the tree. That groan became a pained sound when Telok dropped onto the creature's backside and grasped the spear jutting from its flank.

"Soon, Ivy," Ketahn rasped.

Hooking his claws into the yatin's side, Telok reached out a hand to Ketahn. Ketahn took hold of it and swung himself up onto the beast's back.

Snarling and grunting, the yatin bucked and thrashed in an attempt to dislodge its unwelcome riders. Ketahn latched on with his leg claws and a grabbed a fistful of the thick fur on the yatin's back. Pulling on the rope, he raised his spear high and plunged it between the yatin's shoulders. The spearhead glanced off the hard bone of the beast's spine and sank deep into the muscle of its neck.

The yatin's movements became more frenzied, its sounds more intense. It slammed into the tree repeatedly, shattering bark and making twigs and leaves rain from overhead.

Telok clawed his way into place directly behind Ketahn and took hold of the rope. Together, they drew back on it hard.

Heaving its bulk up, the yatin stood on its hind legs; it was easily three times as tall as a male vrix in that stance.

Ketahn relinquished the rope to Telok and swung himself down, grabbing onto the side of the beast's neck. He moved his face close and snapped his mandibles together on the relatively soft hide of the beast's throat. His fangs tore through flesh.

He twisted as he pulled his face away, tearing out a chunk of the yatin's throat. Hot blood sprayed his face and chest. An agonized sound rumbled from deep in the beast's chest, emerging broken and strained.

Thrusting himself off the yatin, Ketahn landed heavily on the ground, but he managed to remain upright. Telok leapt down a moment later. The yatin's breaths were ragged and sputtering, each weaker than the last as the beast stumbled and spurted blood from its ruined throat. It finally sagged against the tree, unable to support its own weight any longer.

Ketahn did not wait to watch the creature die, and he did not allow himself to acknowledge the sorrow that had replaced the fury in the yatin's eyes. He was already moving toward the next obstacle between himself and Ivy—the yatin that Rekosh and Ahnset were facing.

Ivy's scream echoed in Ketahn's mind, each repetition pulling his heartsthread impossibly tighter.

His eyes swept over the scene, and his instincts offered immediate understanding. The yatin's hide was shredded and bleeding with dozens of cuts both from vrix weapons and the nearby thorns, blood flowing from the wounds in rivulets, but it was Ahnset's first blow that had inflicted the real damage. Only half her war spear's shaft jutted from the yatin's side. At least one of its lungs had been pierced.

Though the yatin had backed away from the thorn snarl, it was still far too close—far too close to Ivy.

Ahnset had the creature's attention. Her claws and fanged club were dripping with blood, but some of the crimson spattered on her hide looked to be her own. Rekosh still held his spear. It was also bloodied, and half the shaft was missing. With his free hands, he was spooling a thick silk strand drawn from his spinnerets.

The strand would do little on its own, but…

"Telok, with me," Ketahn called.

Telok fell into place beside Ketahn, and they sprinted to the yatin, which had its side turned toward them. Just as it lunged at Ahnset, Ketahn and Telok threw their bodies against the beast. It felt like slamming into a solid stone cliff face, but it did not hold against the might and weight of two vrix. The yatin snarled and tumbled over, landing heavily on its side.

Ketahn and Telok sank their claws into the beast, using their momentum to roll the creature onto its back.

Rekosh was atop the beast immediately. His spindly limbs moved in a blur as he wound the silk strand around the yatin's thrashing legs; Ketahn was reminded of the patterns Rekosh sometimes made by stretching a loop of thread between his hands and hooking it repeatedly with his fingers.

Ketahn and Telok dove clear of the beast. Rekosh continued his work until the beast's struggles heaved it back onto its side, narrowly avoiding a swinging tusk as he tumbled away.

The beast finally righted itself, bracing its hooves on the ground. Dirt and plant debris clung to its blood-slicked hide. Its small, dark eyes fixated upon the vrix in front of it—Ahnset—and it tried to charge. Rekosh's strand pulled taut the instant the beast's front legs moved forward. The yatin's hind legs buckled, and its rear crashed down again.

Ahnset released an undulating battle cry and lunged at the yatin. She slammed her club down on its head, burying the blackrock shards in its flesh with a sickening crack, before grasping its horns and tusks with all four hands. She braced her legs wide and heaved the beast aside, twisting its head. The snarling yatin fell again, this time into the edge of the snarl, crushing vines and thorns beneath it.

All three male vrix pounced upon the creature at once. Ketahn and Telok attacked with a torrent of claws and fangs; Rekosh thrust his spear into the underside of the yatin's jaw. More bone cracked. The yatin jerked, creating a tremor that must have shaken the entire Tangle. A rattling breath escaped it, and its chest sagged.

The beast stilled.

The tang of blood dominated Ketahn's senses of taste and smell, leaving room for nothing else, and his hearing rang in the absence of the yatins' thunderous noise. But the silence didn't last for more than a few heartbeats. The shrieks and hisses of xiskals mixed with frantic human voices reached Ketahn with new clarity.

Ketahn's hearts stuttered. He leapt off the yatin before even freeing his claws, tearing up chunks of flesh that he cast to the jungle floor with flicks of his wrists. Without hesitation, he darted into the now mangled opening in the thorn snarl through which Urkot and the others had gone. Vines caught on his limbs, and thorns scraped and snagged his hide, but he barely felt any of it as he clawed across the ground to get to those sounds. His hearts beat faster with each passing moment, and his breaths were ragged and strained.

The same thoughts repeated in his head over and over, like the simple blessings and prayers sometimes chanted by spiritspeakers.

Be all right, Ivy.

Almost there.

Be all right.

The low passage opened on a place not unlike one of Takarahl's understone chambers; a den the xiskals must have cleared amidst the thorny, tangled vines. The humans were clustered at the center, several holding their metal knives—bloody metal knives. The carcasses of many xiskals were scattered around them.

A few of the beasts were still alive, growling and gnashing their fangs at the humans.

Urkot's hulking form was visible on the far side of the group, but Ketahn didn't see Ivy. Where was she? Where was her scent? All he could smell was blood, human sweat, and the musty stench of nesting xiskals. Any traces of Ivy were buried.

Ketahn lunged at the closest beast. His lower hands struck the xiskal on its underside, claws punching through flesh before the strength of the blow lifted the creature into the air and flipped it over. It yelped in pain and came down hard.

A human leaned out of the group, driving a spear into the fallen xiskal. The beast writhed, but its struggles rapidly weakened; it was motionless within the space of a few heartbeats. The human turned her head toward Ketahn, her sweat-dampened golden hair brushing her shoulders. Despite the gloom, despite the dirt and blood smeared on her cheek, Ivy's blue eyes were bright—with fear, yes, but also with relief and something far deeper.

With a growl, Urkot threw himself to the side, driving three of his legs down on the only surviving xiskal. The creature's agonized cry blended with the sharp sound of crunching bone.

Ketahn had already closed the distance between himself and Ivy. She released her spear, leaving it stuck in the dead beast, and turned to face him fully just before he caught her in his arms and lifted her against his chest. She wrapped her arms tight around his neck as his claspers hooked around her backside. She immediately lifted her legs to either side of him.

"My heartsthread," he rasped. His inner heat intensified, but now it drained the strength from his limbs rather than bolstering it. He smoothed a hand over her tousled hair again and again. Ketahn might have been content to sink to the ground right there, curl up around his mate, and hold her until the Tangle swallowed them up.

"I'm okay," Ivy panted, her breath hot on his neck. "I'm okay. We're all okay."

He breathed her in, willing her sweet scent to battle away the stench of blood, to overcome the xiskals' musk, to soothe the fear that had lodged in his core. He'd lost friends and family aplenty during his lifetime. He'd seen them wrapped and buried in the wet jungle dirt, had seen them left to rot in the mires, had seen them laid in holes deep beneath Takarahl, but his sorrow for those loses hadn't been anything like his fury and panic at the thought of losing Ivy.

She was okay. She was here in his arms, and she was okay. He hadn't been too late. He hadn't failed.

Ketahn was unaware of how much time passed—he knew only that his breathing eventually eased, his hearts slowed, and his instinctual need to destroy everything to protect Ivy retreated to the recesses of his mind.

Reluctantly, he pulled his head back to look down at her. Her pale skin was smeared with blood and dirt. His mandibles fell, and the ashes of those inner fires stirred, threatening to rekindle. "I am sorry, my *nyleea*. I have covered you in blood again."

She smiled and ran her fingertips down the side of his face. "It will wash away."

Ketahn's fingers flexed, and he clutched her tighter as he tipped his cheek into her touch. The gentleness of her hand was at odds with the ferocity and brutality of moments before.

Will hissed. "Fucker got me."

But it seemed those bloody matters were not yet done.

Ketahn lifted his eyes to look over the humans. They'd already been sweaty and dirty from their long trek through the jungle, and now they were bloody too, all bearing glimmers of fear in their eyes though the immediate threats were now gone. That fear could consume them if left untended—but it could also be shaped into a tool as readily as a piece of blackrock or a block of wood.

Will had a hand clamped on his left arm over a long, deep gash. Blood seeped from the wound and dripped onto the ground.

"Let me take a look," Diego said, carefully taking Will's arm and examining it. His brows were pinched as he gently prodded the cut. "Spread your fingers for me and then squeeze them in a fist."

Will did as instructed, baring his teeth in pain. His fingers moved stiffly but seemed not to have lost any flexibility.

"Good," Diego said, using one hand to grasp the strap of his bag as he shrugged it off his shoulder. "It's a nasty cut, but it looks worse than it really is. I'm going to get you patched up, all right?"

Will nodded.

Diego looked over the others. "Anyone else hurt?"

Lacey dropped to her knees, breath heavy, and swept her hair out of her face. "Just a few scratches."

The other humans replied similarly; minor cuts, scrapes, and bruises, but nothing else as severe as Will's wound—and nothing worse.

Cole chuckled; the sound was laced with a hint of bitterness. "Guess we got lucky."

Will snorted, cocking a brow. His expression was somewhere between pained and amused. "If this was good luck, I don't want to see what bad luck looks like."

"Now you know," Ketahn said in measured English, gently lowering Ivy to her feet. "There is danger, always. Death, always. But we are most strong together."

"I can't help but feel like we skipped a couple steps between being *ama-chur* survivalists and fighting wild animals to the death," Callie said. She was bent forward, hands braced on her thighs, as she caught her breath.

"Sometimes the best way to learn is to do," said Ahmya, her voice small and soft but somehow not weak. "You know…kind of like sink or swim? At least that's how my dad taught us." She raised a hand and tucked her hair behind her ear. "Anyway, are you okay, Ella?"

Ella nodded; beads of sweat dripped down her face. "Yeah, thanks."

"Is there still some light out there, Ketahn?" Diego asked.

Ketahn nodded. "For a little longer."

"Will, clamp a hand on that cut. Let's get you out of here."

"Let us all go," Ketahn said, waving them onward.

The humans left the way they'd come in, a couple of them glancing back before doing so. Ketahn could not help but wonder if this was the first time some of them had ever fought for survival. He could not imagine the sort of lives humans led on their world, even after all Ivy had told him, but he would not have complained about a lack of excitement if it meant his mate never had to look her potential death in the face again.

His hold on Ivy lingered until the last of the humans, Cole, had entered the low, thorny tunnel. Ketahn bent down, tipping his headcrest against her forehead. She briefly reached up and twined her fingers in his hair, standing on her toes to peck a kiss on his mouth. Then she pulled away. He let her go and watched as she crouched and entered the passage.

"I should have known," Urkot rumbled behind him.

Ketahn turned to look at his friend, mandibles sagging.

"Should have seen the signs, should have smelled them," Urkot continued, thumping a leg on the ground. "But I did not. I…I was too focused on…"

"Enough, Urkot," Ketahn said softly. He extended a foreleg, brushing it against Urkot's. "You did what was necessary to protect them. Any closer to the edge of the snarl, and the yatins might have reached them."

Grunting, Urkot brought his upper forearms together and sank into a low bow. "You entrusted me with your mate, Ketahn, and I—"

Ketahn turned to face his friend fully and thrust his upper arms out, catching Urkot by his broad shoulders and forcing him to straighten. "You kept her alive. You fought for her, bled for her, and for that you forever have my thanks. As though you had not already earned my thanks a thousand times over before this day."

The vrix held one another's gazes for several heartbeats before Urkot finally looked away. His voice was low and gravely when he spoke. "They attacked because we were in their nest, but…I think they smelled sickness on that female. Ella."

The dread in Ketahn's gut—which should have vanished when he was reunited with Ivy—coiled tighter through his insides. "They sought to separate her from the others."

"Yes. Had the *hyu-nins* not grouped around her…"

There was no need to complete the thought; they knew what would've happened. The silence spoke loudly enough for the direness of what might have been.

A tired trill sounded in Urkot's chest. "Come. This place stinks. I am ready for the fresh jungle air once again."

Standing aside, Ketahn waved Urkot on. As the other male crawled into the passage, Ketahn turned to survey the nest. Normally, he would have dragged the carcasses out, skinned them, and carved what meat he could, but the group would be busy enough with the other harvests—and the meat and hides of yatins were far preferable to that of xiskals.

Releasing a slow, unsteady breath, Ketahn exited the snarl to rejoin his mate.

The humans were gathered several segments from the yatin that had died at the edge of the thorn snarl. Diego was tending Will's wound with his strange human tools, using one hand to work while holding Will's hand with the other, and the two males looked up at each other every few moments.

A curious smile formed on Will's lips. If he was still in pain, it no longer showed.

Ella was on the ground, lying on her side with her upper body and head leaning on one of the bags they'd brought on the journey. Though she seemed to be sleeping, her eyes sometimes fluttered open to glance at the others; even such a tiny movement seemed to tire her.

Ahnset, Telok, and Rekosh joined Ketahn and Urkot.

"Are you hurt?" Ketahn asked, studying his friends and broodsister.

"No wounds that could not be bound by some silk," Telok replied.

"We will all have aches in the morning," Ahnset said.

Ketahn chittered. "New and old."

His body was already pulsing with some of those aches, which would grow stronger as he put distance between himself and the battle that had taken place here.

"That tool he is using," Rekosh said, gesturing toward Diego, "it seals the wounds like webbing, only faster and cleaner."

"Human *technology*," Ketahn replied in English. His eyes had settled upon Ivy, who was helping the others wash their wounds in preparation for Diego's attentions. There was a slight tremor in her hands, but she held her composure well.

He could not wait to have her alone so he could rain upon her all the tenderness and affection she deserved—and more.

"Are we meant to understand that word?" Telok asked.

Ketahn turned his palms skyward. "No. But it is the word, all the same. I have told you, many of their tools are beyond our imagining."

After the humans had tended their wounds, Diego, Lacey, Ahmya, and Ivy walked over to the vrix. With Ivy translating, the four offered to help the vrix tend their injuries.

Ketahn's friends seemed caught off guard by the offer, but they accepted gratefully. Ketahn and Ivy both had to hold in their laughter at the way his friends fidgeted as the humans touched them and cleaned and sealed their cuts and scrapes.

Soon, only Ahnset's wounds remained untreated. She looked at Ketahn questioningly every time Diego spoke to her or was about to apply one of his strange tools.

When all was done, everyone looked tired—both human and vrix.

"That was fucking crazy," Cole muttered, surveying the dead yatins.

"These things make elephants look small," said Will.

"Fuck them." Cole waved his hands dismissively. "I'm ready to collapse in my pod and sleep for two damn days."

Diego knelt over his bag to put away his tools. "I finally agree with you on something, man."

Ketahn trilled. "We cannot leave."

"What?" Callie asked as all the humans looked at Ketahn.

"Don't tell me there are more of those things," said Will, wide-eyed.

Raising his mandibles in a smile, Ketahn dipped his head

toward the fallen yatins. "Their meat and hide is very good. We cannot leave it."

"Are you serious?" asked Lacey. She looked at Ivy, then Ketahn, then back again. "He's serious, isn't he?"

Ivy laughed. "He's serious."

"Fuuuuuck," Cole groaned, shoulders sagging.

"Be fast, humans," Ketahn said with a chitter. "The jungle is dangerous at night."

"Was that sarcasm? Is he being sarcastic?" Callie put her hands on her hips and cocked her head, regarding Ketahn closely.

"Maybe it's better when he's serious," said Lacey with a shrug. She drew her knife from its little holder on the leg of her jumpsuit. "From beekeeper to butcher. Not the career change I'd planned on."

As the group converged on the nearest yatin, Ketahn's dread eased. For all that had gone wrong, this had been an encouraging day. There was promise here. There was potential for a future of cooperation and prosperity. There was potential for he and Ivy to live a long, happy life together in peace.

They just had to, as a human might have said, get the fuck away from Takarahl first.

CHAPTER 20

EVERYONE, including Ketahn and the other vrix, felt the aftermath of their battle with the yatins and xiskals the next morning. The meal they shared outside the ship was quiet but for the crackling of the fire and the occasional soft groans from those sitting around it—sometimes in pain, sometimes in appreciation of the freshly cooked meat.

The humans wore their bruises plainly. Thanks to Ivy, Ketahn had grown familiar with such wounds, and knew they were typically minor. Otherwise, he'd have been alarmed as he surveyed the humans and seen the starkly discolored patches of their flesh—especially those on his mate's body.

The injuries on the vrix were, as expected, less noticeable, especially after Diego's efforts. Whatever he'd used to treat the vrix's cuts and scrapes had done its job well. All their wounds were healing clean and quick. Even Ahnset and Urkot, who'd taken more punishment than the others, seemed only mildly bothered by their healing injuries.

Waking up inside the crashed human ship surrounded by so many slumbering forms had been strange for Ketahn. He'd not shared a sleeping space with anyone apart from Ivy in a long while—not since the war against Kaldarak. Falling asleep had been difficult; though the humans had dimmed the lights, the room had maintained an unnatural glow, and he'd been more aware of the faint thrumming under the floor than ever.

His roving eyes had often fallen upon the unopened pods. The humans had found blankets to drape over those pods, making them remind Ketahn of death shrouds. He knew the other vrix—even Ahnset, Rekosh, and Urkot, who spent most of their time understone—were also uncomfortable.

But this was necessary. The sooner everyone grew accustomed to sleeping near one another, the better…and for now, the ship was the most secure place to den.

The relative silence around the fire was broken when Callie said she missed something called *cawf-ee*, prompting a conversation between the humans. Many of the others agreed with Callie. They quickly concluded that there should have been *cawf-ee* in the ship's emergency supplies—apparently, it was just as important as medicine and food. Ivy laughed when Ketahn asked her about it and explained what this *cawf-ee* was and why humans drank it.

Based solely on the way these humans looked, he had to agree with them. They could all use some *cawf-ee* to get them moving.

Despite the humans' weariness and injuries, Ketahn could not allow them more rest. Not yet. Only the sight of Ivy wincing as she stood up might have swayed him; it was hard to bring himself to push her now, after he'd done it so much since he'd woken her. It was hard knowing he would only bring her more suffering.

But sometimes suffering was necessary to win peace, to create security, and to earn those quiet, intimate moments.

Ketahn was met with a chorus of groans when he told everyone to gather their bags and weapons so they could climb out of the pit.

238

"We have many to do," he told them. "There is not time to make tears."

"He just told us to quit crying, didn't he?" Will asked Ivy.

Ivy chuckled as she raised her arms over her head and stretched. "Yeah, basically."

"So what's the plan for today?" Lacey asked, rising to her feet.

"Lessons," Ketahn replied, smiling.

Cole pulled on his pack. "Let's hope these *lessons* don't try and kill us today."

"I think it's an *awwtoe matik eff* if you die," said Diego.

"Must be one of those pass or fail kind of *klassiz*," added Ahmya. "You either get an a plus…"

"Or you never get another *grayd* again," said Lacey, sweeping her red hair out of her face and tying it back with a leather string. She looked at Telok and pointed up. "Am I going with you again?"

Her meaning must have been clear enough; Telok's mandibles twitched, and he waved her toward him with a low but pleased trill.

It took longer to get everyone to the top than it had the morning before, but there was less fear and uncertainty in the process today. Ketahn could only hope it meant there was trust growing between the vrix and the humans; they would need a lot of it to succeed in the coming trials.

Though he longed to keep Ivy in place on his hindquarters with her arms around his middle, Ketahn set her on her feet once they were at the top of the pit, told the group what he intended for the day, and led them into the Tangle. The humans' pace was a bit slower than before, but they seemed more confident in navigating the jungle's obstacles. As small as the improvement was, it was an improvement nonetheless. Though they were battered and weary, the humans were also more alert

—perhaps too much so, as a few of them seemed to start at any sound.

They would find the right measure of wariness as they learned more about the jungle and its many signs and sounds.

The vrix continued teaching as they went, focusing on finding material to craft and repair weapons and foraging food that would keep fresh during their upcoming travels. Ketahn did not lead them nearly as far from the pit as he had during their previous trek, instead setting a path around it in gradually widening circles. Should anything happen again, he wanted a fast, direct route to their shelter.

Ella again rode on Ahnset. Though she'd been the only one to have escaped the yatins and xiskals without a single wound, she looked no better than she had the day before. While she was awake, her eyes were often bright and curious—but sometimes they were unsettlingly distant and empty. Many times, Ketahn had glanced at Ella to find her eyes closed and her cheek resting against Ahnset's broad back.

The other humans checked on her occasionally, none more often than Diego. After midday, as the others sat with Telok and Urkot and learned to shape shafts for their spears, Diego approached Ivy and Ketahn and asked to speak with them alone.

The three walked a short distance away from the others and rounded a tree.

"Ella's getting worse," Diego said, casting his eyes in the direction of the others, whose voices drifted over in light, humorous conversation.

"I know," Ivy said, frowning down at her upturned palms. "I don't know what to do. Ahmya said she could barely wake her up this morning."

Diego's mouth fell into a frown, too, and he brushed his hand across the tiny, abrasive hairs that had grown on his cheeks and jaw, making a rasping sound. "It's stasis sickness. That's what the signs have pointed to from the beginning, but I didn't want to believe it, and kept praying it wasn't true. There's no denying it now."

"What can we do for her?"

"About all we can do is force her to rest. That's the only thing that might help, but even that..." Diego sighed heavily, his shoulders sagging. "Her organs are failing."

Ivy caught her bottom lip between her teeth and flicked her eyes, which were now glistening with tears, up to Diego. "So it's just a matter of time?"

He nodded and pressed his lips together.

Ketahn released a low growl and reached back to grasp his hair, tugging on it hard enough to produce a flare of pain across his head. Though it had only been a few days, these humans were Ivy's people—and because of that, they were *his*, too. He'd come to know them a little better in this short while. He'd caught glimpses of who they were. He'd seen their kindness, their compassion, their anger and bitterness. Their hope and determination.

These humans really weren't so different from the vrix. They had so much more in common than he could ever have imagined.

And Ketahn did not want to lose any of them. He'd lost far too many of those who'd been following his lead during the war.

"All your technology," Ketahn said, waving a hand. "Cannot that help?"

"She needs a *hosspit uhl*," Diego replied, "or at least the kind of equipment they'd have in one. They had all that stuff on the ship, but we don't have access to any of it now. All we've got is a bunch of fucking first aid kits that won't do her any damned good."

Frustration had seeped into Diego's voice as he spoke, adding force to his words, and Ketahn understood that emotion on a primal level. He understood that sense of helplessness.

Ketahn gently placed a hand on Diego's shoulder. "We will do as you say. When we go back, she will rest. She will rest until we go from your ship forever. Whatever you need for her, say. I will make it done."

Diego clenched his jaw and nodded.

Ketahn tapped his foreleg against Diego's leg before placing a hand on Ivy's lower back and guiding her toward the others. "Come. There is much to do before sunfall."

Though everyone was still at work on their spear shafts, Ketahn did not wait long before telling them to gather their things so they could travel. The group's numbers would ward off some threats, but as the yatins had demonstrated, not all beasts could be frightened away. With so few weapons, the group was more vulnerable out here than ever. It would be wisest to finish their work in safety. The pit was the best place if they had to remain stationary for a prolonged time.

But that did not mean an end to the day's lessons—or to Ketahn measuring the humans' skills. Once everyone was packed and standing, he gestured to the humans. "Guide us back."

They responded with blank stares, a few incredulous utterances, and one muttered *what the fuck?*

"Guide us," Ketahn repeated.

When Rekosh asked what was happening, Ketahn explained. Both Rekosh and Telok chittered; Urkot thumped the ground and grunted.

"Is this the time to jest with them?" asked Ahnset. She stood with Ella on her hindquarters, her lower hands covering the human's—which were pressed to the sides of Ahnset's abdomen. The little female's arms couldn't even wrap fully around Ahnset's middle.

Ketahn sketched a quick gesture of apology. "It is no jest, broodsister."

"Just a test," Telok said.

After a couple false starts—which the humans corrected themselves—they began their return journey. Ketahn and the other vrix offered no guidance, and neither did Ivy, despite some of the others asking her to do so. She seemed to understand Ketahn's aim and exchanged knowing smiles with him whenever the group paused to discuss their intended path.

Ketahn couldn't help chittering when she came to him during one of those stops and said, "You do realize I have no idea which way to go either, don't you? I'd get us lost."

"How could that be?" He lifted a hand, brushing his knuckles gently down her cheek. "So long as I am with you, my heartsthread, I can never be lost."

Though her cheeks were already pinkened from walking, they darkened further. She smiled and turned her head to press her lips to his fingers. "I'm never lost with you either."

The humans' process was interesting to Ketahn. They spoke at length, suggesting various means by which they might determine the direction of the pit, offering a great many reasons for why each idea was right or wrong. A couple times, those discussions teetered on the edge of becoming arguments, especially as Cole seemed to think his opinion was correct simply because he spoke louder than the others.

Somehow, the group meandered in the right general direction. Somehow, their voices did not attract any curious, hungry beasts.

But it was Ahmya who impressed Ketahn most during the journey—and it was her who set them firmly in the correct direction.

"It's this way," Cole said, jabbing a thumb toward distant Takarahl.

Callie shook her head. "That can't be right."

"We just walked in circles all day. It has to be this way."

"Yeah, but which way were we walking in circles?" asked Diego.

"It's that way," Ahmya said, lifting a tiny hand and pointing straight toward the pit. "At least…I think."

"No way," said Cole.

Callie looked doubtful.

Rekosh was staring at Ahmya intently, undoubtedly having no idea what she was saying but understanding what was happening all the same.

"Why that way, Ahmya?" Ketahn asked gently.

She dropped her hands to her stomach and looked down at them, brow furrowing. She shifted her weight on her feet, fidgeting the way a broodling who'd been caught doing something wrong might have. "Because…of the flowers."

"What flowers?"

Ahmya glanced up at him and pointed toward a cluster of plants several segments away, where hundreds of tiny suncrest flowers were drooping in the late day shade, their petals in the slow process of closing. "I've seen those flowers all over as we've walked, today and yesterday. In the morning, they're always directly in the sun. By midday, they're in the shade, and they start to close. Every time I see them, they're always facing the sunrise.

"And, well…I've paid attention to them today, and used them to keep track of how we were always turning. So I think it's that way." She again gestured toward the pit.

The humans all looked at Ketahn, some of them with expressions of disbelief, all seeking confirmation. He glanced from Ahmya to the suncrest flowers and let his gaze linger there as he made a slow, thoughtful buzz in his chest.

"What did she say?" Rekosh asked, his eyes still on Ahmya.

"She used the suncrest flowers to mark our direction as we traveled," Ketahn replied in vrix, smiling.

The spark that had appeared in Rekosh's eyes when he'd first seen Ahmya the day before intensified. "I knew there was much behind those shy eyes. She is quiet, but she is keen."

Telok stepped up beside Ketahn and cocked his head. "These *hyu-nins* learn swiftly."

"Um… Why are they staring at me?" Ahmya asked, looking at Ivy.

Ivy rolled her eyes in that disturbing human way and nudged Ketahn with her elbow. "Oh, just tell them already."

Ketahn chittered, bumping a leg against Ivy's backside. "You are right, Ahmya. About the flowers and our path."

"Woo! Way to go, Ahmya," Lacey said with a grin.

Ella smiled. "You're on your way to becoming our nature guide. Guess working with flowers really paid off."

Cole kicked at the ground, tearing up some of the vegetation beneath his boot as he muttered, "Fucking flowers."

Diego grinned. "Guess we better start paying attention to those fucking flowers, huh, Cole?"

"Maybe we can keep some flowers on that bad-ass deck you're going to build," said Callie.

Despite himself, the corner of Cole's mouth twitched up. "Maybe. I've thrown together a few pretty sweet planters in my time."

Ketahn took the lead for the rest of the journey. There was still light in the sky by the time they were all safely at the bottom of the pit—not that any of it reached them there.

They lit the fire, set more meat to cooking, and continued working on the spears. With the help of the vrix, the humans selected pieces of blackrock from those Urkot had brought, honed them, and fastened them to the shafts with tight-wrapped silk threading.

Weary as everyone was, there was far more conversation during this meal than the one they'd shared in the morning—and more laughter and chittering.

At one point, as the darkness grew ever deeper and shrank the world into the range of the firelight, Diego said, "Wish we had more light."

"We can set up a bunch of those solar lanterns," Callie suggested.

Will grinned, extended an arm, and bumped Diego's knee with his fist. "I have an idea. Don't know if it'll work, but…" He climbed to his feet and hurried toward the ship. "Stay there. You'll know if it works or not in a few minutes."

The others watched Will navigate the debris-strewn ground until he'd disappeared into the ship.

"Wonder what he's doing," said Lacey.

"Don't know," Diego said distractedly. Something had softened in his smile; he continued to stare in the direction Will had gone for a few heartbeats after the other human was out of sight.

The conversations resumed—until a sudden light glared across the pit.

Ketahn heard gasps, hisses, and at least one grunt as he slitted his eyes and raised a hand to shield them from the unexpected light. He turned toward its source—the crashed ship.

His vision adjusted slowly, revealing the bottom of the pit in a way he'd never seen it before. The light shining from the ship was the same sort of pure white that illuminated the chamber within, and out here it created long, deep, harshly contrasting shadows. Its luminescence was far greater than that of the fire; this was like having the cresting sun beaming directly upon them.

It also shed more light upon the outside of the ship. Many of the humans were staring at it now—at the dirt-caked metal and the moss, vines, and muck clinging to it. The human writing there was just visible from where they all sat.

"That's still…it's just crazy," Diego said somberly. "A few days ago, I was looking up at that ship, and it was gleaming. Fucking gleaming, bright as the sun. I was so nervous and excited I thought I was going to puke right there."

"I was excited too," Ella said with a small smile. She sat with her back leaned against the side of Ahnset's hindquarters. "I couldn't wait to see a new world and discover new plants and animals." She looked at Ketahn and his friends and then up to Ahnset. "But I think this is even more amazing."

Ahnset glanced from Ella to Ketahn. "What did she say?"

Ketahn took a few moments to consider Ella's words—and the meaning behind them. It was impossible not to look at her now and recall what Diego had said, that this little human was dying. "She is glad to have met us and seen the Tangle."

Mandibles twitching, Ahnset looked down at Ella again. Ketahn and Ivy had not told anyone else what Diego had shared, but he knew the other vrix could smell it on Ella—the sickness Urkot thought had worked the xiskals into a frenzy.

Ahnset tipped one of her bent legs toward Ella, brushing it against the human's arm. Ella's smile grew, and she leaned her head on Ahnset's leg, closing her eyes.

"I was biting my nails while I waited to get in, just staring at it," Lacey said, looking down at her splayed fingers. "I haven't done that in years, but the habit came right back because, at that moment, I knew nothing would ever be the same again."

"I almost changed my mind," Callie said. She had a small stone in one hand, rolling it between her fingers slowly, contemplatively. "I just had this...feeling that something bad was going to happen."

Diego chuckled. "Proof of *sykik* powers?"

Callie laughed and shook her head, closing her fingers around the stone. "Nah. Just nerves. What the hell had I done before getting on that ship? I spent my whole life in school, learning in these safe, controlled environments, and then I went into training with the *Ee nih shuhtiv*. Getting on that ship meant actually *doing* something. Something no one else had ever done."

"Which is terrifying," said Ahmya, who sat with her knees up and her arms wrapped around them. "But...it's exciting, too.

Somnium means dream, and that's what the ship was. The dream of the human race."

"And now look at it." Cole fed another stick into the fire. "Nothing more than fucking scrap metal."

"No, it's not," said Ivy quietly. "It's a *toom*. And a…a *mehmor eeul*. To all those people, to all the dreams we'll never achieve, and to all the dreams we never knew we had." She turned to look at Ketahn, gazing up into his eyes. "My dream."

Ketahn placed his palm on her cheek, sliding the tips of his fingers into her golden hair and stroking her soft skin with the pad of his thumb. "My heartsthread."

Cole cleared his throat. "Yeah, well, my dream sure as fuck wasn't to crash here."

"Really? That's the whole reason I signed up, man," said Diego. "Who doesn't like getting attacked by giant *pig eluh fentz* and crazy shit like that? Makes life interesting."

"It actually worked?" Will's excited voice came from the broken ship, calling everyone's attention to him. He'd emerged from the hole and was staring up at the brilliant light, a broad smile on his face as he walked back toward the group.

The humans cheered. Ketahn was fairly certain Diego started it, but the enthusiasm spread through the group quickly —even to Cole—and it seemed to Ketahn that it was about something more than the light.

Will was laughing when he sat beside Diego, eyes downcast and smile stretched even wider. "I didn't do much, really. I'm just glad I have all these years of *ai tee* training under my belt. It's all worth it to have turned on a single light."

Diego raised an arm and gave Will a little shove with his elbow; the gesture seemed just as playful as any time Ivy had done something similar to Ketahn.

"I have no idea of what they are saying," Rekosh said, "but find myself fascinated regardless."

"Strange creatures," rumbled Urkot, "but I like them."

"There are things to admire about them." Telok was watching Lacey, who, like the rest, was laughing and smiling.

Rekosh had settled his gaze on Ahmya. "They are very different from us. From each other, also. Yet there is undeniable beauty to them. Unexpected beauty."

"There is," Ketahn agreed, looking at his mate.

Even as the jungle above fell into total darkness, the vrix and humans at the bottom of the pit remained around the fire, talking, laughing and chittering, growing more comfortable with one another. Ivy and Ketahn bridged conversations between their kinds by translating. With the white light shining from the ship, everyone seemed to forget their weariness.

Soon enough, Urkot approached Callie. He gently indicated the stone in her hand, and, insisting that Ketahn and Ivy allow him to communicate with her on his own, coaxed her to move a little away from the fire. He sank down beside a patch of cleared ground and opened one of his hands, displaying a collection of little stones on his palm.

Urkot used a claw to draw a circle in the dirt. Backing away about a segment, he took one of the little stones—marked with a black streak of charcoal—between forefinger and thumb and tossed it into the circle. He then gestured to Callie.

She looked from him to the stone in her hand. Scooting back, she positioned herself beside Urkot, pressed her lips together, and tossed her stone into the circle.

Urkot's second stone struck Callie's, bumping it out of the circle with a little clack. She watched him as he made a mark on the ground before him. Then he divided the remaining stones on his palm, handing her the half that weren't marked.

"Wait…are they playing *marbulls?*" asked Diego.

Ivy laughed. "Looks like it."

Callie grinned and plucked a small, round pebble from her palm. "Oh, it's on now."

The two played back and forth with greater speed and intensity; Urkot remained largely quiet save for the occasional grunt or trill when Callie bumped one of his stones out of the circle, whereas Callie was rather vocal, teasing Urkot good naturedly and celebrating her plays.

In the end, they counted the stones each had remaining in the circle, tallying them with their marks for knocking each other's stones out. Urkot chittered—he'd won by three.

Callie leaned forward, scooping up her stones. "All right, big *gai*, we're going again. Come on." Grinning, she gestured at Urkot's marked stones.

He chittered and gathered his stones. Their second round went fast, the turns blazing by like blows exchanged between two warriors. The other humans and vrix continued watching, jesting with one another and the two competitors while both Urkot and Callie grew more and more intense.

Callie's final toss knocked out two of Urkot's stones, granting her the win by a single mark.

"Ha! Take that!" She jumped to her feet and danced with her arms in the air, declaring in a singsong voice, "I'm a winner! I'm a winner!"

Rekosh leaned toward Ketahn. "Is that some kind of mating dance?"

Ketahn could only look to Ivy for an answer, who burst out laughing.

"Does that mean…no?" Rekosh tilted his head.

Still snickering, Ivy brushed the moisture from her eyes and shook her head. She replied in vrix. "It is called a *vik toree* dance."

Urkot watched Callie closely, his expression unreadable. The twitch in his mandibles might have meant anything—or nothing at all—but there was just a hint of heat in his gaze…

Suddenly aware that Urkot was staring, Callie stopped her dance. "What? You're not being a sore loser, are you?"

"I think you're celebrating a little too soon," Lacey said. "You're one and one. Need to have a tie breaker match."

Callie growled and dropped back down, eyes on Urkot as she picked up her stones. "Fine." Her grin returned. "Let's go, big *gai*. One more round."

Urkot's chitter was deep and rolling. "This female is small but fierce."

So is my Ivy.

Ketahn turned his eyes toward his mate, whose eyes were bright with laughter and lips were curled in a smile as she watched the game and cheered the players on. Ivy was happy amongst her kind. She was happy with humans and vrix together, bonding over the many things they had in common. Despite the hardships they were facing, despite the burden of all they'd done and yet needed to do, Ivy was thriving.

And Ketahn would do everything he could to ensure this group—his tribe—remained safe and whole. He would do everything to ensure his mate was happy.

CHAPTER 21

THE SPEAR STRUCK the rotted stump with a dull *thunk*, knocking dark splinters off the wood. The shaft quivered with the impact. Telok strode to it, grasped it with one hand, and tugged it free. More pieces of wood fell, these with a reddish hue from deeper inside the decaying stump.

Backing away from the stump, Telok gestured to it, and then pointed at Lacey.

She pressed her lips together and glanced uncertainly at the spear in her hand. As she changed her grip on it and raised it to throw, Telok walked over to her. Her uncertainty seemed to intensify as she stared up at Telok, but Ketahn saw a flicker of something else in her eyes, too. She didn't flinch when Telok extended two arms and, with a light touch, adjusted her hold on the spear.

He stood beside her and, with hands on her arm, slowly guided her through the throwing motion, pausing her arm during the peak of its arc. "Release here," he said in vrix, holding up a fist and opening his fingers. Then he continued the forward arc of his arm, aiming his fingertips at the stump. He released her and retreated a few steps.

Lacey nodded, and her features hardened in determination before she returned her attention to her target. She muttered something to herself that sounded like encouragement, released a breath, and threw.

The spear soared in a short arc, coming down on the stump at a skewed angle—but the head plunged deep into the wood.

Lacey spun around and raised her fists over her head. "Yes!"

Will and Diego, who were standing nearby, cheered and clapped. Lacey smiled, and her cheeks pinkened.

Bowing his head, Telok tapped his headcrest with his knuckle—a sign of respect between vrix who were not intimate enough to touch headcrests directly.

Lacey cocked her head at him, brow creasing, and mimicked his gesture. Though Telok's delighted trill was soft and low, Ketahn did not miss it.

As Lacey went to retrieve her spear, Telok waved Diego over for his turn. Ketahn folded his upper arms across his chest, tucked his spear in the crook of his lower right arm, and leaned a shoulder against the tree beside him. He let his eyes roam for a few heartbeats, scanning the jungle, before bringing it to rest on the other group.

Urkot and Rekosh were with Callie and Ahmya, teaching the females to wield their spears in close combat. They were running through exercises to familiarize the humans with the feel of their weapons—weapons that would serve as their most important tools here in the Tangle. They would need to become so comfortable with those spears that the weapons felt like extensions of their bodies, no different than claws or fangs were for the vrix.

Ketahn wished there was enough time for the humans to achieve that before they would have to delve into the unknown.

Movement from behind caught his attention, but he did not turn to look; Ahnset's familiar scent drifted to him on the still, humid air, mingling with the smells of wet dirt, rot, and growing things.

"All is quiet," Ahnset said softly, stopping beside him. She dipped her chin in the direction of the humans. "Apart from them, anyway."

"They are encouraging one another," Ketahn said.

Rekosh thrust his spear at Ahmya with deliberate slowness. Wide-eyed—and looking tiny as ever before the tall vrix—she shifted her weapon to deflect the thrust with her spear shaft, flinching as wood struck wood. With a gentle chitter, Rekosh demonstrated a potential counter, showing her how her size might aid her in striking his vulnerable underside.

"You really mean to leave the day after tomorrow?" Ahnset was regarding the humans too, mandibles twitching as though undecided on whether they wanted to rise or fall.

"Yes," Ketahn replied.

"They are not ready."

"Neither was I when first I ventured out with the Claw." Ketahn's mind flashed through memories of Ivy—of how frightened she'd been, of how incapable she'd seemed, of his certainty that she would have died without him. But she'd learned so much since then. "The Tangle is a swift teacher."

"Because those who do not learn die," Ahnset rumbled. On the edge of his vision, Ketahn saw her hands curl into fists.

"Telok, Rekosh, Urkot, and me will serve as their shields, Ahnset."

"No shield is impenetrable. They can be broken or bypassed." There was a subtle growl in her voice, a hint of frustration that she rarely let in.

Ketahn turned his head to look at her. The stiffness in his broodsister's posture was not the sort she assumed as Ahnset the Fang; this was not born of discipline.

"Ella is safe," he said, lowering his mandibles and shifting a leg outward to brush against hers. "I would not have left Ivy behind with her otherwise."

The hairs on Ahnset's leg rose, and she produced an unhappy buzz in the back of her throat. "I know, broodbrother. But…I should have remained behind to watch over them both."

"Every thread of me longs to be with my mate." Ketahn glanced in the direction of the pit, which was obscured by undergrowth and jutting roots. "I could toss a stone and hit the place in which she shelters, but even that distance is unbearable."

"Then at least allow one of us to go to her. To them. It would ease my thoughts, Ketahn."

Ketahn turned to face his sister fully. "This is necessary, Ahnset. I must lose these moments with Ivy to ensure I have as much time with her as possible in the years to come."

Ahnset lifted a hand, pressing her fist against Ketahn's chest. "Our friends are skilled. They are teaching the *hyu-nins* without us even now. The *hyu-nins* will learn what they must whether you and I are here or not."

"And we must watch, broodsister. These lessons and the jungle alike." Ketahn placed a hand over hers, curving his fingers around the top of her large fist. "You and I will make more of a difference here than down there."

Diego had volunteered to remain behind with Ella this morning after it had become clear the sickly female was not fit to travel—not even a short distance, not even with Ahnset's aid. He'd said he had a responsibility to Ella because she was his *patient*; Ketahn had the sense that Diego had not meant that word as his willingness to wait.

Ketahn had been hesitant to let Diego miss a day of learning and preparation. All the able humans needed to learn as much as they could before facing the ultimate test—before they were out in the Tangle with no promise of a safe place to sleep, no promise of fresh water and food, no promise of anything but danger.

Ivy had broken the standoff by saying she would stay with Ella instead. Ketahn had only barely suppressed his rage at the notion. It had been hard for him to leave her at the best of times, but after everything with the queen and the encounters with the yatins and the xiskals, he had no intentions of leaving her alone.

Ivy must have sensed his turmoil, for she'd reached up, taken his face between her hands, and drawn him closer, looking into his eyes. "Ella needs someone with her, and Diego needs to learn. I have a two-month head start on everyone else. It makes the most sense, Ketahn."

An immense pressure had built up within Ketahn. He might have snarled and thrown her over his shoulder in that moment, dragging her up into the jungle to stay with him regardless. He might have insisted upon staying with her, much like Ahnset had tried to do.

But he had not.

Ivy had told him she would stay in the ship with the chamber door sealed. That they'd be safer there than anywhere else. And he'd known she was right, but it had been so hard voice his agreement. It had been so hard to walk away.

There'd been a storm building inside Ketahn as he'd led the others outside and they'd made their ascent; he barely remembered what had been said, what had been done, until the sunlight had taken on the golden tint of midmorning.

"Ella is ill, Ketahn," Ahnset rasped, dragging his attention back into the present. She flicked her gaze toward the others. "Everyone can see it."

"I have never said otherwise."

"You have not, but you know more about it than the rest of us." Rather than the accusation those words should have contained, Ketahn heard only weariness and sorrow in his sister's voice.

Ketahn's hold on his spear tightened; he angled the shaft farther away from himself and Ahnset, unsure of what to say. Another spear struck the stump nearby, and the humans cheered again.

Releasing a heavy breath, Ketahn grasped his bound hair in one hand and tugged on it—as though the tiny flare of pain it produced could somehow clear his thoughts and coax all the right words out of his mouth.

"I do." He gestured toward the humans with a wave of his hand. "Diego told me and Ivy."

"Diego," Ahnset repeated, drawing out the syllables in typical vrix fashion. In time, she would grow more accustomed to the human words, and—

No. She would not. The day after tomorrow, Ketahn would lead these humans and his three friends deep into the Tangle to seek a place of sanctuary beyond everything he knew...and Ahnset would return to Takarahl.

The sadness that struck him in that moment seized his hearts and chilled his blood.

"He is a healer," Ahnset continued, "knowledgeable in the *hyu-nin* ways."

Ketahn let out another breath, this one slow and quiet, and tore his thoughts free of that sadness. It would linger for a time —likely for the rest of his life, never quite fading. But he still had no doubts or regret for what he intended to do. Ahnset understood.

He fixed his gaze on Diego, who was grinning as Will walked over to him. Diego raised a fist to chest level, and Will, also grinning, tapped his own fist against it. Ketahn had seen them perform the gesture several times; he would have to ask about it eventually.

"Yes," Ketahn said. "Their word is *nurse*."

"What does he say of Ella's illness?" Ahnset asked, leaning closer to Ketahn.

"That he might fix it if he had the right tools, but he does not."

"If we have to tear that *shit* apart to find those tools, Ketahn, I will—"

Ketahn gave her hand a squeeze, and she fell quiet.

"Ship," Ketahn corrected gently. "And they do not have the tools, broodsister. There is nothing he or the other humans can do. Ella is more than ill. She is dying."

Ahnset stared at him, her mandibles slowly twitching upward and spreading. A growl rumbled within her. "No. There must be something to be done. Must be a way."

Though he knew his sister well, he could not have anticipated how quickly she'd grow attached to these humans—more specifically, to Ella. Ahnset couldn't have understood more than a few human words at most, and she'd only known this group for a few days, yet she was determined to protect Ella.

"There is not, Ahnset."

"Not for the *hyu-nins*." Ahnset stepped back and swept her gaze around, fine hairs standing on end again. She spread her upper arms. "But we vrix have our ways. We…we can cleanse her, or make offerings to the Eight for aid. We can… We can…" Her eyes widened, and she snapped her hands into fists again before whirling back toward Ketahn. "Mender root, broodbrother! The *hyu-nins* must not know mender root, but we do. It cures many ailments."

"The last of the mender root I had, Ahnset, was used to occupy the Fangs in the queen's sanctum."

He'd smashed the roots and left them as a distraction when he infiltrated Takarahl to speak with Zurvashi—and the queen herself had crushed the batch before that. He could not help a pang of regret at that now, but how could he have known?

How could he have anticipated any of this on that fateful Offering Day when he'd taunted Zurvashi in front of the entire city?

"With you and Telok, we can find more," Ahnset said.

Ketahn clicked his fangs together and shook his head. "The closest I know of will take more than two full days to reach, collect, and bring back, if the patch has not already been torn up by beasts. And Diego told us there is nothing to be done, regardless."

"He does not know our kind, Ketahn. He does not know our ways."

"And you do not know these humans, Ahnset."

"I know them enough to understand that Ella"—she jabbed a finger in the direction of the pit—"does not deserve this slow death. She requires aid."

Ketahn held his ground. "And we are giving all we can to her."

"If there is more that can be done, we must do it."

Keeping his voice as steady as possible, he replied, "This matter is not so simple, broodsister."

"It is very simple, broodbrother." She stomped a thick leg on the ground as though to emphasize her words. "She requires aid. We may have a way to provide it. How would the Eight look upon us if we did nothing?"

"And by their eightfold eyes, what have *they* done?" he demanded in a harsh whisper. "While our kind suffers under Zurvashi, what aid have the Eight offered? If they care so little for the vrix, do you truly believe they care at all for the life of a single human?"

Ahnset's mandibles spread in anger, and she stood taller, squaring her shoulders. "The Eight are not to blame for the woes of our kind, Ketahn."

"Yet they may pass judgment upon us?"

Her mandibles clacked together dangerously close to Ketahn's head; he didn't flinch, didn't blink, didn't react. He just continued to hold her stare.

Something rumbled in Ahnset's chest. "That…that is not

what this is about. And it is unlike you to speak so."

"I have spoken so about the queen for years, broodsister. I have stood in the heart of Takarahl and conveyed as much to her directly."

She growled, but her mandibles fell suddenly, and her eyes rounded again. She turned her head—looking in the direction of the city. "There is mender root in Takarahl, Ketahn. And vrix healers who are experienced in its use."

Ketahn's heartsthread pulled taut, and his hearts thumped faster, harder, louder. "Ahnset, the mender root in Takarahl is controlled by the queen."

"And I am of the Queen's Fang, Ketahn."

"She will not relinquish any root to you, broodsister, and even if she did…" Ketahn threw three of his hands up, keeping one on his spear, and gestured to their surroundings. Spear shafts clacked together in a slow, steady rhythm as the humans continued practicing. Animals made their calls from much farther away, and birds gifted their songs to the sky. "You have been gone for days, with no one knowing where you went. If you were to return and request mender roots only to disappear again, she will suspect something. You will be followed, and it will not be by one or two Claws who can be easily eluded."

Ahnset growled again and turned away from him, stalking forward several segments. "So…so then we tell her, Ketahn. Tell her about the *hyu-nins*, tell her that one needs aid."

Heat skittered beneath Ketahn's hide, crackling like lightning to the ends of his limbs and reverberating back to roil at his core. His reply came out in a low snarl. "No."

"I have seen but a sliver of what these *hyu-nins* have wrought, Ketahn." She paced from side to side, eyes downcast. "Our kind would do well to work alongside theirs. To learn from each other and grow. Imagine what could be achieved if we had the same knowledge, the same capability."

Ketahn slammed a fist against the tree behind him. The bark crunched with the impact, crumbling to the jungle floor.

Ahnset stilled, snapping her gaze toward him.

"I said *no*," he growled. "Not a single word about the humans is to be uttered within a thousand segments of Takarahl."

"Queen Zurvashi has made our city strong, Ketahn," Ahnset said, facing him again. "Our ancestors warred with Kaldarak for generations, gaining and losing ground. She crushed them."

"*We*"—Ketahn pounded his chest with two fists—"crushed them, broodsister. We fought that war. We were the victors."

"And she was there to lead us, to spill her blood and the blood of our enemies at our side!"

"Over *fucking* roots!"

Ahnset's mandibles clacked together and twitched apart. "And now the thornskulls dare not attack. She will recognize that these *hyu-nins* can solidify Takarahl's power further, Ketahn. She will…she will see that a sacrifice of a few mender roots to heal Ella could be to the benefit of all the vrix under her rule."

Ketahn swept his arms to the side, cutting the air. "No, Ahnset. She will see either a way to solidify her own power…or a threat to it. And she does not tolerate threats."

Ahnset bent her forelegs, kneeling on the ground before Ketahn, and bowed forward. "She is as you have said, Ketahn, but she can be more. She is capable of more. But it will never come to be if you do not give her a chance. The queen knows that Takarahl's strength and prosperity is her own. She will see the benefit of helping these *hyu-nins*."

"She will have them slaughtered."

"I know your grudges, broodbrother, but all the queen has done she has done for Takarahl. Being a leader means making hard choices. It…means making sacrifices of the few to protect the many."

Ketahn huffed and stared into his sister's eyes, searching

them for the truth of her words. For her belief in them. "If you think Zurvashi has ever made a decision with the good of Takarahl in mind, Ahnset, you are more blind than I ever could have guessed."

"You judge her too harshly."

"And you do not judge her harshly enough!"

"The words of a male who does not know his place," she snapped.

Her voice struck Ketahn with the force of a charging yatin, blasting the heat out of his chest and stealing his breath for the space of a stilted heartbeat.

Ahnset recoiled, her mandibles falling uncertainly, and averted her gaze.

The fires flooded back into Ketahn, blazing along his heart-sthread and filling his veins. Fury thrummed within him. Yet who was he angry with? Ahnset? Zurvashi?

Himself?

Whether it had been laid out before him by the Eight or he'd spun it as he went, Ketahn had walked the tangled web that had brought him to this moment, and yet he could not unravel those threads to determine how he'd reached this. He and his brood-sister—along with the third of their brood, their brother Ishkal—had been inseparable as broodlings.

But he'd lost his broodbrother seven years ago, and he hadn't felt that sense of harmony with Ahnset in nearly as long. And curse the Eight if they were responsible, that hurt.

"Broodbrother, I—"

"I know what it means to lead," he said, his raw voice emerging like a frightened beast clawing out of his throat. "I know what it means to see those following me suffer. To see them die. I know how it feels to have their blood on my hide, on my hands, overpowering every other accursed scent.

"I was out here"—he jabbed his spear into the ground and released it, leaving it to stand on its own—"with our friends, with our broodbrother, leading them against an enemy *she* provoked."

Ahnset lifted her gaze to him, her eyes bright with concern and pain of her own. "Ketahn…"

"Understand me, Ahnset." His mandibles shuddered; the tremor continued along his spine and into his hindquarters, and he squeezed his eyes shut against it. "I held Ishkal as his blood pooled on the ground, I felt his grip on me weakening with each beat of his hearts. And I pleaded."

Ketahn opened his eyes, his voice faltering into a rasp. "I begged for the Eight to preserve him. The Protector, the Hunter, the Broodmother, the Rootsinger. The Delver, the Flamebearer, the Weaver, even the Shaper. I begged them all. And we both know what good that did. I will not go through that again, broodsister. Especially not with my mate."

Ahnset's posture sagged, and she looked down as though seeking something on the ground before her. Ketahn felt…tired. His anger was already fading, even if it wasn't gone, and he was just tired.

He brushed a leg against Ahnset's. "Ella is dying, Ahnset. I trust Diego's knowledge in that. We cannot change it."

With a low, rumbling trill, Ahnset turned her head toward the pit.

Ketahn moved closer to her. He braced his other foreleg against Ahnset's and reached up to catch her face between his hands, directing it toward him. "All we can do is ensure her death comes with as much comfort and joy as we can provide." He drew her head down, tipping their headcrests together. "That is more than most of us will ever get."

They remained like that for a time. Ahnset's scent familiar as always, even with that hint of Korahla lingering within it, and Ketahn drew comfort from it.

Would that he had eightdays more—years more—to speak with his sister, to address the pain of loss he knew they both carried. To find true understanding with one another and repair their bond fully.

When the siblings withdrew from each other, Ketahn wasn't sure what he felt. A heaviness in his spirit, yes; lingering sorrow in his hearts; fear for what was to come. But he would not relinquish his hope. And his feelings for Ivy, as powerful as they were complex, only strengthened his resolve to continue onward.

He scanned the surrounding jungle, silently admonishing himself for having grown lax in his duties as watcher, before finally looking at the others, who were still training.

"They are eight now," Ahnset said softly, "but...they will be seven soon. That is a bad omen."

"I will not let omens stop us, Ahnset. Nor will I let Zurvashi..."

There'd been more to that thought, but it dissipated into the still, stifling air before Ketahn could grasp it. The humans were eight strong—of course he'd noted the significance of that when he'd first realized their number. Two had remained at the ship this morning.

But there were only five here now. Will, Diego, Callie, Lacey, and Ahmya.

"Curse my eyes," he growled, striding forward.

The others faltered in their exercises as they noticed Ketahn's approach, their attention falling upon him.

"Cole." Ketahn spoke his question in English and repeated it in his native tongue. "Where is he?"

The humans exchanged questioning glances with each other. The other male vrix tilted their heads. Rekosh's mandibles twitched, and Urkot scratched absently at the scar on his side.

"He was not with Ahnset?" Rekosh asked.

Ahnset stopped beside Ketahn. "No. I was keeping watch of the jungle."

"How could I have lost track of one?" Telok asked, snapping

his mandible fangs. "How could I not have noticed one missing?"

"Because there were already two staying behind," Urkot replied.

"I thought he was with us," Diego said. "I remember seeing him while we were waiting to ride up."

Callie nodded. "Me too."

"But we all went to the top in one trip," said Ahmya. "Five humans, five vrix." As she said it, she moved her hands; fingers splayed, she placed one hand on the back of the other and lifted them higher.

Will pursed his lips and arched a brow. "So, he just stayed back? Was he feeling all right?"

"Yeah, it doesn't seem like his style to miss out on this kind of stuff," said Lacey, looking at the spear in her hand. "He's been all-in with all this *fizikull* training shit so far and trying to show us up."

"He didn't say anything about staying behind though, did he?" asked Callie.

Diego rubbed the short, dark hairs on his cheek and jaw and shook his head. "Not that I heard."

Rage bubbled in Ketahn's gut, gaining heat and density with each passing moment. He'd been too distracted to note the simple discrepancy that morning—with six humans meant to accompany them out of the pit, one of the vrix should have gone back down after the initial climb.

And Ketahn had meant to do so himself. But he'd been so focused on not wanting to leave Ivy behind, on fighting his need to return to her, that when he'd looked down to see no one at the bottom of the pit he'd not put another thought into it.

He'd immediately thrown all his focus into monitoring the training and the jungle. So much focus that he'd not realized they were short a human—a *particular* human.

"What is wrong, broodbrother? If he remained in the pit, he is safe," Ahnset said.

Cole had remained in the pit.

Snarling a curse that might have been in vrix—or might have been in English—Ketahn raced toward the pit, crashing through the undergrowth. Increasingly frantic energy suffused his limbs, pushing them harder, faster. His hearts thumped as rapidly as his legs struck the ground.

Cole had remained in the pit *with Ivy*.

CHAPTER 22

Ivy RUBBED her hand over Ella's back in slow, soothing circles as the woman dry heaved over the side of her cryochamber. Anything Ella had eaten the day before had been expelled last night, and she'd had no appetite since—not that she would've been able to keep anything down.

Helpless, Ivy stood by through Ella's pained retching and shuddering convulsions. The only comfort she could offer was in making sure Ella knew she wasn't alone. Ivy didn't know what else to do, didn't know how to ease the woman's suffering.

"You're okay," Ivy said, tasting the bitterness of the lie as soon as the words left her mouth and hating it.

"No, I'm not." Ella shook her head, making her hair pull loose from its bun and tumble around her face. Her body trembled, and a choked sob escaped her. "I'm not okay and I'm not… I'm not getting any better."

She clutched the side of the pod and dry heaved again.

Chest constricting, Ivy gathered Ella's hair and held it back. Tears stung her eyes as despair and guilt flooded her. She couldn't help but feel like this was her fault. She'd woken Ella from stasis; had she done something wrong?

I woke them all the same way.

But why was this happening to Ella and no one else?

We knew there was a chance of stasis sickness when we were put under. It was explained to us. We accepted it.

Because they said they could treat it. They said it could be fixed.

Ivy pressed her lips together.

If I'd just let her sleep, she could have died peacefully. She wouldn't be going through...this.

How could I have known? I couldn't have. I just... I just wanted them to have a chance. I wanted them all *to have a chance.*

Ella drew in a few shallow, wheezing breaths, and struggled to sit up. Ivy helped her to lay back against the cryochamber's cushioned interior. Ella winced, hissing through her teeth as she clutched her side.

Ivy didn't rush her, pausing whenever needed until finally she was settled down with a blanket tucked around her.

Ella closed her eyes and was still except for the erratic rise and fall of her chest with her rasping breaths. It was crushing to see her lying there, so thin and pale, her cheeks hollow, and deep, dark circles beneath her eyes. One of her hands rested on her chest, looking skeletal with its knuckles and tendons standing out through her skin. The woman's cheeks were wet with tears.

She looked nothing like she had when she'd awoken from cryosleep only a few days ago.

Ivy brushed damp hair off Ella's forehead.

"I'm dying, aren't I?" Ella asked, opening her eyes to look up at Ivy. Despite her sickness, there was such clarity within their green depths.

Unable to lie again—but also unable to speak around the tightness in her throat—Ivy nodded.

"I...I thought so. I mean how could I not?" With tear filled eyes, Ella looked up at the pristine white ceiling. "I saw it in Diego's eyes. The fear, the pity. I see it in the way everyone looks at me. And I… God, I can feel it, too. I can feel myself dying."

Ivy placed her hand on Ella's. "I'm so sorry, Ella. I didn't mean for this to happen."

Shivering, Ella turned her hand over and clutched Ivy's, giving it a weak squeeze. "I know. I just…" She turned her head and looked at Ivy, her tears spilling. "I wish I had been able to see more of this world. To explore it. I wish I could have known more about the vrix. I want to learn their language, their culture, to just…get to know *them*. They're so, so fascinating, Ivy."

Ivy couldn't help the soft smile that curled on her lips as she thought of Ketahn. Of how far they'd come since they first met. "Yeah, they are."

Ella smiled in return. "I can see why you care for him. I've seen how protective he is of you, the way he looks at you, cares for you. I guess deep down, we're all the same. Our souls see what our eyes can't, and they connect no matter what's on the outside. Our bodies…they're just shells."

Our souls see what our eyes can't.

Ivy hadn't been able to see past the exterior, not at first. By all appearances, Ketahn had been a monster. How could she have seen the male beneath when she'd been so fearful of his looks? But once that fear had subsided, once she'd allowed herself to get to know him, her attraction to him had been overwhelming. It hadn't mattered how much she'd fought it, hadn't mattered how wrong it should have been.

She was irresistibly drawn toward Ketahn. And now…now she was forever bound to him by an unbreakable thread.

"You make it sound like we're soulmates," Ivy said.

"Maybe you are. How else could you have found each other?"

"All it took was a trip through space and one hundred and sixty-eight years." Ivy grinned. "And well…he was pretty much the first guy to come around, and a woman has…*needs*."

Ella chuckled, though it was cut short as she stiffened in pain.

Ivy's eyes widened. "I'm sorry!"

"It's okay. Worth it." Ella smiled and took a deep breath, releasing it slowly. "I'm glad you woke me, Ivy. I'm glad I got to see something so amazing before the end. I get...I get to be one of eight humans in the whole universe to have met the vrix."

Ivy squeezed Ella's hand. "And more than that, you befriended them. I think Ahnset really likes you."

Ella smiled, her eyelids drooping. "I can't believe how big she is. And she's so kind with me. I just wish... I wish I could have had a real conversation with her. You'll tell her thank you for me?"

"You can tell her later when they get back, and I'll translate. I think she'd like hearing it from you."

As her eyes drifted shut and her grip on Ivy's hand loosened, Ella spoke again; her words were slightly slurred. "Yeah. I... think so...too."

The door hissed opened, claiming Ivy's attention. Cole entered, sweeping his eyes over the chamber before they found Ivy. She brought a finger to her lips. He looked at Ella and nodded, crossing his arms over his chest and leaning against the wall. The door closed soon after.

Ivy waited for Ella's labored breaths to even out before carefully pulling her hand free. Stepping away, she retrieved her own folded blanket from the floor and returned to Ella, draping it over her for extra warmth. She hadn't missed the subtle shivers coursing through the woman's body.

Sighing, Ivy turned away and picked up one of the waterskins from the gathered supplies. She opened the top and took a drink.

"How is she?" Cole asked quietly.

"Worse."

"She sleeping now?"

"Yeah." Frowning, Ivy sealed the waterskin and glanced toward Ella. "Even just talking tires her out lately." She looked back at Cole, brow furrowed. "You're back early. Where are the others?"

"Uh, yeah." One corner of his mouth pulled back as he scratched the back of his neck. "So…I didn't go up with them."

"Why not?"

"I wanted to explore the *Somnium* a little more. What's left of it. You know, before we leave in a couple days and never see it again?" He dropped his hand and pushed himself away from the wall. "And I actually found something in one of the other rooms."

Ivy returned the waterskin to its place and cocked her head. "What'd you find?"

"I think it'd be better if I showed you. I'm not really sure myself."

Ivy returned her gaze to Ella. The woman was likely to sleep for a while, and she'd be safe inside this room. Ivy could step out for a bit in the meantime.

"Okay, but let's be quick." Ivy walked toward Cole. "I don't want to leave her alone for too long in case she needs anything."

Cole pressed the button on the doorframe. The door slid open. "We shouldn't be long."

He stepped into the corridor, and Ivy followed close behind. Though the air here was warmer and more humid than that in the stasis room, it was also moving, and its flow over her bare arms and legs raised goosebumps on her flesh. Since she hadn't accompanied the others out of the pit, she'd worn the silk dress Ketahn had made her instead of the jumpsuit. After weeks of traveling in light, minimal clothing, the jumpsuit made her feel restricted and uncomfortable, especially in the jungle heat.

As they passed one of the doors, Ivy's eyes flicked up to the red light over it. No matter how many times she'd walked this crimson corridor with its deep, dark shadows, she could never quite shake the chill that crept beneath her skin whenever she was inside it.

Cole hadn't gone far before he stopped at a door that was stuck halfway open. Unlike the other doors in the corridor, this one was totally flush with the wall, and it didn't have a light over its frame. There was a soft white glow coming from within the room.

Turning his body to the side, Cole looked at her and flashed a smile. "In here."

He squeezed through the doorway.

Once he was inside, Ivy slipped into the room and looked around.

This room was much smaller than the stasis rooms, no more than fifteen feet by fifteen. Each wall had two beds, one over the other, built into sleek recesses, and beside each set of bunks was a large cabinet. Like the chamber that had housed Ivy and the other survivors, this room was free of dirt and water damage, but there was no air flow within—and the white glow was produced not by overhead lighting but by a solar lantern from the emergency cache placed at the center of the floor.

That lantern created strange shadows, giving the space an ancient, otherworldly feel. This room should have been mundane—the bunks, the posters and pictures on the walls, some of which were curling with age, the articles of clothing and the blanket scattered on the floor. But like the rest of the ship, it was only sad, lonely, and more solemn than it ever should've been.

"What room was this?" she asked, looking at the photographs on the wall. Most of them appeared to be of wives, husbands, and kids. Families.

"Crew quarters," Cole replied from directly behind her. "Me and Will opened it up the other day while we were looking for supplies, but he got all weird about it and pretty much shoved me out after he looked around. The door jammed when he tried to close it."

Because Will knew the people who'd lived in here.

Ivy's heart went out to Will. Had he recognized any of the faces in the photos? Had he known the crewmembers who'd bunked here when the crash happened, had he known their families? Had he brought along photos of his own?

"I hadn't even noticed the door." She turned to face Cole. "So what did you want to—"

Ivy's words were cut off by a gasp that itself was silenced as Cole caught her by the back of the neck and slammed his mouth over hers. Her eyes widened, and she stood frozen, stunned, as his other hand smoothed over her hip to grab her ass. He tugged her closer, groaning as he ground his pelvis and his already hardening cock against her. In that moment, Ivy was aware of everything—his rough stubble abrading her skin, the flick of his tongue in her mouth, the heat of his flesh, his callused fingers on her neck, the smell of sweat and male.

And all of it disgusted her.

"How does it feel to have a real man kissing you?" Cole rasped against her mouth, clenching her ass to pull her even closer. "Did you crave it, Ivy? Did you crave this?"

Flattening her hands on Cole's chest, Ivy tore her mouth from his and shoved him away as hard as she could. "Let me go!"

Cole's hold on her broke, and he stumbled backward a step, eyes widening in shock an instant before her fist connected with his mouth. His head snapped back as his feet met the blanket on the floor—one landing atop it, the other catching on its folds. Between the blanket and Ivy's punch, it was enough to send him to the floor. Cole landed on his ass with teeth-clacking impact.

Ivy hissed, hugging her hand against her chest as pain radiated into her bones. She glanced down to see blood oozing from a cut on her knuckles.

"What the fuck!" Cole brought a hand to his mouth, which was also bloodied.

Fury roared through Ivy. She vibrated with it, and she had to clench her hand to her chest to keep herself from lashing out at him again. She took a step toward him and glared. "What the fuck? Shouldn't *I* be asking that? No, Cole, *you* what the fuck?"

Cole drew his hand away from his mouth and looked at it. Blood glistened on his fingertips. "Why'd you hit me?"

"Why the hell do you think?"

With a scowl, he snatched up the blanket he'd tripped over and stood, touching the corner of the cloth to his split lip. "Was just trying to spend a little time with you now that *he's* not breathing down your neck."

"So you brought me in here to assault me?"

"I wasn't assaulting you!"

"You kissed me! You put your hands on me and forced your mouth on mine. That's assault, Cole."

"I thought you might like to be with a real man. I wouldn't have told him."

"Did you really think that just because Ketahn is busy and you got me alone, that I'd want *this?*"

"I just thought…"

"You must not be thinking very hard. When have I given you *any* hint that I wanted you?"

He threw his arms out to the sides. "Come on! You can't really want to be fucking that thing, can you?"

Ivy growled and stalked toward him. Cole retreated several steps, dropping the blanket to hold his palms up in surrender. But Ivy didn't stop until she stood directly before him, head tilted back, furious eyes locked with his.

"I am with Ketahn because I choose to be. *He* is who I want. He is my *choice*. And I'd never betray him in any way." Her skin still crawled from Cole's touch. "It doesn't matter what he looks like, or what you think of my relationship with him, it's what I feel here"—she struck her fist against her chest—"that matters.

"I've been with someone like you before, Cole. A man with a handsome face and pretty words. He was more of a monster than Ketahn could ever be."

Cole's brows were drawn low, and his lips, still bleeding, were downturned as he stared at her. "You…really care for him, don't you?"

Ivy rolled her eyes and threw her hands out. "Yes!"

How dense could Cole be?

Cole groaned and thrust his fingers into his hair, combing the strands back from his forehead. "Still fucking weird you're banging a spider though."

Ivy crossed her arms over her chest. "Yeah, well, no one asked you, and as I've said, it's none of your damn business."

He chuckled, shaking his head.

"He's also not a spider," Ivy said. "He's vrix."

"Not human, either way. None of them are."

"And what does that matter, Cole? They're not human, but they're helping us anyway. Maybe we could've survived this place on our own. Maybe…maybe we could've figured it all out. But more than likely, we would've all died trying—not that any of us would have ever woken up without Ketahn."

Frowning, he dropped his gaze and shifted his weight uncomfortably from one leg to another and back again. "We can't afford to forget who we are here, Ivy. Humans. On an alien world. Doesn't matter if it's not the planet we were meant to colonize, this place is ours now."

"That's not how it works, Cole," Ivy replied with a sigh.

His short laugh was a little bitter, but there was no real bite to it. He met her eyes. "It works however we want it to, Ivy. We're all that's left."

Ivy's brows fell, and she jabbed a finger at him. "Yeah, well, what you just tried to pull is *not* how it's going to be. Do you understand?"

Again, Cole put his hands up placatingly. "I get it. You're not interested. I just…" As he lowered his arms, one of his hands eased forward, and he caught a lock of Ivy's dangling hair between his fingers. "I'm not coping with this well. I'm…angry. Frustrated. Lonely." He stroked her hair between index finger and thumb.

"Did you seriously not listen to—" Ivy was reaching for his hand, meaning to snatch her hair away, when a huge, dark shape appeared in the doorway behind Cole, silhouetted by the corridor's blood red glow.

A shadowy monster out of nightmare—but Ivy had no fear for herself in that moment.

CHAPTER 23

KETAHN SNARLED, forced the door fully open with a groan of metal grinding metal, and lunged through the doorway. Ivy didn't have time to think. She completed the motion of her hand, grabbing the front of Cole's jumpsuit, and tugged back with all her strength, swinging him around so she was between him and Ketahn. Were he not caught so off guard, she doubted she could've moved him.

The maneuver spun Ivy so her back was to Ketahn. She turned to face him and threw her arms out, making herself as big as possible—which was laughably small compared to him. He skittered to a halt, spindly legs darting out to either side of Ivy.

"Oh fuck," Cole breathed.

"Move, Ivy," Ketahn growled in vrix. His blazing violet eyes were fixed on Cole, and she knew he could easily reach around her to get at the human if he wanted to.

"No. I'm not going to let you kill him," Ivy said.

Ketahn's mandibles spread wider, but he lowered his gaze to her. A rumbling sound pulsed out of his chest as he cupped the underside of her jaw with one hand and tipped her head farther back, leaning down to examine her—to examine her lips, which still throbbed with the lingering, unwanted sensation of Cole's kiss; to examine her chin, which was irritated from the scrape of Cole's stubble.

The words he spoke were so guttural, so bestial, that Ivy nearly shuddered. "You chose *him*."

Ivy flinched as though something had pierced her heart. Did he really think so little of her? Keeping her eyes locked with his, she poured all the fierceness of her love and conviction into her voice. "No, I chose *you*, Ketahn."

His hold on her jaw tightened infinitesimally. "You protect him. Why?"

"To protect you."

"He cannot harm me."

Ivy brought her arms in and circled her fingers around his wrist. "If you kill him, all the trust the humans have in you will be gone. They will fear you. They will fear the others. And none of this will work."

Ketahn moved his face closer to hers, drawing in a deep breath. "You say you did not choose him. But his scent is on you." His thumb brushed across her lips, shaken by a faint tremor. "His *mark* is upon you."

"He kissed me. He tried for more—"

Somehow, Ketahn's already rigid body tensed further, radiating heat and fury. Ivy braced her hands against his chest before he could charge forward.

"But I already took care of it!" Ivy rushed to say. "I fought him. I fought him because I am yours."

Ketahn's eyes lingered upon her for the space of a few thumping heartbeats before shifting up to look beyond her. He dropped his hand from her jaw, took hold of her upper arms, and lifted her off the floor effortlessly, setting her aside. Before she could move back, he blocked her with one of his long legs.

"Ketahn, please…" Ivy pleaded.

He stepped forward, and Cole backpedaled—but his retreat was halted by the wall.

Cole put his hands up. "Look, Ketahn, this was just—"

Faster than Ivy's eyes could register, Ketahn's arm darted out. The cabinet behind Cole buckled with the force of the blow. The man started, his wide eyes shifting from Ketahn's huge fist, which had landed barely an inch to the side of Cole's head, to Ketahn's face.

Ketahn leaned down slowly, placing his head just above Cole's, with his mandible fangs almost close enough to touch the man's cheeks. "Ivy is mine," he said in English, his accent thicker than normal. "Do not touch. Do not look with want. Do not even think. Understand?"

When Cole just continued to stare, another of Ketahn's hands rose, this one wrapping around Cole's throat and shoving him back against the already damaged cabinet door. Ketahn growled, "Touch again, and it is done. *You* are done."

"I-I got it!" Cole rasped, his hands clutching Ketahn's arm. "I won't!"

"Now go." Ketahn dragged Cole away from the wall, releasing his hold as he shoved the man toward the door.

Cole stumbled and pitched forward, preventing himself from falling on his face only by briefly planting a hand on the floor. Before he was even fully upright, he scrambled through the doorway, disappearing into the corridor without a backward glance.

Ketahn's attention was already on Ivy. He strode toward her, closing the distance between them like it had never been there at all and driving her backward until she bumped the wall. His mahogany and spice scent filled her nose, and his hungry growl vibrated into her.

"Ketahn, I—"

He caught her chin, making her breath hitch, and forced her face up. "Mine."

281

Ketahn's hard mouth came down upon hers. The brush of his rough flesh, the insistent press of his tongue against her lips, and the heat he emanated burned away the memory of Cole's unwelcome touch. Ivy parted her lips with a heady sigh and welcomed Ketahn's alien kiss, winding her arms around his neck to pull him closer. Heat flowed through her and pooled between her thighs.

His fingers slid along her jaw and delved into her hair to cup the back of her head, anchoring her in place while he ravaged her mouth. He seemed determined to blast away all traces of Cole. And Ivy returned the kiss in full, offering everything. Her sex clenched with need as the emptiness within her core expanded.

Mine.

The echo of that claim sent a delightful shiver through her, making her moan.

A low vibration rattled in Ketahn's chest, a lustful purr and a possessive growl blended into one hungry, thrilling sound. It was the only warning he gave for what came next.

With the same speed he'd used to lash out at Cole, Ketahn hooked his lower arms under Ivy's knees, caught her wrists in his upper hands, and lifted her. He pressed her against the wall with her hands over her head, pinning her in place with his body. Cold air caressed her bared sex as his claspers curled around her ass.

Spreading his other legs to brace himself, he bent his forelegs, brought them in close, and brushed them along the backs of her thighs. When he angled his hips up, the tip of his cock bumped Ivy's already slick pussy. Her nipples hardened, aching to be touched, to be caressed, amplifying her need for him more.

Trapped in place and softly panting, Ivy looked up and locked her gaze with Ketahn's. The lantern light behind him only enhanced the darkness of his hide, making his many violet eyes glow amidst the shadows on his face.

He was that shadowy monster all over again—*her* shadowy monster.

And God, it turned her on.

"Do it," Ivy breathed. "Fuck me. Claim me. Take my body."

Like you've taken my heart.

Ketahn's fingers flexed, and his claws prickled her, sending exquisite thrills along her flesh. With a snarl, he thrust into her the same instant he slammed her down on his cock, forcing her to take all of him.

Ivy's cry was short and sharp. She tilted her head back against the wall, but kept her eyes locked with his. Her hands clenched against the pain of his entrance, against the slight burn as he stretched her, as he filled her to the brink and beyond. But there was a restless energy thrumming inside her—a craving for more.

He lifted her, shuddering as her sex gripped his thick cock, and drove back into her with equal force to that of his first thrust. This time, he did not stop. His body surrounded her utterly, keeping her trapped, ensuring she was his to use, to take, to claim. Ketahn's frantic, merciless rhythm blasted her with waves of heat and pleasure that ebbed and flowed with each movement of his hips, always building higher and higher.

The room filled with her moans, her cries, her panting breaths, filled with his grunts and growls. She was vaguely aware of the open doorway, aware that anyone could pass at any moment and see them, but she didn't care. She wanted them to see. Wanted them to know without any doubt that she belonged to Ketahn—and that he belonged to her.

The claws at the ends of his legs scraped the floor, and his rhythm grew more frenzied. Dipping his head to her shoulder, he ran his tongue along her collarbone and neck to lick away her sweat.

"You are mine," he rasped in her ear.

"Yes," she moaned.

He growled and pressed his headcrest to her forehead. Their eyes met again, narrowing the world down to just the two of them. "My *nyleea*. My heartsthread."

"Yours, my *luveen*. I want no other."

"Shaper, unmake me," Ketahn groaned.

He released her wrists to cup Ivy's face between his palms. His hard mouth met hers as he adjusted the angle of her hips, making his thrusts strike her in a new way. The altered sensation rocketed her to the verge of climax. Her entire body strained for that last nudge, that final spark to finish her off. Ivy whimpered against his mouth and looped her arms around his neck.

Snarling, Ketahn slammed her down upon him, driving himself deeper than she'd ever thought possible. He held her there as his body tensed and his cock swelled. The heat radiating from his hide intensified, seeping into her, just before his seed—even hotter still—erupted inside her.

That was all it took. The pleasure that had been escalating within her burst, overcoming her completely. Ivy's cries were drowned out by Ketahn's roar of release.

Her fingers delved into his hair, grasping the strands; she needed something—anything—to hold onto while wave after wave of euphoria consumed her. He clutched her, his claws digging into her skin, his claspers gripping her ass, and all Ivy could do was succumb as Ketahn's curious, fluttering tendrils pushed her to new heights.

And when Ivy finally floated down and regained awareness, Ketahn was there, holding her, cradling her in his arms as though she was the most precious thing in all the world. He brushed the seam of his mouth over her lips in the lightest of caresses, and his hair, now loose from its tie, fell forward to brush over her skin.

She opened her eyes. The intensity that had burned in his gaze had softened but had not diminished, and she knew there was nothing and no one else in all the universe he looked at the way he did her.

You make it sound like we're soulmates.

Maybe you are. How else could you have found each other?

She had no idea if soulmates were real, if fate existed, if everyone in the universe had one person they were meant to be with. But she knew with all her heart that *she* had chosen Ketahn to be her forever—and he would be imprinted upon her soul for all eternity.

Ivy softly smiled and caressed Ketahn's jaw. "My heartsthread."

With a gentle trill, Ketahn tipped his headcrest against her forehead. "My Ivy."

CHAPTER 24

IVY EMERGED from beneath the water, smoothing her hands over her face and hair. She opened her eyes and inhaled deeply, taking in fresh air that was perfumed with flowers, clean water, and earth. The sunlight shining through the broad opening in the cavern's ceiling warmed her skin and made the beautiful turquoise pool sparkle like it had been dusted with crystals. Soft, soothing sounds created by the rippling water echoed off the cavern walls.

For the last several days, there'd been few quiet times—at least not relaxing ones.

She tilted her head back to look up. The opening in the ceiling was perhaps fifty feet wide and nearly that high over-head. The walls curved inward toward the hole, creating a natural dome over the pool. Vines and roots dangled down all around it, their vibrant emeralds and fuchsias a perfect comple-ment to the color of the water. She could make out the boughs of a few towering trees up there, too, their leaves shimmering as they turned in the breeze, but most of the view was taken up by blue sky and soft white clouds lazily drifting by.

Smiling, she turned toward Ketahn, who was lounging on a low ledge that hugged one side of the pool. Though the sunlight didn't reach him directly, its reflections from the water's surface danced across his hide.

Nearby him was the break in the wall by which they'd entered—an overgrown crevice that angled down into the cavern from outside, likely carved by rainwater over thousands of years. At the moment, there was only a trickle flowing through it, creating a teeny, tiny waterfall that made Ivy think of the fancy fountains that were always put up for decoration in office buildings back on Earth.

It felt like so long since she and Ketahn had had a moment like this. Some of her favorite memories were of the times he'd taken her down to the stream so she could swim in the cool water and relax in the sun beside him.

Ivy swam toward Ketahn until her feet were able to touch the bottom. Rivulets streamed down her naked body as she stepped out of the water. Her skin prickled with awareness as Ketahn's gaze trekked over her, and arousal flared in her core. She still felt the aftermath of their rough mating the day before, and that reminder only increased her desire, making her ache.

Once she was standing on the ledge, which was partially overgrown with vegetation, she pulled her hair to the side and wrung it out. Water splashed the ground at her feet. "How far have you traveled from Takarahl?"

Ketahn ran his claws through his loose hair. "Five days' journey. Perhaps six. It was difficult to track time while we fought the thornskulls."

"How far will we go?"

"Well beyond that. Beyond the Claws' will to follow. Deeper into the unknown than any vrix of Takarahl since the first queen." He dropped his hand with a sigh. "Until we are safe."

Ivy straightened, tossed her hair back, and stood in the sun, allowing its rays to dry her skin. "Will we ever be safe? Will she just let you go?"

"Nowhere is truly safe, Ivy." Ketahn shook his head. "And she will not give up. Not soon. We must go so far that they will never find us, and even then, she may look for a long while."

Ivy worried her lip as she looked down, nudging a vine with her toe. "Do you think the others are ready?"

He snorted; the sound became a chitter that drew her attention back to him because something about it *seemed* like it should have been hopeless or bitter, but…it wasn't.

"None of them are ready. They are clumsy as broodlings. Loud. Weak. Too slow and too small."

Crossing her arms over her chest, she arched a brow at him. "Ah. So that's what you thought of me."

The light in his eyes pierced straight into her heart as he lifted his mandibles in a smile. "I have told you that before, female. I will not lie to you."

Ouch.

Ivy lifted her chin. "Those don't seem like qualities you would like in a mate. Don't the vrix prefer their females big and strong?"

Ketahn trilled. "I like my female clever, kind, and determined. Small and soft of skin but with a heart that is as tender as it is strong. I like my female to laugh and smile."

And smile she did as warmth spread through her.

"And I like her kisses and her soft, fleshy chest mounds. Her hips, her legs. Her ass. Her delicious slit, and the songs she makes while mating."

Ivy laughed, that warmth turning into a different kind of heat as it burned her cheeks. She pressed a hand to her face and shook her head. "I can't believe how much that sounded like something a human man would say."

"You need only look upon me to know I am not human… But I am your male, Ivy. And you are my female. My mate."

"Yes, we thoroughly established that yesterday." Ivy's smile slipped as a pang of doubt cast a shadow over her happiness. She dropped her arm.

Her expression must have alerted Ketahn of the change in her mood. He leaned forward, his stare intense and solemn. "Hear my words, my heartsthread—we will reach our destination, wherever it awaits. And we vrix will do all in our power to protect the humans."

"I know you will."

Ketahn raised a hand and curled his fingers, beckoning her. "Come, my *nyleea*."

Ivy padded toward him, leaving the sunlight, and lowered herself on the bed of leaves he'd gathered for her between his forelegs.

One of his lower hands smoothed down her back as though to comfort her. Curling a finger beneath her chin, he tilted her head back until her eyes met his. Fire blazed in his gaze. "I will let no hurt come to you."

Ivy smiled and kissed his finger. "I know, Ketahn."

He shifted his hand up over her cheek and to her damp hair, through which he gently combed his claws. When those claws reached the back of her head, he returned them to her hairline and repeated the process, gradually easing out the knots and tangles. His ministrations were soothing, aided by the comfortable silence that stretched between them. There was only the rustling of leaves from outside, the slow trickle into the pool, and the subtle lapping of water against the walls.

Tomorrow, they would leave behind everything both Ivy and Ketahn knew on this world. But today they had a little time to enjoy peace, quiet…and each other. Today they could enjoy being two people in…in…

"Can I ask you a question?" Ivy asked, breaking that silence.

"Anything, my *nyleea*."

She looked up at him. "What…does it mean to be a mate for the vrix?"

His mandibles twitched, and he cocked his head. "Explain."

Ivy caught her bottom lip between her teeth and looked down. She plucked up one of the large leaves from the ground and twirled it by its stem. "On Earth, there are many kinds of relationships. There are friends, boyfriends and girlfriends, friends with benefits, and then there's marriage."

"Is that…like *marry*?"

"Yes. Friendship is what you and me had in the beginning. Friends with benefits are people who remain friends but share pleasure with one another without promises or commitment. Boyfriends and girlfriends are people who are in a relationship together, but there is no…no binding commitment. But marriage is binding. It's like I told you. Two people make vows of love and promise to remain true to one another, through sickness and health, till death do they part."

With brows drawn low, Ivy tore the leaf along the veins. "I guess…I'm just unsure where we fall. And I'm worried that maybe someday, you might…might cast me aside. That you won't want me anymore."

Ketahn covered both her hands with one of his, stilling her fidgeting fingers. "To vrix…a mate can be many things also. But when a male calls his female *nyleea*, it is more. When a male calls his female his heartsthread, it is…*everything*. I want only you, Ivy. My hearts beat for you."

Ivy's chest constricted. Tears stung her eyes and blurred her vision. She blinked, forcing them to spill. "You hurt me yesterday."

His mandibles fell, and he cradled her chin in one hand, tilting her head back and sweeping his gaze over her. "I was too rough. Where did I hurt you?"

She released the leaf, turned her hand to take hold of his, and pressed his palm over her heart. "Here."

An uncertain, unhappy buzz vibrated in his chest. His voice was low when he said, "Because of what I did to him?"

"No, it's because of what you thought I wanted with him. You thought that I betrayed you, Ketahn."

The pain that had caused her had only grown since then. She'd been restless last night, unable to fall asleep despite her exhaustion and despite being right where she wanted to be—in Ketahn's arms. But he'd…he'd questioned her faithfulness, her loyalty. And that hurt.

Ketahn brushed his thumb across her cheek, sweeping away her tears. "Ah, my Ivy. It was I who betrayed you. I let my rage blind me to what I have long known in my hearts… that you are mine and mine alone, and I need never question it."

He wrapped his arms around Ivy, lifted her off the ground, and pulled her against his chest. She felt his strength, felt the thumping of his hearts and the rasp of his hide on her skin. It was her soft curves against his hard ridges. Unbidden, her nipples tightened into achy points. His claspers hooked her hips as his forelegs bent around her, teasing her with their fine hairs. Once more he wiped away the tears from her cheeks before combing his claws through her damp hair.

"I ask that you forgive me, my heartsthread," he said thickly.

Ivy trailed her fingertips along his mandibles, following them to their joints. "I do."

"Some vrix take mates for pleasure, as Zurvashi has always done," he rumbled. "Some take mates only to breed, to keep their blood alive, and have little to do with one another after. But some, as my sire and mother, became mates for something deep and lasting. Because they saw in each other something neither could live without."

Ketahn curled forward, pressing his mouth atop her hair, and inhaled deeply. "I cannot live without you, Ivy."

Ivy closed her eyes against the surge of powerful emotions

filling her chest. She slid her fingers into his loose hair, clutching the long strands. "Humans call that love."

"Love," he echoed, stroking her with his fingers and claspers. "That is what I have for you, Ivy. And it will outlast the Tangle, the stars from which you came, even the Eight themselves. You are my *nyleea* always."

"I love you, Ketahn." She raised her head, forcing him to do the same. Her lips stretched into a smile even as her eyes brimmed with fresh tears. "And I can't live without you either, my *luveen*."

"My beautiful, beautiful female," Ketahn rumbled. He carefully wiped another tear from her cheek. "Why do you cry? I am here with you. You will never have to live without me."

A small laugh escaped her. "Promise?"

Ketahn made a low, rolling trill, soothingly sweeping his thumb across her cheek again. "*Kir rayathi kir'ani ikarex elush ul sythal*, Ivy." *I weave my word into a bond, Ivy.* "I *promeese*."

Ivy's smile softened, and she ran her fingers through his silky hair. "Though I miss our nest, I can't wait to find somewhere safe so we can build a new one together."

He dipped his head, pressing his face to her neck, and breathed her in. His hand trailed along her jawline while the other three slid down her back. "I cannot wait to have you to myself again, my heartsthread. I tire of sharing you."

A thrill coursed over her skin as his callused hands and the tips of his claws rasped over it. When his palms dipped lower to curl around her ass, the sensations strengthened, coalescing in her core, growing into a yearning ache.

"So you can have your wicked spidery way with me any time you want?" she asked.

One of his hands slid lower between their bodies, parting her thighs, and worked its way into the folds of her sex. Ivy gasped, her fingers curling against his back as he worked a finger over her, stroking her clit and spreading her slick.

A purr vibrated in his chest and into her. "A male must see to his female's needs." The pressure of that finger increased, striking her with a fresh wave of pleasure, as he scraped his mouth over her shoulder. "All her needs."

Even as he spoke, his claspers twitched and tightened their hold on her, pressing her thigh against his slit, which parted and radiated heat. His cock forced its way out, shaft sliding over her flesh unhindered.

Panting softly and undulating against his hand, she asked, "What of her male's needs?"

Though already hard as silk-wrapped steel, his cock stiffened further. It throbbed against her thigh, matching the rapid beating of his hearts, which she felt through his chest. His breath was hot on her neck.

"I will take all I require"—his tongue slipped out to dance along her neck, tickling her skin but leaving delightful fire in its wake—"as I give everything to you."

Ivy caught her bottom lip between her teeth, closed her eyes, and let her head fall back as the pleasure rippling through her grew stronger and stronger. Her nails dug into his back. "There is...another way females like to...to mate with their males."

It was so hard to concentrate on speaking as he continued to sensually work that finger around her clit, but this was something she had been curious about for some time, something she wanted to do.

Ketahn raked a sharp tooth down her neck, making Ivy writhe in his hold. He growled in satisfaction. "Of what do you speak, Ivy?"

"I...I want to—oh God, Ketahn." Trembling, she whimpered and arched into his touch, her hard, aching nipples rubbing against his chest as she rocked on his finger. She was so wet, and so, so close. Her essence dripped down her thighs and soaked his hand.

But she wanted to do this for him. *Needed* to do this. And… she also wanted to know.

Ivy raised her head, forced her eyes open, and grasped his wrist. "I want to show you."

Another sound rumbled through him, this one softer and more curious but no less hungry. His finger halted, its pad remaining on her throbbing clit as he pulled his face away from her neck and met her gaze.

Between that finger, which made her want to writhe in abandon, and his passionate, intrigued eyes, Ivy was utterly trapped.

Ketahn removed his finger from her sex, and she released him. With a slowness that made her breath catch, he raised his hand and extended his long, purple tongue, licking her essence from his fingers as though it were the greatest delicacy in the universe. Seeing that only turned her on more.

"Then show me, my *nyleea*," he said, voice low and gravelly.

Ivy released a shuddering breath, torn between begging him to touch her again, to finish what he started, and her want to pleasure him. Her clit pulsed with unfulfilled lust.

"I need you to…to set me down, and then stand," she said.

His fingers flexed, and his claws pressed on her flesh, their wicked points only amplifying everything she was already feeling and leaving her desperate for more. But she could not pursue that temptation; with clear reluctance, Ketahn set her down on her feet. His palms rasped across her skin as he shifted the positions of his hands and unfolded his legs, rising to his normal height. His glistening, violet cock twitched in the open air.

Ivy dropped to her knees amidst the piled leaves—though she wasn't sure if it was because her legs were too weak to hold her up in that moment or if she'd done it on purpose. Either way, she didn't care.

She wrapped her fingers around his claspers and gave him a

gentle tug. He grunted and followed, moving closer. She straightened until her face was level with his shaft. The tip was weeping pearlescent white seed. Ivy looked up at him, and he stared down at her, his dark hair hanging over his shoulders.

"I've wanted to kiss you, Ketahn." Ivy released his claspers and moved her hands to his cock, trailing her fingers along the shaft lightly until she gripped him at the bulging base. He was too thick for her to wrap her hand around completely. "Here."

A tremor wracked his body, and the fine hairs on his legs stood on end. His upper hands curled into fists, while the lower pair fell to cover her hands. His mouth opened, revealing the sharp teeth inside, and his gleaming eyes were wide. "Ivy…"

Those wicked mandibles, which she knew were capable of inflicting terrible damage, twitched and fell limp at the sides of his face.

She leaned forward, and while keeping her eyes locked with his, twirled her tongue around the tip of his cock. "I want to give you pleasure, my heartsthread."

Ketahn groaned. The sound made her pussy clench and flood with heat. His hands tightened over hers, and he drew in a ragged breath.

"Trust me." She pressed her lips to the head of his cock in a gentle kiss. "Let me love you this way."

Movements stiff, Ketahn lifted his hands from Ivy's and reached toward her. He ran his fingers along her jaw and settled his palms over her cheeks. His claspers stretched forward, running lightly up the outsides of her arms. "I trust you."

Anticipation thrummed through her, twining with her desire to please him, to get to know him fully.

With one hand clutched at the base of his cock, Ivy parted her lips, took his tip into her mouth, and sucked. He was warm, throbbing, and tasted of salt on her tongue, but there was something more, something subtle, sweeter. His mahogany-and-spice scent was stronger than ever, filling her senses, arousing her further and driving her to widen her mouth to take more of him in. But he was much too big. So, she took as much of his shaft as she could, stroking her tongue along its underside, teasing the slit at its tip, and pumping her other hand along its length.

Ketahn's fingers flexed. More spasms rocked his body, and his breath came and went in short, rough pants. He rumbled something—a stunned curse, perhaps, followed by Ivy's name— before sliding those clawed fingers into her hair. One of his forelegs curled around her back, trembling, before he stamped it back down on the ground beside her.

Spurred on by his reactions, Ivy closed her eyes worked his length at a steady pace, drawing upon his cock hungrily, licking and sucking, lightly grazing him with her teeth. Over and over, she teased his slit, eager to discover what it was she'd felt within her time and again.

And though she had been denied her release, hearing his pleasure as she performed this act only increased her own. Her core ached, her clit throbbed, eager to be touched, and hot slick dripped down her thighs.

She imagined his cock inside her as she sucked him into her mouth, imagined it thrusting, stretching her wide, filling her so completely that there'd be no room left between them. She longed to be part of him—to be one with him. A moan escaped her, vibrating into Ketahn.

"Ivy," he rasped. His claws lightly raked her scalp, and his pelvis bucked forward, eliciting another low, pleased sound from him. Just like that, whatever control Ivy had held over this vanished.

Ketahn's big, strong hands guided her to meet the thrusts of his hips, which first matched the pace she had set but soon surpassed it. His breathing also quickened and grew ever more ragged. Ivy knew the erratic, powerful pulses coursing through him; she knew he was on the cusp of his climax, and it only made her hunger all the more.

Dropping a hand between her thighs, Ivy stroked her clit in time with his vigorous thrusts. She moaned, letting him use her, wanting him to use her, uncaring about the discomfort in her jaw. All that mattered was this. Him.

She came quickly, her body tensing as her core seized and flooded her with heat. Pleasure sizzled through her, sparking every nerve, consuming every bit of her in a blissful inferno.

"Ah, Ivy. My mate, my *nyleea*," Ketahn panted. Suddenly, his body went rigid. "Shaper, unmake me," he growled as his leg swept behind her again, and, along with his claspers, drew her toward him, forcing a little more of his shaft into her mouth. It was almost too much.

The bulge near the base of his cock expanded in her hand, producing even more heat. It thrummed with tension, with pressure, and Ivy relished the imminent explosion.

Ketahn came with a roar, his hot seed filling her mouth. She hadn't known what to expect, but his taste was a shock—a delightful one. It was spiced and rich with a hint of sweetness, and she swallowed it swiftly, moaning again at how delicious he tasted.

Until something emerged from his slit, unfurled, and vibrated against her tongue and the roof of her mouth.

Ivy pulled back abruptly. As his cock slid free of her mouth, seed jetted from him again, spraying her chest. Finally, she saw them—three black tendrils fluttering in the air, like the feathered antennae of a moth. Her breath hitched, and her eyes flared. It was those she'd felt pulsing inside her, those which had sent her to the brink again and again.

Tentatively, she reached up with her other hand, grasped the head of his cock, and brushed her thumb along the open slit and up to those tendrils. They were firm and soft at once. She stroked their lengths, following them back down to his slit.

Fresh seed flowed from his tip.

Ketahn drew in a sharp, shuddering breath, and his body shook. "Ivy," he rasped, one of his big hands cradling the back of her head while the other clenched her long hair. His claspers quivered on her shoulders.

The tendrils were sensitive.

She grinned and, unable to resist, closed the distance between them, dragging her tongue along Ketahn's length, licking up his delicious, spiced sweetness. When she reached his tip, she closed her mouth over it and twirled her tongue around those tendrils.

He made a desperate sound—a roar, groan, and growl combined—that became something infinitely deep and primal as it bounced off the cavern walls. His leg joints buckled, and his hips jerked back, tugging his cock from her grasp even as he sank to the ground—but not before Ivy was rewarded with a fresh eruption of his seed, which she drank greedily.

Ketahn's torso pitched forward, stopping only when he braced all his hands on the ground. His shoulders heaved with his heavy breaths. The tips of his headcrest grazed Ivy's skin just beneath her breasts, and strands of his loose hair tickled her belly and thighs.

Ivy sank down on her heels and chuckled, tracing the violet and white markings on his headcrest with her fingertips. "I take it you liked it?"

Ketahn chittered and exhaled; his warm breath fanned over Ivy's stomach, toward her still throbbing sex. "I..." He chittered again, lifting his head to meet her gaze. "You have unmade me, Ivy."

Leaning back, Ivy propped an arm behind her and parted her thighs. With a self-satisfied smile, she trailed the fingers of her other hand through the warm, pearlescent seed on her chest and smeared it over her breast, twirling it around her nipple.

The Ivy of a couple months ago would never have recognized the woman sitting here now. She would never have thought herself capable of embracing this openness, this passion, this…this wickedness. But having his essence on her body, marking her, branding her with his scent, aroused her on an instinctual level. The ache between her legs intensified, and fresh heat raced to her core.

"Did I tire you too much?" Ivy asked, moving that seed coated finger down her belly and toward her sex.

His eyes followed her finger; his gleaming gaze was that of a hungry predator fixated on its prey. It made her skin tingle in awareness and her heart quicken.

"No." His long tongue slipped out and ran across the seam of his mouth, and his mandibles spread wide before dropping low and angling back. "You have only awoken my hunger, my heartsthread."

He gave no other sign of his intentions before he acted—there was no tensing of muscle, no refocusing of his eyes, not even the barest shifting of his legs in preparation. One instant, he was on the ground before her, propped up on his hands. The next he was pouncing on her, a dark blur of violet eyes, claws, and thrilling power.

His upper hands caught her forearms, his lower hooked behind her thighs. He lifted her up and swung her legs out from beneath her. Briefly, Ivy felt weightless, and her stomach flipped with anticipation and excitement. She giggled.

Ketahn lowered her onto her back with unbelievable gentleness considering the speed with which he did so. The leaves provided a soft cushion to protect her from the stone. He held himself over her, his torso wedged between her thighs, his body casting a shadow over hers that made his eyes shine like eight amethysts suspended in space. His claspers teased at the tops of her thighs as though not quite sure whether they wanted to latch on or explore.

Legs spread and braced to either side, Ketahn leaned down,

pressing his hard, ridged flesh against her soft body. His deadly mandible fangs brushed Ivy's collarbone as he trailed his tongue down her neck. That downward motion continued, and his whole body shifted with it; his upper hands slid along her arms from wrists to elbows, from elbows to shoulders as his tongue crept through the valley between her breasts.

Ivy arched her back, thrusting her chest toward him when his mandible fangs grazed her budded, sensitive nipples and triggered an overwhelming explosion of need inside her.

But his head continued its trek down her body. His tongue forged a path across her belly, tracing a delicate ring around her belly button that had her quivering with want. And his hands shifted again, those rough palms cupping her breasts. He held them still for a moment; it was long enough to have her writhing in desperation, trying to brush her nipples against his hide and take whatever sensation she could get.

Ivy covered his strong hands with her own. "Ketahn... Please."

His tongue swept over her pelvis, crossed the small patch of hair with a whisper light touch, and dipped down to tease her clit, circling and flicking it. Ivy's breath hitched. Only then did his hands move again, kneading the tender flesh of her breasts, fingers pinching and twisting her nipples.

She hummed, smiling as her lashes fluttered, though she willed her eyes to remain open.

Ketahn drew in a deep breath and released a growl. "Now I will tend to your needs, my *nyleea*."

He pulled her thighs up, hooked his mandibles beneath them, and cupped her ass with his lower hands. Before Ivy could fully register any of that, he pressed his face to her sex and speared her with his long tongue.

Ivy's head fell back as she cried out. Closing her eyes, she gave in to the pleasure her mate bestowed upon her until, finally, he withdrew his head, lifted her off the ground, and drew her down upon his throbbing cock. Their moans echoed off the stone walls, growing into a song that enveloped them both—a song of passion and love, a song born out of the impossible odds of two souls meeting despite the unfathomable expanse of time and space that had separated them.

CHAPTER 25

THE HUMANS HAD DIMMED the lights in the chamber some time ago, leaving only the softest white glow that shrouded most of the space in shadow. The cryochambers were dark shapes even to Ketahn's keen eyes, as black as the holes in which the dead of Takarahl were placed to rest. But he knew that was his wandering mind seeking darkness in every corner, searching for gloom, for danger, for death. He knew it was the work of instincts with roots deeper than the Tangle's oldest, tallest trees —instincts that saw doom hiding in every shadowed recess.

And for once, his instincts could not be trusted. Fear was natural to all creatures. Vrix were no more immune to it than any other beasts, no matter how large or small. This night, perhaps more than any other in Ketahn's lifetime, was one when all those fears threatened to rise to the surface.

Something as murky and foreboding as the water that had flooded the ship's corridors lurked at the edges of Ketahn's mind, slinking from shadow to shadow. It openly presented itself only in the lump of dread sunken low in his belly—a weighty feeling that something would go wrong, that all this would be for nothing, that Zurvashi would have her way in the end.

That Ketahn would fail, and all these innocents, including his mate, would suffer for it.

But he would not allow such fears to lay claim to him. At dawn, the new life for which Ketahn had so long yearned would finally begin. And his mate, his Ivy, would be there with him.

Ketahn tightened his hold on her and glanced down. As always, she was sleeping upon him, chest to chest, her spun-gold hair draped across his hide and disturbed only by her slow, soft breaths. Delicately, he hooked some of that hair with a finger and lifted it away from her face.

His little mate was as beautiful as ever. The gentle light caressed her skin, which was no longer quite as pale as it had been when he'd first seen her. That seemed a lifetime ago now.

Her face was tilted toward his. One of her cheeks rested upon his chest, over his hearts, and her eyes were closed, making her lashes look even darker and fuller than usual. Her brow was relaxed, freed from the worries she so often carried during her waking moments. And her lips...

Still swollen from their mating at the cavern earlier, Ivy's full, pink lips beckoned Ketahn, calling to those desires that never would—or could—be satisfied. At first sight, he'd likened her lips to a pair of plump grubs, but even then, they'd fascinated him. Disgust had become curiosity; curiosity had become longing. And after the way she'd used those lips to pleasure him today, that longing was now closer to need.

He was suddenly much more aware of her weight atop him and of her delicious warmth, which was trapped beneath the silk blanket draped over her. His hands, unbidden, trailed down her back and slid to her sides, following the flare of her hips to sample the yielding flesh of her backside, which was bare thanks to her skirt having ridden up to her waist.

Yet he was also aware of the quiet sounds in the room—the

low, ceaseless humming he always felt through the floor; the slow, hushed rhythms of humans and vrix breathing in their sleep; the huskier, more erratic sounds of Will slumbering in his open pod. The humans called it *snoring*.

Ahnset, Telok, Rekosh, and Urkot were scattered on their own makeshift nests, all asleep as far as Ketahn could tell. His broodsister had settled herself with her back against Ella's cryochamber. One of Ella's arms hung past the edge of the pod's bed so her hand, so small and frail, could rest upon Ahnset's broad shoulder.

Even in this unnaturally cool, dry air, even in the depths of night, the sheen of sweat on Ella's skin was apparent.

Everyone else was sleeping securely in this human built chamber, taking advantage of what might well have been their last safe night for a long while. And yet here was Ketahn with his mate nestled against him and his mind overcome by swirling chaos, unable to choose between his desire for Ivy and his many concerns about what tomorrow would bring—most of which were no more than vague, partially formed imaginings.

Barely holding back a growl, Ketahn forced all the thoughts out of his mind and narrowed his focus to his senses. To the feel of Ivy's body, to her sweet, familiar scent, to the faded but unmistakable traces of her delectable taste upon his tongue. He closed his eyes; the darkness almost reached its fullness behind his eyelids, but golden threads danced in his mind's eye.

Heaviness settled over him, bringing a sense of peace and certainty. Tonight, Ketahn had his mate. He could face everything else tomorrow.

He finally succumbed to sleep.

A sound roused him, reaching through the fog of sleep to brush against his awareness. Movement. But even as his eyes slitted open, he knew the rustling of movement hadn't been what woke him. His hearts had beat scarce once more before the first sound repeated—coughing.

His instincts told him it was not yet morning, but he could sense the impending suncrest like it was a familiar vrix spied from the far end of one of Takarahl's long tunnels.

Ivy stirred in Ketahn's arms as he turned his head to look at Ella and Ahnset. Absently, he smoothed his hands up and down his mate's back, watching as Ella grasped the side of her pod and, trembling, drew herself into a sitting position. The blanket that had cocooned her—Ivy's blanket, which she'd lent to the ill female yesterday—fell away from Ella's shoulders and chest. Her body shook with more muffled coughing.

Ahnset rose and twisted toward Ella, placing a supportive hand on the human's back. That hand spanned Ella's back from shoulder to shoulder and nearly top to bottom. In vrix, Ahnset whispered, "Easy, little one. Breathe."

Only a few of the others seemed to have awoken—Telok's green eyes were alert from his place near the door, Rekosh had pulled himself upright using the cloth-shrouded pod beside which he'd slept, and Lacey had lifted her head off the bed of her cryochamber to look bleary-eyed through the gloom at Ella.

"You okay?" Lacey asked.

"Just... Just need some air. F-fresh air," Ella managed to say softly between coughs.

With a troubled light in her eyes, Ahnset glanced at Ketahn.

He tilted his head toward the door and gestured with one hand.

Ella's coughing subsided, but she looked little comforted by the respite. There were frantic patches of color on her cheeks that stood out harshly against her sickly pale, sweat-slickened skin, and her breaths were shallow, labored, and rapid.

Ahnset shifted her huge body toward the front of the pod. Gently, she hooked a bent finger beneath Ella's chin and guided the female to look at her. Ahnset pointed to herself, then to Ella, before waving a hand toward the door.

Ella nodded and offered a smile; the expression looked thin and strained, genuine but made at some unseen cost.

Rising fully, Ahnset bent over the cryochamber, carefully gathered Ella in her arms, blanket and all, and turned toward the door. She paused only to collect her war spear and her bag before striding forward.

Telok was watching Ahnset when she reached the door. He cocked his head, eyes narrowing slightly, and a brief, uncertain tremor coursed through his mandibles.

Ahnset reached forward and pressed the button on the doorframe. The door made its usual hiss and slid open, allowing red light to spill in from the corridor beyond. She hesitated for three heartbeats, attention locked on Telok, before she hunched down, twisted aside, and—with more than a few contortions of her limbs—squeezed through the too small opening.

Lacey laid her head down again. Rekosh eased back onto the floor.

Telok stood up, braced a hand on the doorframe, and leaned through to glance into the corridor. His suspicion should have roused Ketahn's, but Ivy made a sleepy, confused sound and began to push herself up off Ketahn's chest.

"Is Ella okay?" she asked.

"Shh. She is okay." Ketahn dropped his gaze to his mate, resuming the soothing up-and-down motions of his hands on her back. "Back to sleep, my heartsthread."

With a sigh, she relaxed and sank atop him, rubbing her cheek against his chest. He could not help again noticing the press of her warm, soft body atop him.

The door whispered shut, and Telok's hide rasped against the wall as he lowered himself to the floor. Ketahn meant to look at his friend, to wordlessly pose a question and find out what had passed between Telok and Ahnset, but a weariness beyond any he'd known crashed down upon him. Ketahn's eyelids fell. Somehow, he kept his hands moving until the darkness swallowed him utterly.

"Ketahn."

The deep, familiar voice dragged Ketahn out of sleep, splashing alertness over him as surely as if it had been a pot of cold water dumped on his head. Though he felt as though he'd only just closed his eyes, he knew time had passed on an instinctual level. Not much time, but time all the same.

Ivy still lay atop him, languid and sleep warm, and he swore he could still feel her body thrumming from their mating the day before. But Telok was here, too, his legs bent so his underside was almost on the floor.

"They are gone, Ketahn," Telok said.

"Who?" Ketahn asked, but he knew the answer before that tiny word had been fully shaped in his mouth.

The cold, hard lump within him expanded, pressing up into his chest and making it hard to draw breath.

"Ahnset and Ella. I went to check on them when it felt like they had been gone too long. But they are not outside."

Ketahn braced a pair of hands on the floor and pushed himself into a more upright position, keeping a snug hold on his mate. Ivy stirred again, tensing as she stretched against him. He pressed the tips of his mandible fangs together and fought back his rising panic.

"Has the sun yet crested, Telok?"

"Only just," Telok replied. "But a storm came during the night and has yet to cease."

Ivy covered a yawn with her hand and combed her fingers through her hair, sweeping it out of her face. "What's going on?"

The words of Ketahn's response sounded as though they were laced with hurt and uncertainty, even to him. In English, he said, "Ahnset has taken Ella."

Ivy braced her elbow against his chest, driving her weight upon it as she shoved herself up. Her eyes were wide and disbelieving. "What? What does that mean, Ketahn? Taken her where?"

Any signs of grogginess had been banished from her features. Ketahn felt her heart quickening through all the contact their bodies still shared; it could not match the pace of his already racing hearts.

"Ahnset has taken Ella away from here," he replied.

"Why? To where? Ketahn, what is—"

Cold certainly flooded him, undaunted by the fear in his mate's voice, undeterred by the confused murmurings as the others woke.

"She is taking Ella to Takarahl, Ivy."

Panic glinted in her eyes, threatening to overwhelm their clear, calm-skies blue. A thousand unspoken questions danced in her gaze like the loose threads of a hastily spun web in the breeze, none strong enough to take priority over the others.

It mirrored Ketahn's emotions; he was overcome by a thousand feelings, all conflicting, a thousand thoughts, all spiraling out of control, none of them helpful. There was doom in that tangled web, death. Betrayal. But all the same, he knew he had not been betrayed.

Words he'd once spoken to his broodsister echoed from his memory.

You have always seen things as they should be, Ahnset, rather than as they are.

Ketahn had initially argued against waking these humans. He knew his sister would have sided with Ivy, though she had not known any of these beings.

As quickly but gently as he could, Ketahn slid Ivy off him, setting her on the floor. She got onto her knees, watching as he twisted, gathered his legs beneath him, and rose.

"Ketahn?"

"She means to help." He reached aside to take his spear from its place against the wall. "But she is mistaken in how to do so."

"What's going on?" asked Ahmya, sitting up in her cryochamber.

"Something's wrong," said Callie.

"No shit," muttered Cole.

"Not helpful, man." Diego had already swung his legs over the side of his pod and was rubbing the sleep from his eyes.

Ivy was on her feet now, staring up at Ketahn with more unease in her eyes. "Ketahn... What's going to happen?"

Bending down, Ketahn took hold of her arms with his lower hands. Ivy clutched the undersides of his forearms.

He used his free upper hand to smooth her tousled hair. In that moment, she seemed so small, so vulnerable, so lost and alone. Ketahn's every instinct roared against that; even seeing hints of such upon her face was too much to bear. And yet... In her concern, she was as beautiful as ever. That compassion and caring made her spirit so radiant that it shone brighter than any star, than either of the moons, than the sun itself.

He brushed his mouth against the side of her neck and breathed deep her scent, making no effort to quiet the hungry, appreciative rumble in his chest. At the same time, he stroked a foreleg against her calf. He needed as much of her fragrance upon him as possible before the rain washed everything away.

Ketahn wanted nothing more than to stay here with her forever. He wanted to stop caring about everything and everyone else. He wanted to be free of the responsibility, the guilt.

But each thump of his hearts marked another moment closer to disaster.

"Tell them that my broodsister has gone to get aid for Ella," he rasped in vrix.

"Why can you not tell them yourself?" she replied shakily in the same tongue. He knew by the resignation in her tone that she already understood.

He drew back to meet her gaze. "I will do all I can to find Ahnset before she reaches Takarahl."

"Let me go instead, Ketahn," said Telok gruffly. There was something hard in his eyes, a determination with which Ketahn had once been quite familiar.

One of the humans—it sounded like Will—asked Ivy what was happening. She turned her head toward him and responded in English, relaying Ketahn's message.

"We are all friends with her." Rekosh spread his arms to either side, palms up. "Any of us could go in your stead."

Telok gnashed his mandibles, fine hairs bristling. "You are needed here, Ketahn."

The humans were all awake and out of their pods now, wearing their worries plainly on their faces. Some of them spoke to one another; their voices held no meaning to Ketahn now.

Ketahn looked at his friends one by one. "In this, it must be me. This matter... It runs to my broodsister's core. Only I have any hope of changing her path. And she could not have journeyed far in the time since she left."

Urkot grunted and tapped a leg on the floor. "Yet should Ahnset get to Takarahl—"

"Tomorrow is the day I am expected to fulfill my word to Zurvashi," Ketahn said, holding down the flare of rage that had erupted at the center of his dread. "Today, I still have some grace. The queen will be of no concern."

"Unless she sees you." Though Ivy had not raised her voice, her words filled in all the empty space within the chamber, making the air impossibly thick and heavy.

Ketahn returned his attention to her. His heartsthread pulled taut, quivering beneath enormous pressure. This was not how things were meant to go. This was not how they'd laid out their plans, not how they'd prepared.

But there was one lesson Ketahn should have learned over

and over again throughout his life if no other—the Tangle had no interest in anyone's plans.

And his mate, for all her softness, all her kindness, was certainly no fool. He could not argue with her concern. He could not tell her not to worry—the words wouldn't even form in his throat.

Lowering his head, Ketahn tipped his headcrest against Ivy's forehead. She slid her hands up the backs of his arms, her nails raking his hide, until they were at his shoulders.

He took in another lungful of her scent and rasped, "I will return to you, my *nyleea*. I promise."

She closed her eyes, digging her nails a little deeper into his flesh. "You had better weave those words into the strongest bond in the universe, my *luveen*."

Despite everything, Ketahn chittered. It eased some of his tension, if only briefly, and he lifted his mandibles in a smile. He wrapped his arms around her and pulled her small body against him. A voice in the back of his mind, far too quiet, insisted that this was not a farewell, that everything would be all right.

That he would return to this place soon enough with Ella and Ahnset alongside him.

Love was not unknown to the vrix, though they did not have a word to encompass the feeling—which to Ketahn seemed more like a collection of feelings, all woven together into a single web, unfathomably strong and large, warm and secure, comforting and maddening. But Ivy giving name to it had put all the pieces into place for him. It had solved a puzzle he'd not known he'd been staring at for so long.

Two moon cycles ago, he'd been content to meet his eventual end having never had a mate. Now he would do everything he could to ensure his final moments, whenever they came, were spent at her side.

"My hearts beat for you, Ivy."

"And my heart beats for you. I love you, Ketahn."

Ivy stood on her toes, tipped her head back, and kissed him on the mouth, gifting him another taste of those soft, yielding lips, though the kiss was born of desperation. Ketahn trilled, low and rolling, just for her. He told himself that he'd have another taste soon enough.

She leaned her forehead against his headcrest. "Please come back to me," she begged, her voice breaking.

Ketahn trailed a finger along her delicate jaw, tilting her face up so her watery eyes met his. "I will, my heartsthread."

He adjusted his hold on the spear and slung his bag over his shoulder on his way to the door.

CHAPTER 26

UNDER THE DARK STORM CLOUDS, the jungle shadows were even deeper than they would have been at night. The plants gave off no light now. No cool blues or vibrant purples, no bright yellows or fiery oranges. There was nothing to light the way but erratic flashes of lightning—all of which were too weak and distant to overcome the gloom.

There had been no sign of Ahnset's recent passage. Both down in the pit and at its top, the ground was too riddled with tracks to pick out anything specific, and those tracks had been further obscured by mud and rainwater. Finding and following Ahnset's path during this storm would be a slow, tedious process.

Ketahn did not have the time to spare. Ella did not have the time.

So, Ketahn had pressed his only advantages—he was faster than his broodsister, and he knew where she was going.

The heavy rain limited his vision and left every surface slick and unreliable, but Ketahn could afford nothing but haste. He leapt from root to branch and back again, tore across mighty trunks with no regard for the damage wrought by his claws, and plunged through tangled plant growth with lashing arms and gnashing mandibles. Each segment he traveled was won with a pounding beat of his hearts. Each moment gone by intensified the heat coursing beneath his hide.

A weight he'd not fully felt in a long while fell upon him. It sought to drag him down, to make his limbs as heavy and stiff as stone. And though he had long been spared the fullness of that sensation, he recognized it—the burden of having others dependent upon him. The burden of lives beyond his own and his mate's being at risk because of his actions, the burden of their fates being woven with his.

Everything was for Ivy. He would fight harder for her than he'd fought for anything. And he would allow himself to fight no less fiercely for any other member of the tribe that had formed around himself and his mate—especially those who could not defend themselves.

Protector, let me be their shield.

Hunter, let me be their provider.

Delver, let me be their guide.

By your eightfold eyes, watch over my new kin... Or stand aside that I may do so myself.

Ketahn pushed on harder still in response to that burden. His muscles strained, flooded with unbearable fire despite the chill in the rain, but they did not falter.

His breath was ragged by the time he reached Takarahl, and he knew his hearts were not likely to slow. That persistent dread mingled with a fiery swell of rage when the mouth of the entry tunnel came into view. Heat and cold skittered across the surface of his hide, thrummed in his bones, and warred with one another in his chest.

Never again. He was never supposed to have seen this place again.

Growling a curse, Ketahn strode to the entrance—and the pair of Queen's Fangs guarding it.

They watched his approach with a strange blend of wariness and confidence in their eyes.

"I seek one of your spear sisters," he said, easing his tone as much as possible. "Ahnset."

"She has not come this way," replied one of the Fangs.

"No one has come today," said the other, dipping her chin toward the jungle, "though some hunters have gone."

Ahnset hadn't come this way, but she might have used a different entry—one closer to the queen's sanctum, perhaps. It would have meant less chance of Ella being seen.

But in his haste, Ketahn might well have arrived before his sister. What then? Wait, relying upon the tiny chance she would use this entrance?

He could not risk standing idle while it was possible she'd already entered the city with Ella.

Ketahn hurried forward, ignoring the fresh flare of fury and unease that blasted him as he crossed from the storm's gray gloom into Takarahl's eerie blue glow. One of the Fangs said something behind him. He didn't care what it had been.

These tunnels had never felt so cramped, this stone had never seemed so cold, these shadows had never looked so cruel, this place had never been so unwelcoming. Ketahn's quarrel had always been with the queen, but over the years, he'd come to see Takarahl as some twisted extension of her. It was as though Zurvashi's malice had seeped into every rock, saturated every shred of cloth, and burrowed into the core of every crystal.

And once again, he was rushing right toward her.

He drew the attention of many other vrix as he moved—a lone male, bearing those rare purple markings, clutching a spear and dripping water everywhere as though he'd brought the storm inside with him. Their hushed conversations were meaningless to him. Their faces blended together as he raked his gaze across them, searching for Ahnset, for Ella, disregarding everyone and everything else.

With his every step deeper into Takarahl, his heartsthread pulled tighter. His spirit cried out with need—need to be back with his mate, his Ivy. Its increasingly desperate, troubled song echoed in Ketahn's bones.

He needed to keep Ivy safe, needed to keep her—and her kind—hidden from his enemies. For Ahnset to bring Ella here...

Ketahn's dread hardened further and expanded as brighter blue light became visible ahead—the combined glow of countless crystals in the Den of Spirits, putting out their own light in the absence of the sun.

His mind's eye tinted that glow crimson.

"I will return to Ivy," he rasped. Each step was heavier than the last, each was harder, and he was forced to draw upon strength from deeper and deeper within himself. "This is not the end."

Today was the beginning.

Though it was not Offering Day, the large entrance to the Den of Spirits was guarded by Queen's Fangs, their gold and gemstone adornments gleaming cold in the blue light from the chamber beyond.

"The queen is holding private audience," said one of the Fangs, stepping forward with a palm outthrust. He knew her; she was called Nahkto, a veteran of the war with Kaldarak. "Turn aro—"

Recognition sparked in her eyes.

"Go on," Nahkto said, her voice tight. She stepped aside, planted the butt of her spear on the floor, and waved Ketahn onward.

He felt no shame in that his first instinct was to flee. Zurvashi was the last thing he wanted to get tangled up with—

not just now, but always. His previous encounter with her had been meant to be the final one. He was never supposed to see her again.

Fuck.

Clamping his jaw shut, Ketahn squared his shoulders, fixed his attention ahead, and strode forward.

He was halted by another Fang when she stepped into his path. Though her spear remained to the side, her solid, wide stance spoke of a readiness for action, and one of her thumbs was hooked on her belt just above her fanged club. He knew this one, too—Irekah, who had thrown an innocent male against a wall for carrying a weaver's knife when last Ketahn had seen her.

"Your weapon, hunter," she growled.

Ketahn squeezed the shaft of his spear. Water oozed from the damp leather grip, running between his fingers and dripping to the floor. In his mind's eye, he saw a fleeting image of his spear buried in the queen's throat. He stared up at the female looming before him, unsure of whether he kept his hatred and lust for blood from showing outwardly.

Her adornments clinked softly as she adjusted her stance by a thread's breadth, and the grip of her war spear creaked in her fist.

For Ivy. For Ella.

For the future he'd never dared imagine but now dangled so close.

Angling the head of his spear toward the floor, Ketahn turned the shaft so it stood vertically and held it out to the Fang. Irekah snatched the weapon away with a snarl. For a few more heartbeats, the female held his gaze, her eyes intense and fine hairs bristling.

Finally, Irekah huffed and stood aside. "Make haste. We are not interested in sharing your company, hunter."

When Ketahn walked past her, she gave his back a hard shove, making him stumble through the entryway.

He denied his anger's demand that he turn around and show Irekah that he did not need a spear to inflict damage. But it was a close thing.

The Den of Spirits was largely deserted; that fact made Ketahn's gut twist into knots. On most days, there were always numerous vrix to be found here perusing the tales carved into the stone, basking in reflected sunlight, or quietly paying homage to the spirits of their ancestors and praying to the Eight. The only other vrix here now were all gathered on the central dais.

Fangs stood along the edge of the dais like gold-adorned statues. A small group of spiritspeakers were positioned a couple segments in from that edge, their silk-shrouded figures just as large but far less imposing than those of the Fangs.

The middle spiritspeaker wore garb different from that of her two companions—Archspeaker Valkai. She was talking in soft tones, her white coverings swaying with her gentle movements. Despite the echo in the chamber, Ketahn could not make out her words; her voice was nothing more than a musical hum by the time it reached him.

Beyond the spiritspeakers, perched at the highest point of the dais, was the queen. Two Claws stood close behind her. The black furs over their shoulders hung low enough down their backs to brush their hindquarters.

Ahnset was nowhere to be seen. Relief and renewed dread clashed within Ketahn, making his chest constrict and his gut churn. She was not here, but that didn't mean she wasn't in Takarahl. That didn't mean she wasn't on her way here even now.

Zurvashi's head turned toward Ketahn. Even from such a distance, he did not miss the ravenous glimmer in her amber eyes. Her mandibles twitched outward and snapped together, and she raised herself a little higher. The long, flowing ends of her purple silk coverings trailed across the stone beneath her.

Ketahn's broodsister was not here, but he was trapped.

The queen turned toward him fully without so much as acknowledging the disrespect to the Archspeaker, who had still been talking.

"My bold little hunter," Zurvashi called. The cavern built her voice into something booming and ominous, and Ketahn's stride faltered. Her eyes—and her tone—darkened. "Have you not made me wait long enough, Ketahn? Come. Now."

Ketahn's teeth ground together as he forced his legs into motion. The tension crashing through his body was stronger than ever, threatening to overwhelm him utterly.

Once more, he had to play the game. Once more, and never again.

Never again... How many times had he told himself that? How many times had he failed to make it true?

The queen waved a dismissive hand at the spiritspeakers. "We will resume our discussion at another time."

The spiritspeakers flanking Valkai sank into low bows.

Archspeaker Valkai offered only a shallow dip of her head, glancing toward Ketahn as she did so. "My queen, if I might ask but a few more moments..."

Zurvashi snapped her head toward Valkai, granting the motion an enhanced sense of power and finality with a sharp clack of her mandible fangs. She said nothing; her stare was more than adequate to send her message.

Archspeaker Valkai held the queen's stare for five of Ketahn's heartbeats; far longer than he would have expected. Then she bowed deeply and backed away with impressive grace, her silk coverings moving fluidly.

Somehow, Ketahn found more hatred for Zurvashi within himself. Whatever questions had arisen in his hearts about the Eight, he had seen only kindness and respect from the Archspeaker—not only for the queen and other vrix of high station, but for every vrix in Takarahl. She'd always seemed to nurture genuine care for all the Eight's expansive brood here in the realm of flesh, blood, and bone.

The three spiritspeakers retreated from the dais just as Ketahn reached it. Valkai again met Ketahn's gaze, this time crossing her forearms in the sign of the Eight.

He returned the gesture, wishing he could imbue it with the appropriate reverence.

"May they watch over you favorably, hunter," the Archspeaker said softly.

Gold jingled and silk rasped atop the dais. Ketahn looked at the queen, who was approaching him with the leisurely air of a predator toying with its prey; she was followed by the Claws.

"I see no gifts. Shall I voice my disappointment, Ketahn?" she purred. Though she was still several segments away, her scent thickened in the air, beginning what was sure to be a relentless assault on Ketahn's senses.

The Claws behind the queen flicked their eyes toward her, their claspers twitching.

Ketahn forced the memory of Ivy's scent to the forefront of his mind and wrapped himself around it. "You are the queen. Have you not made it clear you will do as you wish?"

Six Fangs stood on the dais, including Prime Fang Korahla. There were undoubtedly more at each of the cavern's entrances. Escape would not be possible without the queen's permission.

Zurvashi's chitter was low and rumbling, as unhurried as her pace. "I know not whether to praise you for learning or punish you for insolence. Yet either shall be a joy to me."

She stopped at the edge of the dais and slid one foreleg forward, freeing it from the confines of her long silk covering. Ketahn was forced, as always, to look up at her. She brushed her leg against his shoulder. Her fine hairs teased his hide, sparking a wave of revulsion that swept through his entire body in an instant.

"That strange scent is upon you again..." She tilted her head, mandibles swinging outward and back in.

Ketahn's hearts stuttered. That scent was Ivy's; the rain had not been enough to wash it away. He couldn't help taking some pride in that—though his alarm for his mate was much stronger.

He stepped back, breaking the contact with her leg. "Many strange scents are upon me. And, as ever, none of them are yours."

In the back of his mind, some part of Ketahn protested. What could he possibly gain by provoking Zurvashi? For his pride, for his bitterness, was he really going to further endanger Ella?

There'd be no protecting anyone if the queen tore his throat out.

"Your little taunts mean nothing, Ketahn. They are no more than feints thrown to feel out the skills of an enemy warrior."

Ketahn curled his hands into useless fists. Where was Ahnset? How much longer did he have to find her?

How long could he bring himself to pretend?

"Is that what we are to one another, Zurvashi? Enemies?"

She trilled thoughtfully. "You have seemed eager to make us such."

"I am eager only to prove my worth," he said, somehow keeping his voice steady. "There is no female like you, my queen, and conquering you is the greatest challenge any vrix could face. Yet thus far I have earned only your disappointment."

"Ah, you foolish little male," she said in a light tone. "I am disappointed only because you have not arrived laden with gifts, as you promised. That means you will need to make extra efforts in other matters to appease me."

Everything inside Ketahn twisted and shrank back at the

thought of the *efforts* she'd implied. "Your patience will bear fruit. But I must point out that no matter how much you wish it so, my queen, seven comes before eight. Tomorrow is your day."

She chittered again. There was far more humor in it than Ketahn could have hoped to hear—and it was unsettling. Sweeping the long silk cloth aside, Zurvashi stepped smoothly off the dais. "Every day is my day, Ketahn. And according to our dear spiritspeakers, eight comes before all."

Zurvashi strode toward him, the two Claws not far behind. Her fragrance wafted from her, coalescing around Ketahn in a cloud thicker than any jungle mist he'd ever encountered. It raked its claws against his instincts, seeking a weak spot on his hide to overwhelm his senses and lay claim upon him. He held her stare as she approached—and held his place.

The queen halted less than half a segment from Ketahn. She lifted her upper hands; one went to the thin braids dangling over her shoulder, toying with them delicately, while she brushed the knuckles of the other up along Ketahn's arm. Her maliciously mirthful eyes shifted toward the nearby spiritspeakers. "Of course, I say *one* comes before all."

Those amber eyes returned to Ketahn, smoldering with hunger. "You may yet convince me that two"—her hand drifted over his shoulder and up his neck—"is the better number."

She slid her forelegs forward, rubbing them along Ketahn's, and purred.

A shiver threatened to course through Ketahn from backside to crest. Instinct roared within him—*this is not Ivy, not my mate!* He focused on that rage, on that wrongness, on the promise he'd made to his mate. With a huff, he expelled the air that had been tainted by Zurvashi's scent from his lungs.

Ketahn closed the distance between himself and the queen, rising high on straightened legs to look her eye to eye.

On the edges of his vision, he saw the Fangs who were still on the dais heft their spears into two handed grips, their attention fixed upon Ketahn. The Claws who were following the queen had lowered their hands to the blackrock axes on their belts, but their eyes were upon the queen instead of Ketahn, gleaming with barely masked lust. Undoubtedly, they were also struggling against her scent.

"There will be no question of it when I am through, Zurvashi," Ketahn said.

Zurvashi searched his gaze. "Such arrogance."

"Confidence," he corrected. Fully aware of her huge mandibles so close to his face, he leaned closer still and lowered his voice. "You are as good as conquered, my queen. Tomorrow."

Her hand stilled in its trek along Ketahn's jaw. The heat from her body intensified, and the tension in her muscles vibrated in the air. That heady scent intensified further, lashing out in retaliation to Ketahn's resistance, battering down his defenses, forcing a response from him.

He drew his claspers in as tight as possible, squeezing his slit shut against the involuntary desire her scent instilled. He would *not* betray his mate, instinct be damned.

Her fingers curled slowly; the change poised the claws of her upper hand against the relatively tender flesh of Ketahn's throat. But she didn't put any pressure on those claws. Not yet.

"Tomorrow," Ketahn repeated. "I will not break my word."

His word to Ivy. To the humans. To himself. The queen had earned nothing from him—not loyalty, not honesty, not even a sliver of respect.

There was movement on the other side of the cavern—the side that led to the queen's sanctum. Heavy steps, thumping spear butts, and clinking gold.

Zurvashi spoke in a voice just as low as Ketahn's, but her tone was laced with menace. "Has my generosity led you to believe that you may dictate the terms of our relationship, Ketahn?"

Ketahn kept his eyes locked with hers, betraying nothing. "I already have been."

The sounds that had entered the cavern drew rapidly nearer. Zurvashi's mandibles twitched as though in time to the approaching steps. Pricks of pain flared on Ketahn's hide beneath her claws.

But there was a flicker of lust in her eyes.

"My queen," said one of the newcomers, "please forgive the interruption."

Neither Zurvashi nor Ketahn looked away from each other, even when one of the newly arrived vrix gasped.

"Later," the queen growled. She did not ease her hold on Ketahn's throat, but she did not strengthen it, either, and her leg stroked his lightly, teasingly.

"My queen, it is a matter of—"

"Later!" Zurvashi's mandibles swung inward, halting only when her fangs were but a hair's breadth from Ketahn's face. He granted her not so much as a flinch.

"This is not to be ignored, my queen," Korahla said in a voice both commanding and uncharacteristically thin.

Ketahn guessed it was her tone more than her words that pierced the queen's focus; it was certainly what captured his attention. Releasing a low growl, Zurvashi turned her head toward the newcomers. Ketahn's eyes fixated on the queen's throat for a moment—a terrible, tempting moment—before following her gaze.

He might have likened what he felt then to a net snapping shut around his insides and pulling so tight that it all seemed about to burst. The cold that flowed out from his core made the snow Ivy had once told him about sound balmy in comparison.

Flanked by a pair of clearly confused, unsettled Fangs stood Ahnset. She held something against her chest, bundled in a familiar silk blanket. Water was dripping off her hide, her wet braids hung in limp disarray over her shoulders, and her wide, desperate, apologetic eyes were fixed on Ketahn.

Though she was larger and broader than either of her escorts, though she had fought countless foes to the death, though she was elite even amongst the queen's elite guard, there was something woefully innocent about Ahnset in that moment. Something that reminded Ketahn of a broodling.

Something that felt like a knife sinking into one of his hearts.

The queen snarled. "Ahnset?" Her fingers flexed just enough for Ketahn to feel a claw bite into his hide. She tore her hand away from his neck and spun to face his broodsister fully. "Explain. Now."

Ketahn's lungs were ablaze, but his throat was too tight to draw in air—and that had nothing to do with the queen's relinquished grasp. The sorrowful gleam in Ahnset's eyes deepened; she hadn't looked away from Ketahn despite now being the focus of the queen's attention.

There were no words to express the torrent of emotion raging within Ketahn. A thousand weavers could have worked at it for a thousand years and not unraveled the tangle.

"Do not ignore me." Zurvashi stepped toward Ahnset. The Fang escorts retreated an equal distance. The queen paused, her anger faltering as her eyes dipped. "What are you carrying?"

I am sorry, my nyleea.

I am sorry.

Ahnset took in a heavy breath and finally looked at the queen, the softness fading from her eyes. "A creature in need of aid, my queen."

She lifted the bundle in her arms. The creature within stirred, and part of the cloth fell away, revealing a small, pale skinned face, lank brown hair, and exhausted, terrified green eyes.

Human eyes.

The nearby females gasped and uttered shocked curses. One of the spiritspeakers whispered a brief prayer to the Eight. A few of the Fangs turned their spears toward Ella and Ahnset, as though the tiny, sickly human could possibly do them any harm.

But only one reaction scared Ketahn—only one reaction fed directly into his cold, heavy dread.

Zurvashi stared at Ella, completely silent, totally unmoving. And Ketahn felt his world shattering around her.

CHAPTER 27

THE QUEEN'S mandibles rose and fell, and she tilted her head aside by the barest degree. The only sound in the chamber was that of the storm raging far, far above, amplified through the hole in the cavern ceiling, and the slow, echoing drip of water falling through that same hole.

Ketahn's hearts lurched into motion again. His blood crawled through his veins like mud sliding down a hill, thickened by that impossible mix of hot and cold.

"What is this creature?" Zurvashi asked. The buzzing underlying her words might have been curiosity—but it might as easily have been disgust.

Though the movement was subtle, Ahnset eased back from the queen. "She is a *hyu-nin*."

Zurvashi summoned her Claws closer with an impatient gesture. The males advanced warily, eyeing Ketahn and keeping their hands on their weapons as they did so.

"Have you seen such a creature as this?" the queen asked.

"No, my queen," replied one.

"Never," said the other.

"Only the finest hunters for your Claw, my queen," Zurvashi

said mockingly. "Were it not for his loyalty, I would have crushed that fool Durax long ago." She dismissed the Claws with a brisk wave and looked at Ketahn. "And you?"

Ketahn did not answer.

The queen chittered. "You have. It is plain in your eyes, Ketahn."

"W-what's happening?" Ella asked in a small, worn voice. The light in her eyes was more than just fear. It was a sputtering fire that was burning through the last of its wood, brighter than ever as it entered its final moments. And, whenever her gaze drifted away from the vrix to take in the cavern around her, that light took on a hint of wonder.

"It has a strange call," remarked one of the Fangs.

"Quiet," snapped Prime Fang Korahla.

"Ahnset?" Ella looked from Ahnset to Ketahn, a pleading crease forming between her eyebrows. "Ketahn?"

Zurvashi released a disbelieving huff. "Did this creature just speak your names?"

"It will be all right, Ella," Ketahn said in English; he did not look away from the queen.

"Words," Archspeaker Valkai breathed. "Those are words in another tongue."

"The *hyu-nins* are intelligent," Ahnset said, bolstering her voice with fresh confidence. "My queen, befriending these creatures would benefit all Takarahl. The tools they are capable of creating are beyond anything we have imagined."

The queen stepped closer to Ahnset and Ella. The human female shrank in Ahnset's arms, curling close against her chest.

"K-Ketahn, what…what is this place?" Ella asked, trembling. "Why did Ahnset…bring me here?"

The words Ketahn was about to speak formed low in his gut, taking the shape of a thorny vine. They shredded his insides as they rose, leaving his chest and throat torn and raw; it was not the alien tongue in which he spoke them that made them so painful. It was the truth of them.

It was the futility of them.

"For healing," he said. "Ahnset...wants to help."

"You understand this creature, Ketahn?" the queen asked, looking at him again. "Tell me what it is saying."

Ketahn curled his hands into fists, pressing his claws into his palms. "Ahnset, take her out of here."

"You will do no such thing," Zurvashi snarled, thrusting a finger toward Ahnset like it was a war spear. "Bring that thing to me."

Ahnset's mandibles twitched and fell, hanging at the sides of her face. Her posture was stiff with tension and uncertainty. "Ketahn, I..."

"Your queen has commanded you," Zurvashi growled. "Do not ignore me."

Ella's trembling had only worsened in the face of the queen's anger.

As large and powerful as the queen seemed to him, she must've been terribly more so from Ella's perspective. Ella was a small, soft, ill thing in a world of giants—and none were quite so large as Zurvashi.

Ketahn did not care if Ella's death was mere days away or years in the future—he would not allow the human's final moments to be here. Not with *her*.

"Do not ignore *me*," he snarled, darting into the space between Zurvashi and Ahnset.

The Fangs shook their apparent stupor. In a burst of movement, four of them took position in a ring around Ketahn, leveling their spears at his neck. The two Claws behind the queen had their axes raised now, mandible claws gnashing.

Ketahn did not look away from Zurvashi.

The queen dipped her chin to glance at him, narrowing her eyes.

Ahnset rasped his name.

Ketahn's chest and shoulders heaved, breath growing ragged as the fire inside him finally beat back the cold. "We have not finished, Zurvashi."

Queen Zurvashi made a thoughtful trill. "No, little Ketahn. We have not. Remove yourself from my path."

Ivy... Forgive me.

"No."

"Curse your stubbornness, hunter," Prime Fang Korahla growled. She stood behind the queen, eyes shifting repeatedly between Ketahn and his broodsister. He'd never seen her look so troubled.

The mask of calm that had settled over Zurvashi's eyes shattered. She lunged at him, reaching with both left arms. Her long, wicked claws were blurs racing toward Ketahn's head, each as capable of piercing his hide as a sharpened blackrock shard.

Ketahn ducked under Zurvashi's reach and shifted to her left side. He put up one of his arms, hooking it around both of hers, and swung himself behind her, using his hold to throw himself against her back.

Between the momentum of her attack and impact of Ketahn's weight, Zurvashi's forelegs buckled. Her leg joints hit the floor heavily. Gold and gems rattled and clanged, some of them striking the stone, and she was forced to twist her torso to catch herself with her right hands.

Drawing himself fully atop her, Ketahn latched his legs around her hindquarters and torso, hooking his leg claws into her hide. She snarled in pain and shoved herself upright far too quickly.

The faces of all the vrix he'd seen fall over the years flashed through Ketahn's mind's eye. With a growl of his own, he curled his upper left arm around Zurvashi's neck and sank his claws into her cheek to anchor his hold. Hot blood trickled over his fingers.

There was shouting all around, hulking figures looming nearby, but Ketahn couldn't make out any of it; that chaos did not matter.

Protector... Avenger. If he could not save Ella, he would at least ensure Zurvashi would never pose a threat to any of his other friends, any of the other humans.

Zurvashi lifted her upper right arm over her head and bent it back. Her groping hand came down on Ketahn's back between his neck and shoulder. Her claws pierced his flesh like it were no thicker than a leaf.

He did not feel any pain, but the strength drained from his arm all the same. Zurvashi bent forward, dragging Ketahn off with raw force. His body flipped over her shoulder, his claws tearing furrows on her cheek, and he hit the floor on his back with enough force to steal the air from his lungs.

Zurvashi shook her head. Droplets of blood spilled from the cuts on her cheek, falling on Ketahn.

The Claws were upon him first. The edges on their black-rock axes gleamed in the blue light of the crystals as their groping hands caught Ketahn's arms.

"Do not kill him," Zurvashi barked.

With no attempt at hiding their frustration, the Claws growled and tightened their holds on Ketahn, dragging him up. When he tried to get his legs beneath him, one of the Claws kicked the backs of his leg joints, forcing the limbs to buckle.

"Please, Ahnset, I want to go back. P-please. Take...take me... take me back." Ella's words were broken, weak, desperate. Labored and fearful. Tears glistened in her eyes.

"Shh. Be easy, little one," Ahnset soothed. Ketahn recognized the cracks in her outward calm, the faint wobble in her voice.

"Was this a challenge for rule?" the queen demanded, locking her gaze on the Archspeaker. "Were we battling beneath their eightfold eyes to determine the fate of Takarahl?"

Valkai lowered her head. "No, my queen."

"No." Zurvashi spun toward the Fangs, fine hairs bristling. "So why did all of you stand and stare as your queen was attacked? Boulders would have offered me better protection!"

"He was unarmed," replied Prime Fang Korahla, "and you have ever chosen to meet your attackers with your own hands. My queen."

The queen walked to the Prime Fang, fingers flexing as though preparing to lash out. Zurvashi's voice was dangerously low. "When all this is through, Korahla, we will have a spirited discussion concerning the loyalty and effectiveness of the Fangs under your command."

Something flickered in Korahla's eyes—unease, perhaps even shame—but it was gone before Ketahn could determine what it was.

The Prime Fang made a gesture of apology and bowed her head. "Yes, my queen."

Zurvashi lingered there for several more heartbeats; Korahla stood her ground but did not raise her head again. Finally, the queen stepped in front of Ketahn.

Crimson oozed from her cheek as she leaned down and grabbed his jaw, holding his head still. She purred, "We are *not* done, you and I." She raised a bent foreleg, pressed it against his side, and slid it down slowly, deliberately, spreading her strong scent along his hide. "Bending you to my will be the greatest challenge I have ever faced, Ketahn. But when you finally crumble, when you finally admit to yourself that you belong to me… That moment will be sweeter by far than any other."

"By the Eight," Ketahn rasped, "I will end you, Zurvashi."

"A foolish male who needs to learn his place. It is fortunate for you that your place is as my mate and sire to my brood." She relaxed her hold on his face and patted his cheek. "But I must attend to my other guests before I see to you, little hunter."

He snapped his head forward, seeking the queen's forearm with his mandibles, but one of the Claws grasped a fistful of

Ketahn's hair and tugged him back hard. The jagged edge of an axe pressed against his throat.

"Do not move," the Claw to his right growled.

Zurvashi chittered as though it were all in jest and turned back toward Ahnset. "I will say this but once more, Ahnset. Bring the creature here."

Ahnset drew in a deep breath that made her chest swell. Ketahn watched her harden—her eyes, her stance, her very spirit. She closed the distance between herself and the queen in two strides.

Queen Zurvashi folded her arms across her chest. "Place it down."

Stiffly, Ahnset lowered Ella. The human clutched at Ahnset, fighting to remain close, to remain in the shelter of her arms, but it would have been an unwinnable struggle for Ella even if she were at her prime.

Ella's feet touched the cold stone floor; they were bare. She staggered back against Ahnset, making as though she meant to twist toward her.

The hardness in Ahnset's eyes shattered. She looked away as she placed a pair of hands upon Ella's shoulders and gently forced the human forward. Ella's struggles ceased as she found herself looking up at Zurvashi. The flesh around her eyes was dark and sunken, in stark contrast to her terribly pale skin, and there was a blue tint to her lips. She drew the blanket around herself more snugly, shivering.

"As I said, my queen, there is much we might learn from them," Ahnset said.

"From something so tiny and frail?" Zurvashi leaned closer to Ella. "What is wrong with it?"

"She is ill. I had hoped…to acquire mender root, my queen, to heal her."

"Are they all like this? Soft and weak?" The queen lifted her gaze to Ahnset. "This creature looks like something we vrix would hunt, though it would barely make a single meal."

Ketahn's gut churned at the thought of humans being food— of his Ivy being food.

"Do not touch her," he growled, throwing himself forward. The Claws restraining him grunted and pulled him back.

Zurvashi turned her head, regarding Ketahn. His hearts hammered in his chest, his rage swirled in fiery waves that had nowhere to go, consuming him from within, and his heartsthread thrummed mournfully in the absence of his mate.

"There are more, yes?" Zurvashi returned her attention to Ahnset.

Ahnset's mandibles drew together, fangs grinding against one another.

The queen reached for Ella. The human female let out a meager cry and shied back, but she could not retreat; Ahnset's firm hold kept her in place.

Zurvashi's hand caught the underside of Ella's jaw. Ella's breathing, already shallow and strained, became quick and ragged, panic lighting in her eyes. Zurvashi tipped the human's head back, turning it from one side to the other.

"Ugly things. Like misshapen grubs crawled out of the dirt." The queen grasped the blanket and tore it away from Ella. The damp cloth brushed along Zurvashi's foreleg when she released it.

"She is as harmless as a broodling," Ketahn said. "Let her leave. She is no threat to you."

The queen's body went rigid. A low growl rumbled in her chest as she hooked the fallen blanket with her leg claws and lifted it to one of her hands. She pressed the fabric to her face and drew in a deep, heavy breath.

Realization struck Ketahn harder than any blow Zurvashi could've delivered.

That was Ivy's blanket. The one she'd used most every day

for several eightdays before gifting it to Ella. The one that bore Ivy's scent down to its tiniest fibers.

Mandibles spreading wide, Zurvashi leaned down and sniffed at Ella, who closed her eyes and turned her face away.

"Leave her, Zurvashi!" Ketahn snarled.

"I know this scent." The queen shifted her hand to wrap around Ella's throat.

Ella let out a choked cry, throwing her hands up to grasp futilely at Zurvashi's arm.

"I have smelled it on you"—Zurvashi thrust a finger toward Ketahn, fire flashing in her eyes—"many times. One of many jungle scents, you said. But I had never smelled it before, and I have walked the jungle, Ketahn."

Ahnset's arms tensed, tremors rippling through them. "My queen, please. She has done no wrong to you or any other vrix. She and her kind mean us no harm."

Zurvashi tore Ella from Ahnset's hold, leaving the Fang to stumble forward. Ella's feet dragged on the floor as Zurvashi, holding her by the neck, spun to face Ketahn. "You have mated this creature!"

Ketahn pulled against the hold of the Claws, hearts thundering. "I have not!"

Ella's face was turning red. Ketahn knew some of that color on human skin was healthy, but there was nothing healthy about this.

He roared and twisted his torso fiercely to the side, wrenching his arms free from one of the Claws and throwing his weight against the other. The blackrock edge sliced across his throat. The searing pain was distant, the wound minor—and his fury was unleashed.

Instinct drove him, demanding blood, demanding death, demanding savagery to protect this sickly member of his tribe. His claws lashed out wildly, shredding the flesh of the male he'd knocked down.

The other Claw had maintained his hold on Ketahn's hair. He pulled on it now. Ketahn resisted for an instant before throwing his weight in the same direction. The sudden shift in momentum disrupted the Claw's balance, and Ketahn fell upon him. In the span of a heartbeat, he wrestled the male's axe away.

A huge figure approached from the side. Ketahn lashed out with the axe, burying its head in the gut of the Fang who'd tried to intervene. It slowed her down, but she did not stop.

A storm of grabbing hands and pummeling fists enveloped Ketahn, obscuring his vision, reducing his mind to the most primal of all thoughts—kill or be killed. He thrashed and clawed, gnashed his mandibles, and kicked his legs, doing as much damage to his foes as he could.

But they were too many, too strong. The Fangs managed to get hold of his arms and legs, lifting him off the floor completely to deny him the leverage solid ground would have provided. They bent his limbs, putting so much pressure on his joints that he might have wailed were it not for the battle haze dulling everything but his rage.

The Fangs swung him around so he was facing Zurvashi again.

Ella's round, terrified eyes, showing so much of their whites —and the weblike veins running through them, now more noticeable than ever—met Ketahn's gaze.

"You mated this abomination," Zurvashi snarled. "You have spurned me for this creature! This worm! You have been offered the best of our kind and you chose an animal instead." She shook Ella hard; the human's limbs flopped against the force, but somehow Ella held on.

"Release her," Ketahn roared, straining against his captors.

The Fangs swayed, shifting their legs to better brace themselves, and tightened their crushing grips on him.

"Please, my queen," Ahnset begged. "It is not as you say!"

She lunged forward, but Korahla intercepted her, blocking Ahnset's path with her own body.

"Still you fight for this creature's life?" Zurvashi lifted Ella high. The human's feet dangled and kicked weakly nearly two segments off the floor. Zurvashi was still staring at Ketahn. "I will not allow our kind to be tainted by these vile creatures. I will no longer be made to look a fool in my city."

The queen stepped forward and wrapped a hand around Ketahn's neck, squeezing tight enough to cease the flow of air into his lungs. She forced his head up. "I will no longer allow you to believe you have any choice, you sniveling jungle worm. Takarahl is *mine*. The whole Tangle is mine. *You. Are. Mine.*"

Ketahn tried to choke out words; he did not know what they might have been, did not know what he could have said, and it didn't matter. They wouldn't have changed anything had he been able to get them out.

She did not allow him to look away as she clamped a hand on the top of Ella's head. She did not allow him to look away as she squeezed Ella's neck and skull. Did not allow him to look away as she pulled her hands in separate directions.

"No!" Ahnset cried.

Ella's agonized scream was cut short by the wet crack of bone and the tearing of flesh. Ketahn had heard such sounds countless times, but this time, they pierced to his core. They were burned into his spirit, into his heartsthread, and they would haunt him forever. There was shouting, Ahnset crying out in shock and rage, but all Ketahn could hear was cracking bone, tearing flesh, and that short, horrifying scream.

A choked moan was Ella's final sound. It was little more than a whisper amidst a raging storm.

Blood gushed between Zurvashi's fingers, and bits of shattered flesh and bone oozed out with it. Her amber eyes bored into Ketahn as she tore what remained of Ella's head away from her body.

"Shaper, unmake me," someone rasped.

Ketahn stared at Ella's unmoving body, stared at the blood running over her jumpsuit, stared at her dirty bare feet as that blood ran down to drip off her toes and pool on the floor. For an instant, his imagination presented Ivy in Ella's place—and he knew the Eight were nothing like what he'd been taught. What benevolent gods would allow such an atrocity to take place here, in the very cavern where they were worshipped?

Zurvashi jerked Ketahn's face back to her and leaned close— close enough that he could've caught her with his mandibles, close enough that he should have done so, but he couldn't feel his body, couldn't move, couldn't think.

"I will have every one of those creatures brought to me," she purred, trailing the tip of a claw along his jawline, "and you will watch as I tear them apart, one by one. You will watch as I paint Takarahl's stone with their blood. And you will give me every-thing I demand and more, because you belong to me, Ketahn. You will spend the rest of your days redeeming yourself for what you have done. You will spend the rest of your days in your place, beneath me."

She shoved his head down hard and released her grasp. Ketahn sucked in air through his burning throat, mandibles flaring wide.

"I will give you everything you deserve," he growled. "Blood for blood."

The queen tossed Ella's remains aside like a soiled piece of silk, shaking excess blood from her hands. "Take him to the deepest, darkest hole in Takarahl and ensure he remains there until I see fit to use him."

The Fangs hauled him backward, carrying him away from the queen. Ketahn struggled and hissed, but he could not break their grips. His hearts beat like rolling thunder, and his rage was hot enough to melt stone, but it was all for nothing.

"As for you, Ahnset…" the queen said, turning her back toward Ketahn.

Prime Fang Korahla shifted so she was more fully in front of Ahnset. "Zurvashi, she—"

The queen silenced the Prime Fang with a click of her fangs. "She is going to lead my Claws to the rest of these creatures."

Ketahn roared in useless fury; it echoed in the cavern, building and building, shaking the crystals as it became something as powerful as it was meaningless. He roared until his throat was ragged, and even then, he did not stop until there was no sound left to emerge from him.

And the Queen's Fangs dragged him down into the dark.

AUTHOR'S NOTE

Look. We understand if you don't want to talk to us right now. We'll see you with the next book.

Cringes

Just kidding. Don't hate us! Please? Believe us, it made us sick knowing what was coming as we wrote this, knowing that it needed to happen to move the story forward. We didn't like doing it. But we never said this series was going to be fluffy. At least take comfort in the fact that there is only one more book in this trilogy, so there will be no more cliffhangers after this. That's a good thing, right? Right?!

Anyway, thank you so much for reading Enthralled. We hope that you enjoyed it—aside from the ending. And as we always request (or is it called begging?), if you loved it, please leave a review, share the series in your favorite reader group, on social media, or with a friend. Word of mouth is the best way you can support an author.

We also wanted to say thank you to those of you who loved and enjoyed Ensnared. We were blown away by the response we received for that book, and the excitement for this trilogy. We can only hope that you are still eager for the next despite…the way things have gone so far. Also, come join our Facebook

Reader Group, Tiffany Roberts' Ravagers! We'd love to have you there.

Turn the page for the blurb and cover of *Bound* (*The Spider's Mate #3*).

BOUND

THE SPIDER'S MATE #3

Ketahn will protect his mate at any cost.

Queen Zurvashi will not rest until everything Ketahn cares about is gone and he belongs to her.

His sweet, compassionate Ivy, his sister, his friends, his new tribe of humans—all are in danger. He fears nowhere is far enough away to escape the queen's wrath.

But Ketahn will see the whole jungle burn before he lets any harm befall his mate. Even if he must stand against Zurvashi and her army, even if he must face every beast in the Tangle, even if he must defy the gods themselves, he will not surrender his female.

Ketahn and Ivy are bound, and no force in the universe will sever the threads that connect them.

Get it here!

ALSO BY TIFFANY ROBERTS

Lover from the Waves

ALIENS AMONG US
Taken by the Alien Next Door

Stalked by the Alien Assassin

Claimed by the Alien Bodyguard

STANDALONE TITLES
Claimed by an Alien Warrior

Dustwalker

Escaping Wonderland

His Darkest Craving

The Warlock's Kiss

Ice Bound: Short Story

ISLE OF THE FORGOTTEN
Make Me Burn

Make Me Hunger

Make Me Whole

Make Me Yours

VALOS OF SONHADRA COLLABORATION
Tiffany Roberts - Undying

Tiffany Roberts - Unleashed

VENYS NEEDS MEN COLLABORATION
Tiffany Roberts - To Tame a Dragon

Tiffany Roberts – To Love a Dragon

ABOUT THE AUTHOR

Tiffany Roberts is the pseudonym for Tiffany and Robert Freund, a husband and wife writing duo. Tiffany was born and bred in Idaho, and Robert was a native of New York City before moving across the country to be with her. The two have always shared a passion for reading and writing, and it was their dream to combine their mighty powers to create the sorts of books they want to read. They write character driven sci-fi and fantasy romance, creating happily-ever-afters for the alien and unknown.

Website:
https://authortiffanyroberts.wordpress.com
Facebook:
https://www.facebook.com/AuthorTiffanyRoberts
BookBub:
https://www.bookbub.com/authors/tiffany-roberts

Sign up for our Newsletter!

Printed in Great Britain
by Amazon

31541752R00202